KATE O'Bl

(1897–1974) was born in Limerick, Ireland, the fourth daughter of Catherine Thornhill and Thomas O'Brien. Her mother died when she was five and she was educated at Laurel Hill Convent, Limerick, and at University College, Dublin. Kate O'Brien lived in London for some years where she made her living as a journalist and began to write stories and plays. She also worked in Manchester, on the *Guardian*, and spent a year as a governess in Spain: a country she was to return to and write about often.

Kate O'Brien originally became known as a playwright, her first plays being *Distinguished Villa* (1926) and *The Bridge* (1927). But it was with the publication of her first novel, *Without My Cloak* (1931), that her work became widely acclaimed. Described by J. B. Priestley as a "particularly beautiful and arresting piece of fiction", it won the Hawthornden and the James Tait Black Prizes of 1931. This was followed by eight more novels: *The Ante-Room* (1934), *Mary Lavelle* (1936), *Pray for the Wanderer* (1938), *The Land of Spices* (1942), *The Last of Summer* (1943), *That Lady* (1946), *The Flower of May* (1953) and *As Music and Splendour* (1958). Two of these novels, *Mary Lavelle* and *The Land of Spices*, were censored for their "immorality" by the Irish Censorship Board. Kate O'Brien dramatised three of her novels, *That Lady* also being made into a film starring Olivia De Havilland; she wrote travel books: *Farewell Spain* (1937), and *My Ireland* (1962); an autobiography, *Presentation Parlour* (1963); *English Diaries and Journals* (1943) and a monograph on Teresa of Avila (1951). Her works have been translated into French, German, Spanish, Czech and Swedish.

After a brief marriage at the age of twenty-six Kate O'Brien remained single for the rest of her life. In 1947 she was elected a member of the Irish Academy of Letters and a Fellow of the Royal Society of Literature. She lived in Roundstone, County Galway until 1961 when she moved to Boughton, near Faversham in Kent, where she died at the age of seventy-six.

Of her work Virago publishes *Mary Lavelle*, *That Lady*, *Farewell Spain* and *Without My Cloak*. *The Ante-Room*, *The Land of Spices* and *The Last of Summer* will be published in forthcoming years.

WITHOUT MY CLOAK

KATE O'BRIEN

WOODCUT DECORATIONS BY
FREDA BONE

WITH A NEW INTRODUCTION BY
DESMOND HOGAN

PENGUIN BOOKS – VIRAGO PRESS

Penguin Books
Viking Penguin Inc., 40 West 23rd Street,
New York, New York, 10010, U.S.A.
Penguin Books Ltd, Harmondsworth,
Middlesex, England
Penguin Books Australia Ltd, Ringwood,
Victoria, Australia
Penguin Books Canada Limited, 2801 John Street,
Markham, Ontario, Canada L3R 1B4
Penguin Books (N.Z.) Ltd, 182-190 Wairau Road,
Auckland 10, New Zealand

First published in Great Britain by William Heinemann Ltd 1931
First published in the United States of America by Doubleday & Company, Inc. 1931
This edition first published in Great Britain by Virago Press Limited 1986

Published in Penguin Books 1987

Printed in Finland
by Werner Söderström Oy, a member of Finnprint
set in Baskerville

TO
M. S. S.

Why didst thou promise such a beauteous day,
And make me travel forth without my cloak,
To let base clouds o'ertake me in my way,
Hiding thy bravery in their rotten smoke?
'Tis not enough that through the cloud thou break,
To dry the rain on my storm-beaten face,
For no man well of such a salve can speak,
That heals the wound, and cures not the disgrace:
Nor can thy shame give physic to my grief;
Though thou repent, yet I have still the loss:
The offender's sorrow lends but weak relief
To him that bears the strong offence's cross,
    Ah! but those tears are pearl which thy love sheds,
    And they are rich, and ransom all ill deeds.

Sonnet xxxiv: William Shakespeare

INTRODUCTION

It has always seemed to me that there are two languages in Irish literature apart from the obvious ones of Irish and English. The languages of the East and West of Ireland. At the end of "The Dead" by James Joyce, a young bespectacled and intellectual-minded Dublin man, after arriving home from a New Year party, in their bedroom, with the rumoured imminence of a deluge of snow outside, questions his Galway wife about a boy, now dead, with whom she'd been close in Galway, his memory having been conjured by a party lament.

"I suppose you were in love with this Michael Furey, Gretta," the young man tremorously asks.

"I was great with him at that time", is his wife's desultory reply.

Two languages that can never meet. And after putting down *Without My Cloak* it occurs to me that there are two other languages in Irish literature, that of men and that of women. James Joyce and other male writers were credited with the great weight of Catholic Irish expression but it can now be seen that there are three women who, to use George Moore's phrase, tilled the field of Irish nationalist, Catholic identity and who summoned up their own field in Irish literature, which in a way they share. They each write of low-lying land bordering on hills or mountains. Mary Lavin of Meath and Athenry. Edna O'Brien of South East Clare. Kate O'Brien of Limerick, bordering on South East Clare. But the troubled and visionary heroine in the pagan, metallic-lighted air of Edna O'Brien's *A Pagan Place* would be a stranger to the populace of

Kate O'Brien's novels; she is looking in an opposite direction to them. The populace of Kate O'Brien's work have their own troubles; upper middle-class Irish people, they came into being on a wave of opportunity open to Catholics after the Penal days. By the Pope's jubilee in 1877 we are alarmed to find many of their members travelling to Rome "in order to look on the living face of His Holiness and kiss his authentic toe". This ethos, this code of conduct, has its victims, girls startled out of their virginity in Spain, lapsed and garrulous clerical students in nineteenth-century Rome. They talk a lot. They think a lot. But their troubles and their agonisings are rimmed by a code which would be alien to the spare-boned woman, addled by promiscuous flights of thought, traipsing home to her mother's funeral in Edna O'Brien's short story "A Rose in the Heart"; it is a code determined by nuns lost in Belgian convents and fruity-tongued priests always about to don stoles. No matter how far they depart from it, Ana in *That Lady* and Clare in *As Music and Splendour* are aware they are departing from a touchstone. Right up to the end, in an extract published in 1972, from a novel *Constancy* Kate was working on at the time, the heroine is bound by background.

"I'm not a good anything—but I am a Catholic."

Christina Roche, the bastard servant girl, is the only one who gets away in *Without My Cloak*. This, Kate's first novel, published on her thirty-fourth birthday in December 1931, is her most complete statement about family. At one point in the novel it is insinuated that a Considine can only have a life as part of a collective, he or she is always answerable to an amalgam. Caroline and Denis try to forage their paths away. But there is no escape. The result of Caroline's attempt anticipates that of Denis which is not given. "Love, that Caroline had so long forgone, then found and flung aside and wept for, had now become a thing she hated to consider." In Kate's later novels the heroes and heroines would make many forays towards escape, Mary in *Mary Lavelle*, Clare in *As Music and Splendour*. In *The Land of Spices* there is a strange reversal where a woman flees her father's exultant homosexuality into a convent. But the argument is always there, as for Caroline in *Without My Cloak* who, having run away to London and on the threshold of adultery, is confronted by a hallucination.

> She saw those generations come whirling towards her now as on that river's flood. All Mellick she seemed to see, men and houses, quick and dead, in an earthquake rush to overtake her. Faces whose names escaped her, clerks of her father's, old beggar-women, shopgirls, ladies with whom she drank tea, her confessor, Father McEwen, pretty Louise Hennessy, Mrs Kelleher the midwife, and Tom with his stole on, ready to preach, and Molly picking bluebells ...

At the moment of release, of sublimation, there is the wraithe of "the hideous kitchen cat".

It was that woman, Elizabeth Bowen, who slipped in and out of Irish literature, who said that Kate O'Brien could be the Balzac of Ireland. *Mary Lavelle* and *That Lady* are outsiders to Kate's gleanings from provincial Irish life; Mary and Ana are versions of the one being, Ana older than Mary; they are women trying to unite their own passionate natures with the fixtures of family, church, God— and land. *Without My Cloak*, *The Ante-Room* and *The Land of Spices* form a trilogy of provincial Irish life in an ascendant order of power. There is a rocky, distanced, Balzacian edge in *The Ante-Room* which is only elusively present in *Without My Cloak*. In *The Land of Spices* language and theme merge to create a Pissarro-type subtlety of landscape, both of exteriors and of the soul. But *Without My Cloak* has a gaucheness and a charm which the other two novels lack; it has the breadth of extreme and unselfconscious daring; it is very much like Denis Considine, going forth without his cloak, only a dazzle in his eye and a lock on his forehead, with the admonition of Uncle Eddy, echoing Henry James in *The Ambassadors*, vaguely in his ear—"At your age young man, you should be free and selfish and quite blind. You should be trampling over this and that and everything to reach yourself—you should tolerate no cramping, masterful, enduring love"—and a thousand stories reeling in his head, "stories of Matteo Ricci and Benedict Goez and Father Benoit". In short it gathers many of Kate's future virtues and preoccupations into one stable piece. The stability is soon to be broken. Whatever happens to Denis Considine after the novel finishes?, one fearfully asks. But it is a mirror for the Irish middle classes to look at themselves and say "We weren't that bad", forgetting that an ancestor of the Considines was a horse-thief and rode out of an amorphous dark to create their lineage; a dark not unlike that in "The Dead" in which Michael Furey lies dead, a threatening, unstable, haunting dot in the consciousness.

"The Dead" is a good point on which to start talking about *Without My Cloak*. In "The Dead", in a city edged by poverty, the Misses Morkans' table is laid out—

> A shallow dish full of blocks of blancmange and red jam, a large green leaf-shaped dish with a stalk-shaped handle, on which lay bunches of purple raisins and peeled almonds, a companion dish on which lay a solid rectangle of Smyrna figs, a dish of custard topped with grated nutmeg, a small bowl full of chocolate and sweets wrapped in gold and silver papers and a glass vase in which stood some tall celery stalks. In the centre of the table there stood, as sentries to a fruit-stand which upheld a pyramid of crepes and American apples, two squat old-fashioned decanters of cut glass, one containing port and the other dark sherry

—as often are the tables in *Without My Cloak* in a land of poverty—

> Cold fowl, cold game, cold ham, salmon mayonnaise, lobster salads, cucumber salads, sandwiches, olives, salted almonds, petits fours, éclairs, cherry flans, fruit salads, the famous Considine trifles.

"Quadrilles. Quadrilles", a rosy-faced woman commands in "The Dead" while at the party before Honest John dies in *Without My Cloak* Molly says to Caroline "Do you think we could have a quadrille?" In "The Dead" Gabriel Conroy intuits her coming death in the face of Aunt Julia as she pipes "Arrayed for the Bridal". Death interchanges with merriment in *Without My Cloak*. There is almost a sacramental, elected rhythm to this interchange. But such rhythms, as in "The Dead", are governed by the indissoluble, ancestral dark.

Kate's grandfather only came to Limerick after the 1845–48 Famine, one of the many unlanded peasants heading on the cities, and the rise of the O'Brien horse-breeding business was breathtakingly rapid. Already it was in decline when Kate was a child. *Without My Cloak* draws on and encapsulates the afterglow in her childhood of this business at its hiatus. The history and lore of the nineteenth century obviously lapped on her childhood mind and created a solidity of texture which she would draw from again in *The Ante-Room, The Land of Spices* and in *As Music and Splendour. As Music and Splendour*, her last novel, like her first, is mainly about youth and its contradictions and agonisings, but in her first novel the image of youth is expressed through a young man, Denis Considine. It is Denis's story which is the crescendo of the book and the goal towards which the book goes. In retrospect he could have been the author of the book. A kind of Roderick Hudson figure, on the threshold of many experiences. "He flung off his nightshirt and raced across the room. He was as beautiful as the morning and as innocently unconscious of his beauty."

It seems to me that at the point in the novel when Christina Roche finally takes leave of Denis in Gansevoort Street in New York two parts of Denis's character divide. The part that stays in America through the character of Christina Roche, exposing itself to the vastness and unpredictability of a new continent, is Kate O'Brien, the novelist. The part that returns to Ireland is the conscience which adheres to the mainstay of family and tradition. The American episode in the book is its highpoint, the point which dominates the book, towards which all the action flows. Kate is addressing herself in a simple, intellectually uncontaminated way to an archetypal Irish experience. That of exile and pursuit of the exile. Especially across the divide of the Atlantic. Christina Roche is driven to the perils of the New World because she has transgressed the social code in Ireland. Denis pursues her. In Mary Lavin's impressive story "The Little Prince" a woman, about to marry, plots to send her embarrassing brother away:

Far away though that new world might be, to be reached only by crossing the vast Atlantic, what other remedy was there for a spendthrift like him: who had no sense of what was due to his family? Many a young man like him went out in disgrace to come home a different man altogether; a well-to-do man with a fur lining in his top-coat, his teeth stopped with gold, and the means to hire motor cars and drive his relatives about the countryside.

The Atlantic is the solution to all problems, a liner on it framed in an advertisement in her father's shop which, like many Irish country stores of years ago, is also an agency for trans-Atlantic tickets. Forty years after her marriage she and her husband pursue her brother whom she has not heard from in that time and catch up with him as a corpse.

But if it was her brother, something had sundered them, something had severed the bonds of blood, and she knew him not. And if it was I who was lying there, she thought, he would not know me. It signified nothing that they might once have sprung from the same womb. Now they were strangers.

In New York Christina and Denis realise they are two different people from what they were at home. Denis's embrace is newly negotiated by the New World and falsity is revealed in it. A momentous experience is inaugurated for Christina. Exile and turning her back on all that she was familiar with. Denis patters home. It is a situation, which by order of Irish history, must have been repeated in millions of Irish lives.

And what does Denis return to? The Catholic, upper middle classes of Ireland. That elusive band. In *Without My Cloak* the Hennessys and the Considines jostle for credentials. The Hennessys can claim ancestors among the Wild Geese, the aristocrats of Ireland who went out on the tide after the Irish defeat of 1690 and 1691; some of the Hennessy numbers tossed around with the armies of Europe as part of the legendary Irish Brigade during the eighteenth century, in Austria, in France; they seem to have returned at the tailend of that century. During the worst of the Penal Laws there

was still trading by Catholics. Even wealthy Catholic merchants
could be pointed out. Traders with the guile for big business got
around the Penal Laws where no one else could. This was especially
true in the remote West of Ireland, say, among the O'Connells of
Derryvane. During the eighteenth century smuggling was a large
part of the relish of business. The same ships that smuggled goods in
from and out to Europe brought the Latin and Greek inculcated
goslings of the merchants to Europe to be educated. Daniel
O'Connell and his brother got out of France on the same ship which
brought the news of the guillotining of Louis XVI to England. But
the new freedoms of the nineteenth century gave Catholic
merchants the room to move more freely; the professions were still
mainly with Protestants (Catholics were banned by their church
from going to Ireland's illustrious university, Trinity College,
Dublin), but the first half of the nineteenth century saw the dramatic
rise of a new, wealthy Catholic merchant class, like the Considines.
Oliver Saint John Gogarthy could claim three generations of
doctors on his father's side of the family. That was almost unheard of
for a Catholic. But his mother was of a wealthy Galway merchant
family. It was she, incidentally, who initially stopped him from
attending Trinity College, where his father had graduated. The
tradition on his father's side bathed Gogarthy in a confidence which
distinguished him from most Catholics of his time. But by the end of
the nineteenth century families like the Considines had
accumulated their own kind of confidence and arrogance about
their place in Irish society. John Aloysius Hennessy, that old man in
Without My Cloak, with Wild Geese and Irish Brigade gurgles in his
blood, stands for "the autocracy of wealth and the supremacy of the
bourgeoisie". In *The Flower of May*, her second last novel, Kate gives
a picture, which oddly seems enamoured of them, of the Irish
Catholic upper middle classes at the turn of the century. They are
the same class which prompts the young hero in Michael Farrell's
Thy Tears Might Cease to write under an inscription of his
grandmother's "To the Glory of God and the Honour of Ireland".
They are the people, along with his own background of genteel,
parlour-song piping Catholicism, which Stephen Dedalus turned

his heels on at Dublin Bay. It was partly them too that Francis Stuart, married into a wayward version of Catholicism, fled from to Germany in the 1930s. The conglomerate which makes Christina Roche tremble when she contemplates Denis's marriage proposal to her:

> Indeed for one who was a stranger to the proud middle classes, she formed a surprisingly accurate picture of how that class would regard her tentative of entering it. Beyond the first storms and the first piercing humiliations, she saw the long array of years that she would have to live at the centre of that great, possessive horde, unforgiven by them, unaccepted, but forever hemmed in; felt their contemptuous eyes on her as she fumbled to learn their superficial tricks, not for their sakes but for Denis's, fumbled and failed because of them standing by; saw their resentment if she made Denis happy, their sagacious head-wagging if she didn't; heard their anxious comments on Denis's children, tainted with her lowliness; felt her own gnawing terror of them that would never lie easy in her to the end of her days.

They survived, as the possible meat of literature, into the late 1940s, but now they seem to have been absorbed into the ubiquitous nouveau riche of Ireland. But sometimes a house at the end of an Irish street, turned convent, or a mansion become mental hospital, is a monument to them. *Without My Cloak*, like the stained-glass windows of Evie Hone, is a monument to them; it has a recessive quality; it can be brandished with rugby triumphs of long ago or a photograph of a young scintillating forelocked merchant in a gleaming new white shirt at the turn of the century, a schooner or two outside the background window maybe, as a testimony of something we imagine, like the arbitrator Kate O'Brien was as a child, once existed.

For a real understanding of Kate O'Brien's work it is essential to read *Without My Cloak*. Its presence is always there in her other work. In it she swore the affidavits of her fiction. The luminousness and the force of its energy are a surprise set against some of her later work; it is a book written with an Irish accent rather than with the English accent Kate O'Brien actually later adopted in real life. There are minor embarrassments, but the elegant flow of the novel sustains itself against these. It is a book about being young and the effect of first sexual experience on life.

In her last novel she returns again to the theme of youth. The two young Irish opera singers in Italy meet the heights of success in their art. But the quotation from Shelley at the beginning of the book makes it seem that Kate O'Brien distrusts success.

As music and splendour
Survive not the lamp and the lute
The heart's echoes render
No song when the spirit is mute.
When hearts have once mingled,
Love first leaves the well-built nest.
The weak one is singled
To endure what it once possessed.
Oh love who bewailest
The frailty of all things here,
Why choose you the frailest
For your cradle, your home and your bier?

Shelley got it wrong. Music and splendour do have reverberations. Kate O'Brien's work is picking itself up again and presenting itself to a new public. The face of Denis Considine merges into that of Kate O'Brien as she accepts the Hawthornden Prize of 1931, an event reported by a number of newspapers of the time. It is on that level we must accept *Without My Cloak*. As a work of youth. With some of the guilelessness and all the trust of youth. A young woman is giving us a book again much as Denis Considine wanders into parties and gives his love to ephemeral beauties. There is the shock and the immediacy of youth about it. Writing about young people from the vantage point of her later middle years Kate O'Brien injects obvious sadness into the theme; Clare in *As Music and Splendour* is doomed either to be a loser in love or else to be blanketed in what she considers amorality, a tawdry life of reaching out to her own sex, accruing sins. But neither is Denis Considine safe from a similar fate.

We know that the music and splendour of his life at the end of *Without My Cloak* will fade into acquiescence to the Irish Catholic upper middle classes. The moment of music and splendour, the moment of love, is a barrier against the presentiment of age, the inevitability, intrinsic in the moment, because it has not been insured against by the fibre of the spirit, of the failure of the resources of the imagination and the spirit. Clare in *As Music and Splendour* stands up and takes her moment of glamour too but her taking it is qualitatively different because there is a creative dignity in her action which will ward off the worst ignominy of loss. The novelist has learnt along the way. The nerves have been racked, the choices made; the rest is the legacy of those choices. But Clare, Ana, and Christina will always have the moral weight over Denis Considine because theirs have been the braver and the more consuming choices. Denis Considine's choice, then, given to us with Jamesian delicacy, for all its momentary allure, seems to have been a tragic one.

Most of Kate O'Brien's books end on a note of retreat. At the end of *Pray for the Wanderer* the hero (a male writer), on the verge of returning to England after a visit home, looks from the family homestead to the "river and the shining water" by a Limerick weir and finds that all, in the late 1930s, is still apparently well with the Catholic upper middle classes and their land. "The harmony within this house, for instance,—is that representative and does it promise anything? The uncrowded landscape, flowing peace." But *Without My Cloak*, like *Sons and Lovers* in a different way, ends on a note of entering, of participating, of making a vulnerable gesture of acceptance.

At the end of *Without My Cloak* we are told that John Aloysius Hennessy has reckoned with the nineteenth century. We are now in a position to reckon with Irish literature of the first half of the twentieth century. The men have had their say. Stephen Dedalus has reared his head over the horizon of Irish literature. Frank O'Connor and Sean O'Faolain have let loose their often brilliant characters in their parables and their short stories. Francis Stuart, their contemporary, wrote his major and jostling work in the sixties (that is not forgetting his earlier and imaginatively soaring novels *Pillar of Cloud* and *Redemption*). But from the 1930s, forties, fifties and early sixties it is the women who now, mainly, seem to have the ascendant voice. That era in Irish history which John McGahern named "the dark". Mary Lavin's small-town business people toed and froed on the Atlantic during this "dark". They seem to have suffered from concussion in regard to lost lovers, memory momentarily and jaggedly revived. Edna O'Brien's girls were growing up, waiting for moments of sublimation of memory in a foreign city. Kate O'Brien, with her novels, challenged the "dark" and was rapped for it. She returned to live in the "dark" between 1949 and 1961. Her last thirteen years were spent in Boughton, near Faversham, almost forgotten by the world which had earlier dazzled her with recognition, a friend to the local Irish vicar, a luminous visitor to the White Lion pub. Shortly before her death her masterpiece *The Land of Spices* was reissued by an Anglo-Irish publisher. It was the first hint of an initially slow but now apparently enduring renaissance. Perhaps like Reverend Mother in *The Land of Spices* we should not judge, but Kate O'Brien's place in Irish literature now seems fixed for the seriousness, the evenness and yet the witty detours of her voice; she was a Saint Teresa of Avila at a drawing-room party, a meditative for whose rich meditations on their predicaments her race should be grateful, a writer in whose opus *Without My Cloak* is a delicious and Chopin-ballade lightsome beginning.

Desmond Hogan, London, 1984

PROLOGUE

1789

The Horse-Thief

PROLOGUE

THE light of the October day was dropping from afternoon clarity to softness when Anthony Considine led his limping horse round the last curve of the Gap of Storm and halted there to behold the Vale of Honey.

The Vale of Honey is a wide plain of fertile pastures and deep woods, watered by many streams and ringed about by mountains. Westward the Bearnagh hills, through whose Gap of Storm the traveller had just tramped, shelter it from the Atlantic-salted wind, and at the foot of these hills a great river sweeps about the western valley, zigzagging passionately westward and southward and westward again in its search for the sea.

A few miles below him on this river's banks the traveller saw the grey blur of a town.

"That must be Mellick," he said to hearten himself and his horse.

In the south two remote green hills had wrapped their heads in cloud; eastward the stonier, bluer peaks wore caps of snow already. To the north the mountains of St. Phelim were bronzed and warmly wooded.

Villages lay untidily about the plain; smoke floated from the chimneys of parked mansions and the broken thatch of cow-men's huts; green, blue, brown, in all their shades of dark and brightness, lay folded together across the stretching acres in a colour-tranquillity as absolute as sleep, and which neither the breaking glint of lake and stream nor the seasonal flame of woodtops could disquiet. Lark songs, the thin sibilance of dried leaves, and the crying of milk-heavy cows were all the sounds that came up to the man who stood in the Gap of Storm and scanned the drowsed and age-saddened vista out of eyes that were neither drowsed nor sad.

Bright, self-confident eyes they were indeed, deep-set and brilliantly blue, seeming all the bluer because of the too black, too thick bar of eyebrow that brooded quarrelsomely above them. In spite of these savage eyebrows the eyes and face of the man were gay and his whole body had a coarse beauty. He was tall, and black-haired, with white skin, white teeth, ruddy cheeks, and heavy shoulders. His thick hands supported the indication of pugnacity in his brows, but they were nimble too, the hands of a horseman. One of them, playing lightly now on the neck of his strawberry roan mare, seemed to have hypno-tised her restive weariness into peace. His hair was wild and his ragged clothes were stained with sweat and dirt. But he wore his rags and the three days' beard on his chin with as much ease as he carried his strength, all these things being natural to him.

They were a contrast, this horse and man who seemed so much in harmony. His was the beauty of a peasant, something flung up accidentally by life. A root his bodily fineness might be called, but the horse he caressed was a flower. He was nature's heedless work, but she, taking her inbred and high-bred quality from generations of great blood stock, was a work of art. The breeders of Rose Red had brought beauty, through her, to the threshold of degeneracy. She was superb, she was the end of beauty in her kind.

Anthony Considine looked tenderly at her now and dropped his hand from her neck to caress her injured fetlock, laughing contentedly to think of the clever way he had stolen her.

She had a stud-book name, this strawberry roan, a noble name, which revealed her great descent, and was written above her loose box in the aristocratic stable she would never see again. But Anthony Considine, the first time he laid his thief's hand on her neck, murmured "Rose Red" to her, and named her for himself for ever, as a lover names his mistress.

Now he had ridden her and led her seventy-two hours' jour-ney and more from her aristocratic stable, and the Bearnagh hills were a shelter at their backs. The tramp and his stolen

love were tolerably safe, so long as they did not return to the
treeless, lovely west. If they were to stay together they must
descend into the Vale of Honey that was strange to them, and
see what chances there were of free stable and bed in that grey
smudge of a town called Mellick.

The man tossed back his curly, greasy hair.

"The Vale of Honey!" he said softly. "I've often heard 'tis
a grand, rich, easy-going place. It's like a saucer, upon my
word, the shape of it, or like a dish, the way the little hills come
up all round it. Faith, if it's a dish, I hope it's got our supper
on it, Rose Red!"

He stood up and drew the bridle through his arm.

"Can you do it for me, asthore?" he asked the horse. "Can
you limp five or six more miles along with me, God help you?"

Dusk was past and it was already full starlight when the
horse-thief led his lovely roan past the crumbling gates of
Mellick and along a well-paved and lighted street, which was
called "Kilmoney Street" on its cleanly painted name-board,
and which had a lively and a prosperous air.

BOOK I

1860–1861

Honest John and His Children

THE FIRST CHAPTER

A NTHONY CONSIDINE paused in the office doorway and
sniffed the evening good-temperedly. Good humour had
been a suppressed excitement in him all day, and was rising
now a little out of his control, so that he was conscious of
his heartbeats and hardly able to withhold from singing. The
April air touched his face serenely, and though he barely perceived the caress it heightened his mood of jubilation. He
smiled into the street and tipped his hard high hat to an
audacious angle.

"I'll want the gig at No. 30 in half an hour," he called backwards to the gaslit office, and without listening to the flustered
assent of a roomful of clerks he strode away up the southward slope of the street.

The evening was of that tender kind that is frequent in Ireland in the Spring. Behind the Bearnagh hills the open sky was
luminous where the sun had passed; afternoon rain glittered
on roofs and in cart-ruts; smoke plumed from chimneys and
the air was warm with noises of the relaxing day.

Anthony splashed along the puddled footpath; if he perceived the gentle evening, if he heard the rattle of cart-wheels,
the thudding and laughing of boys at play, the scrape of a
fiddle, the bark of a dog, the hoot of a coal boat; if he smelt
lime and horse-dung and porter, hay and new-milled flour; if
he saw night, not an hour away now, creeping up to his little
town—he did all these things only with the slight sensibility of
habit; for his observation, dominating the private pleasure
that disturbed him on this evening, was now as always reserved

9

for the men who walked the street with him, and for their business and their manner of setting about it. Anthony was a business man and a citizen and moved consciously in rivalry, friendship, and pride among his fellow citizens of Mellick.

Charles Street and his direction along it now went parallel with the seaward flow of the river. At the crossings, where short streets cut the New Town symmetrically from east to west, he could glimpse the great stream to the right of him down a short hill and observe the regular hurry of its course past the unhurrying docks; carts and ships and cargoes he noted, his own and other men's, and all he saw refreshed his knowledge of the town's business life and kept the surface of his mind in motion with trade affairs. When he looked eastward up the wide crossing streets, he snatched, one block away, a fragment of the life of King's Street, where the shops were gay at this hour, and where broughams and phaëtons splashed arrogantly through the mud, bearing wives and daughters of the town to and fro between the tall brown houses at the southern end and all the fripperies and agitations of their social habit. The street in which they rode was a lively place compared with its long grey parallel where Anthony was walking. Charles Street consisted mainly of stores and offices; it wore the grave, grey look of commerce, an aspect increased by the dusty pallor laid on the street's face by two or three great flour mills. Drays and carts were its chief traffic, interspersed by the occasional phaëtons of the merchants.

It was only nine years since John Considine, Forage Merchant, had moved his premises from Kilmoney Street in the declining quarter to their present admirable position in the New Town; but, standing now between Hennessy's Mills and the Passionist Church, with its back windows opening on the Dock Road and the river, and on its face a look as blank and sad as any worn by its more venerable neighbours, the store managed to exude an air of ancient permanence.

Anthony left it behind him quickly this evening; went at top speed past Hennessy's Mills too with their familiar swishing music, and their workmen flour-whitened to the eyelashes, nodded briefly to old Honan, drowsy at his perch in the Coal Office window, appraised the episcopal carriage-horses as they stamped on the cobbles outside his Protestant lordship's dwelling, crossed the road by the theatre with a quick eye for Cummins's play bill, turned into Lower Mourne Street and rattled the knocker sharply on the door of No. 30, his father's house.

His sister Agnes let him in and took his hat.

In spite of the open secret that John Considine's daughters must have at least eight thousand pounds apiece, no one had come courting Agnes—no one, that is, whom a Considine would desire or be permitted to marry. She was thirty now, only three years younger than Anthony, and there was nothing for it but to accept her as an old maid. Her virgin state irritated Anthony at times, as it irritated other members of the family. It did not suit Considine pride that any bearer of that name should appear to the world as flouted and unimportant, and Anthony could not help admitting that old maids were unimportant. However, his thoughts were not on Agnes to-night, and as, taper in hand, she climbed a chair to light the hanging lamp, he went past her quickly to the dining-room.

He found his father there. Honest John Considine, as the townspeople called him, was sitting upright in his leather and mahogany chair, that had been drawn away from the fire this evening and towards the window. He had a newspaper in his hand but he was gazing past it at what he could see of the street.

No. 30 Lower Mourne Street fronted north, and so the thin brightness of the April afternoon could not do much to illuminate the house. Beyond the windows the green buds opening on the sycamore trees gave a flicker of gaiety to the wide, brown-façaded street, whose further pavement sparkled in sun now after the shower. But from within John Considine's dining-room this prospect was curtailed by bamboo window-screens and by looped curtains of red serge. A gilt cage stood on a table before one of the windows; its door was open and two green finches flew in and out of it.

"Good-evening, father," said Anthony, and his voice brightened the room.

The older man turned towards him without graciousness.

"I didn't expect to see you here this evening," he said.

"Well, I can't stop long. I only thought maybe you'd change your mind and come out and have dinner with us after all."

"I had my dinner at half-past two, thank you."

"And then you had a tea-party, I see," said Anthony, teasing him affectionately. "You're a regular old woman for tea-parties."

Honest John conceded him a slow, jibing smile.

"Caroline looked in with a couple of the children," he said.

"The fact of the matter is that your daughters spoil you, Mr. Considine," said Anthony. "What's Caroline's news? How did she enjoy Dublin?"

"Bought the town up, by all accounts. And she had a new emerald bracelet on her that cost two hundred guineas if it cost a halfpenny."

The old man's eyes smouldered proudly as he recalled the silky, jewelled beauty of the daughter lately departed from this room.

"Fine for the Lanigans!" commented Anthony. "Money to burn, seemingly!"

"Like yourself, my fine fellow. Building yourself a country mansion more suited to a duke than a forage merchant!"

"I don't know what dukes like," said Anthony, "but if it's good enough for a son of yours it's good enough for anyone." He sat down by the table and wheedled his father. "Come on out with me now like a good man, and help me eat my first dinner in the place!"

"One dinner a day is enough for me, thank you, and that at a decent hour."

"And no wonder you've no appetite if you've been sampling all this stuff!"

Anthony helped himself to a long, thick finger of plum cake and waved a mocking hand at the remains of the tea-party still spread on the big table. Tea was always excellent at Lower Mourne Street, served in old Irish silver and big Rockingham cups. Always muffins and toast and soda bread and plum cake and seed cake and two or three kinds of jam, for John Considine was a sweet-tooth and, after his carriage with its splendid pair of horses, the trimming of his respectability that he liked best was afternoon tea.

Honest John was a heavily built, unprepossessing old man. His large head was thickly covered with grey hair; his forehead was low and deeply wrinkled; enormous black eyebrows beetled together gloomily above his sombre eyes. He wore neither beard nor moustache, but bushy side-whiskers grew low on his cheeks and chin. He had thick, plain features and excellent teeth. His suit of broadcloth was untidy; there were stains on his waistcoat, and his big, freckled hands, with their dirty, broken nails, were discoloured like a manual labourer's.

He had had a successful life. He was born in Lady's Lane, off Kilmoney Street in the old part of Mellick, in the poverty of poor folk of the seventeen-nineties. By singular good fortune he had had about two months' schooling, and in manhood was proud that he could sign his name and read a newspaper.

There was no portrait anywhere of Honest John's father, who had died in 1790, and his grandchildren often wondered what he was like. Though they talked little, and never in public, of his unedifying history, they knew its outlines, how he had come into Mellick one night from the west without a penny in his pocket and leading a lame and beautiful horse that he called Rose Red, and that everyone said he had stolen. The legend was that the first person in the town he spoke to was the widow Dooney, who kept a potato and crubeen* shop in Lady's Lane. He put his head through the door of her shop while his horse was helping herself to hay off a wagon outside.

"Will you give me a supper of crubeens, woman of the house," said he, "and chance my goodwill to pay you for them sometime?"

Whatever came over Ellen Dooney to make her so foolish, she gave him the supper of crubeens, and while he was eating it, he put the come-hether on her. She always said, and so did the neighbours, that he was a beautiful figure of a man. She married him, and had eleven months of storm with him, for all he cared about in the world was his horse, Rose Red, and boasting about her and drinking, and fighting all that vexed him with envious talk of her. One night he found the roan horse poisoned and dead in her stable. He went from her down into Friar's Well, where some lived that coveted her and mocked him, and he raised a great fight in the street. All the men of Friar's Well joined in, and it was never known exactly

---

*Pig's feet.

who gave the blow of a crowbar that stretched Anthony Considine dead, but he was carried home to the crubeen shop in Lady's Lane, cold and stiff on a shutter, in the hour that his son, John Anthony, was born. That was all that his grandchildren knew of the horse-thief from the west.

Ten years later that son John Anthony, looking older than his years, was weighing potatoes in his mother's shop and counting out crubeens. Youth was over.

John worked hard and seemed to have no desire to do anything else; his only weakness was a hankering after stablemen and horsey gossip. He liked to hang round the horse-fair and appraise good-looking horses. Sometimes he longed to buy a horse, and had to mock himself out of so absurd a dream.

From his association with the men who followed fairs it happened that when he was sixteen he negotiated a deal between two farmers for a load of hay. In the following week he arranged a larger deal, and made fifteen shillings for himself on it. He saved this sum, and watched his chance to make another deal in forage. It came within three weeks and brought him a profit of nineteen shillings and ninepence. An idea began to form in his head. He invested all the money he and his mother could spare in six sacks of oats that were going cheap. When he bought them he had no purchaser in view, but within a week he got rid of them at a good profit.

On his twentieth birthday he opened a small store in Kilmoney Street. The sign above its door announced uncertainly that he was "John Considine, Hay, Strau and Forrage Deeler." When he was twenty-three he sold the crubeen shop, took a long lease of the old house above the forage store, and brought his mother from round the corner in Lady's Lane to live there. In the same year, he brought a wife to his new house, a plump and pretty girl from a neighbouring lane. He married her at six o'clock on a dark March morning of 1813, and opened his store in the usual way of business at seven o'clock.

He prospered in Kilmoney Street. His wife was docile, his mother thrifty. He had himself a tireless capacity for work and an inclination to take risks. As he grew older, he ceased to talk more than was necessary with stablemen, and lingered only as business required around the precincts of the horse-fairs. He seemed to forget his dream of owning a good horse.

In any case he rapidly grew too heavy and too busy to ride one. He became a silent, self-reliant man, whose wife feared and venerated him and whom even his mother approached with caution. Uncouth and simple he remained in his own life, but growing rich, loaded his womenfolk with silks and gauds, and became a great buyer of jewels and trifles for them.

His wife bore him thirteen children, of whom eight, four sons and four daughters, reached maturity.

His forage trade expanded, in spite of fluctuations of his luck, and before he was fifty he had to be accepted, however reluctantly, in Mellick as an important citizen. He possessed the more ordinary of the civic virtues; he was sober and honest, moderately generous, and with a sufficiency of local patriotism; he was proud to be a Catholic in days when that was not easy; and he always showed the courage of his rather staid opinions. He had only one enthusiasm and that was for Dan O'Connell, "the Liberator," as he unfailingly called him. After O'Connell's death he lost such interest as he had had in national affairs, and watched them, and the affairs of all the world, merely for their material reactions on his business and family. Political agitators, Ribbonmen, Young Irelanders, and such like filled him with rage, and he was not shy about cursing them when he got the chance. The Potato Blight concerned him chiefly in that it was disastrous to his trade; the Crimean War brought back prosperity and was remembered with affection. During the Indian Mutiny he was vaguely and sardonically amused at what he guessed of England's difficulties, but his native inclination always to think and act as an Irishman was perpetually impeded by a secret sentimental tendency to admire the sturdy little Queen. He inclined to like Mr. Gladstone better than Mr. Cobden, and he distrusted Lord Palmerston in all things. He was a hard master, a good Churchman, and an affectionate father—undemonstrative with his sons, but genial and courteous to his daughters. And as with every year his respectability grew in the town, so with every year he learnt to take a greater pride in the accident of his surname. To be a Considine seemed to Honest John a very special and magnificent responsibility. And all his children had grown up to agree with him.

He was seventy now, the autocratic owner of "John Considine's," the most extensive forage dealer and exporter in Ireland and one of the wealthiest men in the south. His wife was dead these fifteen years, and the doctors were telling him that his heart had become a very uncertain organ and needed care. These were his only visible troubles, and to the latter, however his children besought him, he refused to pay any regard. He was rich and respected in Mellick where once he had been a barefoot nobody; his carriage was drawn by a superb pair of high-stepping bay thoroughbreds; he inhabited a fine house in the best part of the New Town; his eldest son was a doctor, his second son a priest; two sons were in his business with him; two of his daughters were honourably married in the town; one daughter was a nun, and his youngest, Agnes, was the companion of his fireside; he had twenty-five grandchildren and possessed the means to provide well for all of them. Above these advantages, he had the love of his eight children, who had feared him in youth, and now, in their riper years, gave him a great affection.

It was not easy therefore to account for the depths of sadness in the eyes of Honest John below the too-black, beetling brows, or to say why his great shoulders sagged sometimes as if under a heavier load than seventy years.

Anthony, who stood at the dining-room window now in the failing light, was in his thirty-fourth year and was Honest John's youngest son. He looked as if nothing could be more satisfactory than to be a Considine.

He was not only the best-looking of the family, with the exception of his sister, Caroline Lanigan, but he showed himself the most vigorous and forthright too, with a sweeping intelligence that often irritated the others. When he was more than usually on their nerves, if they happened to be strictly in family conclave, and shut off from even the most sympathetic relatives-in-law, some of whom might well have enjoyed but would never have been permitted a dig at him, his brothers and sisters allowed themselves the acid pleasure of comparing him to "Grandfather," the horse-thief. But the comparison never wounded Anthony. When Dr. Joe, John's eldest son, ponderous as his father and not nearly so shrewd, thought to impress the younger man and to give him pause in his arrogance, he hinted heavily of the strange belated visitations known to medical books of the sins of the grandfathers. When Tom, the priest, planned more concisely to put his brother in his place, he shook a warning head over Anthony's port, and asked him, between sips, what he thought it would profit a man, etc: when plain, intelligent Teresa felt herself too enviously stung by his high-spirited beauty, she accused him of having "a drop taken."

Anthony was dark-haired with a clear and vivid face; he was clean-shaven, except for small, picturesque side-whiskers, an adornment which the family inclined to condemn. His eyes were bright blue and deep-set, his teeth flashed finely when he laughed. He had John Considine's weight of shoulder, but greater height with which to carry it, and lighter hips and legs. His thick hands were better kept than Honest John's and though he was too self-confident and impatient to be a dandy, he wore good clothes and wore them well. He had vitality, quick wits, and charm.

As the two men talked now in the heavy twilight of the room, the kinship of their bodies was more apparent than their individualities. Certainly, peering through the thickening shadow, an observer could have guessed from them that their stock was on the up-grade, for the light was still enough to show the younger man as the finer and more civilised type, but father and son they were branded there, for any casual eye, by those innumerable blood subtleties which none of life's after-chisellings can efface. Something of this visible bond was stirring too in Anthony's mood to-night; the hour was one of special emotion for him, and in such times his feelings were open to irrelevant attack. The pressure of his mood had characteristically brought him hurrying round to his father's house, when, in fact, his eagerness could not easily spare the half-hour; and now, as he looked down into the gloomy, noncommittal eyes of Honest John he was touched with a filial love, half pity, half veneration, for this ageing man, his father, who had made the Considines.

"And anyway you needn't have dinner. Tea, or a glass of port, or whatever you want."

"I can get whatever I want in my own house, Anthony."

"I know that, sir. But won't you come? I'll come back with you myself in the carriage."

"I'll stay where I am to-night and thank you, my boy."

It was one of John Considine's peculiarities that he was able to soften his manner as his purpose strengthened. Anthony saw that happen now as he had often observed and admired its effect in business. He answered his father's smile with a twinkle as he gave in.

"You're an obstinate man. I thought that maybe you'd like to see us shaking in."

"So long as I don't live to see you shaking out I'll be satisfied," said John.

"You won't do that, sir."

"Please God," said John morosely. Silence fell as Agnes and a servant entered with lamps.

"There's the trap outside," said Anthony. "I'd better be off."

"Nice little cob you have there," observed his father. And then he turned genially to Agnes. "The young blackguard has no better sense," said he, "than to be trying to drag me out of my own house this cold night! Out to dinner, if you please, late dinner, at his new country mansion! What's this we're to call the place—River something-or-other!"

"River Hill, sir," said Anthony.

"Too many River-this-and-that's round here for my taste—silly name! Be off with you, sir—you and your late dinner—and let Agnes and myself have our tea, if you please!" He seemed happy now with a daughter clucking round him.

Anthony made ready to go. "It doesn't feel right, you not being there for our first meal in the place, father. And we owe it all to you."

Old John was grateful for that.

"You're welcome," he said fussily, "you're welcome. But keep your head and mind what you're about. I've no love at all for showy extravagance and I never thought you had. I'll say this, that up to now you always seemed to have a head on your shoulders. What's got you lately I don't know, to be pouring out my money like water on builders and masons, after I buying you one of the best houses in the town four years ago."

"You can afford it, sir."

John grunted. "Maybe I could, if I saw the reason for it.

Well, well, it's my own fault to let you have the money. But I'd like to know what your brothers are thinking of my folly!"

Anthony laughed. "If that is all that's bothering you you're a happy man!"

"H'umph! I'll trouble you not to sneer at your brothers, sir!"

"I'm not sneering at them, father."

"Off with you, then. Don't keep that valuable cob standing all night."

"Anyhow, sir, you're all having dinner with us next Sunday, aren't you? That's fixed, Agnes."

"Maybe," said John, "if you have it at a rational hour of the day."

"Two o'clock."

Agnes demurred politely. "It is too soon for the whole family to go out to you, Anthony. There's a lot to be done, moving into a new place. Molly will never be ready."

"Of course she'll be ready. Didn't I tell her to be ready? Why wouldn't she, with servants eating their heads off all round her?"

"All right, young fellow," said John impatiently. "We'll come out, since you're kind enough to know us these days, and you so high up in the world!"

Anthony twinkled at him and went out in even happier mood than he had come in, since now for the first time his father had allowed himself to be genial about River Hill. He was smiling as he gathered the reins and nodded dismissal to the man at the cob's head.

The gig clattered smartly into King's Street, and headed northward through the town, taking Anthony home for the first time to the new house by the river. The air was blue-grey now, and the lamplighters were out. King's Street was very lively; many of the shops were still open, and Anthony admired the up-to-date gaslight in the better-class ones; English redcoats swaggered at every corner, some shouting in hilarious groups with the bolder girls, some coaxing the shy ones in doorways. Stars pricked the sky; a hawker's fire glowed on the kerb and a smell of roast potatoes floated up from it deliciously.

Anthony clicked his tongue at the willing horse. There were many to be saluted, for the citizens liked to parade their handsome street on fine evenings. He missed no acquaintance, and though few resisted an inward, envious gibe—"too big to live in the same town with us now, it seems"—all were glad to be acknowledged by him in public. He was indeed a personage, as was proved by the cordial bow of his worship the mayor, Mr. John Aloysius Hennessy, rolling past in his victoria. The mayor's wife, his second, who sat at his side, was English and had her name in Debrett, and she smiled even more kindly than the mayor when this handsome merchant doffed his hat to her.

But Anthony was not thinking of these people or of the flourishes of courtesy. They were welcome to their gibing and their calculated friendliness; it all sat easy enough on him. Indeed, if he had reflected on the half-jealous, half-placatory regard in which his acquaintances were beginning to hold him, he would have understood it, and regarded it with more pleasure than rancour. But to-night he smiled at them abstractedly, and it is even possible that the mayor's lady brightened her eye for him in vain.

Soon the gig was rattling up the Carberry Road, and soon after that the trees that edged the new estate shut out the dimming west. "Gate!" Anthony called to the lodge-keeper as imperiously as if his ancestors had been doing so since the rout of the Danes. While he waited the "Wet Paint" notice on the iron gates waved welcome to him through the dusk like a ghost's hand. He swung in under the budding lime trees, peering this way and that at his sleeping fields with the eyes of a homesick child. A dog barked from the stables, and gravel crunched under the wheels. He drew up at the doorway of the warmly lighted house.

He hurried to the porch. If it had been daylight he would have had to linger to survey the external glories of the place, although he must already have known them by heart. He would have chosen daylight for this first return, but filial piety had delayed him. And now tumultuously he felt that it was better this way, better to come to it when it was glowing with evening life, when his wife was quiet by some fire within it, and his children were curling down to their first sleep under its fold. Time enough in the morning to count its windows again for the fiftieth time, and its chimneys, and compare its northerly aspect with its northwest, and its southeast with its south—oh, all its entrancing aspects, time enough for them, a hundred mornings now, a thousand mornings. He made out the window of Denis's nursery before they opened the door, and then, slipping past the exhausted-looking maidservant into the paint-smelling chaos of the half-furnished hall, he whistled contentedly for Molly.

THE SECOND CHAPTER

A NTHONY had done well perhaps to come home under the veil of the dark. The truth is that to impartial eyes the most pleasant aspect of River Hill was the nocturnal one, for with the best intentions in the world, he had built an ugly house. He was no æsthete, but only a man with progressive ideas. All that he wanted in his house, as in other things, was the best that his epoch could give him for his money. And the best that 1860 could give him in domestic architecture was not felicitous. He thought it was, and it would be pleasant therefore to let the matter go at that, but he built consciously for his posterity and so it is necessary to consider the house from posterity's angle as well as his.

Anthony, whose father thought him an encyclopædia of culture, had had, even by Mellick standards, only a very average education, and perhaps the world beyond Mellick would have said that he was not educated at all. The Christian Brothers did their best for him, and did it firmly, leather strap in hand, but, emerging wearily from penal laws and hedge-schoolmastering, had little time to mince round the fine arts with their pupils. So, whether for reasons of nature or education or both, Anthony, brightest in his class at reading and writing and arithmetic, and more susceptible than most men to the beauty of women, of old simple songs and of the rivered landscape he was born in, had, as they say, no taste.

The architect whom he employed, however, a gentleman from Dublin with condescending manners and a reputation which almost justified them, was renowned in his own country, unlike most prophets, for the impeccability of his taste.

Mr. Cleethorpes Downey—that was the architect's name—attempted no old-style reproduction in River Hill, his object being, as he said, to give Anthony a "high-class up-to-date gentleman's residence." And that was exactly what Anthony wanted. It was not that Mr. Downey was incapable of setting up a Doge's Palace or a small Versailles on the Considine acres; indeed he would have revelled in giving Anthony a bit of each, with a dash of Tudor thrown in and a Moorish tower, but that sort of thing "runs into money, Mr. Considine" and Anthony's funds, though large, were limited, and did not seem to impress Mr. Downey.

Between them, however, and pretty quickly—for Anthony called the tune—the man of taste and the man who had none reared up a large house of bright red brick on a tranquil dreamy hill, below which a great river murmured.

There were three storeys of this house in front, and four at the back, where Mr. Downey allowed the servants' quarters to get the light of day. It fronted westward, throwing out its pathetic new colour across the curving waters, to streaky old bogs and the wine bloom of the Bearnagh hills. Fortunately, through an oversight of Mr. Downey's, who liked "lofty effects," it turned out to be considerably longer than its height, and this accident gave it a certain steadiness, which counteracted the absurd red grin, as of a good-natured toper, that the fanciful might have seen on its façade when the sun dazzled the windows.

The house was gabled at the north and south corners, so that the rooms at these points were enlarged and had "bays" instead of ordinary windows. Mr. Downey had wanted also to "throw out a round bay" from the south wall of the drawing-room, but Anthony intended to have a conservatory there and made him compromise with a French window, which would be useful when the dream came true. The architect was sympathetic about the conservatory, but it must be domed, he said, in many-coloured glass—and he quoted a line from "Adonais".

Such was the new house. Old elms and limes were gathered about the sweet long slopes of its fields, to shelter it; rooks wheeled and homed above it, and the river, curving impetuously below on its north side and its west, sent up a solemn music to it night and day. So life's inescapable beauty floated about

Anthony's crude new mansion, even for this first homecoming, and had even crept indoors where fires were burning and cakes were baking, where children had fallen contentedly asleep, where a woman mused before her mirror in the candle-light.

Anthony whistled softly in the hall.

§ 2

THE whistle brought Molly from her dressing-table into the corridor. Anthony sprang up the carpetless stairs softly, like a cat, and they went back to their room together. She kissed him and he held her on his arm as they walked.

"You're worn out, my little girl."

"'Twas a big move, I can tell you."

"That means that you disobeyed me. Didn't I order you not to lift a finger this day? Amn't I paying for men and women enough to move the County Asylum from here to China? How dare you tire yourself out?"

She sat down before her dressing-table again.

"I didn't, Anthony. Everything happened the way you arranged it, and I hardly did a thing. But the confusion——" She leant her head on her hand and smiled wanly at him.

"It's over now," he said. "And you must take all the rest you can in this good air. You're feeling all right—in general, I mean—except for being tired?" He looked at her anxiously; she was in the third month of carrying a child. But she smiled a lazy reassurance at him.

"Are the children in bed?"

"Oh, yes."

"Is Denis asleep, do you know?"

"I hope the three of them are. No one in this house wants to hear another sound out of them to-night, I can tell you."

He laughed. "I'll believe that. They like the place, you think?"

"Well, we didn't bring them out until their rooms were ready, and that was fairly late—and considering anyhow that Denis is three and a half——" It was her turn to laugh.

"Ah, but he is old enough to know what he likes."

"He was tired when he got here—the drive made them all sleepy." She ran a comb through the curls on her forehead.

"I see," said Anthony. "And are you better pleased with the move, do you think, Molly?" His voice was kind and conciliatory.

She shrugged good-naturedly. "Well, we're here anyway. And it's a fine big house. But King's Crescent was good enough for me."

"Nonsense. Buckingham Palace wouldn't be good enough for you if I could afford better."

"King's Crescent was a grand place, I thought."

"You've thirty acres of ground now, and the best air in Munster."

"It's the back of Godspeed."

"It's nothing of the kind, Molly."

"Well, I feel buried alive here, I know that."

"How do you feel that, I'd like to know? Haven't you carriages and horses, and aren't you only a mile from Mellick?"

"Oh, I don't know. I'll get used to it, I suppose."

"You will, of course. It'll be the making of you. But my father got used to it before you. Joking about it this evening, if you please!"

"Easy for him. He hadn't to upset himself and come out here to live."

"He had to give me the money, though."

"King's Crescent are the best houses in Mellick. Just as genteel people live there as outside the town. It's good enough for Lady Roundstone."

"Maybe. And that's no reason at all why it is good enough for Mrs. Considine."

"Anyhow, we can't afford a big place like this."

"May I ask how you know what we can afford?"

"Well, I don't see how we can."

"Neither can Tom see how. Neither can Joe. Neither can Sophia or Teresa, I daresay. You've been drinking tea with your 'in-laws,' Molly—that's what's wrong with you. But I'll tell you what—the very first time you're short on your allowance, or that your housekeeping books aren't paid on the nail, you start talking about what we can't afford. That'll be time enough, my girl. And for the present, I'll manage our affairs."

He wasn't angry and she knew it. He was amused at the crisscross of family gossip that was visible behind her grumblings.

He wanted her to be happy in her new house, and he understood her well enough to know that eventually it would give her pleasure; she was not a person to bear long grudges, and she had a natural liking for space and ease and for playing the fine lady. She had been happy in King's Crescent, because, as she said, its houses were among the best in the town, and residence in them gave definite prestige. She had liked her snobbish neighbours, had liked the nods and becks of genteel town life, the tattle and the tea-drinking, the pretty posing to and fro in her carriage, the flattery that twittered unceasingly about her frou-frou elegance, and the envy that derided it. And now, although in her heart she must have known that as mistress of an imposing country house these things would multiply for her, and that her excursions through the town behind the stepping greys must henceforward gain in impressiveness what they might lose in frequency, she chose for the present to deplore her isolation from her familiar life and to punish Anthony's lack of confidence with her disapproval. Very natural. But her husband did not like to see her even transitorily unhappy, and this disagreement had been troubling him for the best part of a year now, in fits and starts. He would be glad when it passed. He might have cleared it away before now by revealing to her how the possession of River Hill would aggrandise her in Mellick society, but he would not condescend to exploit her little snobbery; he knew only too well that she would find it all out for herself and aggravate him in the doing.

Anthony was a snob himself perhaps, if it is snobbish to take a too emphatic pride in lowly origin. He exulted, as did all the Considines, in the hard story of his father's life and attached a value that was at least debatable to its material achievement. But more than the achievement he valued the simple virtues in his father that had made it possible, and if it was his dream to push that achievement further in his own time he would take care to do so without sacrificing or deriding the honourable simplicity of its beginnings. Molly might play the great lady to her heart's content, she might be as full of whims and petulances as any tired beauty of a decadent aristocracy; these foibles attracted him and ministered delicately to his own especial glory; but when she tried, as once or twice he caught her trying, to gloss his father's simple origin, when he glimpsed her tendency to dismiss as embarrassing man's power to climb without losing the common touch, he let his temper fly above her frightened head. Their snobberies were not compatible.

He smiled at her now and laid a hand on her hair and she, leaning against him, looked up to the warm affection in his eyes and let him have the last word. Their bodies relaxed; Anthony's hand moved over her hair and neck to her warm, silk-covered breast. Familiar, sensual peace crept into them, and they rested a minute together. The man's eyes dreamt over her reflection in the mirror, and she took pleasure in it too.

How lovely she was! Five years of marriage, three births within that time and this new pregnancy, had indeed dimmed the morning radiance that Anthony had wooed, but the warm candle-beams made little of that to-night. Cloudily the two saw her reflected. Her waist was not modishly clipped in at present, but there was small outward sign as yet of her fruitfulness; her skirts of night-blue silk billowed to the floor; her little bodice, beribboned up and down with velvet and inlet with lace, was faithful to the lovely line of her breasts; pagoda sleeves engulfed her arms, but little jewelled hands gave pretty pledge for them; chatelaine and mighty topaz brooch weighed touchingly upon her slenderness. Her chignon lay softly on her neck, and dim curls clouded her forehead. Blue eyes, misty as Anthony's were bright, smiled faintly from the pool of glass; the curve of her mouth had a dream's outline, and over her indeterminate soft face shone the appeal of lovely transience. She was all woman, all fragility, of the type that flowers enhance, and parasols and jewels; pouring out tea she could look adorable, or dancing a quadrille, or singing at the piano; but beauty unfolded from her voluptuously in hours like this; evening and quietude adorned her like a crown.

Anthony's thoughts turned back inconsequently to the first time he had stood beside her dressing-table; he remembered the rapturous excitement of that hour.

He had courted her in his quick style of conqueror. Brought
to her father's house in Dublin for the sole reason of his
eligibility, he had been mightily pleased to play his expected
part, once his eyes had fallen upon Molly. Her virginal beauty
that hinted so sweet a promise sent him home in a storm of
desire that December night of their first meeting. And on the
twenty-fifth morning of the next April, five years ago this very
month, he waited for her at the Communion rails of her parish
church.

His wedding day had been too full of emotion for easy
remembrance, but he saw that Winterhalter dress come swaying
up the aisle to him again, crinoline, orange blossom, Mellick
lace—all white as the bride's white bosom. He saw her later
in the carriage, saw rice and flowers and slippers in the air,
and a receding group on the steps of her father's house; he felt
again the soft blue cloth of her going-away dress and smiled
at the shy face in the cabriolet bonnet. Before they went abroad
they had made a long pause in their London hotel, drowsed
and exhausted in their happy consummation. Memory touched
him warmly here. He roused himself with a little laugh and
took his hands from her. Raptures of five years ago were
sweet enough, but he was hungry.

"Don't you want your dinner, Anthony?"

"Indeed I do. Half-past six seems a queer time to be thinking of it."

"It's only an hour later than you had it at King's Crescent."

"Oh, I know—I'll get used to it. But I'm a hungry man
to-night, I tell you. And you've all the house to show me
afterwards, my little girl!"

"Come on down then." They moved to the door.

"I'll look at the children first," he said on the landing.

"They're sound asleep."

"I won't be a minute."

He sped to the next floor, still with his catlike spring lest
he should wake the slumberers.

§ 3

THE nurseries were on the south side of the house. He crept
in at a half-open door. Windows and curtains were flung

wide in obedience to him, though nurses trembled for his madness. The moon was up, mocking the babies' night light. Anthony looked benevolently at Jack, and pulled the coverlet straight over the fat and dark-haired two-year-old. At Mary, aged ten months, he peeped more cautiously. And then he crept through another open door to an adjoining room. Denis, his eldest son, slept here. Light haloed the child's bed, but he lay in radiance, undisturbed, offering his baby beauty to the moon without a quiver of foreboding. Anthony fell into immobility beside him and studied the lovely little head that was so like his wife's. The child's face was lifted to the moonlight, and wore a shadow of wistfulness now in the composed gravity of infant sleep. The small, compact mouth was closed and breaths came and went in peaceful rhythm. All seemed to be well with Denis in his new bed in his new house. But Anthony still watched him, without moving.

He loved this child inordinately. He loved him with a grave and apprehensive love for which there was no clear reason and which seemed out of place in his forthright character.

There had been nothing unusual in the circumstances of Denis's birth. He was born after fourteen happy months of marriage. His parents had been pleased and matter-of-fact in their expectancy. There was satisfaction in spreading the news through the family, some members of which had already begun to wag their heads over the delay in this part of the wedding programme. All went well with the pregnancy; Molly had fits of weeping, of course, and fits of petulance and other woman's symptoms, but married sisters and married aunts and all the married bosom friends of all these ladies saw everything to rejoice at in these developments of her state and circled about with smiles and whisperings and a hundred contradictory counsels. As her time drew near she grew extremely senti-mental and made Anthony promise that if the child was a son they would call him Denis. The name offended him; he would have chosen from the plain names of his family; but Molly had come on it in novel-reading, and thought it very gentle-manly. "A lovely Irish name," she said it was. She was in no state to be crossed just then, and so he agreed to call the child as she desired.

In the night of Molly's labour, Anthony bore the historic

pain of husbands in such hours, and when it was safely over they allowed him to take a look at his little son. He was a weary, almost an indifferent, man as he bent over the child that some woman held out to him. He wanted sleep and silence; wanted to get away from clucking midwives and forget the screams of his young wife. He was not ready to be interested in his son, with the mother's ordeal still shaking him. But as he looked, to satisfy the women, the child gave out a little thin thread of a cry. A small, unearthly sound, hardly a sound at all, but it shivered through Anthony as nothing had done before; it shocked him; it jolted all the wild sensations of the night and overthrew them; it jabbed through his old self down to a nerve of tenderness that the rest of life had left untouched.

Women murmured on all sides. This was Denis, his son. He walked away with a tired step, but aware that a new, untravelled region of his heart was opening for the child they held.

Life crept back to the usual round; the house in King's Crescent emptied itself of old wives; a procession of Considine carriages took Denis to his christening at St. Peter's. Denis John Mary they named him when they washed away his original sin—the third name being added so that the Queen of Heaven might be his especial patroness. Gold mugs and silver plates were engraved for him by uncles and aunts; Honest John bought gilt-edged securities in his name, and Anthony laid down Burgundy. Molly revived and suckled the child contentedly among her pillows. Summer beamed on Mellick and Mellick's river sang a lazy song. But at the store in Charles Street there was no indolence. This year of Denis's birth was the most prosperous that Considine's had known.

"He's lucky," said Honest John. "That fellow will bring luck to the place."

Anthony's love for his son, that had taken hold of him in hysteria, at the end of a long strain, did not relax as might have been expected when normal life returned. It changed indeed. The first raw tenderness became a gentle habit of thought; a joy that was content to flow within and be secret ran now below the man's habitual geniality; his new preoccupation gave a more sober richness to that all-round happiness of his that men might see and envy. He found a use for

thoughtfulness, and looked with new eyes at his world, sometimes, to see how it might strike his son.

Anthony had never in his life wondered about how things
struck people. He was an impetuous fellow, of straightforward habit; he estimated life in what he saw and felt and
bothered little with subtlety. He had a flair indeed for understanding men, but it was a swift, intuitive flair to which he
gave no meditation. He never paused before the human mind.
He visualised Molly, for instance, tenderly and kindly, as his
dear little wife who loved him and whose life and thoughts
were bound up irrevocably and uncomplicatedly with his. She
was all-in-all to him, he might have said in the phrase of his
day, and outside of that span she had no existence for him. He
himself was what Molly saw, what other men saw, except for
the trivial secrecies of family and business life which he supposed they might have the wits to take for granted. And of the
spirit's hinterlands he had never heard. That people who were
closely associated, who loved each other, who were intimate,
could live apart as well, could keep a space withheld, could have
a separate vision on the world and a celibate life in it he never
realised. Molly was married to him and happy—that was all
he needed to know. He was her husband according to the
canons of his day; his brain was a sound one and his personality forceful. He led, and his wife followed. It never occurred
to him that she should not, or that there was anything else for
her to do; he had not loved her quite enough for that.

He was to love Denis more. He was in fact to love him with
a love which, if it was paternal, would bear no resemblance
to the orthodox fatherly feeling inspired by his other children.
They would grow to be more like him; younger sons would
have more of his simplicity, more of his audacity and sense of
fun, more of his engaging insolence and family pride. Beautiful daughters would gratify and amuse him. He would be
generous and cheerful with them all, a conventional autocrat,
glad to do his duty for them, fond even of indulging them
when that occurred to him. Such education and opportunities
as were open to the wealthy in Ireland they would have at his
hands, and welcome. An excellent firm father he was indeed,
just as he was an excellent firm husband.

But, by some freak of emotion, his usually self-confident

spirit was destined to hover anxiously round Denis. There was a poignancy and strangeness in the child's attraction for him. Delicacy and something as foreign to him as shyness stood on guard before the new emotion. He was not shy of it in his own thoughts; he accepted that this love for his son was greater and more unmanageable than he had expected it to be; in time he saw how it differed from his attitude to his other children, and that it transcended the love he bore his wife. He did not examine it more than that; he simply felt it. But he was shy of it before the world, and for deeper than diplomatic reasons. He would not bear that anyone should enter into this love of his for Denis. No one must brush near to it, not Molly or any other. If family talk touched close sometimes, he was cunning to wave it off to safety again with a light hand. The infant Denis taught him subtlety, and by its use he was able to make it apparent that he loved his children equally and his wife above them all. Even she, who loved him with jealousy, saw no more in his preoccupation with Denis than that extra proprietorship that any head of a respectable family might feel in his heir-apparent. Anthony was glad to let it go at that.

It was for Denis that he had built this house that Molly said she did not want and that the family in general considered an extravagance.

It had occurred to him one day during some slight illness of the child's that this strangely endearing son of his would be happier among green and growing things and in the clean, soft airs of the Vale of Honey than behind a brown façade in King's Crescent.

The idea grew with that speed which characterised all Anthony's ideas. While it was still shooting, he happened to drive by the estate of River Hill, which had been on the market since its house had been blown up in '48. Its invitation was irresistible to his immediate mood. He drove in through its ruined gates and over the grass-grown avenue under a long tunnel of old lime trees. He stumbled about among the sad stones of the broken house; he ranged the long slopes of meadow and lawn and strained his eyes to catch every detail of the open view, southward between the elms and limes to the grey, slumberous blur of Mellick and westward over the water to the subtly coloured bogs and the quiet Bearnagh hills. He trampled through the undergrowth of the little birch-wood that sloped down on the north side to the water; he smoked a cigar as he paced up and down the curving river-path. For a while he dreamt there, trying to see the beauties of this place through Denis's misty eyes.

But dreams were of little use to him.

He bought River Hill, and put the King's Crescent house up for sale. He got the money for his new house from his father; he got the services of Mr. Cleethorpes Downey. In short, he got his way as he always did, while everyone grumbled at his obstinate impetuosity. But no one guessed, because he would never let them do so, that all this fuss and extravagance rose out of a sudden whim to please his small, first-born son.

To-night then, with at last a half-hearted blessing on it from his father and a good-humoured dropping of the argument from Molly, Anthony had come home to take possession of River Hill. His veins beat quickly again as he looked down at Denis round whom it all had grown, to whom it would all be given. He heard the river sobbing below the fields and wondered if he would ever get used to its voice so near him. He breathed the delicious air and smiled at the moon in the elm tree.

"He'll love it," he thought. "Oh, Denis, you'll simply love this house."

Then he tiptoed downstairs to Molly and to dinner.

THE THIRD CHAPTER

A T TWO o'clock on the following Sunday twelve Considines
sat round the dining-table at River Hill, and addressed
themselves to clear soup and an excellent sherry.

Mahogany, serge hangings, Turkey carpets, gilt-framed oil
paintings; no opulent fitting of the 1860 convention was
absent from this new dining-room. But three tall windows let
in floods of tender light, spilling it on wine and silver, on
polished wood and swaying daffodils, on Caroline's emeralds,
on Molly's hair. There was a breeze too, since where Anthony
sat there must be open windows. A wood fire crackled, voices
hummed, and silky crinolines sighed demurely; daffodils
swayed in a monumental centrepiece. Far off the river crooned.
The commonplace setting was somehow edged in beauty.

A lively group the twelve around the table made in all their
panoply of contrast and resemblance, with their ties of blood
and marriage plaited up and down between them, binding and
straining them apart and binding them again, making them
eternally interesting to one another, eternally irritating,
eternally important.

It was a highly nervous organism, this united family. All
twelve of them were tremendously alive, even Danny Mulqueen,
alive to the fingertips. That was evident from the torrents of
their talk—they were great talkers—and from the frequency
of their disagreements. Their common vitality, which kept
them in sympathy with one another, made them irritable too
and jealous, made them sardonic, exacting, sentimental, mocking and faithful and harsh. Individuals all, they were held

together in a strange and much multiplied Siamese-twinship
of the spirit, but they kept sane because of their freakish
ability to take pleasure in the inconvenience of the state. To-day
the sad garland of the Spring was binding them in an unexpected mood of softness and the dominating presence of
Honest John distracted them somewhat from their nervy
interplay of cut and thrust. More than one of them may have
felt that the occasion was suspiciously like the opening of a
new chapter in their story—Anthony's chapter—and that
thought frightened them and **made** them solicitous to keep it
from visiting the mind of the dour, beloved old man, whose
eyes seemed now with every day to gather a darker brooding.

Anthony indeed was more afraid of this possibility than
any of them. He addressed himself with care to the rôle of
unimportant youngest son.

"I hope this sherry is all right, Joe," said he. "I'm always
afraid of your expert palate."

Joe was pleased. "Pretty good, Anthony. Just about dry
enough, I think. Just about. Donovan ships it for you, I
suppose?"

"Yes. I find him reliable."

"Quite sound on sherry. But take my tip and never trust
him to buy port for you, my boy. He knows as much about
port as a new-born kitten."

"Well, James," Agnes was saying uncertainly, "as a rule
I don't drink wine."

James Lanigan set down the decanter. "That settles it,
Agnes," said he. "A principle's a principle."

"Wine and wenches empty men's purses," said Danny Mulqueen, who spoke mostly in proverbs, and who even seemed to
think in them. His whole face would lighten if anyone said
that it was no use locking the stable after the horse was gone.

Caroline and Eddy were enjoying a private joke.

"London will be the ruin of you, Ted." Her voice was soft
with fun. James Lanigan looked across sharply at his wife.

Anthony had arranged his guests at table with respect for
the tradition of Considine parties but also with an eye to peace
and compatibility. Honest John, of course, sat at Molly's right
hand, a place that always pleased him well, for he had a soft
corner for this pretty daughter-in-law. And Father Tom, by

reason of his Roman collar, had pride of place at her left side.

This admirable, handsome priest had a knack of boring his young brother Anthony. Father Tom was hard-working, virtuous, courtly, zealous and intelligent—a credit to his cloth and to Maynooth. He was also pompous and a bit touchy, liking to lay down the law and strike attitudes, liking to gossip advisorily with ladies. He could sit a horse superbly and it was his secret grief that the Bishop of Mellick, with whom he was eager to find favour, disapproved with violence of fox-hunting priests. Therefore he might never hunt the fox, a pursuit which seemed to him to be the best of all legitimate earthly pleasures. But there were compensations. Father Tom was becoming renowned as a pulpit orator and could preach as eloquent a sermon as any cleric in Ireland. Fair-haired, tall, suave, careful in dress, careful in behaviour, he cut a fine celibate figure in the world. He had kept the whole of his difficult bargain with the Church, and in the effort he had come by now, in middle life, to lay an over-emphasis on the horribleness of those sins of the flesh which he must never know outside of theological books, training himself to believe that the sensualities were an incomparably greater evil in the world than cruelty or dishonesty or greed. He was inclined to harp on the Catholic's Sixth Commandment, preaching sermons for which he was already locally famous on the horrors of night-walking and company-keeping and the loathsome goings-on in the lanes round Mellick after dark. On the subject of "morality," which he seemed to take to mean exclusively man's conduct of his sexual life, Father Tom was fanatical. He could be hair-raising about the night life of cities he had never seen, and his hints as to the prevalence in Ireland of what he called "the social evil" were nightmarish. He went in perpetual sorrow, poor Father Tom, for the decline in purity among Irish girls—but somehow still the adventurous were finding that, for all his stimulating guarantee, the historical chastity, or coldness, of Irishwomen was not yet entirely a matter of history.

Anthony was not interested in Tom's purity mission, but sometimes, if he was feeling mischievous, he liked to start him on his hobbyhorse. Mischief indeed was what Tom was always rousing in Anthony, when he wasn't rousing his temper.

"Did you have two collections at St. Peter's, sir, this morning?" he said innocently to his father.

"I believe we did," said John indifferently.

"And so did we in this parish," Anthony went on. "Going to Mass is as expensive as going to the theatre these times."

Tom bridled.

"The second collection was exceptional, Anthony. You may not be aware that the Bishop himself preached the charity sermon for it at the Cathedral and that it was taken up in every church in the diocese."

"I was not, then," said Anthony. "And what was his lordship begging for this time?"

"There was a notice in every church porch." Tom seemed to wish to leave it at that. But the table obviously expected him to go on. His colour mounted.

"The money is needed to found a refuge for fallen women," he said courageously.

The ladies resumed the clatter of knives and forks with tactful unanimity, but Danny Mulqueen lost his head and knocked his into his lap.

"Fingers were made before forks," he said cheerfully as he recovered them.

"Are there fallen women in Mellick?" asked Anthony, ignoring a grimace from Molly.

"God help us all!" prayed Sophia, who sat on charity committees and was the wife of Dr. Joe Considine.

"That will do, Anthony," said Teresa, who sat on more committees than Sophia. But Tom addressed himself quietly to roast lamb and mint sauce.

"Anyway, I'm glad I wasn't let in for his lordship's eloquence on that subject," said Honest John suddenly. "We'd a nice plain address from Father O'Malley at St. Peter's."

"I know. No floweriness—just plain sense," said Anthony —-"that's what I like."

Now floweriness was Tom's great quality as a preacher. Indeed, he was at present giving a series of Lenten Sunday evening sermons at St. James's Cathedral, where he was senior curate, and these sermons were so particularly flowery and were creating such a sensation that he had thoughts of having them printed in a little book. He said nothing now, however—and really, this first roast lamb of the year was delicious.

"I think I like our priest here," Anthony went on. He and Molly had made a state attendance at their new parish church that morning. "Short sensible talk he gave us. The best sermon I've heard in six months."

Molly shook her head reprovingly at him and he subsided with a smile. Perhaps that last was too much, since only a week ago he had had the enforced privilege of listening to the second of the flowery Lenten addresses at the Cathedral. Poor old Tom!

§ 2

THE day was just sharp enough for perfect enjoyment of the carefully warmed claret, a smooth and lovely vintage, not to be wasted on the women, who had their favourite sweet sauternes. All except Caroline. "Red wine, please," said she to the servant. "Ahem!" said James Lanigan, across the table—"and do you really think it will agree with you, my dear?" The only answer went to him from her eyes, over the rim of her garnet-burning glass, and a man might have been forgiven if that language baffled him.

The grape did its work, and so for that matter did the sugared grape, if the slight roll of Sophia's eye meant anything. The party shook down into itself and grew happy. Molly's eyes strayed less often to Anthony and the servants and she was able to give her attention to the kindly, growling jokes and compliments of Honest John.

Dr. Joe stroked his Jehovan beard—he looked as if he had been Doré's model for Jehovah—and lifted his glass affectionately from time to time towards his wife, Sophia. Agnes seemed positively interested in what James Lanigan was saying about English goings-on in a place called Tien-tsin, and even Tom appeared to be forgetting the thorns that hide in floweriness.

Danny Mulqueen sat next to Tom, for no other reason than that he had to be seated somewhere. Danny had no appearance to speak of, simply looked small and fat and older than his age, which was forty-four. He had thin red hair and a freckled skin. He was stupid and without viciousness, very much the sort of "in-law" that turns up in most families at one point or another. The best day's work he ever did for himself was when he set the notion going in Teresa Considine's head that she would marry him or know the reason why. And he didn't do that deliberately.

There had been an unforgettable family quarrel when Teresa announced her intention of marrying Danny Mulqueen. She was twenty-three at the time, but had about her already a slow and formidable deliberation of purpose. Anthony remembered the wild storms that had raged in the dining-room at Kilmoney Street, and how her impregnable obstinacy had infuriated him, fifteen-year-old though he was, and no one asking for his opinion. How Honest John had raged at her, how their gentle, ailing mother had implored, with the sere of death already in her face. And quite in vain.

It was a monstrously bad match, and even at that date a sad come-down for a Considine. For although the family and the business were still in Kilmoney Street, Honest John was an alderman, and sat on the Harbour Board and in the Chamber of Commerce. There was no reason at all why a good alliance should not be arranged for his eldest daughter with some well-thought-of young man in the New Town. Granted her face was plain, her fortune would be handsome.

No. Nothing would do Teresa—Teresa, the proudest of them all!—but she must marry Danny Mulqueen, who was a nobody, you might say, without place, appearance, or family—a mere clerk in some hole-and-corner office. Nobody even knew clearly how he first set foot in the house. But there he was, and he had put some sort of a spell on Teresa with his proverbs and his smiles. She married him and as a consequence her fortune had to be larger than it would have been in happier circumstances, since no Considine could be disgraced by a poor establishment, and Danny had nothing to bring. House and carriage and furniture were provided by Honest John, as well as a safely invested dowry. And Danny was forced to leave his obscure occupation and perch to better purpose on a stool in Considine's. He fell on his feet, in short, and now after seventeen years he had forgotten that he was ever anything but a shrewd and successful merchant and the invaluable counsellor of Honest John. He had a high opinion of his own business ability.

The family had long given up wondering about Teresa's inexplicable passion—and indeed if any of them had guessed the truth, which was that her morbid young awareness of her plain face and consequent lonely dread that no man would ever seek her out had caused her to reach frantically towards Danny's timid admiration, Teresa, at this distance from her own youth, would honestly have believed that they were mad. After her marriage she became once more and remained the strongest pillar among them of the family pride. Danny and she had so far contributed eight to Honest John's quota of grandchildren, the eight plainest perhaps, but indubitably eight grandchildren.

It was unfortunate that two years after this unworthy marriage, Mary, the second Considine daughter, who had a certain prettiness, should have startled her world by wishing to cast it aside and be a nun. There was another quarrel over that; it seemed as if none of the girls could behave reasonably. But the quarrel had no spirit in it, for Mother was really dying now, and Honest John could find no room for another trouble in his heavy heart. So Mary and her fortune went down to Friary Lane, to the Little Sisters of the Poor, and there they were to this day. Honest John took pleasure nowadays in calling on this daughter and talking over family news with her in the chilly convent parlour. In her life of renunciation she had not renounced Considine blood, and her heart, emptied of worldliness for herself, was greedy still for the prestige and solidification of her father's house. Her sisters and brothers had to bring their families to see her as often as the rule allowed, and she took a burning interest in all their material affairs. She prayed for their intentions, which were generally of that worldly and transient kind that the whole of her own life mutely criticised; she paraded them delightedly before the other nuns; she endured mortifications so that they might suffer none. She was a paradox of unselfish vanity.

Caroline, who was sitting next to Dan now, between him and Eddy, had been the most satisfactory of the Considine daughters. In the first place, she was the only beautiful one, and perhaps she alone ever guessed how much pleasure her beauty gave to her inarticulate father. She and Anthony, and after them Eddy—the three handsomest and least like him superficially—were his three pets, and they knew it, if the others didn't. But Caroline, because she was a girl-child, had carried off the lion's share of this surreptitious favouritism. He adored her above them all, without ever dropping a hint of his adoration.

Her marriage had been staggeringly correct and had come to pass without the least manœuvring. It was on her twenty-second birthday that James Lanigan had come to Honest John in the dining-room at Lower Mourne Street with the news that he had Miss Caroline's permission to present his suit. Honest John was a contented man that night when he drank to Caroline's betrothal. Lanigan had the reputation in Mellick of being a brilliant lawyer; he was thirty and doing extremely well for his age. A bit dry and dictatorial for his age maybe, and inclined to speechify about the movements of politicians; but a fine fellow, of distinguished appearance, and coming of dignified middle-class stock. It was exactly the right sort of marriage for a Considine.

When Honest John gave Caroline away in St. Peter's he told himself that the town of Mellick had never seen so beautiful a bride. That was ten years ago, and she was the mother of six children now, but the old man's affectionate eyes, brooding towards her across the table, saw none of time's changes in her face. Anthony also admired her profile more than once during the meal, and wondered idly, as he had often done before, that ten years of life with that thin-lipped fellow—he didn't care much for Lanigan—had dimmed so little of her radiance.

She was very like Anthony, with his vitality and glow of health, attributes that had brought her gallantly through much childbearing. Her eyes were brilliant lightning-blue; her hair was the fairy-tale raven's wing, and fairy-tale blood-red came and went in her cheeks. But Honest John was deceived in thinking that the years had not touched her, and so was Anthony. For the beauty that had glowed with such softness in her once was burning frostily now and with too crisp a flame had they but known, and the once ingenuous eyes were guarded. Perhaps Eddy noticed these things, on his occasional returns, but if he did he made no comment.

He was always glad to waste an hour with Caroline, who tuned well to his easy-going urbanity, and whom from childhood he had loved especially. But he was an adaptable person, and when it was necessary for him to turn to the left now and then to entertain Sophia, no one could have guessed that he found his sister-in-law a whit less charming than his sister.

Wine, of which she was fond, always roused reminiscent frivolity in Sophia, and she was now entertaining Anthony with vivid but oft-told memories of the social delights enjoyed in the old days by her family, the Quilliheys of Mountjoy Square in Dublin, and of the struggle it had been for a woman of her nature to give them up fourteen years ago to marry Dr. Joe. Anthony's own impression of those social delights was that her struggle, and the struggle of all the genteel Quilliheys, had been to keep them up, and that Joe's application for the hand of the hook-nosed and dowerless Sophia had resembled nothing so much as the relief of an exhausting siege. He smiled indulgently now; the family was used to these innocent intoxications of Sophia. Jingling her bracelets, fluttering femininely, she turned to gather Eddy into her visions of the past.

"Ah, Eddy—you know what it means—the life of a capital city—of its leading families, I mean! Never shall I forget those days—the card parties, the fêtes champêtres, the balls! Ah, Eddy, the balls!"

And Eddy, who cared little for dancing, agreed that the balls were an intoxicating memory.

Eddy Considine was the sort of man who was liked in England for his unmistakable Irishry, and admired in Ireland for his total lack of it. His leisurely, civilised manners belied his business capacities, which were excellent. He had now spent six years in London as Considine's representative, and he seemed to enjoy his bachelor life there. But he never spoke of it with exactitude. He was tall and broad like his three brothers, with softer lines to his face and with less definite colouring than theirs, except for the family blue of his sunken, intelligent eyes. An agreeable, courtly fellow, something of a dandy, something of a faddist. Anthony and Caroline loved and trusted him, and Honest John was proud of his business ability and inclined to indulge his foibles.

But other members of the family were not so easy in their minds about their brother Eddy. There was a feeling that he couldn't be up to much good all by himself over there in London. Indeed, according to Teresa, Tom fretted himself terribly about the probable state of Eddy's soul. She herself thought it odd for him not to marry—thirty-five now and as well-to-do as any of them! Every time he came home Teresa led out suitable victims for him—and so did Sophia. They gave parties for that purpose. And there wasn't a nice girl in Mellick who wouldn't jump at Eddy Considine, they told each other. Would he oblige by proposing to one of them? Not he. Teresa washed her hands of him every year. But hand-washing is a repetitive business, and she never seemed to reach finality with it. And still there remained something about this brother that dimly frightened the shrewd Teresa in her heart of hearts. Something vague and unfamiliar about his ways. He positively ought to marry. There had even once been a rumour, vehemently hushed up by charitable Tom, that Eddy did not always go to Mass on Sunday. But that was sheer slander, Teresa said. None of this talk was allowed to percolate to Honest John of course, and most of it was kept from the virginal Agnes.

Teresa sat opposite to Sophia, at Anthony's left hand, and as the bachelor brother coquetted with Joe's wife, she weighed the problem of him all over again, in the intervals of steam-rollering the political pronouncements of James Lanigan. What that man was speeching about she hadn't an idea—God help us, but wasn't he fond of the sound of his own voice? Palmerston's desertion of Reform meant nothing to Teresa. Reform of what? Maybe his lordship was quite right—the word had an unpleasant ring of novelty about it, anyway.

Being Irish, Teresa obviously couldn't be a Conservative, but being a woman she was spared the necessity of knowing for certain which party was which. In any case, political feeling never ran high in Considine blood. The destiny of mankind, or of any race of it, mattered only in so far as it furthered the interests of an established family. Teresa was inclined to

regard politics as she regarded firearms—things that shouldn't
be left about the house. What in the name of goodness was
James always finding to say about the government? No doubt
about it, Eddy was a fine-looking fellow—now either of those
two girls of Patsy Roche's—"Free Trade, did you say, Jim?"
Oh, well, her father was that, anyhow. A small card party,
maybe. She'd have to talk to Sophia afterwards. "What
Treaty, in the name of God? With Louis Napoleon?" Well,
nothing that you'd arrange with France could be right. A
heathen country. But Lord forgive her—wasn't it called the
Eldest Daughter of the Church? It'd be a thousand pities if
he got into bad ways over there—and could you blame him,
with nothing but Protestants and Masons on every hand?

"Yah, don't be bothering me, James," broke out her
exasperated bassoon of a voice.

"But I will be bothering you," said her brother-in-law, with
that immovable lawyer's courtesy of his, "it's very interesting,
Teresa." And the clipped sentences went on without perturbation. 'Twas true for Tom. That London life had far too many
temptations, and what was more, she reflected grimly, he was
looking very well on it. If they didn't get him married off soon,
he'd be set in his peculiar bachelor ways. "Druses, did you say,
James—oh, I beg your pardon, I thought all along you were
talking about the Jews. Nothing you'd say about those ruffians
would amaze me." Sophia seemed to have plenty to say to
Eddy to-day—it was queer the way a drop of wine always set
her off.

"Cream, Teresa?" said Anthony.

All Considine parties were cushioned in cream, though
James Lanigan was the only one in the company who looked
as if he really needed it. He was a handsome, emaciated man,
with a razor of a nose, high temples, and uneasy eyes. His hair
was touched with grey. He was unmistakably a lawyer and a
prosperous one. Since his marriage he had had charge of all
the Considine affairs and he directed them very well.

He turned from Teresa now and leant towards Agnes to
address Dr. Joe beyond her. He had a great deal to say about
the reaction of Eastern affairs on Palmerston's position, and
Joe, who was nothing if not a many-sided man, listened
solemnly and made a few magnificently inaccurate statements

of his own into the bargain. But these didn't matter to James, who was talking, not listening.

Dr. Joe had studied medicine in Paris and passed all his medical examinations—in his own time, that is. He was no good if you rushed him. He had won the hand of Sophia Quillihey, who had been very highly educated by her governess in Mountjoy Square. And he was now enjoying a large and fashionable practice built up on the phrase: "You never know." He was fond of saying "you never know." Also he was fond of a good race-meeting, a good medical joke, a good glass of brandy and a good run with hounds on a Saturday morning. Obviously he was an intelligent man, and so he liked to talk with James, whom he knew to be such another. But he also liked apple pie. However, he could enjoy it very comfortably while still leaning an attentive ear towards his brother-in-law. As for Agnes, playing dormouse in between them, well, she also liked apple pie, and, as James was most meticulous to pass her both sugar and cream, it is unlikely that his discourse inconvenienced her.

Honest John, the sweet-tooth, shouldering away from Joe and imperial politics, gave his plate to a maid for "more of that pie, my good girl" and leant on his elbow to listen to what Molly and Tom were saying about the children. He liked domestic chatter. Danny piped across at him importantly once or twice with some weighty piece of "shop," but the old man did not hear him. He found Danny's business acumen unexciting, a fact which may have accounted for that son-in-law's exaggerated notion of his deafness.

When he had finished his second helping of pie, Molly laid a kind hand on his sleeve.

"Denis and Jack will be wondering what on earth's keeping us. They've finished their dinner long ago. I can hear them in the garden."

"We'll go out to them so, the ruffians. I don't want any of these trimmings, thank you, Molly Bawn," and he waved away the grapes and pears that were circulating now. He smiled down the table and caught Caroline's bright eye.

"Aren't you finished yet?" he growled. "You've fine appetites, God bless you. When I was your age I didn't have all this stoking."

"It is no good growling, father; I intend to eat every one of these grapes," said Caroline.

"I'm finished," said Anthony, "but won't you have a glass of Marsala, sir?"

"Not I," said Honest John.

Father Tom was dutifully quick with his Marsala.

"We give Thee thanks, Almighty God, for these and all Thy benefits, which from Thy bountiful hand . . ."

Dinner was over.

THE FOURTH CHAPTER

THE children were wandering with a nursemaid about naked, unfinished lawns where the builder still left his trail of bricks and mortar. Mary slept in her pram, but Denis and Jack trotted up sedately to the elders, a grotesque, pretty pair in long drawers and tartan petticoats. Honest John greeted them with friendly noises, and they went to him confidently, as children do to grandparents. The uncles and aunts made amiable comments in respect to the size, weight, and colour of the two little boys. Teresa thought Jack was getting bandy, and Sophia picked him up to "take the strain off his legs." But the solicitous action put a strain on his feelings, and for all her motherly wiles, he had to be returned yelling to his nursemaid.

Joe and Tom lighted immense cigars and stalked apart to get a look at the new house. Anthony, holding Denis by the hand, talked to his father of what he was going to do with the garden; Molly twirled a jonquil in her fingers and half-listened to Sophia's recollections of the view from Sir Timothy Tuohy's house on the Liffey; Teresa sailed down the path where the nursemaid was, to remonstrate with Jack and inspect the sleeping Mary; Danny Mulqueen discoursed in parables to Agnes, whose inattentive eyes kept wandering past him to the children. James buttonholed Eddy about England's fiscal policy. Caroline wondered how one got down to the river.

"Are not your shoes too thin, my dear?" said James.

Molly indicated the path, and moved wistfully as if to take it herself. But Sophia was monumentally happy with her

47

memories of high life in the capital city, and Caroline's yellow-patterned crinoline went swaying alone down the thicket of silver birch, with only James's quick glance to follow it, and the indolent musing of Eddy's eyes.

They drifted about, smoked, walked, laid down the law, and crisscrossed with one another to form new patterns within their unity. The sun warmed them, the birds sang. Smoke-wreathed and grey in the south lay Mellick, their town that had raised them up and now was proud of them. The spire of its cathedral, where Tom would preach to-night, pierced the soft heaven like a prayer, and the old Italian chime came faintly even to here from the square tower of another church that the Protestants had stolen. A scattering of snow gleamed remotely on the high eastward mountains, but all the immediate valley was full of spring. The river danced and colours of renewal gleamed up from the old bogs in the west and from the patterned hills. Wild jonquils starred the unmown grass, and lime and elm trees wore their new green buds. The world was new to-day with Anthony's new house.

But Teresa and Sophia must examine that at closer quarters. They had often gone over it during building, but now that it was furnished there would be much posthumous advice for Molly about her arrangements. She had to throw her flower on the path and take her sisters-in-law indoors.

§ 2

THERE was a drawing-room and a dining-room and a large breakfast-room for the children's meals, and another fine room that was to be Anthony's—"smoke-room," Teresa said, but Sophia, who had had a governess, thought it should be "the library." And no less than ten bedrooms, not counting serv-ants' rooms, and a bathroom with a new kind of hot and cold shower that had a mackintosh curtain hanging from it on a circular ring, for fear you'd see yourself in the mirror when you stood up to use it. Gas was laid on, of course, and there were beautiful modern gasoliers everywhere, except, mind you, in the drawing-room and in Molly's bedroom, places where you'd think there would be no sparing. But Molly explained that that was by her wish—and the sisters-in-law wagged their heads in perplexity.

Molly had not had gas in those two rooms because she was so reactionary as not to like it. Anthony had been disappointed, but, anxious to coax her approval of the house, let her have her way. She could not say why it was, but the flat yellow glare of gas jets gave her no pleasure.

Molly had a shadowed and troubling sense of beauty in some things. Hesitantly, unselfconsciously, she felt certain lovelinesses and took pleasure in them; shadowy moments of candlelight, sudden mirror glimpses, grouping of winter trees, reeds in an evening pool; it made her happy to observe such things. She loved flowers, to carry them, to touch them; Teresa said she had no knack of arranging them. Neither had she; she only fumbled with them dreamily, and let them fall, and gathered them up again, and stood and stared at them. But always they looked lovely where she placed them, and gave her eyes contentment.

It was this dim apprehension of beauty that had made her plead against gaslight and gasoliers, and that gave to her opulent and undistinguished drawing-room an air of wistful quietude. Wood fire and candlesticks; open piano, open windows, breezes from the river; flowers and flowers reflected —somehow by these the ugliness of ottomans and whatnots and antimacassars was veiled, and Sophia vaguely felt a lurking elegance, and Teresa said "weren't servants terrible to leave it so untidy?"

On Molly's new bedroom the visiting ladies made no comment, though the breath of dreaminess floated there almost tangibly. Flowers again, and blue silk hangings on the bed, and over everything the half-murmur of a secret. Why did Teresa say nothing? Did she, for she was intelligent, feel her modesty offended? Did she apprehend that this was the room of a woman much desired of her husband and willing to be desired?

§ *3*

THREE other Considines paced together over the piece of ground that once had been a kitchen garden, and soon was to be that again. Their steps were slow and short out of consideration for that one of them who was not yet four and went in tartan petticoats. He walked in the middle happily, and held the hands of his father and grandfather.

"These old trees are blossoming well for you," said Honest John.

"Diseased, though."

"Ah, very likely." Honest John snapped off a twig of apple blossom and shook his head at it. Denis put up his hand and the old man gave it to him with a smile.

"Lovely flower. Thank you, grandpa."

Anthony was struck for the first time by a resemblance between the eyes of Honest John and those of the little boy who was so like Molly. In the child they were young and clear, and in the old man's face they shone dark and impenetrably sad. But relationship expressed itself uncannily between them as they met above the apple blossom—something in the shape, in the setting, in the folding of the flesh about them for a smile. For half a second he saw it. Then it was gone, and he could not find it again.

"I've a man coming down from Dublin next week to advise about the whole lay-out of the garden," said Anthony.

His father nodded. They talked of other things.

"We'll have to move Danny out of the receiving office, Anthony. Flannery and he are worse than a bag of cats together—and between them they're making a fine mess of things."

"Well, I don't think that's Flannery's fault."

"Neither do I. He's no great shakes, but he's got more sense than our poor old Danny."

"What can we do with him, sir? The receiving's the easiest job in the place."

"Maybe, but it's an important one. Can't afford to have a pair of old women sparring over it, my boy."

Anthony laughed.

"We'll have to find a sinecure for Danny."

"There's never been one of those in Considine's!"

"Then we must invent one, sir. And that's the sort of thing you'd be no good at inventing."

"I'd like you to go down to their office one of these days

and have an eye round and talk to Flannery. I'm tired of playing chess with Danny."

"He's a hardy annual of a problem, and no mistake."

"Well, he'll be your problem soon, not mine," said Honest John.

"We don't want any of that sort of talk, thank you; do we, Denis?"

The old man's knotted hand dropped Denis's little one, and lay for a minute on the child's soft hair. Silence folded the three of them. It was Honest John who broke it.

"There are changes to be made, Anthony, and I'd like to be there to make them."

"Please, sir!"

The other did not notice him. "I built the business from day to day, as it came. There's nothing wrong with it, but it's a bit old-fashioned now—wants reorganising. I'd like to bring it up-to-date, before I leave it."

"There's years of time for that," said Anthony gently.

"Maybe."

"What's come over you, man? Sure, you're only seventy."

"I was a working man when I was ten, my son. That took a bit off my life, I think."

"Father, it didn't!"

"Didn't it? Anyway, Denis, don't you go to work for him when you're ten, do you hear?" The child was trotting in front of them now and smiled back enchantingly when he heard his name. Anthony was heavy with his father's mood. He looked at the great, bowed shoulders and sombre brows of Honest John with new anxiety.

"You're feeling well?" he asked.

"Quite well, but I'm feeling seventy, Anthony—and that's a queer sensation."

"Ah, what's seventy?"

"Nothing much, maybe. But if a man hasn't the gumption to begin to get ready for his end at that age without being forced to, he doesn't deserve a long life."

"Well, you deserve one, and you're going to have it."

"I'm not grumbling at what I've had, my son. But there's no occasion to upset yourself. Simply I'm going to alter things in Considine's, and you've got to help me."

"All depends on what you want done."

"We'll go into it one of these days. There's no hurry."

"That's true anyway," said Anthony.

"I haven't done badly in my time," said Honest John, dreamily, and he paused under a blossoming branch. "But the son who'll take charge of things for me when I go is twice the man I was." His sad eyes were unusually gentle, but Anthony did not see them. Tears came to him easily, and now, as his father's voice died, old man and little child and snowy apple trees were blurred together in sudden mist. He could say nothing; affection was tearing his heart. "I hope you'll give it up to that rascal there as happily as I'll leave it all to you," Honest John continued, and he was trudging along the path again before Anthony's eyes cleared. Even then he couldn't find words for his father, so he stood a minute to look at the two ahead of him. And as he looked, the anguish that he felt before the nearness of death to Honest John was lost in a dreamy thought of his little son. How many springs Denis would play with apple blossom, how many Aprils he had yet to spend! He went forward and lifted the child to his shoulder.

"We're tired out with walking, you and I," he said to him. "We're no match at all for this frisky grandfather of yours."

"Take me back to your fine house," said Honest John, and as they turned down the twisty path he took Anthony's arm, and talked almost dreamily of Denis.

"I don't mind telling you that this small whippersnapper is my favourite," he said. "The pick of the bunch. I wish I could live to see him starting off in Charles Street, the ruffian!" Anthony felt his heart swell with painful love for the child that rode on his shoulder and the old man who leant on his arm.

§ 4

EDDY went to find Caroline along the river-path, and saw her there before she saw him. She was standing on a flat mossy rock by the water and gazing towards the hills. The wind disturbed her hair, and the corners of her little silk shawl flapped about under her joined hands. Her body was relaxed as if a dream possessed her.

"Caro!" her brother called when he was near her.

"Hello, Ted." These two used the abbreviations of childhood still, and their eyes were soft for each other now when he came and stood beside her on the rock.

"Are your feet wet?"

"That's not your question. That's someone else's. Why should they be?"

"Well, with mooning up and down a perfectly dry path," said he, mischievously. He rarely poked fun at Lanigan, but she chuckled now without comment, and became lost in watching the swirl of the strong brown water under the rock.

He lighted a cigarette.

"Come and walk, Caro. It's draughty on this perch of yours." He helped her back to the river-path and they strolled on contentedly.

"I like it here," said Caroline. "Molly's a lucky creature."

"She'll be in her element in this place; all this wetness and moss, and woods and bluebells——" Eddy waved a vague hand.

"She's having another baby," said Caroline.

"So I hear."

"Look how full the tide is. Oh, Ted, did you see that salmon?"

"Where?"

"A huge one out there in the middle. Good times we used to have up and down this river! Do you remember?"

"I do. We're getting on, Caro. Isn't it dreadful? Shall I tell you my age?"

"You needn't. I never forget my own."

"I hate growing old," he said softly.

"So do I. But isn't it hard to believe it? I feel young, Ted. Truly I do. Sometimes in the night I have to din it into myself that I'm thirty-two, that I've six children, and that I'll never, never be young again!"

"But Caro, you *are* young. Young and so lovely."

"Ah, Ted!"

It was becoming Eddy's dilettante foible to search for the sting and the salt in beauty before he would admit it beautiful, but bitterness was sometimes almost too apparent in his sister Caroline. It occurred to him now and then that probably the love that he had felt for her since boyhood would long ago have died if she were happy. "And then how different we'd both have been!" he would muse, half-shuddering at some vision of himself made normal. He was a peculiar fellow.

At this moment her face was too sad for him. He turned from it.

"Do you remember a picnic, Caro—the summer before you were married—up there in Kilcrusha Woods?"

"I was thinking of it a minute ago," she said.

"It was great fun," he went on, with the slowness of one who picks his way by a dim path. "The best picnic we ever had, I think. You and Alice O'Leary—do you remember, the two of you went and got lost, and there was terrible excitement for fear we'd have to face home to father without you!"

"Yes." Her eyes were amused at his memories.

"She was a lovely creature. I'll never forget the pair you made in your muslin frocks that sunny day. What happened to her? Didn't she marry an Englishman?"

"A man called Glenster in the Hussars. She's dead now, poor Alice!"

"I never heard that. I remember that when we found the two of you that evening, you looked so excited, we were all quite sure you'd been up to mischief. Were you, I wonder?"

"We were, Ted." She laughed tenderly back to her youth.

"What was it?" he coaxed.

"It's so long ago and so silly—you won't laugh if I tell you?"

He shook his head gravely.

"We had a secret appointment that day with two officers at the other side of the wood. Lord, weren't we rash, Alice and I!"

"You were. If father had ever heard——"

"You might well say!"

"How did you know them?"

"Oh, Alice met them at some party. You remember the way old O'Leary used to run after the military. Alice and I were great friends then, and used to go for walks together—and so I met them. We used to smuggle letters and do all sorts of things. But that picnic appointment was the coolest thing we ever tried. If any of you had seen us——"

"Did they make love to you?"

"Oh, well, yes! We thought they did anyhow. Ah, looking back, how pathetic it was, Ted! They must have found us rather trying really—such innocents we were!—and we thought ourselves wicked, Alice and I!"

"And what happened that day of the picnic!"

"Well, we walked about the woods together. My lieutenant —no, you're not going to get his name—vowed tremendous vows, I remember, and I was in the seventh heaven. He was a handsome creature!"

"You were in love, Caro?"

"I was in love, I think. Ah, yes, I know. I was in love."

"And then what happened?"

"Why, it went on like that, our innocent intrigue—and we were so clever that even Agnes didn't get to know about the walks and the letters. No one knew. And then, in November the regiment was ordered abroad, and—well, suddenly Alice went to England to marry her Hussar—that's all."

He smiled at her tenderly. "What about yours?"

"He didn't want to marry me, after all, it seemed. He had enough money, you see. What he lacked and had to get from a wife was breeding and I hadn't that." She gave a silvery little laugh; flawlessly bred she looked as her ironic mouth curved in amusement. "So much for vows made in Kilcrusha Woods, Ted."

He was tremendously interested. "Am I the only one who's ever heard this story?"

"The only one. And it's my only story. My first, last love."

"That was the winter you married James."

"Yes. I was a silly girl that winter. Always crying in corners, I remember. Poor James!"

"Well, he wanted you and he got you."

"Ah, this lovely day! It's well you and I don't meet often, Ted, you make me talk too much."

"I wish you'd talk to me more."

"I've never much to say, honestly."

"What do you think about, then?"

"The usual things—James and his food, and the children and the house——"

"They're all very interesting topics."

She looked at him wanly.

"You think I need encouraging—that's what you think?"

"We all need that, Caro."

Her hand slid under his arm.

"Why don't you marry?" she asked him.

"Because I've never wanted to," he said.

She hesitated delicately, then risked a euphemism.

"But, well, I mean, you're not a saint, are you?"

He laughed delightedly.

"No, no, I'm not a saint—but for God's sake don't tell that to Tom."

"Is there no woman you'd marry?"

"If I could find your twin somewhere, maybe." He bowed to her half-mockingly.

"My twin would be your sister."

"True for you. Very well then, in that case I'd rather have a sister than a wife. Come over with me, Caro, and darn my socks and give my parties!"

She stopped dead on the path.

"If only I could," she said, "if only you'd take me and hide me over there!"

"Caro," he patted her hand. "I shouldn't talk nonsense, and you shouldn't look solemn about it when I do. How they'd all love you at my parties, lovely Caro, and how you'd hate most of them!"

"Why would I hate them?"

"Because you have sense, and you're born a Considine. You're best off here, and you know it; children, after all, and security, and an appointed place—and all this lovely countryside about you—if it isn't a perfect life, oh, it's still a pretty good one. Believe me."

"Encouraging me again. Ted, why are you so afraid of me? What do you expect me to do?"

"Your duty," he chuckled, "like Nelson's sailors."

"You're getting worse than Tom in your old age!"

"I'm his brother, after all—the whole lot of us, Caro, are tarred with the same brush of respectability. Thank God for that at least!"

"Before you came down here," she said irrelevantly, "I was wondering what they'd say up in that big house if I threw myself in there, and never came back." She pointed to the rushing water. He pressed her hand closer to his side.

"You and I, Caro," he said gently, "are fond of dramatising ourselves. So is Anthony, a bit. So are many of the nicest people. I often play that game of desperate deeds and build up wonderful scenes of remorse and emotion round my coffin. It's a relief sometimes—but it's only a game, because, after all, you see, we don't really want to make other people feel half so much as we want to go on feeling ourselves, and so far as I know the only way to do that is to stay alive. Besides, we're not just ourselves—we're Considines—and that family isn't given to hysteria. And we've father to think of too. We're very nicely hedged about, thank heaven!"

"Yes, father. I'm not so sure if it weren't for him——"

"You're perfectly sure. And if you aren't, then thank God for him."

"Wise old bird, Ted!"

There was a low grey wall between them and the river now, and she turned and leant against it.

"I couldn't bear to die, really," she said, trailing white fingers dreamily along the stone.

"Of course you couldn't. And even if you could, what of the six most beautiful children in Mellick?"

"You think me very selfish, a bad mother."—-He shook his head.—"But I'm fond of them, Ted. Really, I am. How could I not be? Only——" She straightened herself and looked out across the river. She seemed to be seeking words to explain things that to her native shyness were inexplicable. Eddy wondered how he was able to bear the look of wasting puzzled sorrow on her face. When she did speak again, her voice was dry and weary.

"It's not Jim's fault." She gave a bitter little laugh. "He tries, oh, God, he's always trying to be warm and good. Fusses about what I eat and drink, Ted, and whether my feet are dry—he thinks that that's what good husbands have to do! Poor Jim!"

"Don't, Caro."

"Ah, let me—just to you. His sharp face—so certain with everyone else—so nervous and foolish with me. It makes me cruel, Eddy. I get unkinder every day—and I can't stop it.

But if you don't love your husband, what is there to do but hate him? How can you help it? So near you always, so crushed against your life! Oh, it's impossible, it's crazy, without love!"

"But it isn't, dear. Look at the world! Why, almost everyone is putting up with marriage somehow, without what you call love!"

She shuddered. "What are they made of?"

"Flesh and blood, I think. Your husband is very fond of you, very proud of you."

"Oh, yes, he's proud of me. That's his consolation—to parade me."

"Well, he needs some consolation, doesn't he? I don't think he's a very happy man."

"He doesn't know how to be happy. Why, even in the beginning—— Oh, he can't help it." She relaxed against the stone and flickered a smile. "Whatever happened to make me talk like that?"

He picked up her hand and rubbed it between his two.

"Your hands feel like a woman's, Ted."

"Do they?"

"Yes. You're rather like a woman to talk to. Not that I'm a judge; I never talk to any."

"You ought to."

"I can't. I like Molly fairly well—but there's nothing to say. Now if you were about—if you'd been a sister——"

"Oh, God!"

"Would you hate to be a woman?"

"I think so."

"Do you understand them well?"

"I don't understand anyone well."

She mused over him speculatively.

"I wonder what it's like to be you?"

"Riddle-talker. I wonder what it's like to be you!"

They stood and guessed at each other's secret heart for a breath or two.

"Look at that heron," Eddy whispered suddenly.

Leaning eagerly over the parapet, they watched the gawky bird take its mincing way across the rocks below them, and up the river, out of their sight behind a jutting bush.

"There's a nest of them just here," said Caroline. "Molly told me."

"They're welcome. I prefer dry land. Come in and ask Molly to give us tea!"

They went homewards arm-in-arm along the dimming path, and her soft laugh ran before them sometimes like a sprite in the dusk.

§ 5

HONEST JOHN sat in a big chair by Molly's drawing-room fire and spooned damson jam onto hot Sally Lunn. Joe had brought his father's cup from the tea-table, and stood and lectured him on the sugar and cream that was in it. "With all that jam, father! You'll poison yourself, I tell you."

"A grand death, Joe!"

The doctor grew pompous. "I'm speaking seriously, sir. After all, I have given some study to these things."

"Have you now?" said Honest John indifferently. Joe deflated with reluctance. "There's no teaching an old dog new tricks, is there, Danny?" went on the old man. "I never knew a fellow like Danny," he told the company. "He has more proverbs in him than the Bible, but he's never handy with one when it's wanted!"

Danny, at the other side of the room, turned round in a fluster when he heard his father-in-law, and mouthing anxiously, tried to catch the threads and be apposite.

"You're late, my poor man, you're late," said Honest John, and tackled his Sally Lunn.

Molly gleamed softly through the dimness above her gleaming silver. James stood near her, deft to handle her china. Anthony strolled amicably about the room with Tom, showing him the disposition of the furniture and getting him to admire some new "antiques." The family was strong and haphazard in its feeling for "antiques," but Tom really fancied himself as a judge of them, and was the tribal expert on Waterford glass.

Teresa and Agnes talked happily on a high-backed settee about Teresa's eight plain children, whom they both thought very remarkable. Her eldest son, Ignatius, was a very religious, serious boy, and was going to be a Redemptorist Father. His aunt Agnes regarded him as a saint, but it was Reggie, the second boy, the laziest and least plain-looking of her children, whom Teresa liked to talk about. This Reggie was learning to play the piano, and showing an aptitude for it, and his mother, who loved music with a deep, uncritical passion, wanted to boast about him. But Agnes preferred the religious-minded youth, Ignatius, the saviour of souls.

Sophia and Danny pottered along in another corner with some irrelevant little chat of their own. They were inclined to find each other restful, these two who were not blood Considines.

In spite of the tender breeze, the room was warm with the wood fire and the mixed heaviness of buttered toast and hyacinths. The river moaned under all the talk, but the Considines had grown used to its sad voice already.

When Caroline entered the room with Eddy she went and sat on the fender stool at her father's feet.

"Well," he said to her, "settled the affairs of nations down there, you and your crony?"

She leant an elbow on his knees.

"Settled everything, and now we're cold."

James brought her a cup of tea.

"Thank you, Jimmy," she said with a sudden smile at him. The points of his ears turned red.

"Are you sure your feet didn't get damp, my dear?"

She moved to poke the fire and he got no answer. He went back to Molly's table.

"Is that angel cake you're eating, father?" said Caroline.— "Oh, Eddy, bring me some, please!"

"Bread and butter first, my girl," said Honest John.

"I'm not in the schoolroom now, you silly old man! Molly, we saw your heron, but Eddy wouldn't stop to look for the nest."

"I couldn't find it yesterday," said Molly. "The river-path is lovely, isn't it?"

"You own that bit of fishing, I suppose, Anthony?" said Joe.

"Yes, half a mile—a good stretch of water—I don't suppose I'll want to make much use of it."

"Oh!" said Eddy, "in that case, remember the poor!"

"Fishing!" said Honest John—"I thought you'd some sense anyway."

" 'Poor' indeed," said Teresa. "It's a pity about you, Eddy, I must say! Why don't you get married—then you'd have something to complain about!"

Crisscross, crisscross above the moaning river, until one by one the carriages rolled past the window and gathered on the gravel sweep. One, two, three, four, all closed now against the evening chill, and each with its exquisitely matched pair of horses. Time for the family to break apart again. The women rose with silky swishings to find their bonnets and cloaks. The men poured into the hall. Denis and Jack were brought to say good-bye. There was much clamour of voices arranging the week's activities—for Eddy was not staying many days and must be entertained. Teresa and Sophia had laid their plans.

Out into the cool air against the sunset. Jim and Caroline left first, with Tom whom they would drop at the Cathedral House. After them, quickly, for the horses were restive, Teresa and her Danny, and after them, with more deliberation Sophia and Dr. Joe. They were taking Eddy with them, to see their latest-born, his godchild. Last of all Agnes and Honest John, a lonely-looking pair.

"Good-bye, father, thank you for coming."

"Good-bye, grandpa."

All the carriages were gone from the trampled gravel sweep.

Honest John, looking out at the bend of the drive, waved again to Anthony, who lingered in the evening light, holding Denis by the hand.

THE FIFTH CHAPTER

Anthony had been living in River Hill for eighteen months before those alterations were made in Charles Street of which Honest John had spoken in the kitchen garden that first Sunday.

Eddy and Anthony had been the least expensive of the Considine children, since they were content to enter the firm and earn a living there from the time of leaving school. Therefore the understanding was tacit in the family that they would inherit John Considine's business between them. Both, it is true, had received handsome gifts of money at different times, and Anthony had been given a house in King's Crescent at his marriage, and eventually capital to build River Hill—but even allowing for that, he still had, with Eddy, the greatest claim on his father's estate. That he would govern, if he did not practically own, Considine's, and in that sense become head of the family, when Honest John died was common knowledge, since it was unlikely that Eddy would ever be attracted home again to live in Mellick.

There was occasional peevishness against the chance of fortune that would put the youngest brother so high in authority. No doubt Joe worked off a little of it sometimes into Sophia's devoted bosom, as they settled to that rest which few patients ever had the courage to break with a night-call. He seemed now and then in the few minutes before sleep to find his mess of pottage indigestible. Tom also, picking his way in the dark rain from his cheerful bedroom to bring the oils of Extreme Unction to some spent old crone in a swarming tenement, may now and then have regretted that the call to feed His lambs and feed His sheep had been so strong. As for Eddy—well, it is unlikely that he, in the pauses of whatever most engaged his London midnights, took thought to envy his brother Anthony.

In the main, the family recognised that, by reason of personal talents, and general understanding of affairs, Anthony was admirably suited to step into their father's shoes, and that as in any case he would do so, they might as well face the inevitable and look to the arrogant fellow's future prestige among them with a good grace. They were not blind to the fact that their father must now be at least twice as wealthy as he had been twelve years before and that therefore at his death Anthony and Eddy might be infinitely better off than any of them. But that was in the hands of Honest John and there they were prepared to leave it. It was Hobson's choice, but there was no real perturbation in it. They knew their just and impartial father.

They did not know, however, what he was worth. Eddy and Anthony alone shared that secret with him. The rest had only Danny's proverbs and head-shakings to go on, a code which even Teresa did not trouble to read.

§ 2

HONEST JOHN was in fact a warmer man than his sons and daughters might have surmised. Lock, stock, and barrel in 1860 his business was worth two hundred thousand pounds.

It was his intention to disperse this estate among his children—in a manner that would be safe, just, and conservative and in such a way as to keep a united family still united by centralising their interests. It must be disposed too so that its manipulation would be directed by the best brain among the Considines. It must be kept together, for its own enlargement and permanence, and yet belong to all, in the proportion of their claim on it.

So Honest John cogitated as he trudged up and down Charles Street, or sat drinking tea by the fire in the dining-room at Lower Mourne Street, and so it was that he decided that "John Considine, Forage Merchant" must become "Con-

sidine & Company" with himself as first chairman, for as long
as remained to him, with Anthony managing director and chief
shareholder with Eddy, and with all his children and children-
in-law shareholders also, according to the proportion of their
right. Anthony was to be appointed chairman after his death,
and to have the right to appoint his successor—and there would
be a clause—Honest John looked dreamily down the years—
choosing the grandson who promised most to his observation—a clause which would express his, the founder's wish,
that that successor should be Denis John Mary Considine, the
eldest son of the second chairman. So the patriarch would
bind his house together, and keep that which he had made for
his children the pivot of their children's activities and pride;
so, having established, he would secure his name through as
long a stretch of years as his sad, straining eyes could pene-
trate, even past little Denis's span, deep into the mists of another century.

It came about therefore that on a day of September 1861,
when the sycamore leaves were yellowing in Lower Mourne
Street, Honest John assembled his children and children-in-law
to tea in his dining-room, and before the silver tea-pot was
brought in called upon James Lanigan to read to them the
constitution of "Considine & Company" as the business in
Charles Street was henceforward to be known.

The family listened attentively. With the exception of parcels
of shares to stray cousins, to relatives of their mother and
certain old employees, the bulk of Honest John's estate was
securely and justly divided out in Considine shares among the
eleven who sat round him now, for them and their children.

Surprised at the wealth which the figures revealed, they were
pleased by the just and suitable manner of its disposal, glad
that their father would still hold them so close together after
he was gone, and perhaps unconsciously excited by a vision of
all the skirmishes, antagonisms, and clashes among them which
this precious and difficult unity would bring about. But sadness ruled all these sensations, sadness for the word of finality
that murmured through Lanigan's well-balanced clauses,
hummed in every corner of the shadowy, familiar room and
spoke to them unmistakably from the old man's brooding eyes.
This was his "nunc dimittis," and his four sons and three

daughters were powerless to avert its sweeping sorrow or to
force the hour to be anything but what it was, a grave and
elaborate good-bye.

When Lanigan's voice ceased the green finches answered it.
"Chirrup," said they. "Chirrup." But nobody seemed in a
hurry to take their advice. Affection had the Considines in
its usual easy stranglehold. Molly looked pensively out at the
languid September day and the quiet street; Anthony leant
on the mantelpiece as if he were asleep; Sophia jingled sadly.
The room was heavy with an immense family mood; every
Considine throat was aching; no Considine voice could trust
itself to words. Danny Mulqueen wheezed sympathetically in
his chest.

Father Tom broke the heavy silence at last, but he wasn't
feeling at all flowery. "Thank you sir," was all he said.

Teresa managed then to tell her father in her deep, level
voice that the scheme was just like him and couldn't be bet-
tered. Joe was clearing his throat to say something suitable as
eldest son when Caroline laid her white fingers on Honest
John's dusty sleeve.

"Oh, father," said she, "I wish——" and the quiver of love
in her voice tightened all their nerves to uneasiness again.

"What do you wish, my little girl?" growled Honest John.

But she turned from him swiftly with a shake of her head
and went and stood in the window, to stare at the yellowing
trees through misted eyes.

Joe never got his sentence out. The note of Caroline's voice
had unsteadied his.

"Here's tea at last," said Agnes shakily.

Sophia sniffed at her vinaigrette. Extremely sympathetic,
but possessed of less vitality than the Considines, she found
their emotionalism a trifle exhausting.

"Look sharp with your tea-pot, my girl," said Honest John.
"I've a thirst I wouldn't sell for a sovereign."

The family drew in towards the big silver tray. James Lanigan folded his papers and tied his red tape with precision,
flattening it out in neat bows that he didn't see at all; his eyes
were full of Caroline crying in the window under the green
finches' cage.

"Come on and sample this jam with me, Molly Bawn," said Honest John contentedly.

§ 3

IN THE second week of October 1861 "John Considine's" became officially "Considine & Company."

The day of inauguration was packed with emotional event. In the morning every employee at Charles Street received an envelope containing a bonus equal to two weeks' wages, and Honest John had to visit each department with Anthony, to accept cheers and handshakes, and to answer them with an infrequent smile and with that brooding gaze that most of his dependents found so terrifying.

He was not at his best when compelled to front the world directly; he had no oratory for it and no thought of how to charm it. His people existed in his mind only so far as they were a necessary part of Considine's; he was hard, just, and unsentimental about them, dealing out rises and notices to quit with an equally remote impartiality. He took no more interest in their private affairs than he expected them to take in his. So, when confronted with a feeling from them, perfunctory and of the hour though it might be, he did not seem to know how to answer it, and left most of the smiles and flourishes to Anthony who had a flair for such things. Nevertheless, it was he who had suggested the ceremonial tour, and the making of it probably satisfied the conventional employer in him.

Later, in his own office, he received his clerical staff, but this was easy, since they were fewer, and he was used to talking to them. Peter Farrell, the young bookkeeper whom he had engaged in 1831, chief accountant now, and an ageing man with the longest service record among the clerks, led them into the room, and swayed as he came—he was small and nervous —under the burden of a framed and illuminated address that he was to read. When all the sheepish men and boys had shuffled in behind him, and when O'Halloran was at his side to give him a hand with his ponderous gilt load, Peter Farrell cleared his throat and began the address.

Honest John sat very still at his desk, and Anthony and

Eddy stood behind him with folded arms and listened as attentively as he did.

They heard from Peter, by tortuous ways of eloquence, "that no occasion could be more auspicious . . . that it was their glorious privilege to stand there to-day . . . that the name of Honest John Considine was synonymous in the devoted hearts of Mellick's loyal citizens . . . that it was their fervent and unceasing prayer . . ." Now and then it seemed as if Peter's failing sight would be defeated by the remarkable penmanship of Sister Anastasia, a co-religious with Mary who had done the illuminating. But O'Halloran gave the frame a hitch towards the light, so Peter held on, and rose with feeling to his peroration. . . . "Most beloved and distinguished son of our historic city . . . not so much employer as kindly guide and father and friend . . . honour us by the acceptance . . . pledge of our undying personal loyalty." The ambiguous falsehoods achieved sincerity in the passing belief of Peter and his listeners that they were true.

Panting with excitement, Farrell laid the huge frame on the desk, and shook the hand of Honest John. Eddy and Anthony bent over to see what appeared to be small medallioned portraits of themselves at the top of the address, flanking a larger central medallion of their father. The bottom right- and left-hand corners were adorned by little pictures of Considine's and of No. 30 Lower Mourne Street, with the arms of Mellick emblazoned in between. Honest John was studying all these details with obvious pleasure and having them explained to him by the delighted Peter, when Mickey, the youngest office boy, came up with the clerks' presentation, a case of heavily embossed silver brushes, for hair, coat, hat, and everything. Apt gift for a dusty-looking old man. And Donegan, foreman of the packers, staggered behind Mickey, bearing a massive ormolu clock, that would help Honest John to observe the running feet of Time. He touched the gifts gently with his discoloured, workman's hands, and when he rose to thank the waiting crowd of men, he wore the half-jibing smile that his family knew well but that the rest of the world hardly ever saw.

"You ought to be ashamed of yourselves," said he, "inventing all these lies,"—he tapped the address—"about an innocent man who never did you any worse harm than slave-drive you. And I hear from Peter that 'twas a holy nun you got to write them out in this fine style. I'm greatly shocked. But I'm very thankful, too, and very thankful for these remarkable presents I've got. A clock that our friend Donegan here can hardly carry must be an extraordinary timepiece—and as for the brushes, well, I'll try to be worthy of them. My sons and daughters will say that they're the very thing I wanted. Be off with you now, like good fellows. You'll find dinner waiting for you in the Victoria Hotel—Mr. Anthony knows as well as any of you that I was always the friend of temperance—still, nothing would do him but you should all have champagne with your dinner to-day. Well—you can have it—it's waiting for you at the hotel—but the one of you that can't do his work this afternoon will get no quarter—do you hear that, Mickey?"

The office boy jumped with alarm. Everyone laughed and the chairman of Considine & Company waved his staff from the room.

THE SIXTH CHAPTER

THERE was a party for the shareholders at Lower Mourne Street that night.

When Honest John had announced his intention of giving one, Agnes was flustered to decide what form it ought to take. Her father would give her no advice and saw no cause for debate.

"A good party, my girl, that's all," said he. "And we'll have it late in the evening."

That was easily said, but if all the shareholders were invited, it would be a large gathering. Besides the twelve who made up the real family, there would be Uncle Thady and Aunt Julia, and Charlie Tracey, and Cousin Rosie, and maybe the Garrys, and a few other relations who lived too far out from Mellick to come, it was to be hoped; and then there'd be O'Halloran and his wife, and Peter Farrell and his wife, and old Barrett, and poor old Mr. O'Shaughnessy. Thirty people, at the very least, if he insisted on asking them all. He did insist.

Agnes fled to Sophia and Teresa. Sit-down supper for that number was impossible in the Mourne Street dining-room, she told them feverishly, and they agreed with her and wagged their heads.

"Have it at River Hill," said Sophia, but the two born Considines winced. It was their father's party and he would have it in his own house.

Sophia had put her foot in it. However, she plucked up courage presently to inform the others, out of her knowledge of a higher life, that "running buffets" were all the go now among the titled.

"What the titled do or don't do is troubling us very little, thank you," said Teresa acidly, but she did admit all the same that there were possibilities in this particular rumour of their methods of entertainment.

§ 2

AT NINE o'clock on the evening of the appointed day the party was ready to begin. Teresa, an early arrival, immensely crinolined in purple brocade and carrying a goodish weight of jewellery, stood in the middle of the dining-room and surveyed the fruits of her own staff work. The folding doors stood open between this room and the seldom-used back sitting-room. Along the walls of the two rooms narrow, snowily covered tables stood up without as much as a groan to a magnificent burden of food and glass and plate. Cold fowl, cold game, cold ham, salmon mayonnaise, lobster salads, cucumber salads, sandwiches, olives, salted almonds, petits fours, éclairs, cherry flans, fruit salads, the famous Considine trifles. Coffee-pots and tea-pots of old Dublin silver. Jugs upon jugs of cream. Rows of bottles, rows of decanters, Moselle cup sparkling through Waterford glass.

Teresa knit her brows over that cup. Eddy had insisted upon making it, and although she had warned him that "cup" must be regarded as "the ladies' drink," she was not feeling easy in her mind about it. He might say what he liked, but she had distinctly seen a brandy bottle in his hand when he was making it. Certainly he had given a glass of it all round to each of the maids—to prove his innocence, he said. She eyed those of the starched damsels who were now in the room, and was gloomily thankful that no one would call on her to swear by the Bible that they were sober. Indeed, her own cook, an expert carver lent for the night, and ensconced now in a bower of pheasants' tails, looked alarmingly cheerful.

Well, well, everything was very nice, anyway, and Danny thought so too. "Eat at pleasure, drink by measure," he was murmuring. Teresa smiled complacently at him. He looked dapper and cheerful in his dress suit.

A last look round. Wood fires burning clear, all the lamps in safe places, the green finches covered up for sleep. Dahlias and chrysanthemums in the unnecessary profusion that Eddy liked. Teresa swept Danny out of the room and up the stairs. She wanted to "run her eye" over the rest of the house. The little "return" room, which was only an expansion of the landing, had been made warm and bright. Armchairs, cigars, and ash-trays. The gentlemen would smoke there.

The L-shaped drawing-rooms, back and front thrown into one, were beautifully in order. There was no one in the larger room at present. Wood fire and flowers again, and French chocolates in silver dishes. And over the mantelpiece the new oil painting of Honest John which his children had presented to him for this occasion.

Teresa wondered if that log wouldn't set fire to the over-mantel. Danny poked it into safety. The lamp by the far window was none too steady. With people like poor old Mr. O'Shaughnessy coming—they moved it to the console table. Did Agnes remember to have the piano tuned? Teresa's strong hand rippled an arpeggio with sudden delicacy.

Honest John was sitting by the fire in the inner room with Eddy and Agnes and two expectant green card-tables. He was looking forward to his party. He never wore evening dress, but he had actually troubled to put on a new frock coat, and he called on Teresa now to say if it fitted him properly. He had to stand up before she'd answer him.

"Well wear, father; it's a lovely cut."

"I had to tidy myself in Eddy's room, if you please. Nice thing to do to a respectable man—turn his bedroom into a ladies' boudoir!" He chuckled. "Full of pin-cushions and pertumes puffs I found it when I went up!"

His plain and lonely room, breathing lavender to-night and Parma violet; lighted softly to catch a flit of women's faces in its mirror, and that they might powder their breasts and pin their curls. As vast a change as when the poet's helmet made a hive for bees.

Teresa cast an approving eye over Agnes's new gown of grey and lilac silk and the collarette of amethysts on her unremarkable neck.

"It's well wear to you, too, I see."

Eddy strolled away into the main drawing-room, and his sisters, gazing after him to admire the hang of his beautiful tail-coat, felt a sharp regret that this had had to be so strictly a shareholders' party. It seemed a waste of opportunity, with Mellick full of suitable young girls for him. And that Cousin Rosie coming too, thought Teresa in a mood which really had more contemptuous amusement in it than anxiety. The woman was no class, Teresa told herself, even if she was their own second cousin. And a widow, what's more! As if Eddy—ah, she must be losing her wits to let the idea bother her at all. Still, the fact was that Rosie Phelan was the only woman outside the immediate family whom Teresa had ever seen amuse Eddy for more than a minute at a time. But shrewdness told her that the most pernickety of her brothers wouldn't dream of such a scandalous thing.

Eddy loved parties—anywhere, at any time. He loved to plan them, loved arranging them. Teresa was not aware, because he was tactful, that it was he who had given the gloss and final effect to the preparations for this particular one. He had hovered about her unobtrusively, saying very little, but giving a soft pull here and there to her creation with his more sophisticated hand. He had looked after the wines and cigars, of course; but he had insisted too on taking charge of the flowers, and had written to London for particular kinds of stuffed olives and marrons glacés and foie gras. He had had the expensive Axminster carpet up and the floor polished. He had moved the furniture about, and by emphasising all the best things in the house, and tactfully lifting much of Agnes's bric-à-brac to "a safe place" on the attic floor, had got an air of genuine impressiveness into the haphazard rooms. Now the bright lamps and all his brilliant flowers gave gaiety too and even a sort of excited, festive beauty. He was pleased with the clear, if necessarily limited, result which his accurate touch had brought about, a touch so different from Molly's ghostlier impress, which cast a tremulous shadow about a room, while hardly knowing that it touched at all.

He straightened his tie in front of the console mirror and smiled a little at himself. Then he removed a broken aster from a vase, thinking as he did so how like Caroline its wide-eyed fellows were, with their petulant brave look, half passion and half innocence.

The front door bell rang terrifically as he threw the dead flower on the fire.

"Bet you a sovereign that's your son Joe," he called out to his father. "Come on in here now, your party's beginning."

§ 3

THE party went well. Not an invited aunt or cousin failed to turn up; but then, as Agnes ought to have known, those humble sidesmen never yet disobeyed the infrequent commands they received to step for a while into the proud, warm circle of Considine life.

They were a bit nervous at first, perhaps, and so were those members or pensioners of the staff who had been awarded shares and who were therefore invited to-night. But if the Considines had a disconcerting arrogance, they were also natural and spontaneous, and when they troubled to be hospitable, took pains to do it graciously. Also, the commoner kind of snobbery was not in them. They rejoiced indeed rather splendidly in their kinship with plain and simple people, and only drew the rapier of their pride on those careful upper classes who cultivated them so assiduously nowadays. Their cousins might be dowdy and boring, but at least they were their cousins —surely a saving grace? Their father's clerks might be seedy and insignificant and possessed of rapaciously curious and observing wives, but the curiosity was not unnatural. It was even an amusing flattery. In sum, were not all these little people a bit of Considine's?

It did not take the talkative family very long to set everyone at ease. Honest John indeed, by simply assuming that his guests felt as much at home as he did, contributed much to the result of his children's more studied graciousness.

Molly got poor Mr. O'Shaughnessy into an armchair by the fire. He had entered Considine's when he was thirty and worked there until he could work no more. He was eighty-three now, with a palsied left hand and sagging bloodshot eyelids and the imaginings of a childlike saint. He was devoted to the family, and leant close to Molly as he piped up wonderingly at

her. His breath was unpleasant, but she didn't flinch. Poor old
Mr. O'Shaughnessy!

She set his tea on a little table for him near his good hand
—maids were circulating with cups of tea and glasses of sherry
to thaw the arrival chill—and soon his tears were flowing and
he was talking of the wonderful ways of St. Joseph. A sure sign
he was happy. His dead and holy wife, and the blessed saints
—those were the topics that always had Mr. O'Shaughnessy
weeping and content.

Molly smiled at him and nodded, her eyes wandering the
while over the humming room. How lovely Caroline was in
that green dress! That was Uncle Thady she was talking to—
fatter than ever—he must weigh at least twenty stone. Molly
smiled at the contrast of his grossness with Caroline's star-
like beauty. And Aunt Julia just behind him, nearly as bad—
in her prehistoric rose-coloured satin! What a pair! Molly
could only barely see a corner of little Danny peeping round
Aunt Julia's bulk. Cousin Rosie was talking to Honest John
in the middle of the room. They seemed to be entertaining
each other very well. The old man's growling laugh was quite
distinct in the multiple noise of the room. Rosie, tall and serene
and comely, had evidently a good joke for him. They were
both unaware that Mr. O'Halloran was standing behind them,
squat and polite, anxious to present his little red-nosed wife
to the head of Considine's.

Peter Farrell's wife was having a joke with Joe, her medical adviser. Tom and Teresa had the two gaunt-looking
Garrys well in hand, and Sophia, trying hard not to show how
unused she was to such society, was compromising gallantly
with the too easy manners of Charlie Tracey. Eddy, Anthony,
and Jim moved far off among a vaguer group of cousins, and
Agnes was listening nearby with Peter Farrell to those remi-
niscences of the firm in Kilmoney Street days which were the
conversational speciality of Mr. Barrett, another pensioner.

The room was full. Thirty-two people, drinking and adjusting themselves and finding their tongues. The clash of voices
grew more vigorous every minute. Eddy, pausing by the window he had just opened, surveyed the room with pleasure, and
reflected that there were at least two women in it whose clear

beauty might have caused a stir in more sophisticated salons:
for Molly was decorativeness unflawed, standing by the fire
all white and seductive, with misty eyes and snowy sloping
shoulders, and on her breast the ruby that Anthony had given
her last year—while Caroline, ah, Caroline was strangely radiant to-night, young in her mood, exquisitely dressed, and impassioned to be merry, to enjoy herself, to laugh—even with
Uncle Thady. Eddy's eyes passed from her to Cousin Rosie
and lost their sudden sadness. Dear, lively, vulgar Cousin
Rosie, with her great laugh and springing, shameless bosom—
handsome creature, like some coarse old divinity disguised!
He chuckled with friendliness for her. She might have taken a
place in the capital too, he thought—if hardly in the same
assembly as the others. But indeed he was well aware that his
good Catholic cousin Rosie, the respectably widowed Mrs.
Phelan, would never put as much as her decent, self-respecting
nose inside the sort of place for which her splendid frame was
built. He moved to greet her; it was eighteen months since
they had met.

§ 4

ANTHONY worked his way down the room to rescue Molly
from that "poor old nuisance, O'Shaughnessy." Shameful that
her loveliness should be squandered before red-rimmed eyes
that were blind to everything less bright than visions of St.
Anthony and the holy angels. He smiled towards her as he
drew near. Six and a half years married, and to-night she
was exciting him with the invitation of a bride. How well she
knew it too—he smiled again, standing beside her now, his
hand under her cool elbow. Old O'Shaughnessy took the vivid,
happy smile for himself and greeted "Mr. Anthony" with
wheezy rapture. Anthony bent and was charming and merry
with the delighted old man, greeted Barrett too across
O'Shaughnessy's shoulder, and with a deft word, brought
Agnes, Barrett, and Farrell to stand round the octogenarian's
chair and take on Molly's labours.

A polite murmuring then—"If you people will excuse us—
Molly, I want you to meet——" A smile to them all, his hand

on her elbow, and he bore her proudly away across the room.

"Had enough of O'Shaughnessy's visions, my little girl?"

She breathed delicately into her faint-scented handkerchief and he chuckled at her ladylike comment.

"I'd like a drink of something, Anthony."

"I know. Come on over to this tray and have some sherry."

She sipped the wine gratefully.

"You must be the loveliest woman in Christendom this night," he told her. "I've never looked on anyone so beautiful."

Veiled and soft smouldered her eyes' kind answer to his ardour.

"If I am beautiful," her gentleness seemed to say, "oh, I am yours as well." She knew his mood of desire and was unfolded to it.

"You're like some sort of bird in that dress," he went on, "I'm not sure what bird though—a swan, I think."

She laughed at him softly.

"Hush, Anthony. Someone will hear you."

Tom broke in and shook off the starved-looking Garrys onto them as gracefully as Anthony would have done it himself.

Ever since Molly's fourth child had been born thirteen months ago Anthony had been trying to be abstemious with what the law called his conjugal rights. To fast completely from the passion Molly could rouse in him was out of the question, but he had sought deliberately to discipline it of late and had been surprised and not a little proud over his uncharacteristic restraints. Luck was rewarding his comparative austerity, and Molly had had thirteen months of freedom from conception. Anthony hoped her rest would be prolonged; indeed, if she never had another child, he would be well content with his modest four. So long as he had Denis, the rest of the world was welcome to its overflowing quivers.

Whether Molly guessed the motive of his efforts at asceticism he could not say, but he imagined that she did. Whatever she was thinking she was very tender with his lapses from monasticism. But he and she rarely spoke of these things and never with precision. She knew that he deplored for her the discomfort of incessant childbearing and would do much to lessen it, but saw no help within the social and religious code they both upheld. He knew that childbirth frightened her, wilted and crushed her and gave her in her babies only very slender compensation, for she was by nature far more wife than mother. But it was a problem which they could never thrash out, and it was heightened by the fact that they were both on the crest of life, and if not loving each other very perfectly at all times and in all the regions of love, yet doomed to find a terrible delight, again and again, each in the other's body.

Some of the party were moving to the inner drawing-room for whist. Jim, a demon at the game, was organising the tables. The word was to the Garrys as the snapping of a leash to bloodhounds, and Anthony led them across and gave them in charge to Jim with great alacrity. Molly turned to relieve poor Sophia of that dreadful Charlie Tracey. Her sister-in-law looked eloquent gratitude and sped in the direction of the card-tables. For she was a real exponent of whist—indeed, very nearly a match for Jim Lanigan, to his perpetual horror and disgust.

Charlie Tracey indicated sociably to Molly that he was "very partial indeed to a bit of a dance," and Molly was glad to take any hint that relieved her of making conversation for him. She went to Caroline.

"Don't you think we could have a quadrille?" said she, and Caroline cried radiantly that they would. Teresa was swept to the piano. No one like her to play a quadrille. And away the dance went, merrily, suddenly—cross and set to partners, bow, chassez. Teresa marked the time well, and Honest John marked it too with his heavy boot. Uncle Thady and Aunt Julia sat with him to watch it, and old Mr. O'Shaughnessy blinked at the bright-moving pageant through tears and thought of the blessed saints. Eddy with Cousin Rosie, the only woman he'd ever dance for, he told her blithely, and gaily enough she made him step for it. Caroline dancing like a runaway queen, absurdly partnered by Mr. O'Halloran; and Mrs. O'Halloran with Danny, who was excellently nimble on the dancing floor; and Joe, very stately and benign, with young Eileen Molloy, and Tom Fogarty, who knew none of the figures with Agnes, who knew them all; and Molly, the swan, gliding to the beck of the accomplished Charlie Tracey. Tinkle Tinkle, set to partners; twirl and cross and twirl again and bow.

§ 5

WHEN the quadrille was over the party was alive. Hungry and thirsty ones crowded downstairs; Teresa's cook brandished her knife among the pheasants' tails.

Upstairs hearts were trumps at Jim's table; Sophia, thank God, was at the other for the moment. The woman was impossible to play with. By persuading Tom to take a hand, since Anthony wouldn't, Jim had made up two tables. Mrs. Garry, Peter Farrell, and old Barrett at his own, and Arthur Garry, Mrs. Farrell, Sophia, and Tom at the other. A great game, whist. He settled in his chair.

"Cut, if you please, Mrs. Garry."

Anthony, standing by the fire, smiled softly at such an invitation to a woman who looked exactly like a knife. Jim himself was looking more razorish than ever these days, his brother-in-law reflected; this wasn't the first time in the last two years that he'd noticed the intensified edge of the man's features. Not ageing; not by any means. Indeed he seemed more alert and arrowy than ever, but the tightness about his mouth was getting more marked, and there was a hard strain, even an anxiety, in his eyes. He looked as if he might be secretly ill, fighting some painful disease. Anthony had observed that irascibility was becoming Lanigan's weapon against the world; well, it was less trying than his old, suave lawyer's insolence. But what was wrong with the man? Was it money trouble? Couldn't be that, Anthony decided. Jim was as shrewd and safe as the Bank of England. Ah, well! Anthony shrugged and strolled away. He must manœuvre Aunt Julia down the stairs to supper.

Rosie Phelan, expertly waited on by Eddy, ate lobster salad with great enjoyment on a settee in the back hall.

"I'm sorry you chose that, Rosie; no one should ever eat lobster salad. Besides, you simply have to drink champagne with it and I made the Moselle cup specially for you."

"I'll try it, then."

"You'll do nothing of the sort, you ignorant woman! With lobster salad!"

"Will you get me some, if you please, and stop talking? I'll tell you soon enough if I like it or not when I've tasted it."

"But Rosie, there's brandy in it!"

Still protesting, Eddy departed to obey her.

He found Caroline in a little island of peace, at the far end of the crowded dining-room, eating stuffed olives with enthusiasm.

"This lovely kind you always get!" she sighed gratefully at him.

"Enjoying yourself?" She had always shared Eddy's feeling for parties. She looked at him now as if his question scared her.

"Yes, I hope so. I think so."

"Go on, Caro."

"It's important."—He waited.—"Coming in the carriage I suddenly felt glorious—this dress, you know—oh, one of my attacks!"

"I remember them. When you insist on being happy."

"That's it."

They laughed.

"So I said to myself that to-night was going to be good fun —right up to the end, and that I'd go home feeling—oh, feeling alive, Ted, and not bothering—— So, in thanksgiving, I said I'd have a new era. Our new eras long ago! Do you ever start any now?"

"Every month or so, Caro."

"As often as that? Oh, Ted, how silly. I'm starting a real one." Sorrow that could come so swiftly to her face threatened it now.

"It's a sort of new era for Considine's to-night, isn't it? So it's a lucky time for me to begin one—oh, I hope it is, anyway!"

"Why, Caro?"

She gave him again the candid, anxious look he found so touching.

"Oh, no why. Just something had to be done, one way or another—and a party's always a good starting point for things, isn't it?"

She was perfectly serious.

" 'Course it is, Caro."

She smiled entrancingly beyond him. "Thank you, Mr. O'Halloran. Are you sure they're foie gras?"

Eddy passed on, but her voice followed him as she talked to fat, nervous O'Halloran.—"Look, Mr. O'Halloran, do please look at the lights in this emerald of mine!" Looking back, he saw her white hand under a lamp, and all a child's eagerness in her eyes for the gleam of her ring. But Rosie must be dying of thirst.

They settled down together to have a thoroughly good supper, and "no nonsense about it," said Eddy. After the lobster salad Rosie had pheasant and ham, and after that she had trifle. And generous glasses of Moselle cup. They took their time over it all. Rosie was not the woman to hurry through good food.

Cigar smoke drifted to them from the half-landing, and the boom of Joe's voice as he discoursed to old Barrett. Aunt Julia creaked up the stairs, immensely replenished, with Anthony in attendance. The piano thrummed irrelevantly against the wave of voices.

"Did I forget salt, Rosie? How stupid of me!"

The dining room was quiet now. Young Eileen Molloy drifted out of it with Charlie Tracey. They settled on the stairs behind Rosie and Eddy, halfway up the flight, where it was darkish.

"I don't care what you say, Rosie; chicken is far nicer food than pheasant. But have it your own way."

"That's what I'm doing." She chuckled at him gently. "You're in great form to-night, Eddy—whatever's wrong with you?"

Anthony was singing in the drawing-room, in a firm, untrained baritone made rich and steady by feeling:

> "*. . . My Irish wife has hair of gold—*
> *Apollo's lyre had once such strings . . .*"

Rosie quieted her knife and fork.

"Ah, that's grand," said she. "I like a fine big voice like that."

> "*. . . I would not give my Irish wife*
> *For the Queen of France's hand . . .*"

Joe could be heard moving up to the drawing-room, booming good-temperedly along. Whenever people were being asked to sing he stood around. He had a big jovial singing voice himself and no objection to using it.

Tom's step descended.

"Excuse me, Charlie, if you please." A stern note in the speech told Eddy that Charlie's arm had been round Eileen at that unlucky moment.

"Well, Eileen," the bright sacerdotal tone went on, "aren't you going upstairs to listen to the music?" And Tom passed down, seeking food. But Eileen and Charlie seemed to be lingering still—Eddy thought guiltily of the Moselle cup he had seen the child drinking.

He twinkled at Rosie.

"That Charlie's a bit of a lad," she said softly.

"You don't sound as censorious as a woman of your experience should," he told her.

"God help us, the words you use! And how am I a woman of experience, will you tell me?"

"Widows—nice widows—always are, I believe."

How splendid she was looking, he thought—honest, common, matter-of-fact of speech and derisive in humour—superbly casual about her bodily splendour. She was a tall woman, and her white arms and shoulders were cast in the grand manner—but not excessively so. Under the crinoline Eddy suspected a perfect line from waist to ankle, for she walked as if her hips were gloriously balanced. The full bosom was a shade too full perhaps, but her neck was "like the tower of David builded for an armoury, whereon there hang a thousand bucklers, all shields of mighty men."

"What's that you're saying, Eddy?"

"I was thinking how King Solomon would have liked you." She stared at him.

"You seem to be getting madder every minute."

"Your fault entirely if I am."

"King Solomon, if you please! God help any woman who got into that fellow's clutches."

"A number of them did."

"So I'm told."

Her eyes were full of benevolent life, and her amused mouth

curved back sensually over milky teeth. Her clothes were not cheap—Rosie was by no means poor—but they were showy and ill-chosen. She had no flair for ornament, regarding it conventionally and without relation to herself. Yes, thought Eddy, studying all her drawbacks, King Solomon would have liked her, and if she's good enough for that great man . . . Cloudily, indolently, he felt desirousness engulf him.

"Why don't you marry again, Rosie?"

"Maybe I will—in my own time."

"And when might that be?"

She sparkled with mockery.

"Are you thinking of proposing to me yourself, by any chance?"

"As if I'd dare!"

Upstairs two unsteady voices had launched on "Home to Our Mountains." Could it be Mr. and Mrs. O'Halloran? Eddy thought suddenly of London and of one or two people there. What would they think of this absurd and unkind dalliance? And of the secret, shamefaced amorousness behind it? Or would they recognise the surface fumbling of an impulse towards escape? For there were hours when Eddy's suavity was only a cloak for panic, and when he had to fight against a need to run away for ever from his usual, appointed self and hide and be lost in just such an impossible bastion of remoteness as Rosie's arms might be. He wanted sometimes, or almost wanted, with a great bewilderment, to get back miles and miles from the particular point that he had reached, further back from it than Anthony was or Caroline, back to where the root normality and plainness of his stock was still abounding, where he might learn to feel with simplicity again and to decline and grow old at ease, to be plain husband and father, and genial commonplace small-town man, to be all that his blood taught him to understand with sympathy, all that Rosie would want, in short, and that he could never be.

"You'll be looking for a much better man than me when you take that notion," he told her, and she laughed a little less straightforwardly than usual.

"Anyway, none of us'll ever see you a married man, Eddy Considine," she said lightly, as she rose from the settee.

"Come on upstairs," she commanded.

"Are you afraid that Tom will be rash-judging you?"

"I think even Tom must know that you're not much given to putting your arm round ladies!"

They strolled towards the stairs.

"I was very much tempted to put it round you just now."

"Ah, Eddy,"—was she laughing at him? "You're far and away too good a match for temptation!"

§ 6

HONEST JOHN liked people to sing and play for him and was putting the company through its paces. He called for Rosie's song when she entered the drawing-room with Eddy, and she went good-naturedly to the piano. Eddy looked after her perplexedly in the bright light—hot and uncomfortable to remember that a minute ago he had desired, almost desired, to posses that honest vulgarity.

Caroline beckoned him from far away, and he hurried to her—fastidiousness aching to be consoled.

Honest John had happy memories of "Jack Sheppard" and liked Rosie to sing "The Carpenter's Daughter" for him. She sang it now with a blend of riotousness and cautious innuendo that enchanted the room, and made Father Tom alone look grave. Joe told her with a flourish that she out-Keeley'd Keeley, and those who had never seen the great comedienne agreed with him fervently.

The party rattled on. Uncle Thady and Aunt Julia went home, but that was no great matter. Old Mr. O'Shaughnessy went and then the O'Hallorans, and then old Mr. Barrett. But Honest John had no intention yet of going to bed, and his children knew that he wanted the ball kept rolling. Sleep eluded him often nowadays—for a change he would elude sleep.

Tom came to say good-night to him.

"Aren't you a very delicate fellow, God help you?" said he in return. "Be sure you have your bread and milk nice and hot."

"Dumbcrambo!" said Caroline suddenly.

While they were squabbling over sides, Jim and Sophia and

the Garrys sneaked back to the card-table for a really grim and earnest set-to.

Crazy charades. Caroline was in a crazy mood. Anthony captained one side, and she the other—and they worked out their words in a way that would have been entirely unguessable to any but the family, which knew its own methods. They did the word itself—"dumbcrambo," and "Mulqueen" and "Tennyson," and in four mad acts, "Lower Mourne Street," with Joe in the last scene giving a marvellous version of his father eating bread and jam, Cousin Rosie playing Agnes at the tea-pot, and Caroline and Eddy the green finches in the cage. Honest John was delighted. And he suddenly said that Eddy must sing "The Meeting of the Waters." And Eddy sang it, sitting very still at the piano, and letting his tuneful voice trickle effortlessly through the room.

Honest John stared into the fire as if he heard nothing, but the look of being too old for his years came heavily upon him, and the dark brooding of his eyes was fathoms deep; and Molly, white crinoline crumpled mistily about her, sat as still as if the silver threads of the song were binding her in everlasting sadness; Anthony closed his eyes, and Teresa's practical face seemed to surrender the here-and-now of life to the singer's questioning lightness. Agnes listened too, head bent correctly. Had she some regret to plait in with Tom Moore's? Danny kept his hands behind his back for fear that he'd maybe put them in his pockets and jingle his money by mistake, and Joe cocked his head deifically and hoped that Sophia was listening—she was so fond of Tom Moore.

Sophia was listening, cards laid down and tears not far from her short-sighted eyes; and so were the starved-looking Garrys. And so was Jim, his unrested face turned to where Caroline stood in the doorway. But Caroline linked her hands together on her breast and stared at the wide-eyed asters that Eddy thought so like her, and wished with all her strength that he'd stop singing.

> ". . . *When the storms that we feel in this cold*
> *world shall cease,*
> *And our hearts, like thy waters, flow*
> *mingled in peace.*"

Tom Moore's light cry, trivial, sentimental, easy as a hand-wave in farewell, pierced far deeper into these Irish Victorians than perhaps the curly-headed poet had ever meant, and, twisted somehow into sober earnest by Eddy's singing, shattered their dumbcrambo hour, set wistfulness all of a sudden over gaiety and seemed to be asking them, in the height of their fun, for such an incongruous thing as resignation.

It stopped as gently as it had begun.

Honest John lifted his head; Sophia gathered her cards again and Anthony opened his eyes. It was over.

And so was the party. The most sociable of poets had killed it stone dead. He had ended a bright pause and marshalled back the reluctant procession of every day.

"You've a lovely sad voice, Eddy," said Cousin Rosie.

"My only romantic symptom—isn't it a pity?"

Honest John had no jibes left in him, and was unable to lift the aged stoop that his son's singing had laid on his shoulders.

"Time the last of us were in our beds," said Teresa with a quick look into his weary face.

"What are you looking so tired for, father?" said Caroline, slipping her arm through his.

"Because I've sense enough to want to be in my bed at four a. m., my girl," growled Honest John, touching her dress very cautiously with one big, uncouth finger. "Be off with you now and be a good girl, you silly bit of silk, you!"

§ 7

THE Garrys got a lift home in the Lanigan carriage, which would take them on to their suburban dwelling when it had dropped its owners in Herbert Street. Caroline leant back in the darkness, still hearing Eddy's song, still trying not to hear it. Mrs. Garry made tired but correct conversation—so did Arthur Garry. Jim seemed disgruntled. Could Sophia possibly have beaten him? "When the storms that we feel in this cold world . . ." Caroline smiled. What tiny storms they were, after all—as tiny as a game of whist that goes against us! The carriage jolted, and jolted Jim's ankle gently against hers. He started violently.

"I beg your pardon, my dear!"

The undue nervousness in the man's voice may have puzzled Mrs. Garry. How could she guess his neurotic fear that Caroline would think that gentle touch deliberate, a vulgar, after-the-revels appeal such as he could never make? How could she know that he was nervous and absurd because of a night two years ago, when his wife, without faintest warning, had cried out with a terrible cry as she lay in his arms, telling him with all the insane cruelty of despair that she couldn't bear it, that he mustn't touch her, that he must never touch her again.

Jim had obeyed without a word. Wounded, sick, perplexed, tormented, he had lain beside her silently that night and the next, and all the nights since then, wretched and proud and almost ludicrously baffled by that cry that never seemed to have done vibrating in his ears. He loved his wife far too well not to have been shocked to the last reaches of his heart by the flagrant misery of her voice.

That they were not perfectly happy he had always understood; confident and calm to all the world, he had never felt any assurance at her side; he had bluffed it sometimes, however, and she for her part had been kind—vagaries of mood and word ending always in the same repentant royal tenderness. And he had been dumbly happy in the possession of her, however he had bungled at her happiness; she was the glory and decoration of his life, and the mother of his splendid children. Never had she refused, or seemed to wish to refuse, herself to his persistent desire. Never until that night. But then indeed in her sudden outcry he learnt as much about her feeling for him as if her ten years of acquiescence had been ten years of protest. He was hurt, he was baffled. Near enough to her in his love to feel beyond all doubting the wild urgency that had made her cry out, he yet could not really understand why it had seized her. Ten years together after all, six children, habit, association. It wasn't as if he were repulsive in person or gross in mind. He was on the contrary truly fastidious and considerate, and without the least conceit he could not help knowing that he was a good-looking man. But what did all that matter against the heartbreaking revulsion in her voice? She had asked for mercy at his hands. It came to that—his beloved wife had begged for mercy. He granted it, frightened that he should ever have to hear her beg again. Nothing was said. He did not see how anything could be said. He belonged chronologically and in spirit to a time when the sexual problems of marriage had to be left dumbly to darkness and the night.

Their life went on and no one saw a change in it. They ate and drank and went about together; took and gave perfunctory kisses. Respectability, servants, the far-seeing family eye, above all the enormous silence that had to loom between them, made it necessary that he should continue to sleep in his place at her side. He endured it all without a word, without an appeal—he did not know any word to say to her, he did not know of any appeal that he could find courage to make. And he was too frightened to look in her face and see the self-reproach that flitted over it sometimes and the perplexity, too frightened to see how pity was often fighting there against relief. He asked for nothing, thus laying no burden on her Catholic conscience; he held out no hand, made no reproach. But on every day of his life he desired her and was made weary by the aloof proximity of her great beauty.

The carriage stopped at 19 Herbert Street. The Garrys made their last tired courtesy speeches and rolled away. Jim and his wife climbed up to bed.

As she brushed her hair he sat in remote shadow and stared at her.

They had made no move to light gas or candles and the only illumination of the room as they undressed came from the blue glass lamp that, never extinguished, burnt on the little altar of Our Lady of Victories by Caroline's side of the big mahogany bed. The circle of this little light was small and wavering and hardly made more than a ghost of Caroline, far off before her mirror. But she felt easier so.

She was superstitiously fond of this little blue lamp that was never allowed to go out. It had lighted her through secret places, through her husband's hours of passion, through childbirth's unrememberable woe, and once through the shadow of death; through nights of listening for a little child's cough, through nights of desperate thought, through nights of toothache, through sleepy interludes with sucking babies, through foolish make-believes and brave plans for new eras, through blessed sleep, through all the variegated monotony of the nights of ten married years.

Jim's talk with her was desultory and uncertain as they undressed. Yes, Sophia had actually beaten him. He bent over his shoelaces to confess it, and Caroline understood that that was indeed the last straw.

She dropped to the blue priedieu and bowed her head a minute before Our Lady of Victories. Then she got into bed.

When Jim came to lie beside her she put out her hand to find one of his and held it with generous warmth.

"It's a new era to-night," she said gently. "You must forgive me—I've been very unkind."

The cry that he strangled brought pitying tears to her eyes and she drew his hand up to her breast. Her husband—had she after all been missing his faithful arms? As they went round her, gently, gently, she thought that perhaps she had. But when they tightened, and his mouth was on her neck, she caught back a shudder with skill she had taken long to learn but which two years' disuse had not overthrown.

§ 8

ALL the carriages were in their coach-houses at last and all Considine's shareholders in their beds. Danny Mulqueen was probably the first to raise a snore in his, with Teresa wishing gloomily that he wouldn't, as she had wished now for upwards of six thousand nights. Joe found it more difficult to drop off—for Sophia was restless; she did not know whether to be cross because Joe had only been asked to sing once at the party or to be hysterical because at last she had trampled on Jim Lanigan at the whist table. In the end, nature decided for her, to Joe's relief, that she was mainly very tired. Tom had been asleep, of course, before the party ended, office read, clothes folded, every duty done, and old Mr. O'Shaughnessy had worked his way through many a tearful dream of his guardian angel and the holy souls. Agnes said her rosary from her pillow for this once, with apologies to the Blessed Virgin, because her knees were weary. Eddy sat awhile on the side of his bed, thinking of London and some people there, thinking of Caroline, thinking in perplexity of Cousin Rosie and of the nightmare tricks a man's five senses play, thinking again with troubled eyes of his lovely sister Caroline. And Cousin Rosie turned and twisted, trying to get warm alone in her marriage bed, and wondering what sort of a creature that fellow Eddy really was. And Anthony in his big room in his big house by the moaning river held his swan in his arms at last and felt her happy, innocent voluptuousness fold him close and close. And Denis slept upstairs, untouched by any trouble or any bliss.

Eventually Honest John slept too, and easily to-night in the end, more easily even than the child, more easily than he had ever slept before, heedless of feminine fragrances that still floated unfamiliarly about his sober room, heedless of his more than seventy years. A deep, cold sleep. And the leaves fell in Lower Mourne Street and the watchman cried "All's well!"

THE SEVENTH CHAPTER

IT WAS Eddy who found his dead father. Unable to get more than fitful sleep, he got up when the east was brightening, running downstairs for a spirit lamp to make tea. A vague anxiety directed him to look in at Honest John as he passed his door. He found him blue-lipped and cold, already an hour cold. The old man lay untidily on his back, his arms flung wide and one of his discoloured hands tight-clenched; his mouth hung open and his sombre eyes stared up into eternal darkness. The rising light spared his son no detail of the lonely struggle that was ended now; the bedclothes were disarranged, the body was flung slantwise on the bed; streaks of saliva had crystalised on the chin; all the lines of the heavy face were rigid and violent.

Eddy was quiet externally and in his heart as he looked down on the dignity of his father's undignified gaping mouth and measured the solemn new depths of the blind eyes. Amazement, cold and dreary as death itself, was all that death could wring from him in this first minute. His hour of woe would come, he knew. It would not be easy to **face the re**morse that was in wait for him; to remember that while **he lay** awake in an upper room, fretting egotistically about the absurd, unreal perplexities of little life, his father had been alone down here when death had swooped. It would not be easy to accept that he had been so near the beloved old man in his last hour and yet too far to give him hand or voice. Honest John had taken all the odds of life alone; would it have meant anything to him to have had a son at hand in this last loneliness? Eddy hardly knew.

He opened the curtains wide. Agnes must not find her father in this rigour of agony. There was no time to lose. Eddy's hands, that Caroline thought so like a woman's, had to be a man's now to move that stiffened frame. He straightened the legs and forced the stained left hand to open so that he might fold it with its fellow on the dead breast. He smoothed the pillows and laid the heavy head on them in such a way that the jaw would be forced to close. He drew the reluctant eyelids over the brooding darkness of the eyes. He sponged the saliva from lips and chin, and straightened the quilt and the edge of the upper sheet. Then he drew down the blinds again, and lighted three candles in a silver candlestick. That was all he could do to bring belated peace to his father's death-bed. But a grotesque satisfaction stirred under the cold emptiness of his mood as he looked at his work and thought of how Agnes would say, of how all the Considines would say, that Honest John looked very peaceful, and must have died in happy sleep. The composure which had been forced on the dead man would be the precious consolation of his children now. A happy death. The grace of a happy death, the one last boon that every Catholic implores and counts on. To be allowed to be ready at the end, composed and quiet for the journey. Well, perhaps he had been granted that. What is the poor body, Eddy mused, in that tremendous hour? What can its contortions matter to the inattentive spirit that is gathering itself up to fling them off? Their father had been braced this long while for departure, and however the flesh may have hindered him in his last breath, it was unlikely that the laconic soul of John Considine had gone off without a jibe, his usual signal of acceptance. But Agnes and Tom and all of them would prefer to think that his last banner was a prayer. Well, perhaps it was. He looked majestically prayerful now, eyes closed, hands folded, resigned and unprotesting, ready for perpetual light to shine on him.

Eddy went downstairs, and found old Annie the cook on her knees before the kitchen range. He told her that her master was dead and listened gently to her holy wailings. Then he made tea, and took it up to Agnes's room with his heavy news.

§ 2

"His green finches—ah well, God's will be done."

Teresa turned from the little birds in the darkened dining-room and looked in perplexity at Agnes who was in her usual chair by the fire. Poor Agnes, poor flattened, broken, emptied Agnes, whose noiseless tears had not ceased from flowing in these two long days, whose eyes were cushioned in tender, swollen, weary flesh, whose distended throat made speech impossible, poor lonely Agnes, whose occupation was gone. Teresa was full of pity as she looked at her, and a bit exasperated.

"Where's Tom?" said she.

The other jerked her head ceilingward to indicate that he was in the drawing-room.

"Why don't you go and lie down for a while?" said Teresa. "You're dead tired. I'll send you up some hot milk. Maybe you'd sleep."

But Agnes shuddered and her eldest sister abandoned the one-sided conversation for the moment.

There would have to be a family conference about Agnes, and Teresa thought the sooner the better. Just like her not to go and lie down. But the poor girl seemed to want to be with the rest of them these days. Well, that was easy to understand. They'd have to decide though—she couldn't live on in the place all alone—some of them would have to offer her a home. The hot milk would have got her off nicely. Indeed she looked as if she might drop for want of sleep. Pitiful the way she kept crying like that without a word! None of them would mind having her—their own sister, after all. And still Teresa knew that no one had yet determined to invite her. They were all eyeing the problem. It would have to be discussed. Poor Agnes! Teresa sighed impatiently.

One of the green finches twittered again and started Agnes into a new sob that almost choked her.

"Come up to the drawing-room," said Teresa.

Tom and Joe and Eddy and Danny were there, with Sophia prostrate in an armchair by the fire, her feet on a higher stool than would have seemed decorous at a normal time.

Sophia was worn out but bearing up with gallant patience. She sniffed her vinaigrette and dried her eyes for the seventieth time that day. She was so tired at this stage that the slightest word brought tears. Family bereavements—how well Sophia understood! Why, when *her* dear father, the late Mr. Jeremiah Quillihey, J. P., had passed away in Mountjoy Square—— Sophia dabbed her eyes again. The solemn weariness of Honest John's children in these two days, and the exhausting funeral ceremonies of this morning, had frayed the woman's amiability almost into silliness, and as for the ponderous grief of her great bearded husband—— It really was a great comfort to put the feet up at times like this, she reflected now. A cup of tea would be delicious—but she couldn't be so heartless as to mention it.

The men made way for Agnes and Teresa. Danny went and stood beside his wife, patting her strong shoulder kindly with his little freckled hand.

Languor was on them all. The bright day filtering through the yellow blinds and the passionate blackness of their clothes flung sallow lights and shades about them and made new combinations in the lines of their drawn faces. They might not have recognised each other now, had they looked keenly. But they wanted to recognise each other, they wanted to huddle together for awhile, brothers and sisters. Even if nothing were said, if no one moved, they must stay here awhile. They were too tired to break apart, it was too soon. It was too soon to turn back to everyday, to turn forward, apart, to a new everyday in which there would be no Honest John.

"It's a long time since Mellick saw such a funeral," said Joe.

Sophia handed her vinaigrette to Agnes.

"Wonderfully soothing," she pleaded.

"Sir Thomas Henn spoke very nicely about him to me in the graveyard," said Tom.

"I'll engage he did," said Eddy with amusement.

"Did anyone take a list of the wreaths?" Teresa asked.

"I told the undertaker's men to do it."

Eddy knelt to poke the fire.

"Where's Anthony?" said Tom.

"The man from the 'Champion' wanted a list of the wreaths."

Their words sarabanded among them like leaves on a windless day. Not that they were indifferent to the externals of what had passed in the morning. It mattered indeed overwhelmingly that the town had been lavish of mournful tribute to their father and themselves. If any suitable honour had been omitted from his last rites or if any citizen who might reasonably be expected to be present had absented himself, there would have been anger now among the Considines instead of lethargy. As it was, Honest John had had full measure of posthumous respect. Danny said that he had watched on purpose and that there wasn't a shop or a house in the whole length of the town but had had its blinds down when the hearse passed—even Toffley, that black Protestant at the corner of Prince Street, had had the decency—honour in fact was satisfied, surfeited, and there could be no distraction from sorrow under that head.

The world had seen them grave, collected, and resigned, and so in the main they had shown themselves to each other. They had made his room majestic with candles and lilies; they had stood quietly at his bedside and had knelt to pray there; they had been gentle in receiving the sympathy of an exhausting stream of callers; they had arranged efficiently for mourning clothes; they had driven behind him in their victorias through last night's dusk to see him safely laid in St. Peter's for his one night before the tabernacle; they had followed his Requiem Mass devoutly in their books, had listened unfalteringly to the wail of the "Kyrie Eleison," and had borne the climbing agonies of the "Dies Irae" without much outward sign of an answering anguish. His sons and grandsons had walked behind him then, out into the sunlight at the head of the long stream of citizens, Joe and Tom and Eddy and Anthony, Jim and Danny, the beautiful Lanigan boys, two of them old enough to be there, and three of Joe's boys and three stubby young Mulqueens along Kilmoney Street past Lady's Lane, up to the corner of King's Street and so, through Edward Street, out onto the Dublin road. His sons had walked, and his daughters, forgetting to drive home from the church like ladies, because they wanted to be near him to the end, and because they knew he would wish them there, drove behind him, their beautifully matched horses reined to a very slow step, past the dreamily spired Cathedral to which he had given a priest, past the grey outskirts of his town to St. Stephen's Cemetery, and so up its wide paths—all on foot now, and Honest John travelling once more on the shoulders of his sons —to the wide family grave he had bought, where his mother slept with the horse-thief, where his wife slept and five of his children—open and waiting, the immense, marble angel with the realistic wings standing aside politely to let him in. They had given no noisy sign and said no audible farewell when the ropes dropped him home; they had heard the clay rattle on his coffin, had seen Tom and Father O'Malley shake holy water on it once, twice, three times; they had laid their wilting lilies among the piled-up immortelles; they had prayed again and crossed themselves, and seeing that all was done that Church and children could do, had driven back to his empty house. So here they were, lethargic and resigned, bereft of Honest John as they had known they would have to be one day.

But under the lethargy and resignation, under all the crape banners which they had hoisted to accept defeat, the hearts of the Considines were raw as from a flaying. While they were supporting their loss with admirable composure, none of them really knew how they were supporting it at all. While they were saying that indeed if they had the power they would not call him back, their foolish hearts were crying out for him as infants cry in the night; and while they prayed quietly for his eternal rest, anguish seemed to be shattering all the peace he had built up for them. Death had jabbed down into the great nerve of affection that controlled them. They would survive the blow, and the nerve would not go on throbbing forever, but meantime, large, sedate, mature, husbands, fathers, mothers, wives, men and women of the world, behaving as the world behaved—under all these disguises they were children too who had just lost their father. And they seemed to find some sort of reassurance, some sort of respite in huddling together.

"Where's Anthony?" said Tom again.

"He drove away from the cemetery with Molly," said Joe. "He's coming back later. Don't you think we might have a little more window open?" Eddy crossed the room uncontradicted.

"That was a beautiful wreath the Donellys sent," said Sophia.

"In the shape of a Maltese Cross. Did you see it, Teresa?"

"I did. Paddy Donnelly was one of his oldest friends."

"Solid plate glass," said Danny. "You'd be surprised how heavy those things are." He sighed very heavily.

"The rector of the Jesuits was there," said Joe, who admired that order.

"The least he might do," retorted Tom, who was too tired to-day to be impartial. "All the orders were represented."

"Who was the young priest who sang the 'Dies Irae'?" Eddy asked.

"Father Coghlan," said Tom.

"What a glorious voice!"

"Try putting your feet up, Agnes," said Sophia.

Agnes gave another shuddering sob, and Tom dropped a hand on her shoulder.

"Poor old Agnes!" he said, without any priestly wisdom.

§ 3

JIM came in then with Caroline on one arm and a black portfolio under the other. They were all glad to see him; he had been helpful in the last few days, steady and quick to arrange things, very kind to everyone. His wife came to Teresa, who made room for her on the settee.

There was no colour in Caroline's face to-day; it was pallid as ivory. All extraneousness of curve and light and moving expression had left it; it seemed alive only in one fixed contemplative passion; the loveliness whose great enchantment had been young, quick-changing light and shade and light again, was caught to-day in some place where the unaltering lamp was dim; something had hypnotised it into pale stillness. Superbly it bore the elimination, seeming more beautiful than ever, deprived of beauty's changeful glow. A tragic muse was Caroline to-day, a tragic muse in a chic mourning bonnet.

She was a superstitious creature, always looking for signs

from heaven. On the night of the party she had been certain of receiving one; her gaiety had been a kind of craving of God to vouchsafe a happy omen. She was going to be good; wasn't that what was wanted? Very well then, He would surely set a seal on His own wish. She would not have been surprised if He had made her fall in love with Jim then and there, for that simple thing alone was needed to put her life in order. And how easy for God!

It didn't happen. Instead of love He had sent death to close the door on her past misdemeanours.

Tenderness for her living father had stood between her and all kinds of folly, or so she had believed; now, dead in the very flush of her new resolutions, Honest John seemed to be asking an articulate pledge from her for the first time. He seemed to be preaching a sermon, the old, hackneyed sermon on the old hackneyed death-bed truths, but aimed directly and singly at her this time. And through all the platitudes that thundered up from his cold corpse, platitudes about transience and vanity, about the littleness of oneself and the unimportance of restlessness, which must come at last to this inevitable rest, he seemed to be saying too with an unfamiliar harshness that if in life she had bluffed him, in death she could do no such thing; that he was pure spirit now and would know the recesses of her heart; that he would stand on guard over her new era and make a real job of it; that in fact he had been made God's answer. So while grief held her dry-eyed and lonely, this sermon and this admonition went rumbling on and on through the dark aisles of her heart; the ears of her spirit were straining obediently to catch them; she was steeling herself to meet the most unexpected omen God had ever sent. Childish, superstitious Caroline! Was it only then this naïve fear of the dead, this docile wish to placate a departed spirit, that was carving your deceptive face into a mask of eternal resignation?

"Be off with you now and be a good girl, you silly bit of silk, you!" These words, that had meant nothing, floated perpetually now about her brain. Wearily she answered them, over and over again.

"I will, I will! Father, I'll always be good now."

Jim had to read their father's will for them—a perfunctory

document, dealing only with bequests to old friends and to his grandchildren, and with the disposal of certain portraits and personal treasures—but it had been his wish that the family should hear it on his burial day. Jim spread his papers on a table, but they must wait for Anthony.

Eddy rang for tea, and Sophia sighed with such relief at this that the effort brought new tears to her inexhaustible eyes.

While they were drinking tea Anthony arrived, looking sallow and hard in the darkened room. He was fresh from a quarrel with Molly, who had wept and stamped her feet at him.

Molly did not want to have her old maid sister-in-law come to live at River Hill; she was jealous for the intimate peace of her evenings there with Anthony. Neither did he greatly covet Agnes as a fixture by his fire, but filial instinct was tormenting him with knowledge of what his father would expect of him, whom he had left in charge of all the Considines. Pity raged in him, too, to see one of his own blood left so bleakly unwanted.

"I won't have her in the house, so there!" said Molly.

"You will do as I tell you, madam," he had answered in a shout, and left the house.

Now, taking his tea-cup from Teresa, he went and sat by his old maid sister.

"Agnes," he said to her in a clear, formal tone which all the room could hear. "Agnes, my dear—you can't stay on in this sad house any longer. It'd kill you. You'll come to River Hill to-night, won't you, and make your home there? Molly especially asked me now to say this to you, and to bring you back this evening."

There was a murmur through the room, but he raised his voice against it.

"You'll be happier there, with all the children. They're dying to have you, and we've heaps of room. More room than any of the others have. You can be as free as you like to come and go, of course. You've plenty of money now and need be under no compliment to any of us. But I'd be greatly pleased if you'd call River Hill your home."

He paused and looked at Agnes for her answer. She had none, save a hysterical, helpless nodding of the head.

"That's settled then! We can take the green finches out with us to-night. Then you can arrange later on about whatever furniture you'd like to have from here."

"I had been intending to say, Anthony," said Teresa, "that there's plenty of room for her with us at Roseholm, and plenty of welcome——"

"Or indeed with us, dear Agnes," began Sophia.

"I think she knows all that," said Tom. "Who among us wouldn't be delighted to have our dear Agnes?"

"That'll do about it now," said Anthony, and strode across the room to help himself to cake. "It's settled. She's coming to River Hill."

The family looked at him with gratitude. By his decisiveness and warmth of heart he had shown himself their leader. He certainly hadn't been long about stepping into Honest John's shoes!

With a sense of being relieved and comforted the Considines composed themselves to hear their father's will.

BOOK II

1861–1870

Molly   Caroline   Denis

THE FIRST CHAPTER

LIFE unfolded for Denis in a gentle brightness. He grew merrily at River Hill. The rosy line of his brothers and sisters stretched long and longer behind him with the years. When his grandfather died in the autumn of 1861 he had two brothers, Jack and Paddy, and one sister, Mary, and before he was ten Tess, Joey, Floss and Jim were born. He was at ease in the sociable ups-and-downs of his crowded nursery life and he grew into a graceful and good-tempered boy.

His world, ringed in blue hills and cupped in tender, changeful blue and grey, shone gently for him with a dewy gleam. The voice of the river ran up and down it like a refrain. Its fields were green and daisied, with cows in them and sucking calves; he could hide his feet ankle-deep in the dead leaves of the little wood. He had a pony in a stable, and a saddle in the harness-room. Squirrels, pigeons, bluetits were almost tame to his hand; rooks came home to the elm trees at sunset and larks and blackbirds shouted him out of his bed each morning. The house at the centre of this world was warm with friendly life, had fires in it and stores of apples, and a long slippery banister; there were pleasant, gossipy servants there and brothers and sisters with whom to swap things and run races; there was a misty, white-skinned mother, who gathered flowers in the garden and rode in a carriage behind grey horses; there was a bright-faced father who came and went and whom many of the household seemed to fear; a vast man certainly, firm of voice and foot, but in whose shining eyes, that fascinated him, Denis never saw anything but assurance of happiness,

happiness that would last and was everywhere. If ever for a little while this fact of happiness appeared to be in doubt, Denis sought his father's glance and read it re-stated absolutely there. Thus he was at ease in the unfolding world. He absorbed its serenity, gave it the whole of his awakening heart. His blue eyes shone with its soft, reflected lambency.

Even when the shadow of scholarship crept over the horizon it did not cause great disturbance. Lessons with Miss Wadding in the schoolroom were more of a joke than anything else. It was satisfactory to master the A, B, C, since he soon realised that there was more to be deduced from it by enterprise than that the cat sat on the mat.

But if he taught himself to read real books, Miss Wadding certainly did show him how to understand the face of her watch; she introduced him too, and with him poor, flustered Jack, to the chain of reasoning that begins at "twice times" and ends up nowhere. And she discovered that after the first pains of initiation Denis could not be disconcerted by even the most unfairly sudden enquiries—"Seven nines? Eight sevens? Nine sixes?" He always knew the answer, to Jack's astonishment. Miss Wadding found him "very sharp," she said. "Sharp" is exactly what Denis was not, but he was intelligent and had a welcome in his unmuddied mind for logical information.

The Jesuits kept a day-school in Mellick for the sons of gentlemen, and Denis became a pupil there when he was nine. Thus the blue ring of the world was broken on the south to admit the grey town to its bound of every day. Very importantly Jack and he, with satchels and lunch baskets, climbed up beside their father into the phaëton every morning and were rattled up to school by him before he went to Charles Street; rather less importantly and somewhat the worse for wear, they climbed into it again at three o'clock each afternoon when a servant came to drive them home.

This widened life had more definition and a sharper edge; individuals emerged more clearly in it and not always agreeably. Some of the dew was brushed from the world when school began and there was more than serenity to be absorbed henceforward. Denis's blue eyes were sometimes bewildered now. He saw the drama of crime and punishment played on a more ponderous scale than he had been used to at home. He saw boys refuse to obey a simple behest for no apparent reason, and learnt from lookers-on that there was something brave in their behaviour; he saw masters' faces darken and heard their voices raised against these boys; he saw hands held out, not always steadily; he heard the violent swish of descending cane. He saw stupidity refusing to learn, and anger stupefying stupidity. Once Jack drove home with two proud weals across his sturdy little hand.

These things confused Denis, but in spite of them school was not unhappy.

§ 2

ANTHONY enjoyed the morning drive to school as much as his sons did. Jack's forthrightness and matter-of-fact conversation were amusing, and when he lifted him down from his perch outside the school door, Anthony always stood to watch him march pugnaciously indoors, cocking his dark head, as if to say "Who challenges me here?" Every inch a Considine, seven-year-old Jack. Long-legged Denis needed no help in getting down from the phaëton, and his entrance into the school was less ostentatious than his small brother's; it was even deprecatory. But he always turned to wave on the threshold, "Good-bye, father!" Anthony learnt to watch for that greeting and to wonder how he'd feel if Denis should forget it. He never did. He had an unfailing knack of sweet friendliness for his father.

The elder Considines were always inclined to resent and belittle Denis. It was as if they dimly apprehended his father's hidden engrossment in him, and, vaguely resenting it as unnecessary, sought to snub it in Anthony by bemoaning the boy's physical characteristics as if they were unfortunate. Joe was forever recommending tonics and Sophia even went so far as to give his nurse the pattern of a chest-preserver that her eldest son Victor used to wear when he was Denis's age; Teresa thought, and Agnes agreed with her, that he shouldn't be allowed to look at a book of any kind except his lesson-books and Tom said that he was just the boy to be made into a milksop by the Jesuits. Jim, whose four stripling sons were a delight to the eyes, was not much concerned about Denis one way or another, but he thought he could do with keeping in his place, and Danny felt that he needed plenty of underdone meat in his diet. But instinctively they all resented something in him, some unfamiliar essence, some secret thread of love that ran to him from his father. Only Caroline accepted him naturally; she could not quite forget that when he was five he had spoken to Molly and Anthony of his "pretty aunt," and that when they had asked correctly, "Yes, but which pretty aunt?" he laughed and said, "The only pretty one I've got, of course, but then she's very pretty—Aunt Caroline." Perhaps the story had got round against him to Agnes and Teresa and Sophia, but Caroline enjoyed his accurate discrimination even more than Anthony. She was particularly pretty to him afterwards, in smile and word.

Anthony laughed at all the advice and fault-finding. Watching this son with passion, and caring far too much for him to be deceived, he saw that there was no weedy lankiness in his height, that he was pale only with his mother's live pallor, and that his quietness was not languid but sprang from a peculiarly friendly interest in what was going on round him. It seemed to Anthony that Denis was more at home in the social scene than many who were concerned with getting their say said. He laughed at the cluckings of his brothers and sisters and was radiantly proud of his beautiful eldest son.

§ 3

THE chairman of Considine & Company was a busy man in the exciting years that followed the death of Honest John. These were a time of great money-making, but their stress was not eased for Anthony by having to work with reference to a board of directors that met twice a year and consisted, with himself, of his three brothers, two brothers-in-law, and O'Halloran, the secretary of Considine & Company.

The directors' meetings were great fun and extremely difficult. Anthony and Eddy, who knew their father's business thoroughly, had been trapped between mirth and perplexity when first confronted with the cocksure ignorance of their brother-directors. Danny's cautionary proverbs they had always had with them, and there was nothing new in O'Halloran's perspicacity. But it seemed that Tom and Joe, fresh from Latin and physic-bottles, knew all that was to be known about forage-merchanting, had no need whatever to be counselled in it by younger brothers, and came to the board-room fully fledged in business sagacity. Jim too, admirable as a lawyer, and used to being mysterious as the sphinx with regard to the routine of his own profession, made it clear from the first that he had the affairs of Considine's as readily at his fingertips as if he had spent a lifetime within its walls. They were very amusing, these know-alls, and difficult to handle.

The American Civil War, for instance, had had its reper-cussions in the Charles Street board-room.

Honest John had hailed that war with callous pleasure, foreseeing that American trade would not ride the seas very easily while it lasted. He would cut in at the European ports, with the intention of keeping what trade he could snatch, as was his custom. His main trouble would be to wring the supply from his small and lazily farmed island. That difficulty always fronted him. The uncertainty of the Irish yield and the inertia among tenant-farmers always provided a dangerous element of gamble. He had to contract blindly most of his time, not knowing very clearly where supplies might come from for delivery, or what he might have to pay to collar them. Perhaps his success had lain in his perfect audacity and his willingness to lose on a contract rather than break it. He seldom had to lose. He had an unexplainable flair for buying at the right moment.

He worked at pressure through the last summer of his life. He increased, almost doubling, his contracts with northern Europe, made immense new deals with Liverpool and Cardiff, and opened trade with France; he angled for Italy. He over-worked Eddy without mercy. He took risks which really frightened Anthony. The activities of the Confederate priva-teers, the *Savannah* and her sisters, filled him with amusement. He was entirely cynical about the principles of the war. When his daughters told him that slavery was a shocking thing and that Pio Nono had declared against the Confederates, he said, "Quite right, my little girl; a scandalous state of affairs," and went on eating bread and jam in deep contentment. He enjoyed his own abilities in the summer of 1861, feeling perhaps that this was his last lap and grateful that it should be an exciting one. But he died when the fun was really getting merry and his authority declined onto Anthony at a difficult moment.

From the first the new chairman was decided that what Honest John had intended and begun in regard to European trade must go forward. Risks appealed to him; an element of uncertainty exercised and amused him; and he had Eddy's agreement that Considine's was justified in making a bid for real enlargement now.

But he had to fight heavy moods of depression in his first year, for he was lonelier at his work without the old man than he would have believed possible. He could only hearten himself by remembering how completely Honest John had trusted his judgment and how often he had taken the trouble to say that he would leave things in his hands with perfect confidence. Still he wriggled his toes uneasily in the dead man's shoes.

His board of directors wanted to eat their cake and have it. They wanted him to be Honest John, infallible maker of money and solidity for them, and still to be Anthony, youngest brother whom it was their duty to contradict as often as possible, and whose conceit of himself must not be allowed its head. They were greedy to conserve and enjoy their new rich stake in Considine's, but the idea of plunging about in enterprise to increase it, though startling, had its attractions too. They were desirous of knowing the circumstances of the business through and through, but were disinclined to admit that that fellow Anthony could tell them anything that they hadn't known before he was born. They enjoyed the sound of their own voices at meetings, but were reluctant to be committed to decisions. They wanted risks taken, so long as they were safe risks. They wanted their advice to be indispensable to the chairman so long as he had all the worry. They wanted as large returns with as little impertinence as could be wrung from him. Large returns above all, perhaps. For their directorship was making them greedy, or revealing their actual greed. They prosed and speechified; they bullied and on occasion shouted for their own way; but an undercurrent of their brains was always telling them that they were in the chairman's hands, that he knew the ropes and they didn't, that with Eddy he owned nearly half the shares, and that in fine the best of their play was to trust in God and keep their wives making novenas.

§ 4

IN THE early part of 1864 the novenas must have created a traffic block in heaven. The faces that the directors brought to the May meeting were very stern and wise. Dividends were not what dividends should be.

"I hope you're satisfied, Anthony, that we have not devoted too much capital to Scandinavian trade," said Tom lugubriously.

"I'm satisfied that we haven't yet devoted enough—I'm coming to the question presently. Meantime, let's stick to the agenda, gentlemen. The Bordeaux reports, Mr. O'Halloran, if you please."

Nobody listened to these except Jim and Anthony. All the others were busy preparing the pieces of their minds that they were going to give away gratis at the first opening.

"Mr. Chairman," said Jim at the correct moment later on—he was the only one of them who stuck to board-room formalities—"in regard to our North Sea trade; its extensions have swallowed a very formidable proportion of last year's profits."

"Yes, gentlemen. We agreed here eighteen months ago it should do so."

"I wonder did we?" said Joe.

Anthony smiled.

"We did, Joe. Don't waste your wonder."

"It is correct, of course, that we allowed the outlay. What we would like to know, Mr. Chairman, is whether you still feel justified in the policy to which you persuaded us?"

"Entirely, Jim."

Danny wheezed with astonishing force and Anthony turned to him attentively. But Tom, easier of address, spoke first.

"There has been no profit."

"I said that there would be no profit from the North Sea last year. I also said that there would be no loss."

"No loss! How do you account for the necessity of sinking the profit from other sources in its upkeep?"

"The North Sea trade paid its own expenses for this year. Do try and learn how to read trade returns, Tom, like a good fellow. What it did not pay for, and what it was not asked to pay for, was the immense initial expense of collaring it. We agreed here, gentlemen, eighteen months ago, as we are going to agree now when we have had our customary little tussle, that the cost of the new ships, new agencies, new distributary machinery at the other end, and the very large cost of advertising our unknown name among North Sea dealers would all have to be met out of profits on home and English trade. So it has been done. And on that basis, there has been no loss. If there were, we should not have been surprised, but it would have been necessary to reëxamine my policy and its machinery. Happily, that is not necessary. All that is necessary is to nurse it."

"It will show a profit next year?" asked Jim.

"Unlikely. But it will pay for itself, and its initial expenses being now paid for, it will exact no drain on other branches."

"No profit this year? After all our worry?"

Joe showed extremely worried above his Jehovan beard. Confidence in dividends was luring him nowadays to Punchestown, the Curragh, and the hunting field more often than his practice could have justified. And there were other perplexities.

Jim was worried too. He had always been ambitious for his handsome sons, whom he could not have educated by the humble Christian Brothers as he had been, or by the wily Jesuits whom he detested. But these gentlemen had the monopoly of polite education in Ireland, and Jim had concluded reluctantly that to the Benedictines in England his sons must go. To Downside therefore, expensively, Peter and John had been sent two years ago, in the first flush of Considine dividends, without which the cost could hardly have been faced.

Jim's ambitious choice of school had bred worry for his medical brother-in-law. Clongowes had always been the apex of Sophia's dream for her darling Victor, and after him for Joe and Hubert and Paul and little Gussie. In the face of such a challenge from the Lanigans, however, it was impossible to expect her to lie down. If the Lanigans could go to Downside her boys could go to Beaumont, or if they could not, Sophia would know the reason why! After tremendous curtain clamour, she got her way with the not unwilling Joe, who had really no objection to being as good a man as Lanigan.

Victor Considine went to Beaumont. But from the moment that he did so, it became apparent that Carrington Street was no longer spacious enough to hold the mother of so distinguished a son. *Beaumont oblige* and Dr. Joe had to move his family into the larger seclusion of Finlay Square. The new house required more servants and more furniture, a more expensive upkeep of stateliness. It could all be done, thanks to Considine & Company—just done, if Joe would withhold from Punchestown and the Curragh and the hunting field. That, however, was asking too much of a man, and so Jehovah groaned at restricted dividends.

"But if we are not to see a profit next year," questioned Jim, "what are we driving at?"

"We are driving at large profits five years hence, very large profits ten years hence."

"Mr. Chairman, the American war is fizzling out."

"What does that matter?"

"America will soon be back in her old markets."

"Not in all of them," said Anthony.

Tom laughed incredulously.

"That's all very well," said Danny, getting in his spoke at last, "but what I want to know is this—why did you give a rise to that good-for-nothing, O'Driscoll?"

A rise to anyone but himself was always a disaster for Danny.

"If you were asleep at our November meeting, Danny, will you ask O'Halloran here to let you look at the minutes, like a good chap? We've no time to waste."

"It does seem odd, on reflection," said Tom. "I understand that his department deals with North Sea export. Why add such a gratuitous expense to a department that's already a burden?"

"I seem to have heard you say that before, old man," said Anthony.

"Employees have their rights undoubtedly," the priest was handsome enough to admit, "but we directors have a responsibility to the rest of the shareholders, you know."

"It's every man's duty to cheer for his own side, I quite agree, Tom," said the chairman.

"An ass laden with gold overtakes everything," said Danny, mysteriously, "and with trade at its worst, like it is——"

"Trade was never better."

"If trade was never better," thundered Jehovah, "why in the name of heaven are dividends what they are?"

"Because we're building a business here in Mellick, Joe—not taking a snooze. As to this rise that's fretting the life out of Danny——"

So on, so on. All the directors' meetings were like that.

§ 5

As THE years passed River Hill still wore the look of mildly inebriated surprise that Mr. Cleethorpes Downey had imprinted on it. It did not don a sudden, miraculous beauty as in such surroundings the fantastic-minded might have expected it to do, but it settled down and assumed an amiable liveliness. The conservatory was built onto the south side of the drawing-room, as Anthony had dreamt, and its dome was of many-coloured glass. An expensive landscape gardener did wonders with the thirty acres, twisting deceptive paths about them in the cleverest manner, so that there was no indecent straightness anywhere, flinging up terrific rockeries and perilous rustic bridges, planting monkey-puzzles and ornamental grasses with a lavish hand and even introducing a couple of plaster statues —decently draped females called Minerva and Diana. He built a summer-house too that he said was an exact reproduction to scale of a Chinese temple.

Molly and an ordinary gardener took up the work where this genius laid it down, so that there were crocuses and violets in due time, and daffodils and gillyflowers and lavender and a hundred kinds of rose. For Molly loved River Hill, as Anthony had known she would, and was finding satisfaction not only in the increased regard and jealousy extended to her nowadays by the ladies of Mellick, but in the year's procession of beauty about her feet. She grew attached to the mossy river-path, and liked to watch the nestings and flights of the herons there; she wandered on bright mornings in the fields, gathering dewy chestnut leaves to drench her face and hands; she hoarded pine cones for her bedroom fire; she fed bluetits and robins, never wearying of coaxing them to eat out of her hand; often she greeted Anthony with forget-me-nots twisted in her hair, and when they walked together among the tortuous paths, one eye and one hand of hers were forever inattentive from him, looking for weeds, plucking blown roses.

She seemed happy. Certainly she was having to bear too many children; languor was becoming habitual and her voice was not always silky soft as it used to be; there were permanent lines about the soft mouth, and beauty's full radiance visited her now only upon occasion, rarely and more rarely. But as the years lengthened she kept a mute and subtle grace about her still like a soft halo; she was one of those women who have a shadow-beauty to the end.

For Anthony in certain moods she was still immeasurably desirable.

One night of July in 1866 they walked arm-in-arm along the river-path. He had come home from Holland that afternoon, after three weeks' journeying, and it was heaven to be back, to see the lights of River Hill above them, to have kissed his eight children, to have Denis before his eyes again and hear his happy voice, to walk with his wife now by the moaning river. Ah, it was blessed to be back! And if one small discomfort stirred at the base of his heart, at least she need not know of it. She must forgive what she would never be told; he must forget it.

It was by no means Anthony's habit to be unfaithful when apart from Molly. Indeed in their first six years no separation mattered, for she was always then the end and sum of his desire; but nowadays boredom in foreign cities led him sometimes into casual adventure. Not often, for promiscuity offended his conception of himself and he had no inclination to play the rake. Harlotry had to drape itself in many veils of charm and had to be skilful to wear at least a sham fastidiousness before it could undo him. But a woman in Amsterdam had seemed to understand this very well; indeed, she had frightened Anthony. He did not like to remind himself now that he would be bound to return again and again to Amsterdam. A man may have an adventure and be ashamed of it, but married and happy in Ireland, with eight children, he does not fall in love with a Dutch harlot. Good God, what wicked nonsense. His troubled eyes sought out the light in Denis's window.

"It is grand to be home, my little girl."

She was dreamy now; at dinner she had been gay, full of Mellick gossip and family news, the kind of talk they both enjoyed. In her pleasure at having him back she had let her tongue wag audaciously to entertain and even to annoy him. Yes, Jim and Caroline had dined here on Sunday and Tom as well. Jim and Tom were very angry over what the Fenians were trying to do in America, invading Canada or something. Caroline didn't seem well. That reminded her—young Jack had been heard using the most frightful language—a word beginning with *b*—— "No, Agnes, I won't say it, you needn't be frightened. Oh, it was worse than you think, Anthony—not *b-l—b-u*. Jack must have got it from the men in the stables, of course, but Nurse seemed terribly put out." She'd taken some carnation-slips over to Teresa—those wine-red ones; the Mulqueens' garden was really looking lovely. Danny told her then that the double responsibility at Charles Street was a great strain on him with the chairman away.

Molly purred over that bit and so did Anthony, and Agnes said that indeed it was a shame for them to be always laughing at poor Danny!

During dinner Molly sat with her back to the sunset in a heavenly frame of light. She had made herself very lovely for her returning lord; grey, mistily patterned brocade clung tightly to the sweet line of her breasts, and flowed about her in rich skirts to the ground. There had been presents in Anthony's valise, for how could a man come home from Amsterdam without a diamond? The star he had brought lay on her bosom and glowed as if to burn her heart away. She played with the red roses on the table as she talked, and sometimes pulled one out and smelt at it voluptuously.

"They're lovely, aren't they? Did you see any better in Holland? And did you go to Haarlem about the bulbs? Oh, Sophia's like a cat with two tails these times because Victor's been asked to stay a week with young Algernon Trent's people in Warwickshire these holidays. He's an Honourable, you know. Oh, yes, that's all very well, Anthony, but it really will be rather fun for Victor; very good for him to know people like that. Would you believe me, those dreadful Meeneys have actually bought that sweet little place next to us—down there, you know! Isn't it awful to have that kind of people coming out our way? It even makes Agnes uncharitable! I suppose they think I'll call on them—but you have to draw the line somewhere! Did Denis tell you that Quixote has gone lame—poor boy's had no riding these lovely fine days . . ."

Anthony had listened and chipped in contentedly without even troubling to snub her little snobberies. He was too much ashamed to-night of his own greater shortcomings. All he wanted was this, to be at home where Denis was; to eat what Bridget cooked, to see his father's face again in the portrait over the fire, to watch his wife's pretty trick of preening sideways at her own reflection in the great console mirror, to bathe in her innocence, to drink up all her generous, lovely pleasure in his coming home.

Now on the river-path she seemed to have little left to say. He wondered what was making her look sad.

While he was wondering she spoke.

"We're going to have another baby, Anthony."

They stopped in their walk. His voice was more grave than she had ever heard it when he answered her.

"Oh, my little girl," he said. "I'm sorry for that."

"That's a queer thing to say to me." She laughed uncertainly.

"You know what I mean. You've had your share of that. I wish to God——"

"Don't, Anthony. I'm very glad. It doesn't seem to do me any harm."

His heart raged with an intolerable affection. There he had been gallivanting round the world, insulting her love and her innocence in the arms of a foreign harlot, almost unwilling to return to her, impatient of her harmless follies, superiorly amused by her sweet vanity, egotistical, selfish, cock-o'-the-walk—and here was she waiting gently, without protest or cantankerousness, to bear him his ninth child. She was only thirty-three; her youth had been given over to the weariness and pain of pregnancy; motherhood had taken her vigour and was taking her beauty too—all for him. And he couldn't even be faithful for three weeks!

"But Anthony, you foolish fellow, there's nothing to cry about!" She took his hand and drew him along the path again. Her blue shawl fluttered in a sudden breeze from the water.

"Do you hear that owl, Anthony? Isn't it sad?"

A twig snapped under his foot.

"Ssh," said Molly, "we must be near the heron's nest."

"Ah, my little girl! It isn't as if they mattered so desperately to you, all these babies!"

She took his face in her cold hands.

"Don't go on crying like that, I tell you. Perhaps I don't love them as much as some women seem to. But oh, I love *you*, I love *you*."

THE SECOND CHAPTER

MOLLY died in February. She slipped away suddenly, silently, leaving the brief and futile panic round her bed to subside almost before it had arisen. The ninth child played some bungling trick on her, used as she was to the routine of giving life. It elected to leave her womb three weeks too early, for one thing. But Flossie had done something of that kind, so that the mother of eight could not have been taken completely unawares this time. Perhaps she was too tired to rise to the unexpected; perhaps even when the right hour struck she might have been too tired for her commonplace ordeal. In any case, everything went wrong, and Molly closed her misty eyes and made her escape. The newborn child, her fifth son, only stayed half an hour behind her.

§ 2

ANTHONY had had a busy and difficult winter. He was fighting hard for his European trade. American dealers, reëntering the market, were not prepared to suffer his encroachment without a fight, and he had no intention of yielding recent gains. Meanwhile the air was full of Fenian rumours; the talk of field and shop was of nothing but gunmen and peelers, Ribbonmen and spies. Strangers walked about Mellick, strangers with Irish names and twanging accents, bronzed men back from the American war. Fear and close-fistedness were everywhere. The people, knowing the subtleties of their own air, smelt an old, returning fever on the wind, and waited for it uneasily. Farming was almost at a standstill. The great landowners, cursing an unaccountable country from London clubs, instructed their agents to lie low and take no risks. The small tenant farmers, dejected always, were hypnotised now by the trouble that hovered above the Vale of Honey. It seemed as if nothing short of large-scale bribery would compel them to sow their fertile acres. Anthony was at his wit's end to secure his exports; he had to scour Ireland for them, outbid every rival and buy at seed time harvests that might never be reaped.

He was seriously worried, and his fellow-directors were suffering acutely from panic, becoming enamoured of negation at a time when Anthony could see no hope in any but the most active and positive measures. They were for slumber and folded hands; he was for a fight and a victory. He tired of their dead weight on his shoulders. Only Jim had eyes to see what he was driving after, but Jim was never happy in a gamble, and seemed in any case preoccupied; his eyes had the look of a man who is secretly ill.

Eddy was in London and therefore of little comfort. Indeed he had chosen this time of all others to grow indifferent at his end, an unprecedented happening. The London office had always been of a most soothing efficiency and now it was so no longer. Eddy was out of sorts. Anthony had gone over to see him in November, but could find no definite reason for his vagaries. His brother was always at his office, and seemed as sane and full of interest as ever before. But he looked white and weary. Some personal affair bothering him, no doubt, but he was not to be drawn. Anthony went home again disgruntled and Eddy spent Christmas in Spain, the first time in thirteen years that he had not come home for it. Everyone was hurt at that. Caroline had cried and written him an angry letter.

In January Joe was proved to be losing in a rather large way on the race-course. Joe did everything in a large way, but even allowing for that Anthony was staggered by the amount of a bookmaker's bill that his eldest brother called on him to pay. The money did not perplex him half as much as the stupidity it represented, stupidity which made it necessary for him to find the Beaumont fees also for that term's education of his nephews.

With all these frets, he was perpetually irritated by the necessity for talking politics and listening to politicians at every turn of the busy day. He was much in contact at his office with the wealthy landed classes and the Protestant merchants; and these people were eager to have a man of his prominence echo their vilifications of his difficult countrymen. This was a thing he could not do. He was no Fenian, heaven was his witness, nor had he any patience with the crazy dream that seemed to be forever rising up from Ireland to enshroud her, but his people remained his people, and against all reason he could not be happy abusing any of them, however mad, to foreigners.

At home, where he was used to look for solace from all such woes in Molly's arms, his nerves were irritated by the perpetual presence now about his home of his sister Agnes, and his anxieties were increased by his wife's weary looks and moods of languor and discouragement. He was so universally worried that he could neither observe her symptoms calmly nor always refrain in her presence from expressing some of his general exasperation in words of gloom and impatience that distressed her.

"Anthony, don't stare into the fire with that awful face! It'll all be over soon—only a month or so."

They were in their bedroom, resting in dim candlelight.

"I couldn't bear much more of it!" he said. She smiled. To hear him one would think it was he who was carrying the child. "It seems to have been such an age this time, my little girl!"

"It won't be long now—early in March."

"Teresa and Caroline will have the children to stay, I suppose?"

"Yes, they've promised." She threw a handful of pine cones on the fire.

"I love the crackle these things make," she said. "Oh, Anthony! If anything happens this time, if anything happens——"

"Why will you keep saying that?" he shouted. "Why will you keep on saying these crazy things to me?"

She burst into tears.

"Oh! God, don't cry!" he said on the same cruel note of panic; and then, on his knees beside her, "Don't cry, Molly Bawn, don't cry, my little girl," and he cried despairingly himself, his head on her knees.

§ 3

So, on a starry midnight of frost, after a happy day, in which she had been boastful and merry about her crocuses that were stabbing through the lawn, in which she had driven with Denis and Jack and Mary in their pony trap, in which she had drunk champagne at dinner to crown her mood of well-being: when Orion and Cassiopeia were bright and the river was filling the house with its usual song of silence, the pains she knew seized her and her hour was on her too soon.

Midwives and doctors sprang from somewhere at Anthony's sharp command, and took charge by the side of the blue-hung bed as they had often done before; but this time they were brisk and anxious at their business, and did not pause to make any of the old jokes at his expense that used to sicken him. He would have given his right hand for the consolation of a joke from them now, but Hail Marys were all that seemed to be coming to the women's lips.

She died without a fuss, without scream or cry or prayer. She did not even say good-bye to her husband.

Although Orion was still high when Tom hurried up the stairs, she had already travelled far beyond his help. He laid the holy chrism, however, as a last brotherly grace, on her cold hands and feet and eyes and lips and nostrils, that the sins of her five senses might stay with her earthly flesh, and be no burden to her at heaven's gate.

They laid her out with flowers and candles on her blue-hung bed. And her mother came from Dublin and cried and cried to see her so, and her sisters and brothers came and all the Considines who had made her one of them; and the ladies of Mellick, who had admired and envied her and with whom she had gossiped over the tea-cups, left black-edged cards in the hall for Anthony and came and murmured "De Profundis" at her side. And not a soul but said she looked as lovely in death as when she was a bride.

That was true. When there was peace in their room, when he could get it as it should be, empty of everyone but him and her, Anthony would stand by the blue-hung bed to which he had brought her in her beauty not quite twelve years ago, and looking down on her still face, would wearily marvel that death had taken his wife and given him back his bride, a cold facsimile of his bride.

Mellick mourned her, the wife of an important man, almost as much as it had mourned that important man, her father-in-law, six years ago, when he had gone her road more timely. The streets were silent and respectful as she rode past, more respectful even than when she went gaily in silk gowns behind the stepping greys. The leaves had been falling for Honest John but for Molly, who was young, the soft Spring winds were out. A blackbird sang at River Hill on her funeral morning and a few of her crocuses unsheathed themselves.

Anthony walked behind her to St. Stephen's Cemetery, with Denis on his right side, Jack on his left. Black crape fluttered from the boys' black hats; they looked absurdly young and sad, with streaks on their faces where their black gloves or their tears, or both, had smudged them. Anthony wondered what their thoughts were as they trudged in manful gravity beside him. His own were monotonous enough. They were with Molly, entreating her forgiveness.

She had had faults but he could not remember them. She had been vain and extravagant, prone to gossip, prone to snobbery. Indeed she would have been flattered to know that there were two baronets at her funeral. She had not been remarkably maternal; her children had tired and puzzled her except in moods of gay indulgence. She had been jealous of her husband's smiles, but not intelligent enough to be really interested in his interests. These things escaped his memory now.

He could only remember that she was gentlest of the gentle, that her beauty had far outstripped her innocent notion of it and would have adorned extravagance beyond her dreams. He remembered how merry she was with chatter and flowers and birds, and that when he was harsh to her social follies, she took his rebuffs with a laugh. He remembered, not so much that maternity had been a difficult rôle for her, but that in spite of that she had never been angry with her young, but always vaguely tender, timidly amused. He remembered that there was no roughness in her, and that her love for him, her generous, warm, unquestioning love, which seemed to wait open-armed for all his moods, tenderly, consentingly, voluptuously his—that this love had been a glory about him always, and was their undoing now.

"Oh, I'd have spared you," he pleaded, his eyes on her relentless coffin. "I tried, Molly, I swear I tried. But what does that matter now? At thirty-four you're dead. At thirty-four! Because of me—because I loved you! I took everything you had—I killed you. I, that wouldn't hurt a hair of your head. I killed you. Oh, what's the meaning of it, Molly? Oh, Molly, my little girl!"

He could find nothing else to say to himself, only these few, monotonous sentences.

Molly could have told him what the meaning of it was, as in life she had often longed to find the words to tell him, when he was distressed for her childbearing. She had longed to tell him that she, who was a timid woman, afraid of mice and the dentist, unable to endure toothache calmly or to face his gusts of temper with any spirit, was willing to bear as many children as he gave her, not because she wanted them, but because the risk of having them was the price she must pay for his passionate love. She had often longed to tell him that their fused desire was the only real and perfect thing for her in a world of mists and shadows; that it was not for him to fume and fret, for long ago and with open eyes she had made her own bargain with fate, attesting then that if love killed her as it might, she would have no grievance. She had had to go this way to know his love, and she was well satisfied to have it so.

If she could have said this now as she lay in her flower-filled coffin, it might have explained much that had puzzled him in the past, why his restraints had been made difficult by her sweet, shy invitation, why she had been so reckless in her yielding, why all her tenderness had kept an edge of ecstasy in twelve long years. She had had one courage, the courage of passion. She had made and kept her bargain, but she must keep her secret too. She must not lean back from heaven to comfort Anthony and tell him that it was she who chose to go this way, not he who led her to it, and that she would choose the same again.

She was lowered at last into her lawful place in the huge family grave—mother of eight Considines. The marble angel was standing aside to let her in, the first of a new generation to sleep under his realistic wings. The undertaker's men piled up the immortelles, but Anthony and his sons threw her own snowdrops and violets to her; they would lie for awhile at least between her and the terrible earth. That was rattling on her coffin now—soon, soon, she would indeed be gone.

The voice of Father Tom beat bravely against the thud of clay—"*In paradisum deducant te angeli* . . ." ah, lovely she would look among the choirs of angels, lovely as the bright seraphim themselves. Caroline flung more violets, "Good-bye, Molly," said she on a quivering sob. Teresa covered her eyes and Eddy gathered small, sobbing Jack onto his shoulder. But Denis stood erect with Anthony, and in his eyes, which turned often to his father, there was a sombre, unchildish, compassionate look, that reminded one or two of the mourners of Honest John.

In another minute it was all over. There was nothing more to be done to ease or emphasise Molly's death. Her husband had only to leave her now in that preposterous place, her grave.

THE THIRD CHAPTER

DURING the first months of Anthony's widowerhood his relatives set themselves collectively to the task of "taking poor Molly's place." Their way of doing this was to give Anthony plenty of advice. How were they to know that it had been his wife's pleasure to be wax in his hands and that the giving of good counsel to her husband had never entered Molly's head?

The ladies of the family formed the habit of calling at River Hill; they kept in advisory touch with Agnes and acquainted themselves through her with most of the details of the household. The servants' wages, the children's new mourning and spring flannels, the gardener's accounts, the butcher's accounts, the schoolroom meals and the duties of the institutional Miss Wadding all came under their expert scrutiny. They steered the nursery through an epidemic of measles—from the off side of the carbolic sheet. They were firm and cool in handling a painful matter that came to light in regard to one of the nursemaids and a soldier.

But their main objective was to see that Molly's inky-suited family was fittingly educated. All their affectionate uncles and aunts were bent on turning Anthony's children into the most practicable kind of ladies and gentlemen, with only this unmentioned modification, that none of the counsellors thought it necessary for anyone else's children, no matter whose, to be quite as magnificently educated as their own. (By good education the family understood expensive education, even Jim inclining to believe that the more one spent on a human mind the greater should be its yield.)

Between all their households the Considines had an extensive contact with the Catholic schools of the United Kingdom and, from the welter of their educational experience, advice and to spare could be dredged up for Anthony.

"That fellow Denis wants the stuffing knocked out of him," was Doctor Joe's main contribution in council. And Sophia agreed that life in a rough-and-tumble school was the very thing for Anthony's boys. She did not think somehow that Beaumont would be the right place for them; which was just as well, she added diffidently, since with their father in trade it might have been difficult. . . .

"Indeed!" snorted Joe. "Let me tell you that if my brother's children aren't good enough for Beaumont, I can very easily remove mine!"

But Sophia hadn't meant that. She really hadn't meant anything—an explanation which Joe seemed to find quite normal.

"None of my children are going to England to school," said Anthony one day. "I'd always be afraid of my life, Sophia, that some way or another they'd find out over there that I'm in trade. Besides," he went on, with an innocent smile at Teresa, whose children were at Irish schools, "I've noticed that they train them to be ashamed of themselves very nicely and inexpensively here at home."

Eventually, in the late summer of 1868, eighteen months after Molly's death, Anthony announced that the children were starting at school in September, Jack and Paddy at Clongowes and Mary and Tess at Saint Catherine's, the new French convent a few miles outside the town whose fees were quite expensive enough for honour. Denis, Anthony added, without a flicker of new expression in his face, was staying at home and continuing at the Holy Name School.

"Scandalous!" said Tom. "You'll ruin him."

"You're making a mollycoddle of him, Anthony," said Joe.

Anthony took some trouble to answer that charge.

"There isn't a boy in the whole family can sit a horse as well as Denis," he said. "None of your precious sons could swim like him at his age, or run a hundred yards at his speed, or sail a wag with him."

"Oh, sailing, swimming! What he wants," said Teresa, "to give him character is plenty of boxing and football."

"Boxing is simply magnificent for boys," said Agnes
unexpectedly.

Anthony stood up with a gesture of dismissal.

"I'd thank all you ladies to confine your clucking to your
own eggs," he said vulgarly.

The ladies were much upset by this metaphor.

§ 2

THE death of his mother took childishness from Denis, not
so much by its direct shock of loss or by the effect of her
death-bed and funeral on his startled imagination, but because
it was the first cause he was allowed to see of unhappiness in
his father. In the days that immediately followed his mother's
death he looked in vain to Anthony's eyes for their once
infallible assurance and promise of happiness. Bracing himself against this shock, he pierced beyond it and reached, only
instinctively and half-consciously, to that remorse and sense
of helpless responsibility towards the dead which his father
was enduring. He could not understand, could not even have
named this especial grief of Anthony's, for his notions of the
relationship between a husband and wife were as cloudy and
fantastic as those of the average eleven-year-old boy, but his
nerves were aware of it nevertheless, and it laid a burden of
blind compassion on his great love for his father. Naturally,
since he did not even consciously apprehend it, he was
inarticulate about this feeling, but it found its own tortuous
avenues of expression and made him thereafter more than
ever companionable and friendly towards Anthony.

It was his first half-conscious encounter with emotional
difficulty and it bore him swiftly into boyhood.

Now, therefore, as he read and talked with school friends
and went about his normal pursuits he became conscious and
observant of life's confusing contrasts of good and evil,
pleasure and pain.

He discovered Mellick's slums, for instance—the crumbling
Old Town that looked so gently beautiful at evening, grey, sad,
and tender, huddled on humpy bridges about canals and twisting streams—and found that under its mask of dying peace it
lived a swarming, desperate, full-blooded life, a life rich in

dereliction, the life of beggars, drunkards, idiots, tramps, tinkers, cripples, a merry, cunning, ribald, unprotesting life of despair and mirth and waste. He beheld this life with amazement. With amazement which he struggled to hide he stared into the faces of its creatures, the beggars who huddled in church porches and came to his father's door to plead with Aunt Agnes for a copper or a piece of bread or a pair of boots —creatures whose tales of woe, true or false, could not be more fantastic, it seemed to him, than their visible aspect of hopelessness. Rheumy and filthy-smelling old men, sharp-eyed, wolfish children, lively-tongued women who suckled dirty babies at dirty breasts, the old crone with lupus-eaten face who seemed to live in the doorway of St. Anthony's Church and to whom he could never empty his pockets quickly enough to be sure that while doing so his face showed nothing but friendly casualness—on all these creatures he looked nowadays with a newly inflamed astonishment. It was not so much that they distressed as that they and their implications took him completely by surprise.

Their images did not pursue him to his natural haunts, however. His days were full of a happy activity. School hours were pleasant and leisurely and the soft low line of hills that ringed the Vale of Honey was the boundary of a world that seemed mainly happy. The wide, long, leafy streets of the New Town, the stretching pastures and wet green woods that spread outside it, the bogs and trout streams and great, urgent, tumbling river, all made a wide and changeful playground.

At home he missed his brothers, Jack and Paddy, but in his outdoor life it was his cousin Tony that he longed for most, Tony, best of all boon companions, who had followed his own brothers to Downside now. Still, when Denis had his black pony, Phelim, between his knees and when Mickey Cogan or some other rode beside him on Jack's fat Shetland, and with maybe Bill O'Reilly pressing on behind as well as he could on Mary's Spanish donkey, when their way was set towards the Broody River, through woods so thick that in summer they were like greenlit caves of the sea, past waterfalls over which a grey wagtail might be flitting, by hazel banks heavy with sweet nuts, with these two friends or others, with trout rods and dogs and pockets full of apples, there seemed no cloud over all the Vale of Honey save only a faithful regret for Tony, with whom he had discovered these green paradises.

Lessons came easily to him, and contacts with other boys, quarrels, friendships, and gossips with them, were of tremendous interest.

Denis was at this time the kind of bookworm who will read anything rather than read nothing at all. His father was assembling an odd kind of library, picking it up in large and small lots at auctions, with the vague idea that "Denis would be fond of books." Denis was "fond of books," in almost as haphazard a way as Anthony was a buyer of them, and was accumulating a very confused store of information about life, information both of the furtive and non-furtive kinds, from the rapidly filling shelves of the River Hill library. He found that other boys were doing the same according to the means at their disposal. To exchange views clarified and sometimes more deeply confused this knowledge. Odd and heterogeneous indeed were the conversations that Denis conducted with Mickey Cogan and Bill O'Reilly by the Broody River or in the deep green woods, or in holiday time with Tony, tramping the Bearnagh hills—odd and amusing and pathetic, but very important to the young conversationalists. By means of them and of his father's books, Denis's intellectual innocence began to slip from him easily enough and without his being aware that he was shedding anything especially significant.

Full and variegated days. He came home tired and happy at the end of each of them, Phelim jogging lazily under him and his hungry thoughts running on supper and on the tale of the day that he would pour out to his father. When he turned from under the tunnel of lime trees into the open lawns before the house, he always sang out in his clear falsetto a parody from the Mass responses that announced his mighty appetite:

"Dominic, have the biscuits come?"

Anthony's baritone would chant ringingly from the house:
"Yes, and the spirits too-oo!"

He would dismount from Phelim then and try to race his father who, he knew, would be hurrying from indoors to the steps. But Anthony nearly always won.

"Welcome home, my son," he would say, his brilliant eyes full of pleasure. And Denis, going in with him, was dimly aware that the day that had been so good was best in this ending to it that always seemed the same.

§ *3*

HE FOUND a hero to worship at this time.

His minister of studies at Holy Name School was a young Jesuit scholastic named Martin Devoy who had accomplished twelve of the long years of the Jesuit training and was now within fair sight of ordination. He taught Latin to Denis and was also his choir-master.

Martin Devoy was tall and ruddy-faced, a good athlete and a good musician, a man both simple-minded and intelligent, a gifted, vigorous, zealous, boyish person. Wise ones in the Society of Jesus whispered sometimes that there was a great preacher rising up in him for the order. There probably was a great missionary in him. He had entered the Society on a wave of boyish fervour for the work of Francis Xavier in the East and of the famous old missionaries to the dark, un-measured West. The passion to follow and outstrip these men, who he believed to have been without exception saints, still blazed in him and made the motive of his life.

He had an extraordinary faith in the Catholic Church. No intellectual appeal—and he did not shut his ears to any—could overcome his need of and therefore his belief in the institution that he saw his Church to be. He had sought doubt and deliberately exposed himself to its attacks, but took little from it except a faint surprise at the unreality for him of what he called its dangers. He was in fact enamoured of the Church as a man may be of an incompatible mistress. She could not disillusion him because he carried his own image of her in his heart. He saw her, could only see her, as he wanted her to be, and out of his love was impassioned to defend her questionable history. A reckless and hot-headed apologist, he would be wasted always among the converted or among the sceptical. The news he had was for the innocent to whom he would preach a Church that did not exist, save in the dreams of a few men.

It is a question if ecclesiastical astuteness should have with-held priesthood long from such suitable material, but it hap-pened that to his immediate superiors Martin Devoy appeared a proud young man, in need of protracted chastening. They were right. He was proud, and for that reason gave no one any means of guessing that he was also neurotically humble and the prey of morbid and unbalanced self-distrust.

He loathed his present occupation of teaching Latin to dull boys, loathed it so much that he was subject to tremendous bursts of temper in the classroom, outbreaks so violent and so quickly over that he had earned the name of "Flasher" in the school. It was because of these rages and his inability to eradicate them that he was being given an unduly long period of schoolroom work now towards the end of his training. He accepted authority's discipline in this and found comfort for his restlessness in the fact that the boys liked him on the whole. They forgave him his rages because they were always quickly over, and because he was just and humorous and lively.

When Denis was promoted to Martin Devoy's class he happened to be the only lively-minded youth in four benches full of dullards. He had reached the form sooner than was customary and was eighteen months younger than the youngest of his classmates, but still had no difficulty in setting a pace for them that they did not trouble to emulate. His presence became a source of brightness and relief to the discouraged master, for whom his quick wits rippled like a long-forgotten, merry tune. On some particularly weary mornings, it seemed to "Flasher" that Denis's eager, unfretted face was like a lamp held up to him in a fog. The youngest pupil became almost visibly his "pet," as the others in the class styled it. Denis was teased and pestered and laughed at—but he cared very little. He liked his new, lively Latin master.

Anthony's dinner-table was often entertained with tales of "Flasher" Devoy.

"Why don't you ask him to dinner?" said he.

Thus "Flasher" came to dine at River Hill.

He had thought that he would like very much to meet this father of whom Denis talked so much, and Anthony imagined that he would get on very well with his son's new idol. But strangely, in spite of great outward cordiality, the two men found a wall of reserve between them and felt, though they never seemed, uneasy together.

The scholastic was a complete success with Aunt Agnes, however, and she invited him frequently to River Hill.

It was he for instance who, one wet half-holiday, helped Denis to put the heterogeneous library of River Hill in order. He hardly knew which to be the more amused at, the odd jumble of bad, good, and excellent books of which it was composed or the indiscriminate eagerness with which Denis had already rummaged and read in it.

"Good heavens! Is there anything left in the world for you to read? Except perhaps Milton?"

"Oh, him too," said Denis. "A little onward lend thy guiding hand to these dark steps, a little further on——"

Martin Devoy burst out laughing.

"You're an impossible young prig," he said.

§ 4

IT BECAME the fashion for some of the boys of the school, Mickey Cogan, Bill O'Reilly, Wally Mullens, Denis and others, to take long tramps up into the Bearnagh hills on Saturday afternoons with "Flasher" Devoy. The talk during these tramps was often good and exciting. Martin Devoy had excellent stories to tell, and he told them in excellent partisan fashion, of his heroes, the Jesuit missionaries; stories of Matteo Ricci and Benedict Goez and Father Benoit, and of the great Jesuit Republic of Paraguay. He could talk too and make his companions talk of the life about them, of birds and animals and plants; and for those who were interested, Denis among them, he talked of music, of Bach and Mozart and Beethoven and often of his idol, Palestrina. On wet Saturdays he sometimes allowed the choirboys to come and listen to his organ practice, when he would play whatever they asked for, explaining the music as he played. So, out walking on the hills, what he said of the composers was illustrated in some of their memories, or he would illustrate it for them by singing explanatory phrases.

Denis, listening to all this, was enchanted, but sometimes, especially when the talk was of music, inexplicably oppressed by what "Flasher's" talk revealed to him of worlds of form

and discipline, worlds created accurately out of enlightened
personality, worlds far flung from this tangible one which,
with all respect to God, he was beginning to think had blundered
up in a rather inexcusable mess to its present stage. But mainly
he was delighted, mainly all the excitable, full talk of his
master heightened the beauty of the immediate world by adding
infinite vistas to it. And the personality of the talker grew in
heroism for Denis on these walks. As he listened and tramped
and grew dreamy from the long miles and the hilly air, he
looked into the future of this marvellous "Flasher" and saw
it shining like an old, heroic poem. How fine to be so sure of
oneself, he would catch himself thinking, how great to see
only one possible thing to do, and to rush off and do it, no
matter what it cost! Brave, holy, splendid, "Flasher" Devoy!
And meanwhile, wouldn't it be great to be able to vault a five-
barred gate as easily as that same "Flasher"!

§ 5

ONE afternoon in March 1870, Aunt Agnes stood on a garden
path at River Hill and lectured Denis, who was kneeling near
her in a newly turned bed of dung and leaf mould. He wore
no coat and his shirt sleeves were rolled up, his trousers, hands
and forearms were heavily stained with earth, his hair flopped
over his forehead, his face was flushed and dewy with sweat.
His eyes looked westward of Aunt Agnes, into abstraction.

". . . the cut of you this minute—and all the money that's
being spent in bringing you up nicely. Your poor father! God
help him! If it's another gardener that's wanted, but really
with two eating their heads off in idleness already . . ."

The years were not sweetening Agnes Considine. Life
had given her nothing but money, a poor gift, and she was
slipping into the ways of an ineffectual scold. She had nothing
to do except say her beads, give notice to servants, and order
the carriage. No one paid much attention to her. Anthony
never seemed to hear a word she said; even Father Dargle,
her confessor for twenty years, sometimes asked her lately to
cut it short for God's sake and stop wasting his time about
nothing; her nieces and nephews were leaving behind them the
"googly baby" ways that appeal so pitifully to the empty-

hearted and were putting on personalities as much too strong
for her as those of her brothers and sisters had always been;
indeed, were it not for the long hours spent talking things
over with her darling pet nun, Sister Attracta, in the parlour
of St. Joseph's Convent . . .

"Denis, you haven't heard a word of what I'm saying!"

He smiled.

"Well, not the last few words, Aunt Agnes. I—I was
thinking."

"Of what, may I ask?"

"A fuchsia tree, Aunt Agnes."

"A fuchsia tree! And what'd put a thing like that into your
head? In the middle of March too! There isn't a bit of fuchsia
in the place that I've ever seen."

"No. I'm going to get one."

"Indeed?" she laughed drily. " 'Tisn't a tree, anyway, only
a bit of a bush."

"It ought to be a tree," he murmured.

"It's out playing football you should be, with other boys
of your age."

"But Mr. Devoy is coming to tea."

Aunt Agnes almost toppled backwards.

"And you in that state!"

"Oh, he doesn't mind!"

"Come in and wash yourself at once, sir."

Denis stood up.

"All right, Aunt Agnes."

They walked towards a side door of the house together, she
rustling and jingling in black silk and golden chains, he respectfully distant from her, with his mud and his gardener's basket.
The dusk of March was hurrying upon them, although the
west that they faced was still bright, with its brightness reflected
on the river. A breeze scudded over the dishevelled garden and
the air was clear with recent rain; the puddles shone to warn
Aunt Agnes's tidy feet, and though her eyes were on the house
and its slowly lighting windows, she steered her way dry-shod.
But Denis splashed forgetfully and was scolded. He was
seeing too many things besides the shining puddles—the
watery, wide spread of sunset, the subtle new gleam on grass
that had been winter sere two days ago, a hint of swelling on

the topmost twigs of elms. brightness of sheathed crocuses across the squelchy lawn.

"Aunt Agnes—will you give me your honest opinion?"

"As if I ever did anything else, Denis!"

"Well, don't you think, truly, that that summer-house over there is ugly?"

"Ugly?" She stood perfectly still and took a long, reverent look at the exact reproduction to scale of a Chinese temple. "Ugly? Your father's beautiful summer-house? How could I think it ugly?"

"Yes, but if you did?"

"Don't talk nonsense. It was a most expensive summer-house. When did it come into your silly head that it was ugly, if you please?"

"Oh, to-day."

"Ah, well, God give you sense. And don't go saying a silly thing like that to your father. It'd hurt him very much, I'd have you know."

Aunt Agnes was fond of telling Denis how to avoid hurting his father. He opened the house-door absent-mindedly for her on this new piece of advice, and stayed outside it himself long after to browse in the dimming light on the problems and possibilities of his father's lavishly constructed landscape garden. He was still there, mud caking dry on him and a thousand dreams in his eyes, when Martin Devoy came up the drive to tea.

For the latest trouble about Denis was that he was taken with a craze for gardening, a craze which, in the form in which he developed it, was unknown among young gentlemen of his class in Mellick in the year 1870. One directed one's gardener, naturally—disputing his accounts and pouring scorn on his ideas; one might even supervise him actively sometimes. But this would be done only when one had reached a more authoritative age than just under fourteen. It was understandable too, and quite right, that a householder should insist, if he liked, that no one but himself should cut his grapes or his roses; he might know the exact yield of his cucumber frames and his asparagus bed and he could even be pardoned for pottering vaguely in the greenhouses of an evening. But none of these things at Denis's age. Certainly not.

Denis confused the argument, characteristically, by doing none of these things, but something quite different. Instead of directing the gardener he took off his coat with him and asked his advice; instead of pottering in the greenhouses, he dug and wheelbarrowed and sweated in the rain; he knelt down in mud, where Aunt Agnes was always finding him, to plant bulbs, and he squatted back on his heels, still in mud, to lose himself in a tangle of exciting dreams.

This was how he was spending half-holidays and whole holidays now. Nothing that poor despairing Mickey Cogan could tell him of the size of the trout in Broody River would make him get out his rod. He sometimes even excused himself from climbing the Bearnagh hills with "Flasher" Devoy and his classmates; occasionally he forgot to exercise Phelim. He had become bewitched by the idea of making things grow, of planting new flowers, new groups of trees, of scattering new colours, new harmonies and contrasts, and outlines, new lights and shades, about his father's garden. And as he rooted in the mud and plodded, pencil in hand, through catalogues and gardening manuals, the real architectural art of gardening opened an insidious attack on his unready mind.

His uncles and aunts were horrified at the way in which the chit of a child was being allowed to interfere with arrangements established in the garden long ago by his elders and betters. They heard with something like incredulity of the digging up of the monkey-puzzle—simply because "Master Denis didn't care for it, if you please!"—but when on a Sunday of Lent they all drove out to River Hill for tea, and Jim's alert eye missed the spiky ornaments of white-painted wood that used to stand in regular spacings along the edges of the lawn by the carriage sweep, they understood to what lengths parental indulgence can be stretched.

"We've cleared them away," said Anthony. "Denis said they spoilt the look of the grass."

"Denis said!" Joe gave a great Jehovan laugh and pulled his beard. "I can tell you, Anthony, my sons have to say things more than once before they down any idea of mine."

"And no harm either, Joe," said Anthony, "until they fall into the habit of talking sense."

"Sense!" snorted Teresa. "So this is sense, I suppose?" She flung a scornful hand towards the undecorated grass.

"Well, it's doing *you* no harm anyway," said her host, and then his voice hardened, for he grew tired sometimes of this foolish set on Denis. "It seems, anyway, my idea of sense to let him enjoy his own place and have it the way he wants. Come on into the house, Sophia, and give me my tea." He linked his arm coaxingly in that of his sister-in-law.

§ 6

"FATHER," said Denis to Anthony on the evening of the day that Aunt Agnes had lectured him by the flower-bed, "do you really like that Chinese temple?"

"Chinese what? Oh, the summer-house!"

The two smiled at each other.

"Much good my saying I do," Anthony went on. "It's coming down to-morrow, I suppose?"

"Well," Denis demurred politely.

"It cost a lot of money, my son. Are you sure it ought to go?"

"Oh, not sure," said this very courteous critic. "I only think so."

And the laugh that broke from the two of them sealed the doom of the Chinese temple.

"It spoils the view just there," Denis murmured.

A moment later, from the top of his library ladder he spoke again to his father in soft amusement.

"Aunt Agnes warned me not to hurt your feelings by mentioning that temple," he said.

This joke was of a kind he often made. Its sting was soft, touching gently on the obtuseness of an outsider, and its slanting acknowledgment of a deep, private confidence between the two who exchanged it was very sweet to Anthony.

"And why didn't you take your aunt's excellent advice, young man?"

Denis clattered down the ladder, waving a book.

"There's something here I want to show you, father. Did you ever hear of a palace of Henry the Eighth's called None-such?"

THE FOURTH CHAPTER

THERE was a good deal of gossip and subterranean ribaldry going round the family during the Spring of 1870 on the subject of whether or not Millicent Considine would bring off the coup that she seemed to be threatening.

Millicent was the eldest daughter of Joe and Sophia. She was twenty-three years of age and, having been "out" in Mellick and Dublin society for three full seasons, had nothing to show for it. Inheriting a fine frame from her father she had unfortunately taken her mother's hooked nose without the fluffy youthful fairness and helpless air of femininity that had seduced Joe in that lady. So it had seemed as if the combination of Considine wealth in Mellick with Victor's Trinity connections and the genteel repute of the fading Quilliheys in Dublin would not manœuvre the good-natured girl into matrimony. The family, having had enough of old maids in their one, were beginning to fuss in their minds about Millicent when Gerard Hennessy turned up.

From one point of view—Sophia's—this young gentleman seemed almost too good to be true, and that was why everyone tiptoed round the subject with her now. Sophia could hardly bear to talk about Gerard Hennessy—just yet.

Gerard Aloysius Hennessy, M. A., LL. B., third son by his first wife of John Aloysius Hennessy of Finlay Square, Mellick, and of Rockmount, four miles beyond the town, was some very superior kind of magistrate in India, and had the pleasant certainty of becoming a judge in that country and the pleasanter hope of retiring from it one day, maybe in the guise of a baronet. (Eddy said "Nonsense!" to this. "They always fob those fellows off with knighthoods.") Stonyhurst School and the universities of Edinburgh and Louvain had combined to fit Gerard Hennessy for his dazzling fate. He was thirty-three now, and had come home to his father's house in December 1869 on six months' furlough, with the all-but-avowed intention of choosing a wife. He was staggeringly eligible and all Mellick knew it, and so did he.

How odd are the ways of eligible young men!

Mellick was famous in Ireland for the beauty of its young girls. These young girls, the cream of them, the curled and scented and French-convent-trained young ladies of the higher bourgeoisie were flaunted before Gerard Hennessy now in a feverish round of competition, balls, and card-parties, only for him to stalk among them—they had to admit it—indifferent and self-possessed. And slowly, as the Spring advanced, cautiously, almost imperceptibly, he seemed, of all unexpected things, to be hovering towards plain, upstanding Millicent Considine, as if inclined to pay her some erratic sort of court. Mellick gasped just a little, and then settled down to watch this turn of the unexpected.

Even the Considines could hardly jib at a union with the Hennessys.

The latter, whose mills stood beside Considine's in Charles Street, had been millers, house-owners, and mayors in Mellick in 1650. They had made fortunes, lost them, and made them again before Anthony Considine, the horse-thief, ever turned his handsome face to the south. The Church had taken lord abbots and lady abbesses from their family tree, and Hennessy money had raised two spires in Mellick and built St. Patrick's orphanage. Hennessys had fought with Sarsfield for the Stuart; had flown with the Wild Geese, and officered the Irish Brigade; Hennessys had lost wealth and place but by no means good repute when they scorned to take the Protestant Communion in the Penal Days. Hennessy treasures had been sold to fill O'Connell's coffers for the Emancipation fight, and when it was won, the mills that had never closed began to function merrily again after their old fashion, and house property began to slip back into Hennessy hands. Before 1840 the mayoral chain hung once more round a Hennessy neck. John

Aloysius Hennessy, the father of Gerard, was an arrogant man, austerely civilised of aspect and family-conscious in a reserved and subtle manner that had nothing whatever in common with simple Considine pride. He had been among those who saw something ridiculous in the uncouth figure and presumptuous trade gambles of Honest John in Kilmoney Street days, but he had been quick too, when he saw the point of it, to turn dry amusement into dry respect. He was a prominent figure at the old forage merchant's funeral and in the last ten years the two families were on terms of sociability. His eldest son Dominic was one of Jim Lanigan's few intimate friends, and Dr. Joe was medical adviser now to Dominic's pretty wife. He himself was inclined to like Anthony very much, but that quick-moving fellow, as proud as he in a very different way, never gave him a chance to express more than the briefest courtesies.

It was a historical fact in Mellick that no Hennessy courtship or betrothal was safe until John Aloysius had set the seal of his direct approval on it. He was a fanatical upholder of the strictest code of respectability, and his sons and daughters went in perpetual terror of his objections and decisions. He had mercilessly compelled his son William to break his troth with one of the charming Hallinan girls, because it was discovered that her father drank rather more than John Aloysius could approve of. Vicky Hallinan was an old maid to this day simply because Willy Hennessy was afraid of his father. Dominic, the eldest son, had trembled often during his engagement to pretty Louise Redmond of Dublin, lest any rumour against her gay brothers, Arthur and Tom, should percolate to Mellick. None had done so, but it was common gossip that John Aloysius disliked Dominic's smart and charming wife. There was, of course, no scandal anywhere among the Considines, nor any skeleton in the cupboard—but still, the reputation of John Aloysius as a setter of moral standards made the family additionally nervous now for poor Millicent.

A possible Hennessy alliance was something to set the Considines arguing in private. On the whole, the prospect pleased, but the realisation that it pleased exasperated them. Anthony more or less hit off the family mood when he said that he'd like Millicent to refuse the young man, if only they could pub-

lish the refusal in the Mellick *Sentinel* and the Munster *Star*.
That was about it. The Considines didn't want to be riled by
congratulations on having hooked a Hennessy, but they wanted
the town to know that they could have done it, were they so
minded. In any case, there could be no question of Millicent's
refusing Gerard Hennessy—the only point was, did he mean
to propose for her? There'd certainly be no holding Sophia if
it came off!

§ 2

WHILE the question of Millicent's destiny still floated on the
April air, Aunt Agnes got the quinsy, and Teresa and Caroline drove out to River Hill together to sympathise with her.

The day was all fair and young, without a blemish, a gay
prospect spread before the two matrons in the landau. The
sky was Our Lady's own innocent nursery blue, and little
white clouds were scattered over it like woolly toys about a
nursery floor. Eastward the last snow had vanished from the
mountains, and peeping between the housetops the crazily
coloured west was hanging out a hundred little banners of
purple and blue. Grey Mellick was washed in sunlight and all
her buildings wore the look of having had a pleasant surprise.
Hawkers cried primroses along the kerbs and King Street rang
with the jingle of harness and the chatter of easy-going folk.
Young officers clanked about in splendour, the new spring bonnets twinkled in Kiernan's windows, the porch of the County
and Cavalry Club held its usual fine-weather group of gossiping
bloods, a gallery with more than a passing eye for Caroline,
who sailed heedlessly past it in embroidered shawl of blue and
little cherry-trimmed bonnet.

Caroline was forty-two, but feverish summer glorified her
face, and it was still disturbing to see her pass along the street.
The contours of youth had not left her yet nor its radiance,
though that was only there with a difference now, or so Eddy
thought. It seemed to him that youth shone so gallantly through
Caroline because it had become defiant and was refusing to
lie down until—oh, what were Caroline's eyes and mouth
forever wanting?

She was a good comedy player, better than ever nowadays,

and if this queer defiance which Eddy thought he read every year more clearly in her face, so clearly sometimes that he was annoyed by the folly of such an open clue, if that was really there and was a stimulant of her beauty, no member of her family save only this fanciful brother had observed it. So now Teresa, turning to her in the carriage and catching a look of something almost like anger on the face that she had never given up envying, expressed good-humoured surprise.

"What are you frowning at, Caroline? Doesn't the weather suit you?"

It didn't, as a matter of fact. Each Spring that came to Mellick suited Caroline less well than the one that went before. She was not aware of this with her mind, but so it was. Her nerves had some increasing grudge against the lovely earth and every new blossoming of it oppressed her. She never lifted her face to the sun nowadays that her body was not conscious of frustration. Knowing without even vanity's pleasure but often with faint weariness that she was lovely, she became petulant when she had to contemplate the loveliness of life, as one might be who sees her part in some merry entertainment swept away. Beautiful as she was, life had not asked her to participate in whatever this bright fun might be that kept on dancing just ahead of her. It was as if she saw the shape of joy but was never allowed to feel its warmth. An eager child shut out from a party. No wonder her eyes looked angrily at April.

"Well, if it doesn't, nothing will, I suppose," she answered her sister and her voice was airy and good-humoured. But when the carriage swung round the curve of the River Hill drive and slackened its speed in the sweet, open air beyond the arching lime trees, the gaiety of the westward vista from her brother's house took an unmerciful stranglehold upon her heart. She felt her throat swell as if for a sob that all the courage of the world could not force back; the brightness of river and sky blurred into each other before her eyes, and the hills disappeared completely. She heard Teresa praying heaven to tell her where the calves' feet jelly had been put, and though she knew it was in the well of the opposite seat, her lips refused to frame that easy word. She had to go on staring at an empty smudge of brightness, she had to take her chance with

Teresa's eagle eye. Certainly the weather wasn't suiting Caroline.

§ 3

An hour later Denis, crossing the grass lightfootedly, his arms full of iris roots, came on her unexpectedly round a corner. She was sitting on a log beside the old yew tree, her cherry-trimmed bonnet tossed in the grass at her feet, her gay blue skirts all billowing round, her bright shawl fluttering. She was turned in profile towards him and did not see or hear him come.

He started at first with delight for the picture she made, "like some lovely bird," he thought, but before he had time to call her name he saw her face, and what he saw in it froze speech and movement out of him.

His gay and pretty aunt appeared to be staring across the hills, but without caring much what she saw, for she was sitting loosely, with loose hands in her lap. She held her head upright, but Denis saw that the smooth bright colour had gone patchy in her cheeks, and that tears, immense tears, were racing one another down her face and splashing on her shawl and hands.

The Considines were easy weepers and Denis was therefore not unused to tears. With eau de Cologne and cups of tea he had helped Aunt Agnes through more than one good cry; Jack and Mary and he himself had their own straightforward fits of woe about one thing or another, and when Miss Wadding's uncle, the priest, had died, she sobbed off and on in the schoolroom for days. He had seen tears in his father's eyes too. He was acquainted with grief.

But these tears that he looked at now were a new kind in his experience. They ran down the face like other tears, and were wet and splashy and seemed to redden the eyes—all that was familiar. But their speed and multitude, for one thing— why, they seemed to run as close together as beads in a decade of the rosary. But the change they made in Aunt Caroline's face—it was that that froze and frightened Denis. No face that he knew became utterly different just because it was crying—but that had happened here. Denis had recognised

Aunt Caroline without any possible doubt at his first glance, but now, at second looking, though still sure with one half of his mind that it was she, he could not for the life of him relate this far-staring face to the one his memory painted.

When Aunt Agnes cried she made grimaces; her cheeks became scarlet and her nose swelled. Similar things happened to Miss Wadding in distress—only it took her face the best part of the day to be restored. But somehow in neither case did it cross one's mind to doubt the identity of the disfigured one; indeed, each seemed to become more definitely herself—just Aunt Agnes or Miss Wadding having a cry—unmistakable. But this figure that must be Aunt Caroline—this was no one just having a cry. This face that kept so still and uncontorted, and yet most strangely appeared to the watching boy as if deformed or caricatured or out of focus, this was the face of a trouble beyond the kindest imaginings of fourteen years. This was a figure of woe, if it wasn't Aunt Caroline. If this wasn't Aunt Caroline, it could only be an abstraction called Despair, of which the boy knew nothing.

It was Aunt Caroline, a figure of woe and despair, Aunt Caroline weeping hysterically to the Spring day, weeping for untasted youth, for twenty years of wifehood and nine years, since her father's death, of wifehood so complete as to have lulled a nervy and self-conscious husband to something like complacency. Aunt Caroline was weeping for unimportant things of whose existence she only knew by hearsay—love and frivolity and foolish talk and lovers' friendliness, and the pleasures and satisfactions of passions for which an ironic god had surely built her. Aunt Caroline, aged forty-two, with a son not far from nineteen, was being as silly as Aunt Agnes or Miss Wadding maybe, but doing it with Medusa's face. She didn't look silly at all—she looked most terrible and splendid.

Denis stood and pressed the iris roots against his heart. Neither tea nor eau de Cologne came into his head. He wanted to go away, but could not bring himself to abandon such strange trouble; he wanted to go forward—Aunt Caroline turned and saw him.

She smiled a quick pretence smile, before she even attempted to dry her eyes.

"Hello, Denis."

"Hello, Aunt Caroline."

"You look scared. Did I give you a fright, sitting here?"

"Oh, no, Aunt Caroline." He searched in agony for words to brighten her. "I thought you were a lovely bird at first."

He was rewarded by her low, sweet laugh.

"What a boy you are for saying pretty things! As bad as Uncle Eddy."

"But you're prettier than a bird, Aunt Caroline."

He was distressed to see that the tears, which had stopped flowing, spilt over her face again at that remark that had been meant to give her courage, but she went on laughing all the same, standing tall and bright before him now, holding her cherry-trimmed bonnet by the ribbons and pretending to dry her eyes in her tiny wet lace handkerchief.

"I've a clean one somewhere," said Denis, and he put down his iris roots and found it for her. She took it and turned away from him, swishing her silks and running towards the house with little quick steps.

He did not look at her as she went. He was afraid to. He wanted to pretend that that last shiver of her shoulders was only a final spasm, such as generally wound up Miss Wadding's little scenes, but he knew well that it wasn't. He knew that most probably Aunt Caroline was crying again that very minute, and that there was nothing he could do to stop her.

Oh, what was the matter, what was the matter? Woe unutterable crashed suddenly down on his heart, and kneeling to gather up his roots, he toppled over on them instead and began to cry. He cried a long time under the yew tree, and though he did not know it, the tears ran down his face as close upon each other as beads upon a rosary. He cried for poor Aunt Caroline and for the choking weight she had laid on his own heart, and for troubles that he had never heard of. Indeed, indeed she had scared him, the lovely bird under the tree.

§ 4

FIVE nights later Anthony, hearing movements in Denis's room, next door to his own, found him wandering into the corridor in his night shirt, fast asleep. Tears were pouring down his cheeks as he walked and his hands were held out in entreaty.

"Poor Aunt Caroline!" he was saying through sobs. "Poor Aunt Caroline! Oh, poor Aunt Caroline!"

Anthony took him in his arms, warmed him and woke him and dried his tears.

Three days after that Denis and Anthony met the Lanigan carriage going to the station. It stopped. Jim and Caroline were in it, and Caroline's luggage. She was going to Dublin to shop, and to stay with Jim's aunt, Mrs. Munnings, as she often did. She was to travel with Mrs. Dominic Hennessy for company. She was very gay with Denis, and Anthony, watching them laughing at each other, could see no possible reason why she should have troubled the child's sleep.

Two days later Teresa came unprecedentedly to Anthony's office and gave him two pieces of news that bore more relation to each other, as they both saw, than was on the surface. She told him that Gerard Hennessy had sent Millicent a beautiful box of red roses and that Caroline was not in Dublin with Mrs. Munnings at all but had run away to London.

THE FIFTH CHAPTER

I T WASN'T easy for a lady to escape from Mellick to London
in 1870.

Caroline made her get-away with more dash than cunning.

At breakfast one morning she asked Jim if he had forgotten that that was the day she was going to Dublin to stay with
Aunt Munnings. He had not forgotten, because he had never
heard it. Neither had Caroline until that second, and she could
hardly believe her own ears as she made the announcement.

Jim, who was busy just then, and accustomed to these
seasonal flights to Dublin, accepted easily that the subject had
been mentioned before and that Aunt Munnings was expecting
her and would send a maid and a carriage to meet her at Kingsbridge Station.

"But with whom are you travelling, my dear?"

"Louise Hennessy."

A piece of luck this for which Caroline had to thank her
close acquaintance, as a good matron of Mellick, with the movements of other matrons.

"Ah, of course. Dominic told me that he was to be grass-
widowed for a while. Must have thought it odd that I didn't
mention being in the same case."

"Perhaps he didn't know. I haven't really fixed it with her
yet. I'm sending a note this morning."

"Do, my dear. You shouldn't have left it so late. Supposing
she's altered her plans—then what would you do?"

He stood up.

"I suppose you've been scenting the new French models on
the wind, you and Mrs. Dominic?"

He saw her off that afternoon, safely entrenched in a first-class carriage, with rug, foot-warmer and Miss Braddon's latest, with Mrs. Dominic Hennessy and Mrs. Dominic Hennessy's companion-help. As the train moved out she smiled at Jim, who stood and waved his hat beside Dominic Hennessy, tall, well-tailored, and legal-looking as himself.

"From here they might be twins," Caroline thought irrelevantly.

Mrs. Dominic Hennessy was seven years younger than Caroline but more sophisticated. A Dubliner—one of the Redmonds of Foxrock. She was very pretty and queened it hospitably in a fine establishment in the Serpentine Road. And she seemingly did her duty by her husband, to whom she had already presented seven children. She was a Catholic, of course, that being a sine qua non in Hennessy wives, but somehow there was a feeling abroad that she was "fast." Why did a married woman with no marriageable daughters fill her house with English captains and subalterns? No harm, of course—no harm at all. God forbid! But all the same the matrons of Mellick wouldn't have minded knowing what Mrs. Dominic Hennessy wanted with all her captains and subalterns.

Leaning back in the carriage now, small and round-bosomed, in her sealskin cloak, with long-lashed brown eyes and dimpled pink cheeks, with tiny pearls for teeth and a pair of exquisitely useless white hands, Mrs. Dominic Hennessy looked, alas, what Mellick called her—"fast." It really isn't easy to fool the town of Mellick.

She liked Caroline in a feathery way, much as she liked sunshine and new hats and dance music and a good joke with a handsome man, for Caroline had a quality in common with all those things, a kind of easy chanciness that made Mrs. Dominic's spirit feel at home. They passed the time of the journey merrily together, so Mrs. Dominic thought, never opening their novels, so rapid was the flow of their talk. And the companion-help made tea with a silver spirit-kettle. An agreeable journey, Mrs. Dominic thought.

For Caroline it was nothing, not a journey at all, but simply a smudge of time, the externalities of which she could never remember afterwards, but only the few wild, private thoughts that zigzagged over it like lightning. While it was passing indeed she kept hearing her own voice and laugh, nearly as often as Louise's; she observed the kettle too while it sat on the blue flame, and burnt the tip of her tongue with hot tea. But when Louise said "Oh, Caroline, how killing you are," or, "I should have it in green, if I were you," or "Her third husband? Caroline, you're making me blush," Caroline couldn't catch her own sped remarks to which these answers must have been related. She was probably amusing all the same, since one of the persistent zigzags in her brain was that Louise must be kept off the track. And how, oh, how was she to shake her off at Kingsbridge, without revealing that there was no carriage to meet her and no Mrs. Munning's maid? And if her precious brother, the elegant Arthur Redmond, was on the platform! Caroline gasped with alarm. He, who generally met Louise, was of a chivalry that would allow no lady to slip from his charge unescorted. And Caroline knew that his liking for her was inclined to be less feathery than his sister's.

Her cunning was exhausted. From now on it must be dash until it was all over—until she wrote to Jim. What was she going to write to Jim? What had come over her at this morning's breakfast? Where was she running to and why? "Dear Jim—I've gone to London for a week?--for a year"?—or "Dear Jim—I'm never coming back"?

She didn't know what she was going to write to Jim. She only knew that she must get a breath of air before she died. That was what had come over her at breakfast.

The zigzags went on and the merry talk. All the Considines formed themselves into wiry, burning zigzags, and all the Lanigans, her children, the six most beautiful children in Mellick. She was running away. It was an unheard-of thing, a ruinous, preposterous, inconceivable thing, a sin, a disgrace, a family shame, a scandal, a ringing mockery, a butchering of all their pride to make a Mellick holiday. Torture for Jim, and the jibings of the town. Jibing at both of them—to run away after twenty years—with wrinkles coming already and a son at the University. What a joke for the Junior Club and the Law Society and all the whist parties! Wherever was Jim to hide his head?

Yes, yes, but where was she to hide if she went back? Where could you hide in Mellick from a loving husband? Where could you hide from twenty years of "my dear" and arid passion.

". . . getting his transfer to the Lancers soon, unfortunately. Most amusing person, Caroline; always raving about you. I really don't think I'll let him meet you. . . ."

Arthur Redmond was at Kingsbridge, moustached and beaming, beaming most genially on Caroline.

But where was her carriage? Oh, down the rank, down there—she recognised it. And Mrs. Munnings's maid? Yes, she recognised her too. She even signalled, as she said this, to some ghost in the far caverns of the station, over the heads of the crowd. She blessed the dim lights of Kingsbridge. But he would take her to her carriage, of course? No, no—he must look to Louise—she saw the maid distinctly—she would come to no harm. She clutched the arm of her porter. "Good-bye, Louise." She was gone. Arthur Redmond looked after her, amazed, uncertain.

She captured a "growler," far from her friends' carriage. "Drive to a telegraph office, please, and then to a quiet hotel in Kingstown—a very quiet one."

Cabby and porter exchanged a glance.

"Plenty of very quiet hotels in Kingstown," said the cabby.

She had never sent a telegram in her life but the clerk was kind and between them they got it off:

MEET ME AT EUSTON WITHOUT FAIL TOMORROW EVENING.
CARO.

As if Ted would fail! She laughed as she huddled into the growler again and was rattled away to the quiet hotel in Kingstown.

§ 2

GRAFTON STREET, Dublin, is a queer street, though not in the least that kind of one in which most of mankind dreads ending up. Part of its queerness lies indeed in its being so little like Queer Street.

"It'll be all the same in a hundred years" is Grafton Street's motto, and if, say, twice in every hundred years she has to be emphatic about this, Irishmen being the noisy lunatics they are, she is never perturbed, for she keeps on finding that men and women remain the same, with life's seduction just as sweet to them, however the years recede with their fashions and fanaticisms. If there is a certain monotony in this for her she never betrays it, but it may be that the variations in dolman and slipper and fan and the changes from knee-breeches to peg-top and from plum-coloured coat to sober black keep her as much amused as they do her easy-going strollers—for she is light-minded.

That is why she is a queer street. In a country that never is done with boasting about its saints and doctors, where martyrs are three a penny and crucifixes bleed and statues bow to petitioners as if the eighteenth century had never been, where any rising of the moon may be for a gathering of pikes, where unhoused men die in ditches because a potato-crop has failed; in a country where tinkers, jockeys, and hurley players jostle with nuns, where blood is of no account if there's a Cause to spill it, where chastity is a matter of fact, where wit goes barefoot and exuberant and humorists step warily, where mists are the back-cloth and lamentations are the orchestra, where the name of Jesus decorates back-chat and curse and prayer—in this untidy, irritating country, Grafton Street still slithers easily from Stephen's Green to College Green, flippant and unconcerned, or concerned only to mock at all the passionate haphazardry out of which she has grown and in the midst of which she still remains, very queerly, the unchallenged principal street, a persistent and contradictory piece of Ireland's self-expression.

In April 1870 Grafton Street was no less amused than usual. When Louise Hennessy turned into it with her brother on her first afternoon in town, her eyes, glancing eagerly over the narrow sunlit, unimposing curve of pavement, were bright with an exile's affection. She, like the brother at her side, was one of the street's lovers, one of those who kept it alive and for whom it lived. It had an April welcome now for pretty Louise; preening delightfully because, although the flower girls had only daffodils to sell, it was itself a garden in silk and velvet, its windows deep parterres of flaming bloom, its footpaths herbaceous with crinolines, blue, green, and red; the whole most quiveringly alive with summery hum and twitter. The very sun seemed to approve this joke against himself of a premature blooming and the ringleted breezes caught all the plumes and puff-balls as they rose from the bright-moving pattern and blew them north and south with malicious skill, so that the jibe flung up in Switzer's was soon at Carson's Corner and the scandal of the Gaiety stage-door could be coaxed even as far maybe as the shades of the Provost's garden.

It was on the threshold of Mitchell's tea-shop that Louise and her brother met Mrs. Munnings.

Mrs. Munnings was a woman with a presence; she was sixty-five and lived virtuously in Mount Street, the widow of a once-popular and rakish barrister. She stalked through life nowadays with an expression in her eye that made it clear that if she had, for reasons best known to herself, stood this, that, and the other from Thady Munnings, she was by no means going to stand anything similar from other people. She was wealthy and well-known; and she knew everyone and everyone's business and whether or not they were about it.

It goes without saying that she knew the Redmonds of Foxrock.

"Oh, Mrs. Munnings, how do you do?"

"Mrs. Hennessy! Come up for shopping again, I suppose?"

Mrs. Munnings disapproved of wives who left home to do shopping, perhaps because Thady Munnings had inclined to approve of them.

"Come up for shopping," Louise echoed good-temperedly. "How's Caroline? Is she tired after our journey?"

"What journey?" said Mrs. Munnings on the tone of a grand inquisitor. "And how should I know anything of Caroline?"

"But yesterday——" began Arthur Redmond, curiosity flurrying his wits until he felt the steadying nip of his sister's fingers on his sleeve.

"How could you, after all?" said Mrs. Dominic Hennessy with easy sweetness. "It's a whole week, of course, since we travelled back from Waterford together, but as I hadn't seen her, I thought perhaps you'd give me news."

"Waterford?" Mrs. Munnings's was the voice of inflamed

suspicion and Louise recognised it with despair and cursed herself.

"Yes—lovely place," she said. "We'll be meeting again of course. Good-day, Mrs. Munnings."

The ladies curtsied, the gentlemen bowed, and two frightened Redmonds of Foxrock took shelter in Mitchell's upper room.

So that was Caroline! Louise made wide eyes at her chuckling brother. Lovely, innocent Caroline, the Cæsar's wife of Mellick—a rash and desperate intriguer! It was a shock. It was a most demoralising example to be set before Mrs. Dominic Hennessy. She smiled in deep wonder.

"This is a dead secret, Arthur—remember that. Oh, Arthur, what a gaffe I've made! Poor Caroline!"

§ 3

MRS. MUNNINGS wasted no time in the street of flippancy. She put two and two together with great astuteness in the next ten minutes as her carriage swept her to a telegraph office. She also composed a telegram to Jim Lanigan which would enlighten him as unsparingly as possible while giving nothing away, please heaven, to Mellick's post-office clerks. This is the message she despatched:

> PACKAGE SENT BY YOU YESTERDAY
> HAS NOT COME AND WAS NOT EX-
> PECTED. PLEASE EXPLAIN.
>   MUNNINGS

It is clear that Louise's botching had not mended her gaffe and that Jim's aunt could hit a nail on the head when one presented itself. But when she wrote "package" on the telegraph form, was "baggage" the word that really hovered in Mrs. Thady Munnings's mind?

The nephew may have had some difficulty in interpreting her message. At any rate, although it was handed to him at his dinner-table at half-past six o'clock, in the very hour indeed in which Millicent Considine, round the corner in Finlay Square, was unpacking Gerard Hennessy's red roses, he was still sitting by the dining-room fire with the flimsy paper be-

tween his fingers when towards midnight the maid brought
in another telegram. He read that too as if it puzzled him and
then continued to sit there very quietly with two flimsy bits
of paper in his fingers. The second telegram said:

OUR ADDRESS IS BROWN'S HOTEL
WRITING.
EDDY & CAROLINE

From the peculiar wording of this it will be seen that Eddy
Considine shared Mrs. Munnings's objection to washing domestic linen in the Mellick Post Office.

§ 4

EDDY met Caroline "without fail." The telegram, which he
thought he had been expecting for years, alarmed and exasperated him when it came. It did not reach him until a very few
hours before he would have to meet its sender, for it was
addressed to his office, from which he had played truant a
whole morning.

The lovely day had seduced him when he woke. As he
blinked gratefully at the golden light and drank his morning
tea, he felt no jolt between the recovered world and the deep
dream state from which he had come back to it. This place
in which he found himself seemed for once in a while to Eddy
Considine the place that it should be and not untouched with
dream. It seemed well worth the return. The sun had caught
its familiar surfaces, edging their commonplace with gaiety.
Silver-backed brushes, mahogany chest, a row of gleaming
shoes, a vase of daffodils, a brass hot-water can—how merry
they looked because the April sun was on them! Eddy stretched
to a yawn, and then sprang out of bed. He smiled at the
familiar street and at his own pleasant face obstructing the
branch of plane tree in the mirror. He smiled at the memory
of last night's Madeira and last night's companionship and
though he waked alone felt close-companioned still as he
bathed and dressed in the warming sun.

Soon, modishly dressed and humming a phrase of "La Belle

Hélène" he wandered through the town, taking long breaths of its freshness, his blue eyes alert with morning liveliness.

He bought a flower for his buttonhole; he ordered neckties, and as he found himself in Jermyn Street thought it no harm to have himself fitted for new boots. He called on his vintner merely to gossip, and yielded there to a case of Clicquot and some Napoleon brandy. In King Street he haggled for a piece of famille rose and, since he was the son of Honest John, drove a thrifty bargain. He took stalls for "Il Barbiere" and looked in at an exhibition of sporting prints. He bought cigarettes. He refrained from buying a new hat. He kept humming "La Belle Hélène" and he lunched at the noontide crown of the day with the companion of last night.

A sweet allegro movement. But it had to tinkle away at last into the dull afternoon roulades of Finsbury Square. And here was Caroline, without as much as by-your-leave, breaking calmly into those, as if they had not already been sufficiently interrupted, breaking in with her ridiculous runaway cry that might have been understandable ten years ago.

He spent a busy afternoon arranging for this terrible freak of Caroline's. Life must be adjusted for her. That meant the writing of notes to here and there. Eddy pulled a wry face towards the evenings that still beckoned him, all the evenings and nights that had been seen to shine along the rim of the lovely month and must now be waved back to nowhere. Silly Caro would want time and care and a mood that was not near his hand just now but that he must be quick to fabricate. But even if she hadn't such particular need of him, his secrets were still his secrets, treasures to be folded up and shelved away when inquisitive Considines were round.

And, anyhow, there wasn't only Caroline to be served. There was the family. He had a double rôle to play. He must remember Mellick now, put on the Mellick attitude. He must be at least as much Considine as Ted to this hysterical sister. What scenes and shindies were in sight, what tears and adjurations, what bluffings to the world, what lies and family alarums! And all for a lovely goose who didn't know her day was over!

Petulant at having to be a relative at a moment's notice, Eddy Considine jumped in a hansom and rattled out of Finsbury Square.

§ 5

CAROLINE'S train was late that night and by the time it came in Eddy was thoroughly bad-tempered, having missed dinner and worked himself into frenzied anxiety about the unchaperoned state of his foolish sister. He grumbled and cursed as he looked for her carriage.

She was tired and draggled. She had been seasick. She had been crying. All her dash was used up. She took Eddy's hands with the gesture of one who, had they been denied her another second, would have started all over again to be seasick and to cry. She was almost plain. But she clung to Eddy's hands and as he looked down at her he felt himself being charmed by her foolishness as easily as if she were nineteen again, and pursued by ogres.

"Oh, Caro, this is fun, I must admit."

THE SIXTH CHAPTER

A RUNAWAY wife might seem fun to the lightminded on an April evening in London, but in Mellick the Considines were not amused.

Anthony reacted normally to Teresa's two items of intelligence.

He smiled over Gerard Hennessy's red roses.

"He's getting hot," said he. "We might as well be ordering the wedding cake, I'm thinking."

For the news of Caroline he had no words at first but incredulous and then blazingly wrathful eyes.

Jim had driven out to Roseholm that morning to see Teresa. He had had very little to say, just telling her what he knew and showing the two telegrams. He was expecting a letter from his aunt by the afternoon post and of course there could be nothing from London until to-morrow. Teresa could make nothing of it from him. Naturally she couldn't ask him any questions. He didn't even look very different—a bit tired per· haps. It wasn't for advice he had come to her, either, because he didn't ask for any—simply gave her the bare information, that's all. After he was gone Teresa thought that maybe it was dreaming she was—and a nice sort of dream to be having, too!—but when she drove in to King Street to do her shopping, there was the story, some of it anyway, all over the town before her. The fact was that the paving stones had ears in these parts! The first she heard of it was from Miss Hickey, Kiernan's head milliner, who had it, she said, from Mr. Byrne of the haberdashery department. Teresa had to call in there about an alteration to her new grey toque. "And Mrs. Lanigan is gone off to London, I hear," said Miss Hickey. "Well, now, look at that! She was in here with me on Tuesday—I was keeping my best models on one side for her, so I was—and not a word did she say about flying off from us! And it's to Dublin she was going at first, I hear—changed her mind at the last minute, no doubt! Well, well, isn't it she has the fine life, and you too, of course, Mrs. Mulqueen! Doing exactly what suits you like that at a moment's notice! Well for you, that's what I say. Telegrams flying to Mr. Lanigan yesterday, I hear . . ." Even Teresa had always found it difficult to silence the dreadful Miss Hickey, whose tongue was several inches too long for her mouth.

And then, outside O'Keeffe's whom should she meet but Mrs. Willy Hennessy, whose pride it was to hear a piece of news sooner and spread it farther than anyone in the town.

"What's this I hear about Caroline? Rushed off to London suddenly? But Dominic told me yesterday she'd gone to Dublin with Louise. Even that seemed rather sudden! And now Mrs. Walter Donoghue tells me for a fact that it's in London she is! Mysterious, I call it!"

Curiosity sizzled under each word, but Teresa contented herself with remarking that mysteries came easy to Mrs. Walter Donoghue.

It all went to prove, however, that Mrs. Munnings and Eddy Considine were justified in their respect for the understanding of the Mellick postal clerks and had indeed underestimated it.

Teresa, extremely alarmed, had gone to see Sophia at once so that she too could be ready for the story when it was flung at her. And there she had had to admire Gerard Hennessy's red roses first, and sympathise with a mother's natural hopes. But when Sophia had rallied from the first shock—for the announcement about Caroline's departure upset her most painfully—they had been compelled to agree together that any hint of gossip now, any suspicion of irregularity in their family at this critical juncture, would be enough to wreck all Millicent's prospects. Wasn't it common knowledge in Mellick that no Hennessy had ever been allowed to take a wife from where the breath of scandal passed? At that, Sophia collapsed into fresh tears and Teresa had left her to seek Tom at Cathedral House. He was out and she wrote a note in his sitting-room asking him to meet her in Anthony's office at noon.

While waiting for Tom, Teresa pointed out to Anthony that a jilt from Gerard Hennessy—and it would amount to a jilt since he had got as far as red roses—would not merely mean a disappointment for poor Millicent and her mother, and heaven knew that was bad enough, with the girl so hard to get off. Nobody wanted another old maid, but being one man's leavings wasn't going to help her with the others, Teresa thought, and the poor child's looks were never her strong point. Her dowry couldn't be much, either, with Joe running round to Leopardstown and the Curragh the way he was! But the real sting was that the Considines had begun to accept the Hennessy alliance and that Mellick knew this. Sophia indeed had been unable to conceal her anxious happiness. If it fell through now, therefore, Mellick would laugh, delighted to laugh for once at the invincible Considines. "So they thought they were good enough to marry into the Hennessys, no less? Well, well!" Such a jibe—only imagined—made Teresa and Anthony writhe simultaneously in their chairs. They wanted no Hennessys, but if a Hennessy were to jilt them in their own town . . . ! And the red-roses story was about already too. Oh, yes, Teresa had had it all, and something like congratulations with it, from Mrs. Hanley, who had it from her daughter Eileen, Millicent's bosom friend.

But all that, which was so terrible, was nothing, a mere thimbleful dipped from a sea of panic and astonishment. What on earth had come over Caroline? What was it all about? What did these telegrams mean? Was it a plot? Was Eddy in it? Did it mean that she was staying away, that she was deserting her husband and her home? Disgracing her children for ever, disgracing them all, the sons and daughters of Honest John? It was beyond the span of Considine thought that a wife should leave a husband. A husband might conceivably desert a wife—but—oh, well, what was the good of raving? Caroline, their sister, one of themselves, Irish, Catholic, rich, respectable—had run away from her home two days ago. That was the inconceivable thing they had to face. That was the news they had for Tom when he came across the room to them now, handsome and smiling.

His smile departed as if for ever, like Henry the First's, when Teresa gave him her story. At its conclusion he paced the room as though it were his cage and he the king of beasts. He was dumbfounded, this preacher, this holy man, this binder and looser of sins, because a woman had run away from a marriage vow. No one would think to look at him now that he had been hearing confessions for twenty years; never had he looked less consecrate or wise; all his experience and suavity and priestliness seemed stripped away, leaving him exposed to his brother and sister as a mere Considine like themselves, a Considine whose central nerve had been most hideously jabbed.

Anthony looked at him with sympathy for once and he at Anthony. They would be at one on this occasion. They were at one already. They saw to the last reaches of this offence against them and down to its smallest implications. It would occur to neither of them to set his sister Caroline above his surname. They could be kind, but she must be submissive. This madness! This sudden heaving up of dark, undiscussable things to jeopardise them—panic and wantonness and bedroom sulks, flung out to the world without shame, to make a fool of Jim, begrime them all, and set the town in a laugh! The pitiful antics of a woman not far from her dangerous time! Ah, God!

Tom and Anthony looked at each other gravely across this new abyss. Then the priest's eyes rested on the portrait of Honest John behind the desk.

"It's well he's not here to-day," he said.

"We know what he'd say if he were," said Anthony. And Tom agreed and seemed to find comfort in that.

Maybe all the same they didn't know what Honest John would say, but what would be the good of arguing that?

Tom's priestliness ebbed back slowly after the first shock. His next remark was faintly at least in the character of a statistician of immorality and he had some difficulty in uttering it.

"Who—who is to blame for this?" he said. "Who is the guilty man?"

Teresa started, almost laughed in fact, but Anthony showed no surprise. The question had been hovering in his mind, for barring disease or brutality, which were not to be considered here, he knew only one reason why a woman should depart from a man.

"God knows," he said.

"No one at all," said Teresa.

"But——" Tom hesitated delicately.

His sister shrugged.

"If she's been so mad," she said, "as to run away from one man after twenty years of it for no better reason than to go straight to another——"

Tom and Anthony exchanged a glance which said plainly that as any woman was mad who ran away from a man, this last was obviously no argument.

But theory had to be brushed aside. The time was for diplomacy. There wasn't a moment to lose. Caroline would come back, of course, and in a strait-jacket if necessary, the men's snapping jaws seemed to add. Meantime the story of her escapade must be nailed to some one feasible foundation, which Tom and Teresa would agree upon, and narrate throughout the family, so that Mellick could have it and welcome, if it asked for it. Anthony would see Jim without delay and find out what he was going to do. If necessary, he would go to London with him or for him. Certainly it might be a risk for them to set off together—sure to make talk. Perhaps it would be safer for Jim to go alone, or not to go at all, maybe, but to stay here, just as usual, at his work. Anyhow, they'd have to see what he thought. For the rest, Caroline was safe so long as she was with Eddy.

"Ah, but is she with Eddy?" said Tom, who, now he was giving his mind to it, was showing a handsome knowledge of elopements. "Is that double signature a trick, do you think?"

"She'd never think of it," said Anthony, who understood the fecklessness of Caroline.

"Is she so safe with Eddy, though?" Teresa pondered.

So they toiled at the clumsy darn that had to be made on the face of their garment. Invisible mending—difficult work—but they called out the best of their skill to it, and before long it seemed to be rewarding them with some kind of stimulation. Their eyes brightened as they plotted. If they weren't going to enjoy this affair at least their self-confidence would get a thrill out of affronting it.

One thing was clear. Caroline must be back in Mellick and appearing publicly by her husband's side before Mrs. Dominic Hennessy returned from Dublin with whatever story she'd have. The news would be stale then; Caroline's bodily presence would take the meaning out of it. Meantime they could only hope that she'd write nothing home to Dominic. The Hennessys must not be allowed to grow suspicious. The slogan was to be "Business as usual" and in answer to any curiosity-boxes, yes, Caroline was in London just now. No, she hadn't stayed with Mrs. Munnings. Went to Kingstown for a night to a school friend married there, and had crossed with her. She was staying with Eddy and seeing all the dress shows. Oh, yes, she'd be back before the Assizes, of course. And how could Jim manage all his entertaining without her? But she might run down to Bath and see the children at Downside first. That was all that was needed, thrown off lightly, and only in response to direct questionings. For the rest, they must ignore what they didn't hear—Caroline's return was the only answer to subterranean whisperings—and Anthony would see to that without delay.

§ 2

HE WENT to see Jim that afternoon. He was used to interviewing men on matters pleasant and unpleasant and it was no part of his character to shirk necessary conversation. But he had never before had to talk to a husband about the wife who had deserted him and about the means of getting her back. And when that wife was one's own sister and that husband Jim Lanigan! Anthony was in an unusual funk when he stepped out into the sunlight of Charles Street.

In River Street he met Cousin Rosie. They fell into step together.

Cousin Rosie had taken Eddy's advice and married again. It was bad advice, but the giver might have protested that he hadn't chosen the husband. Tom Barry was a handsome fellow, but he lifted his elbow disproportionately often in the twenty-four hours of each day. In the six and a half years of their married life he had drunk through an alarming amount of Rosie's once ample property, and his main addition to their joint stock had been the four children she bore him. It was three years now since he had attempted any more exacting work than to make an occasional book at a race meeting.

Rosie and Anthony were no strangers to each other lately, for she had had to make many a call on Considine's to get Tom out of scrapes, to get bills honoured at the bank, for the "loan" of fifty pounds and so on. All the usual shifts of the shiftless were Rosie's now, who had once been proud and solvent. She had good reason to bless the generosity of Anthony Considine, who had even gone the length of trying to employ her husband. But Tom Barry broke down under the strain of three weeks' regular work. Killed out he was by it, he told his wife. "A bull couldn't stand the slavery at that place, I tell you, let alone a man of my years." And to correct his exhaustion he drank two bottles of brandy that night and went into delirium tremens.

Rosie had indeed deteriorated. When Eddy met her in these days he didn't quote the Song of Songs. The superb concubine was lost under mounds of untidy flesh; hips, teeth, and bosom that had been glorious were both comic and tragic now; the flashy clothes were shapeless and untidy. But irony was still in the benevolent eyes that had no real look of defeat in them. It was these unflurried eyes that Anthony liked, even while he cursed the good-natured muddling of their owner. For she spoilt Tom Barry, Anthony said—she was as weak as water with him.

Her good nature had somehow gone to seed for her husband. The strength had gone out of it. It was true for Anthony —she was a fool over the man. He was always bothering and disgracing her with his tricks, he had ruined her and dragged her down in the world and he'd drag her further if she didn't change her tune and put a stop to his antics. But there it was—you could say all that to her and she'd agree with it—oh, and she'd cry too sometimes and wish herself dead—but no one could look in her eyes on a sunny day and insist that she was getting nothing out of life. She seemed to have that in her that rode amusedly over every shame, even the shame of increasing indolence and lessening self-respect. She exasperated Anthony.

She didn't exasperate Eddy. He had a notion that she actually enjoyed her appalling marriage, and that that enjoyment had been her downfall. Tom Barry had put the "come-hether" on her for life; brandy bottles, handsome face, self-pity, coaxing talk—the whole man in his uselessness had undone her. She would never be proud again, but Eddy didn't think that she'd ever be miserable either. Tom Barry had ruined and enchanted her. The situation interested Eddy, who was never as much annoyed by other people's stupidity as Anthony allowed himself to be.

"You're fading away, my poor skeleton of a Rosie!"

"Well, if I'm not it's a wonder, that's all. And how are you these times, Anthony?"

Anthony informed her that he was splendid.

"Nothing on your mind?" There was more than customary inquiry in Rosie's voice and Anthony heard the added tone.

"What would be in weather like this?" He gave her his easiest smile. "Unless it's yourself. You're the greatest worry I have, Mrs. Barry, let me tell you. Where's that poor, delicate husband of yours, that he isn't carrying your parcels for you? That's the sort of a job he'd be equal to, I think."

"Leave him alone now, Anthony, if you please. Isn't he going to take the pledge from Father Downing this very evening?"

"Father Downing is a patient man. How many times is that he's given Tom the pledge for life?"

"Ah, what'd be the good of counting them? Sure, taking it every now and then pulls the poor fellow up for a bit anyway." The voice became pathetic. "He was in a terrible way last week."

"Woman dear, I'm sorry," said Anthony kindly, and he took her arm. They walked a few steps in silence.

"There's a bad bit of gossip going round," said Rosie suddenly, "but it won't go further than me."

Anthony looked an innocent question.

"They're saying—God forgive them—that Caroline's after running away from poor Jim, if you please."

"They're what? Caroline and Jim? What in the name of God put that wickedness into their heads?"

"Mischief. Nothing else. There's nothing in it—is there?"

"Of course there's nothing in it. You ought to be ashamed to ask me, Rosie."

"Indeed I ought. But two people had it for me. Old Mr. Rohan was the first, coming out from eleven o'clock Mass at the Dominicans'. And now Miss Short, below there at the baker's shop, is ready to swear to it. One of the young fellows from the post office lodges with her—and she has some story about a telegram, and Caroline not being in Dublin. I told her it was a raving lie anyway, no matter which or whether," said Rosie cheerfully.

Anthony laughed and wagged his head at her.

"The ladies of Mellick say more than their prayers, Rosie."

"They do indeed," she answered, pausing on the corner of King Street, where their ways parted. "When did you last hear from Eddy, by the way?"

"Two days ago. Sent you his love; sends it to you in every letter, I needn't tell you."

"Naturally. You can give him mine when you write." She laughed almost charmingly.

"You and Eddy should have married each other, Rosie," said Anthony, knowing that this would please her and thinking at the same time of the appallingly incongruous pair his brother and she would have made.

"Ask Eddy why we didn't."

"I will. I'm going over to him to-morrow. Good-bye, Rosie."

He strode up the town to Herbert Street, Cousin Rosie's version of the rumour like a spur in his side. This spread of talk was appalling—not to be borne, this cheap and spiteful bandying of the Considine name. She would be brought back at once, the heedless, crazy woman!

§ 3

HE RAN up the steps at No. 19 Herbert Street and swung impetuously through the glass door of the outer office. A clerk led him through to the inner room without delay.

He paused on the threshold and looked round the large, well-furnished room. It was in its usual apple-pie order, and the brilliant day streamed in at the window. Jim stood in the full flood of sun, arranging flowers in a glass vase.

"Oh, Anthony? Just a minute!"

Anthony sat down.

He watched his brother-in-law clip one by one the stems of three red tulips and place them in the vase where their fellows were. He watched him gather up dead leaves and débris and carry them to the wastepaper basket. Queer, precise devil! Doing ridiculous things like that even to-day! Anthony marvelled at him. He didn't look a bit unusual either, not a hair astray.

But when he turned full face in the stream of light, Anthony saw that he did look a bit unusual and that Teresa had been unobservant when she described him as rather tired. "Dead tired" would have been Anthony's phrase for the face that was turned to him now; it was dry and grey with sleeplessness.

The chairman of Considine's plunged straight into his subject.

"Teresa has told me about this caper of Caroline's." And then, abruptly, "Did you have any sleep last night?"

Jim brushed the inquiry away as if it were a fly.

"I thought you'd better know," he said and his voice was dull. He seemed to have no more to say after that.

Anthony was at a loss.

"I wondered if you'd heard anything definite yet," he said.

"A letter just now from my aunt." Jim held it out to him. "Read it."

Mrs. Munnings's letter had a presence, like its writer. It was voluminous, written in uncompromising but ladylike caligraphy on heavily engraved vellum. It reported the encounter with Mrs. Dominic Hennessy in Grafton Street as well as all the implications and judgments arising to Mrs. Munnings from that episode. It enlarged on the duties of a wife and the misfortunes of possessing one who did not understand these duties—it was eloquent and sympathetic but too long to be set down here. Anthony took the facts from it and skipped the fancies. Then he folded the heavily engraved vellum and passed it back to Jim.

It proved that Caroline was guilty—not merely whimsical. She had left Mellick intending to deceive. Jim's aunt had not expected her nor had Jim himself heard anything about the trip until the day of departure. She had actually run away. So much was clear.

"I needn't tell you, Jim, we're all extremely sorry."

Again that gesture as of brushing a fly away. Was the man never going to speak out?

"It's terrible. Was there—I mean—well, had you any special quarrel or anything?"

"No. No quarrel."

"But then—you mean she had no reason?"

Jim looked down his long nose at Anthony as if about to laugh at him.

"Of course she had a reason," he snapped, and his voice rasped as Anthony had sometimes heard it do in the court of law.

"And you know what it is?" he said.

With his eyes on the tulips he had just arranged, Jim rapped his answer at Anthony.

"I do," was all he said.

Anthony stood up and took a shivering breath. This was bad, bad, a worse affair than he had imagined.

"Then she may not be with Eddy, after all," he said excitedly. "Good God, Jim, what a frightful business! What can we do? Where is she likely to be? Where would he have taken her?"

"Where would *who* have taken her?"

"This blackguard, whoever he is. Don't tell me his name if you'd rather——"

Jim's cold laugh interrupted him.

"Romantic fellow you are, Anthony. That wasn't what I meant."

The gleam in Jim's eyes was so strange then that it crossed Anthony's mind that trouble might be unhingeing him.

"What did you mean?"

"That there's no third party, that's all—no one for you and me to horsewhip."

He smiled contemptuously again.

"More's the pity, maybe," said Anthony in upflashing rage. "The town will find something funny, I'm afraid, in a man whose wife leaves him for nothing at all."

If this was hitting below the belt Jim stood up to it.

"The town! So that's the bug that's biting you? Biting the whole family, of course?"

"My dear Jim, if you must have it, the post office seems to have spread your news in royal style. Every old woman in the place is onto the affair. That's why we've got to act quickly, you see."

"Act? How do you mean, act?"

"Simply what I say, man. Get Caroline back with all this nonsense out of her head, before there's any harm done."

Jim stalked away to the window.

"I see. There must be no harm done, of course. Especially now with a Hennessy marriage in the offing."

Anthony thought of several answers to that and rejected them all.

"What is it?" he said instead, on a quick change to gentleness. "Don't you want her back? Is it—is it you who've been unfaithful?"

There was no criticism in the question and Jim did not resent it. He went on staring out of the window, twirling the cord of the blind.

"Never for a minute since I first saw her," he said quite simply.

"Then you'll go over," Anthony coaxed him. "You'll go over and bring her back."

Jim shook his head.

"But, Jim—my dear fellow——"

The man at the window gave another of his dry little laughs. "You go if you like—you're set on going, I know. And I quite understand that the scandal—well, I don't like scandal either, but——"

"It isn't just ourselves we're bothered about, Jim. I can't tell you how we feel it all for you and the children—you've been one of us so long, my dear fellow—oh, we're ashamed of her."

Jim tapped the blind cord on the window pane.

"Go over if you like, Anthony. Do as you please." He paused and then added in a low voice, as if speaking to himself: "This is her house, if she wants it."

"You mean that if she cares to do her duty, you'll take her back——"

Jim wheeled on him, blind and blind cord snapping away up the window with a mad rattle.

"You fool! Please give no messages for me!"

He plunged across the room with long steps. He was like a gaunt old bird that has had a death wound. "Caroline knows —Caroline knows!"

Anthony looked on in contemptuous pity. What sort of husband was this, that knew nothing of love and pursuit? Was it any wonder that a woman left him?

Jim sat down at his desk.

"Do as you think best, all of you. As you think best."

He turned his grey face to Anthony and smiled dismissal, but Anthony came and put a hand on his shrinking shoulder.

"It'll blow over, Jim," he said. "It'll be all right. I'll bring her back."

The grey face flushed in patches; something piteous crept into the unrested eyes. Anthony looked wonderingly again at his brother-in-law and left the room. He went to London the next day.

THE SEVENTH CHAPTER

I N THE cab from Euston Eddy was gossipy and uninquiring with Caroline. He did not want her to talk about herself to-night.

She grumbled about going to Brown's.

"Abandoned creature! Now you've taken to travelling alone, I suppose you'd think nothing of staying in my bachelor's quarters."

He saw her eyes shine with uncertain amusement through the shadows of the cab.

"Look Caro, we're passing the Princess's; there are some good plays for you to see just now."

"Oh, Ted—it's nice to be with you again!"

She slipped a hand under his arm, seeming grateful for his unquestioning ease with her. "You're looking very sunburnt. That's Italy, I suppose?"

He laughed and ran his hand over his face.

"Yes, that's Italy."

"How long are you back, Ted? Whom did you go with?"

"A man called Froud."

"Oh, yes—you were talking about him at Christmas, and I said I liked the sound of him. Shall I meet him now?"

"Not very likely."

"But Ted, what's wrong with me? Why do you never let me meet your friends?"

He smiled at her, his eyes full of flattery.

"Simply because I'm ashamed of you, you hideous, ungainly female! And here we are, turning into Dover Street!"

He had filled their rooms with flowers; freesias, hyacinths, and roses—their sweet breath rushed to Caroline like music. Eddy flung up windows, raised dim lights, and threw wood to the glowing fire.

Caro was tired, uncertain.

Hot water in her room and rare lavender water from France to sweeten it. Another wood fire and a long, low chair; bowls of violets, kind candlelight. Ted on the floor at her dressing-case, more deft than a woman, finding her brushes, finding her slippers, shaking out her dressing-gown.

Sherry and olives by the bedroom fire.

"Hurry up, Caro; I'm hungry—had no dinner to-night because of you, you scamp." He went off to the sitting-room.

"You scamp." But she had been "my dear" for twenty years. She pulled the pins from her hair one by one in slow punctuation of her dragging half-thoughts. . . . You scamp. Dear Jim, I arrived here safely. The fortunes Ted must spend on flowers. Is there any cure for seasickness? Must write to the school about hot lemon drinks for Norrie's cold. That's from "La Belle Hélène," that thing he's singing. Oh, he's poured out the water in the tub—it'll be too cool in a minute. Lovely smell of lavender. Dear Jim, I simply had to do it—oh, poor Jim! . . .

Caroline got into silk petticoats again and a rustling gown of silk; she powdered her face and breast and replaced her emerald ring on her right hand; she laughed at her brilliant self in the long mirror and ran into the next room.

"Ted, I smell mushrooms."

They ate a fantastic supper, the kind they loved, as expensive and out-of-season as could be. Mushrooms, plovers' eggs, langoustes, and ridiculous strawberries that had no taste until they were dipped in Pol Roger.

A remarkable supper, and no doubt the waiters thought they were celebrating a remarkable event—as indeed they were. It isn't every day that an Irish wife picks up her skirts and runs for it.

"What will we drink to, Ted? Give me a toast!"

Her eyes were winter stars. Eddy had been thinking of a broken appointment but he lifted his glass now with a smile that was all his sister's. They were alone in the room with

their exotic strawberries; he ventured suddenly to speak from
his heart.

"I drink to your happiness, Caro. I'd love you to have a
minute or two of that."

She stared at him.

"Then you're not going to scold me?"

"Most terribly—to-morrow. Come to the fire."

§ 2

HE HAD decided to let her talk to-night after all, if she wanted
to. Henceforward her little escapade must peter out. If Eddy
knew anything of his family, she could not hope to beat free
of them for more than another day or two, and these two
days could hold little but tears and wrangling, loud voices and
surrender. Let her get all she could out of it to-night, talk and
laugh and cry and take the centre of the stage. After to-morrow
it was unlikely that anyone would humour her or throw
bouquets. The road down which she had come whirling was
a cul-de-sac, so far as Eddy could see, and the thing she
was seeking was not hidden in it anywhere. But let her take
such trivial things as were. Let her be vainglorious awhile
and taste her own audacity. She had been an ordinary, unhappy
wife and she would go back to being that, but to-night she
could boast all the same of having leapt this once on the back
of a flying impulse and ridden it gallantly a fence or two. A
silly brag, maybe—but if it soothed vanity a little, since her
greater trouble was to go unsatisfied, in God's name let her
make it.

"Oh, Ted, what had I better do now?"

"Lean back in your chair."

"Suddenly at breakfast I decided. Yesterday, Ted—oh, it's
longer ago than that."

"Why?"

"Ah, haven't you always known?"

"There was no new reason then, at breakfast yesterday?"

"What reason could there ever be? What do you mean by
reasons?"

"I don't know. Do you think you'll go back?"

She leant forward, elbows on knees, chin in hands. She stared with wide eyes at the fire; her face was enchantingly comic for a moment.

"It's a fix," she said.

"A bit of a one," said Eddy.

"You never get into fixes." She dismissed him pityingly. And then on a snapping breath she began to unpack her two days' load.

She wasn't going back ever, ever. She had to do this thing —she couldn't help it. What else was there to do? And what did it matter anyway—father wasn't there now to be upset —but Jim-and-the-children—she ran them into one word like that and her listener understood that the hyphened phrase meant something entirely different from the short word "Jim" —it meant her house and housekeeping, her motherhood and social place, gossip, routine and family ties, all precious things in her sight; but the short word "Jim" meant something else. Jim-and-the-children, how was it possible to stay away from them? What was she to do? Must she go on or back? Did Ted know a place where she could hide from these two things— from Jim-and-the-children, that she would always want, and from Jim, that she could bear no longer?

She didn't ask these questions, but others even less coherent which Eddy reduced to these. Very soon the interrogative was flung aside and she tumbled from rhetoric into a trembling story of her heart that was only the story of its emptiness.

It was no news to Eddy. What she hadn't told him before had been easy guessing—and she wasn't explicit now. To speak to her brother, to speak to anyone, of intimate things, even in the veiled terms she was fumbling for now made this modest Caroline choke and catch her breath. She kept her head pressed back against the wing of her chair as she spoke and did not move her eyes from the curling fire. The emerald flashed and blazed on her uneasy hand and her silk skirts whispered together. The flame threw revealing light and easier darkness on her lovely face, but her brother was aware all the time of the beating pulse in her throat and could almost hear her heart when she paused for a word.

He interrupted her hardly at all and he gave no advice. For nearly two hours he let her struggle in the maze of herself.

Sometimes a log crashed softly to interrupt her, sometimes a cab jingled home up Dover Street, sometimes a clock struck or a street-girl laughed, and once a rose flung all its petals on her lap. She gathered these in her restless hand, and went on talking as she crumpled them. They became a part of her speech for the man who watched her.

It was the commonplaceness of her ill-luck that hurt him. All this shy talk was only the plain tale of twenty years in which beauty had been used and left unsatisfied. If only Jim had had the very ordinary fortune to give back to his wife the sensual release he took from her—ah, then, what a happy man he would have been! How she'd have cherished her husband, this simple Caroline, how gaily and prettily she'd have loved him in gratitude for desire set free! Eddy Considine, connoisseur of love and passion, allowed himself to wonder for the thousandth time what manner of man his brother-in-law was, who was either so unversed in woman as not to be aware how he had failed his wife or was too proud and timorous of the flesh to speak to her of such a thing or to try and set it right by a new wooing. Poor Jim! Poor married man, who had no words with which to steer desire, who was dumb and, as Eddy thought, not more than a beast in the country of love! Poor Jim, who had no bridge to throw between night and day, between flesh and spirit! And poor Caroline, poor lovely Caroline who had asked so little of life, only the wedded love that others had, only to be loved in the sun as well as the dark, to be laughed at and teased and companioned in the day, to be shouted at and quarrelled with and called soft names, to see her beauty brighten her husband's eyes unfurtively at sudden meeting, to be loved naturally, as Eddy thought—not snatched in the night and bowed to respectfully by day. That was all Caroline had asked—and here she was, at forty-two, still beautiful and warm, with nerves frayed to tatters from loathing of a man's desire, from disturbance and frustration of her senses. A physiological commonplace—that was all Caroline's trouble, drench it however the silly creature might in tears and modesty and hesitations.

Eddy wondered if he would ever dare to let them take her back to what she'd fled. He saw them all about her—coming to fetch her in large fantastic procession—Anthony at their head of course, Anthony, successful in love himself by instinct and sheer magnetism and with no patience at all for other people's failures, Anthony, blue-eyed and invincible, insisting on the family code; Tom, sad and priestly, all his grim purity in arms for the Considines; Teresa, very stern indeed because a bit jealous maybe of adventuring beauty; Joe making a medical joke of it, and with a tip or two for Jim about how to tame her—and Jim—but Eddy couldn't see Jim. Jim was an enigma. How would she fare, this worn-out, bewildered one, when the crowd of bullies marched her home? How would she take up the old ways under their watchful eyes? How would she return to her husband's bed and open her arms to him?

"But I'm so tired after all these years. Oh, Ted—he tires me so and he won't see. . . ."

The words were like slow sobs and made Eddy shudder. Suddenly he felt he could bear no more of them. He must send her to bed, he must get away from her stabbing voice.

St. James's Church rang two o'clock.

"Do you hear that, Caro?"

"Yes. I'm sleepy now."

He opened the door that led to her room.

"Your fire is still bright in here."

She lingered with him on the threshold.

"Sleep long, dear Caro. A long beauty sleep."

She smiled and leant against him.

"Oh, Ted, if more people were like you!"

"Good God, what a world 'twould be!"

"The fire has killed your lovely roses, Ted."

"We'll get some more to-morrow."

"Yes; we'll have fun to-morrow, won't we? In spite or everything?"

He laughed at the childish common-sense.

"We'll have great fun to-morrow in spite of everything."

§ 3

EDDY's friend, Richard Froud, did in fact appear in their sitting-room next day. It seemed to Caroline that Eddy was not pleased at this surprise, but the visitor cannot have thought so, for he stayed a long while and was very gay. He wound up his visit by compelling them to lunch with him.

They ate roast ducklings in the Carlton. Eddy, as he sipped his wine, looked gravely into Caroline's eyes and was assured that she was having some of the great-fun-in-spite-of-everything that he had promised her.

Richard Froud was thirty-five, looking younger. He had a fine, large head and a face made up of pleasing irregularities —wide mouth, wide forehead, grey eyes set wide and crooked, a jutting chin, brown hair that waved about untidily; an assemblage of features that projected immediate and vigorous charm.

He came of a world that had no link with the Considines. His father was an archdeacon in a cathedral close, his brother a commander of Her Majesty's fleet. Winchester and then Balliol had had charge of him until he was twenty-two. He was in the city now, making a leisurely fortune in a famous tea-importing house, that was owned by his maternal uncle. He was unmarried and interested in all things—food, people, theatres, books, religions, wines, the Fenians, Mr. Swinburne, Mrs. Fawcett's notion about votes for women—everything moving within his orbit seemed to catch the eye of Richard Froud.

He talked about Mellick to Caroline, and she raised her brows at his informativeness.

"But I know everything about Mellick, Mrs. Lanigan—except how it came to produce two people like Ted and you."

"I thought I was the only person in the world who called him Ted," Caroline grumbled.

"Eddy then, or Edward—what you will."

"He was christened Edward Francis Xavier."

Richard and Eddy smiled to each other.

"Xavier." Richard balanced the word delicately. "Yes, that might suit him; pronounced Javier, you know, with the 'jota'."

"What's a 'jota'?" said Caroline.

"A Spanish way of being cross."

"Wouldn't suit Ted then."

Richard leant towards her, still smiling back to Eddy.

"But Mrs. Lanigan—he's been cross all through lunch."

"Well, perhaps the weeniest bit. Are you, Ted?"

"Not now—not the weeniest, teeniest bit."

The smiles that sped between brother and sister were exactly alike, Richard thought, alike in shape and speed and in the sweet comment they made upon each other. They were alike too in their slight enhancing wryness, the true but all the same superficial and temporising smiles of people with a bit of heartache. Something was troubling each of the smilers and Richard did not think that it was something shared. How alike they were! He looked more sharply from the man's face to the woman's, pondering the mystery of blood that could make two souls so different and isolated exchange twin smiles across a luncheon table.

He looked from the man to the woman and let his eyes rest.

"But you didn't tell me why you think that Mrs. Fawcett's right," Caroline was saying.

"Perhaps she isn't."

Richard's answer was vague; all his wits were given up to the picture Caroline made.

She had tilted her face upwards to the light and was resting it on her linked fingers. Superficially she was all straightforward beauty now, just a lovely woman, a bright minute in a spring day. The blueness of her eyes was stressed by the blue note of pattern in her grey gown and the blue-grey feather that curled on the brim of her bonnet. Her red lips were apart and smiling; her cheeks were warm in the sun; she was silky and chic and smelt faintly of a rose. To complete and lighten her pretty moment, so that a man could forget, having enjoyed it, she wanted the gleam of coquetry. Of that she had none. There was no self-consciousness whatever in Caroline's face for Richard, no hint of invitation. And that was why his eyes dwelt gravely on her. It was the shadow behind her beauty that made her imperfect now and held him musing. She was enjoying herself—yes, but at the point of the sword. She was happy in this bright, chattering place only because she was insisting on being happy. A desperate reveller, thought Richard Froud, a ticket-of-leave man. What was the matter with this radiant sister of Ted's?

§ 4

EDDY and Caroline strolled and shopped together after lunch and drank tea at Gunter's in the green shade of Berkeley Square. They both felt sad and uninclined to talk of sadness. They avoided the debate that hung about them and chose instead to be listlessly indulgent of each other. It was as if Richard had been a cause of courage between them and that now he was gone they could not muster up anything more positive than courtesy.

Caroline pondered the letter she must write to catch the evening mail.

Eddy smoked cigarettes and flicked up smiles at her.

"Dear Jim"—she bit her lip in the effort of composition, but it seemed as if she would never know what to write to the man who had limped about his office that afternoon like a wounded bird, crying "Caroline knows!"

Caroline didn't seem to know much.

They went back to Brown's at last. Richard had invited himself to dinner and they were going to a theatre afterwards. Meanwhile there was this letter. Caroline settled bravely at the desk and took a long stare through the window at Dover Street façades.

§ 5

IT WAS there that Richard found her long afterwards, when Eddy had gone to dress and the lamps were lighted. She had not drawn the curtains, and over the opposite roofs the slow-starring sky still held a tattered memory of the day. Framed in this blueness her head was, her bent and troubled head, as the man came in.

She had been very busy, had wasted a vast deal of Brown's good notepaper, had written many fine sentences and scattered a few blots, had tried two kinds of nib and one quill and one pencil, had addressed and stamped a beautiful envelope, had drawn trees and cups and triangles on the blotting pad and filled a wastepaper basket with tearings-up. "Dear Jim—I don't know how to explain——" "Dear Jim—you'd better come over and see me——" "Dear Jim—I hope you're very well——" And now in the heel of the hunt she had missed the mail and was crying. A sheet of paper spread in front of her was wet with tears and with two unblotted words: "Dear Jim."

She turned as Richard spoke her name. He had not known that she was crying, but now the lamplight sparkled on her tears. She rose to welcome him.

"I'm afraid I've come too soon, Mrs. Lanigan."

"Oh, no. Ted's dressed, I think—and I won't be long."

Her voice shrank from him, embarrassed with her trouble. But she dried her eyes quite simply, standing between the twilight and the lamp. With a glitter as of votive candles over her face and the starred blue wisp of sky behind her she might have reminded Richard of the Queen of Sorrows in a shrine. But he wasn't thinking in comparisons. It had happened to him unaccountably that in the space between his recognition of her head and the sight of her glittering tears he had been swung from himself and his assured clear place to the dark heart of her trouble; it became his somehow in a second, this unknown grieving; he was bearing it, lapped in its lead. It was as if her tears were in his eyes. A crazy transference that made him tired and dumb.

She came to him and touched his hand.

"I must fly," she said. "Shut out the sad old day."

He went to the window to obey her, but before he got there she had left the room. He leant on the sash then as if relieved to know her gone.

A yellow chip of moon was swinging out above the Green Park. Smooth, empty Dover Street poured itself out of shadow into the bright flow of Piccadilly, where carriage lamps were flashing. A top-hat loafed beside the kerb; a policeman stood impregnable upon the crossing; an idle cabby cracked his whip.

Richard stared at the scene as if it were new to him and difficult to account for.

". . . Shut out the sad old day," a voice kept saying in his breast. When Eddy crossed the room he drew the curtains and turned to him with eagerness.

THE EIGHTH CHAPTER

MELLICK fired its first shot in the morning. A telegram came from Anthony. He was leaving that day and would be at Morley's Hotel the following evening. Salute across the bows.

Caroline winced when this news was told to her and cried "Oh, Ted!" on a sharp breath. Then she threw back her head as if for a long drink.

Whatever it was, that invisible draught, it seemed to do her good. Once it was swallowed she had done with wincing, but laughed instead and stretched a gay hand to her brother.

Two days, her heart was telling her, two days before—before what? What did she so specially want with two days? She didn't know.

There was no word at all from Jim. This surprised Eddy, but he waited silently for Caroline's comment. It never came. She said nothing about writing to him, either, and made no motion towards the desk. Evidently she meant to abandon an impossible task. If Eddy was faintly shocked at this he did not say so. He sat down and wrote a perfunctory note himself to his sister's husband. That sister, not knowing what he was at, sang heedlessly about the room meantime and chattered to him from the window seat.

"Two days!"—the refrain went on in her.—"We might all be blown up in two days—I might die, Jim might die—anyone might die. All sorts of things happen in two days."

DEAR JIM [Eddy wrote]:
Caroline is still with me here and will remain under my wing of course for as long as you and she desire. She is

well but seems overwrought—is tearful and frivolous by turns. She spent all yesterday afternoon writing to you, but I do not think that she has posted her letter. Perhaps it is as well that she should not do so yet. We shall see Anthony to-morrow evening—meantime perhaps you have written. If there is anything that I can do to help the situation only ask me.

Every good wish, dear Jim,
From yours affectionately,
EDDY CONSIDINE.

§ 2

BY THE time Richard looked in to say "good-day" Caroline was rampant to be amused and getting out of hand.

Eddy grumbled to the newcomer.

"How on earth am I to discipline the baggage, will you tell me?"

He had been trying to make her see that after lunch he would have to spend a few hours in his neglected office and that therefore she must resign herself for that period to a sofa and a novel here in the hotel.

"But I won't stay here, Ted, cooped up by myself—I warn you!"

She was standing near the window and, unsteadied perhaps by the mounting music of the street, she flung an indiscretion to the air.

"Only two days," she chanted. "We mustn't waste a second!" But no one seemed to know whom she was talking to.

"Would it be entirely unconventional, Ted, if I were to suggest driving Mrs. Lanigan somewhere this afternoon?"

So it was settled, and Caroline and Richard stole a long surprised look at each other, the look of children granted a treat they had not dared expect.

She left the room presently and silence came over the two men like a mist.

Richard crossed to the window where she had stood.

Eddy blew a smoke-ring, then another that went through it, then another.

"What did she mean, Ted—only two days?"

"That the hunt is up, I think."

Richard looked sideways at him.

"You might as well know. She's run away all of a sudden —cleared off the other morning without plan or forethought— indeed almost without a reason—and without even knowing whether she really wanted to go or not."

"Left that husband of hers at last, you mean?"

"Yes, left Lanigan."

"But—she said 'two days'?"

Eddy laughed.

"Yes. In two days she'll be cornered. Anthony's coming over—God knows who else. She'll have to face the music then, to-morrow night perhaps. She'll have to go forward or back—insult the family or bow to it. And if that were all!"

"What else is there, Ted?"

"There's herself. To-morrow night she will have to decide between all sorts of things, affections, habits, principles, that are a part of her and another thing that she knows nothing about. Poor Caro!"

"Well, then, when Anthony comes?"

"Ah! She has two days. I believe she thinks that if she lights enough candles to-day in the Oratory God will oblige by bringing the end of the world to-morrow night. She's nothing if not extravagant!"

"And if God did—what would she have got out of it?"

"A run for her money, a letting off of steam, the pleasure of causing a sensation—and maybe"—he blew another very careful ring—"maybe a sight anyhow of the thing she's really after."

"If she asked you, would you advise her to go back?"

"Oh, Richard!" The young man turned and saw a darkness of great trouble gathering in Eddy's eyes. "Don't corner me yet! We have two days."

"You're—you're very fond of her, Ted?"

"She's always somewhere in my mind, I think."

Silence again. Each followed his thoughts of her, Richard moving here and there with vague roughness, as if in pain, Eddy blowing smoke-rings.

"You like her, Richard?" he asked after a while, softly and casually.

The other shrugged to the colourless question; the two men lapsed into a mist of silence.

§ 3

THERE were no mists between Caroline and Richard as they drove that afternoon in his uncle's open carriage. Rather they went as in a palanquin together, a little secret, gaudy world that they had made their own, a canopy of silk from which there was no view of the road behind them or ahead. For that was Caroline's mood and he caught it from her, deft and grateful. The April day was to be their tent, she seemed to say, and wasn't it bright and fair enough? Well, then, there must be no peeping out of it at yesterday or at to-morrow.

He was content to have it so.

"It's very kind of your uncle to lend me his carriage like this."

"My uncle's a delightful man. Nothing would give him more pleasure than to know I am so happy now, in business hours."

"Ah! And what's all the world doing about the tea it wants to buy while you're gallivanting?"

"Silly asses! They'd do far better to go along to Ted and buy mangolds."

"I suppose it'll take a long time to get to Richmond?" she said presently on an ingenuous tone of satisfaction.

"I hope so."

"Why did we say we'd go to Richmond?"

"I've forgotten."

"What's to be seen there?"

"You. And 'maids of honour'."

She gave a greedy little purr.

"Have you ever eaten 'maids of honour'?"

She nodded.

"At Richmond?"

"Yes."

"Sophisticated person!"

"What does 'sophisticated' mean?"

She had snatched this Richard Froud. Without a thought of such intention, without a premeditated word or look, she had been asking for him, claiming him, laying siege, from yesterday's hour of first meeting. She didn't know this. It would have scandalised her utterly to learn that in this very hour the arms of her spirit were stretched wide open for him and would not close again until they took him home. She had found the thing she knew nothing about, had run down her cul-de-sac full into it, but without recognition yet.

The walls of her tent receded as Richard talked. He rolled them back to lead her from it to another vaster, more exacting mood, a place of cool, dim colonnades, high-shadowed, that crossed and diverged from each other in the pattern of a dream. His voice was all that sounded there and the way that he was taking her led to no yesterday or to-morrow that she knew.

And it was nothing for all that, their talk—of passers-by and the budding trees, of Irish accents, of Miss Ellen Terry, of his uncle, of Italy, of a shop he knew where she'd find gloves of the exact "gris perle" she wanted—it was nothing. It was peace, their words its chiming bell.

They paced Richmond Hill as the sun heeled over for descent.

"A monster then, if you insist," Richard was saying, "but I'm sure he must have had some charm."

They had been talking scandal about Henry the Eighth who, Caroline understood, had killed twelve wives and tried to make a pope of himself. "You ought to be ashamed to mention him," she scolded Richard.

Now she wasn't interested.

Native of a riverland, she carried the sound of hurrying water in her heart wherever she went. She didn't listen to it often, but now this panorama of a bright stream, spread out too far below for her to hear its voice, set her listening in spite of herself to the moan of a great water she could not see. The voice of another river came crying to her from the quiet Thames and closing her eyes she saw it again, stream of her childhood on which she sailed and picnicked long ago, over which her father's cargoes went lumbering out to sea, in which her sons had learnt to swim—river of all the generations that she knew. She saw those generations come whirling towards her now as on that river's flood. All Mellick she seemed to see, men and houses, quick and dead, in an earth-quake rush to overtake her. Faces whose names escaped her, clerks of her father's, old beggar-women, shopgirls, ladies with whom she drank tea, her confessor, Father McEwen, pretty Louise Hennessy, Mrs. Kelleher the midwife, and Tom with his stole on, ready to preach, and Molly picking bluebells; she saw the steps of 19 Herbert Street and Mr. Bandon, Jim's head clerk; she saw two green finches in a cage; she saw her four tall sons; and the grey mass of Considine's offices with Anthony swinging out of the front door; Teresa she saw, and Reverend Mother at Friary Lane, and Joe with his racing glasses to his eyes; she saw the statue of Our Lady of Victories in her bedroom; she saw the hideous kitchen cat that she detested; and Norrie and Lucy, her little loves of daughters—and her lumbering old father who smiled at her. Away beyond them all, expressionless and as if borne forward involuntarily on the flood, she saw her husband Jim who looked at her without a plea.

This was indeed an inrush of yesterday and to-morrow, a breaking of the rule she had set. Where was her palanquin now, her safe tent of to-day, her colonnades murmurous with one voice? Poor tattered metaphors, they had availed her noth-ing. Her dress of gaiety was gone and all her bright trappings of make-believe, the curl of her lips, the rose in her cheek, the ironic slanting of her brows. Her face was given over at a stroke to trouble.

Richard looked down at her. She was forty-two in that minute; her brave bluff had given place to a larger bravery. Her features had the shocked immobility they had worn in the month of her father's death, but they were nine years older, nine years more strained and hungry. Some chisel of dis-appointment had touched each corner with every added year, and all its adding and subtracting stood out plainly now in the beam of the sun. So Richard saw a woman seven years older than himself and knew that she was grieving perplexedly for her children and her house, and for her harsh traditions of honour and fidelity, grieving for the warmth of her habitual place, grieving because these things all meant so much to her, and yet did not mean enough. He saw a face full of small personal sorrow for little things of the flesh that would die with the flesh. And yet it was to him very strangely as if he looked on an eternal face, stricken eternally.

Caroline lifted her disconsolate eyes to him, and as he searched them the moment seemed to lay its hand on the sun for him, as God for Joshua. He looked as it were for ever; he looked at Caroline outside of time and space. And if as he looked she was still thinking only foolishly and helplessly of transient things, her husband and children and the desires of her heart of flesh on which time would have no mercy, it seemed to him that of such things the cycles of heaven and earth are made. For Caroline's mortal eyes told him then, most irrelevantly, that man is undying. She gave him a whiff of faith, a flash of prayer. She told him that before and after might be great, small, sweet or bitter, might have been or might never be, but that man was undying simply because a face and a moment insisted that so it must be. She told him that the gates of hell would not prevail for him against these ten seconds on Richmond Hill.

Like Joshua then, his victory won, Richard set the suspended moment free.

He broke their silence with a simple commonplace.

"You're sad," he said to her, "and I'd give my heart to have you happy."

"If I were happy," said Caroline, "I wouldn't be here." She said it with a sudden return to gallantry and as one might who, contented with her cake, is aware that she cannot both eat the lovely stuff and also have it. Gaily she said it, lifting ironic brows to summon back their earlier mood. And as her words ended, she laid a conspiratorial hand upon his arm and left it there.

She did not know of this. So little coquettish was she that she could let a gesture of her own trip her up and expose her heart without being aware that she had made it. She laid her hand on Richard's arm, because her sense of peace with him had already become too soft and natural in her for her inexperience to be on guard against it. Her whole soul was trusting him now, and it was impossible for a creature so unself-conscious to let such a happy, new sensation come her way without the punctuation of a gesture. So her hand went nuzzling into the crook of his elbow as unremarked by Caroline as it might have picked up a piece of bread for her if she were hungry.

Richard knew then that she loved him.

He kept his arm rigid under her fingers; he tried to keep his heart from clashing near them against his ribs. In order to endure the tremendous moment he made himself listen only for ᵤ half-breath, only as in a pause of flight, to the too bright message of this sweet, confiding hand. He dared not linger with its news just then. In self-defence, which had become defence of her, he could only give it a quick "yes, yes" of his bedazzled spirit, and so plunge past it for a space of safety into a contemplation of its afterwards. Here it was easier to stand upright and be still.

For he looked to that afterwards with composure now. It was hers, he had given it over to her. Last night when she stood between lamp and window and burnt his eyes with her tears, he had laid the whole gift and problem of himself, willy-nilly, before her feet. All his hopes and dreams and passions, all the unspent years, all his bonds, traditions, idiosyncrasies, loves and secrets and friendships; his love for himself, his love for the courtly, dilettante life, his balanced love for dark, subtle, changeable adventure and the conventional surface pattern of society's exaction, all these that had been his habit of life, with the days and nights that he had yet to live, he flung down and staked on Caroline.

He was calm, therefore, as a helmsman is who pierces an untracked way through moving darkness. Whatever Caroline might want of him, that was hers already without reckoning. Wife, mistress, friend or memory—which of these was she to be? Richard did not know and would not guess. It was enough for now that her hand was making open confession to him in the crook of his arm, it was enough that she had inexplicably emptied life of all its dear and delicate cross-purposes, that she had changed him in one day from a creature of whim and dalliance and lazy adaptability into one blinded and made humourless by a solitary desire, a desire not even strongly sensual yet, since it was mainly to find and give to her whatever she had come seeking all this way. For that, whether it was to be great or small, he had composedly thrown his world away; for this terrible and maybe brief boy's passion with which Caroline had burnt out his happy cynicism, he was prepared to bargain all the mockery that his coming years and his older self might heap on him; he was prepared for the laughter of his world; he was prepared for his own disillusionment and, if it came, for Caroline's contempt. He saw too, unrelentingly, that her time of enchantment was not long before the slow fading of her flesh and spirit must begin. But that did not cool his heart. He found such radiance in her, such crazy, rapturous, golden charm as made her few remaining summer days seem meanly paid for at the cost of all a man's earthly hopes. When beauty left her—ah, what of that absurdity? Let her be his last love then, his last and dear delight. He had enough casual memories to laugh at, enough infidelities for one man's honour. He only asked now to live for Caroline, to fight for what she wanted and make it hers and, so far back into solemn boyhood had she swept him, even to die for her if that were the needed thing.

"Ah, there's a sky!" said Caroline. "It's going to be the sort of sunset we used to paint at school—with coloured chalks."

"I don't suppose you were much good at chalking sunsets."

"Well, I was always breaking my chalks." Her fingers drummed reminiscently along his sleeve. "Once I chalked Agnes's face and made her look downright pretty, but they stood me in the corner with a notice on my back, 'I maltreated my sister.' Poor Agnes had to go and wash off all the lovely colours!"

So they talked with lame, uneasy dullness, against the muted dialogue of their bodies. Caroline prattled all the way downhill of shepherds' warnings and shepherds' delights, asking Richard what it was that shepherds so feared and desired from the sky. He answered her lightness eagerly but without any skill. Her hand was still arpeggioing softly on his arm.

THE NINTH CHAPTER

W HEN they got back to the hotel they found a note from
Eddy:

DARLING CARO:
Ask Richard to go on amusing you this evening. And
expect me when you see me. It is my wicked intention to
forget all about a brother's duty and come home with the
milk.
Love to you both.

TED.

They had taken stalls for that evening for Mr. Sothern's
new comedy at the Haymarket, as Eddy was eager for Caroline to see the brilliant young Miss Robertson. The tickets
lay folded now within his letter. Caroline fingered them
dreamily and handed the note to Richard.

It was a significant note, Eddy's gesture of self-dismissal
from their affairs. To Richard it read like this: "I have done
with fussing round after the two of you. Find your own way. I
am tired and in any case useless."

And it seemed to Richard too that in his last sentence, "Love
to you both," the sentimentalist cried out to them to make no
mistake but take the way that was forbidden, to take it because common-sense refuted it, because Caroline would soon
be old, and even—this almost, in Eddy's peculiar way, pleas-
urably—because their taking of it wounded him. Richard wondered if Eddy knew how well he would understand his note.

"I'm to amuse vou, he says."

The theatre tickets slipped from Caroline's hands, curvetted like butterflies or like young Miss Robertson's comedy-playing. Richard watched them until they settled on the carpet. Then he looked again at Caroline, who held her hands open in front of her as if they had released a bird.

"I love you, Caroline."

She gave a little cry, a sharp, withdrawing cry, as full of surrender as his voice had been. They came to each other's arms silently.

It was as if that was all that they had ever wanted.

A sculptural stillness invaded them when they stood together, a repose of spirit so final that even the soft blind movements of their hands and lips were but a part of it. It seemed like sleep, their first embrace, a living and illumined sleep, sleep after fever. Outside its arc irrelevancies fluttered and they could sense them, even think of them—the smell of hyacinths, the ticking of a clock, the cries of Dover Street—things recognisable but remote. And beyond those lay indisputably the past and future that must be and must have been. But the space of stillness they had found was not narrowed nevertheless; it seemed impregnable, eternal; they sheltered within it matter-of-factly, just as children say their prayers without having to bother to believe in them. So whether they strained together or relaxed, whether their mouths drank each other or wandered murmuring, whether their hands met or fell apart—was all the same; their spirits were still, they were carved in an attitude of peace that did not even defy the rest of life.

"I love you, I love you."

"Oh, Richard, I love you."

With such a soft astonishment they said these words, they might have sprung new-minted from their lips. Indeed to Caroline, who had probably never spoken them in her life before, even to a lieutenant of Hussars in Kilcrusha Woods, they were maybe as great a marvel as the Paraclete's tongues to the fishermen—they seemed a whole new language to her, a language that said everything, filling and emptying the mind. For Richard the strangeness was that words of late grown dusty to him should now be charged with such a truth and passion as he had forgotten could be carried in a phrase.

"I love you."

"I love you."

The voices dovetailed, nestled together.

St. James's chime rang far away outside their circle of peace, where time and Dover Street were hurrying by, where hyacinths were and clocks and tickets for new comedies.

"Caroline, you're tired."

She sat in her winged chair, and he fell beside her. Her eyes were evening stars.

"What time is it?"

"Love, I've forgotten. I never knew."

"Your hand, Richard—let me kiss your hand."

"How long since I first saw you, Caroline?"

"Yesterday morning, my dear love."

"Yesterday morning! Oh, what was I doing before then? Tell me, Caroline—where was I buried till I saw your face?"

It was their turn to talk the immemorial nonsense. Darkness bewitched the room till even the windows lost their dim banners of light, and Eddy's flowers lived only in a ghostly perfume; there was hardly a whisper from the fire.

So with nothing but Richard's face to look upon, upturned to her from her breast, Caroline revealed as much to herself as to her lover the unspent, unpractised Caroline of passion's tenderness. He had from her then all that he asked and could have had more, could have had at least whatever assuagement flesh can give to flesh. But he was in love with her and a sentimentalist according to his day. He wanted Caroline for ever, and so it seemed to him that he must not take her now. Besides, the hour was full enough. Feeling must wait on feeling; desire must be patient with him; even he was slow in tasting this delight of being at rest with Caroline.

"Richard, it's you, isn't it? The darkness does such queer things to your face—you're sure it's you I'm holding."

"You love me. Say it again! Say that you love me!"

"I love you, I love you. I'll say it until you're deaf and weary from my one tune—I love you."

The long, slow wave of the day's emotion was curving upward to its crest in Caroline now.

She bent her head and spoke to Richard with a new urgency, as if against time.

Richard should not have let her speak. He should have made

this rising moment his. The wave must break, either in passion or in anguish. When it had fallen, she would have been lost or won. If her own past returned to assault her before she had been walled against it by love's final satisfaction, that would be perilous for Richard Froud. He should have swept her to oblivion now, whence she would have returned to meet her memories with estranged and calmer eyes. If he had been ten years younger, ten years less diffident, he would not have seen this danger on the tide of his arrogant desire, and so would have been safe from it. Now perhaps he saw but scrupled to avert it.

"Listen, Richard—I must tell you. I'm forty-two. That's old, isn't it, getting old? Too old to let you love me. Oh, yes, it is—but I've been twenty years without loving anyone. Ah, no, don't look like that!" She laughed reassuringly at him, out of her present safety grown indulgent of the past.

"Oh, Caroline, if you could see your face! You have no age or youth or anything like other people. Bend down to me, Caroline, come here! Tell me that you're safe and happy now, tell me you've forgotten those twenty years!"

"Poke the fire, Richard. I want to see you better."

The flames shot up, and Richard, seated on the floor against Caroline's knees, stared with the wonderment of rediscovery into her newly lighted face. And thinking more of her twenty wasted years than of himself, he made another strange mistake.

"Why did you marry him, Caroline?" he asked.

"I don't know. He was good-looking and father liked him, and every other girl in Mellick had her eye on him. I thought my heart was broken then anyhow—and I didn't know—well, I didn't know what marriage was. You see, Richard"—she gathered him up to her again, grown shy of his staring—"you see, for Catholics marriage is—is a sacrament. It's not supposed to be so much a personal matter as something you undertake to do because it's—well, really I suppose because it's God's will. Don't smile, Richard."

"I'm not smiling."

He was laughing in fact—an angry, hysterical laugh.

"When I went to confession the day before I was married the priest told me that a sacrament is a means of grace—and that the sacrament of matrimony would give me grace to be a good and happy wife. I didn't know what he meant. But often afterwards I wondered what I had done wrong that I hadn't been given that grace. Oh, Richard, I prayed so much! I prayed and prayed and made novenas, and for years I was positive that something would surely happen to make me love my husband. Truly, Richard. But I wasn't always miserable either. I have six children, and my four sons are the handsomest boys in Mellick, everyone says. And Lucy and Norrie —like little fat kittens they used to be, but now they're more like two brown leaves in the wind, I sometimes think."

He saw a darkness in her eyes and he grew afraid. He drew her face down to his.

"Oh, love, stop talking. We'll talk of these things to-morrow. To-morrow—Caroline! Stop thinking of them now!"

She drooped over him; he felt her weight on him as if she had grown suddenly tired. She leant her head heavily upon his hair.

"What can we talk of to-morrow? What's there that we can say about Lucy and Norrie—except that I've given them up?"

He had no answer.

"I've given them up." She laid a hand that shook upon his mouth. "No, Richard, don't be troubled. This isn't your affair. I ran away from them before I knew that you were in this world. I left them all—and they'll say that I've no heart— that's what they'll say, Teresa and Tom. Ah, Tom! He's a priest—and if he saw me now, Richard, he'd say worse things than that I have no heart. Ah, if Tom saw me now, committing mortal sin——" She caught her breath.

"Mortal sin! That strange idea!" Richard mused into her bending face and touched it with gentle fingers. "So this is mortal sin for Father Tom!"

"But it is. You can't get out of it. Oh, of course, I forgot you're a Protestant."

On the last word her voice was anxiously polite.

"A kind of one," said Richard. "What's this nonsense we've got onto now?"

He turned on his knees again and flung his arms about her.

"Oh, Richard, it isn't nonsense. I was telling you why I ran away and what they'll say about me, how they'll say that I'm an unnatural mother and the worst disgrace that's ever happened in our family. They'll say that father will turn in his grave, and that I've made a laughing-stock of Jim. They'll turn my sons against me—oh, and Lucy and Norrie too! They believe that it's sheer hardheartedness and that I'm bad! They'll think I wanted to do it, Richard—they'll actually think I wanted to do this thing! Oh, as if I could! What would I want over here among strangers—if I could only bear to stay at home? What would I want, I say? Ah, father, father!"

Her voice climbed wildly. The wave was breaking in anguish and she wasn't ready for it. She stood up and swept away from him, swept down the room and back again, clasping her hands and flinging them apart and clasping them. The firelight flashed on her hurrying silk skirts and touched the sudden tempest in her face.

With her own love-talk, that her lover had guided so unwisely, she had called up images on which she could not look without great fear. With dangerous, self-explaining words she had summoned her father to this room and her religion and her children, and seeing them, feeling them, could not sit still and play the lover.

Richard, who should surely have taken her then, lay still upon the floor where she had left him and leant upon her empty chair. He stared at her, he listened to her swishing steps, but could do nothing else. Or so it seemed to him. He was hers irrevocably and she knew it. This moment would decide if she was also his, but fantastically he thought that he must leave her to herself in it. It seemed an obligation of honesty. Let her look down the years, alone and temperately, as he had done, measure their profit and loss and take the way she wanted, unconfused by his imploring.

He was not easy as he waited; he felt the wind of danger in the room, the breath of ghosts. But even so he must be passive —for his own sake, believing as he did that all his peace in future possession of her depended on her free will now.

Poor sentimentalist. He ought to have known that Caroline could never stand alone and temperately before her future years, to choose them. He ought to have known that by her sex and training and tradition she was bound to be either the woman that he did not know, creature of her Church and of her filial and maternal and herd instincts, a piece of her own setting indeed—or else a woman transfigured out of all that setting by passionate love. She could not judge alone between the two conditions.

Maybe therefore he had already lost her. Maybe when she rose from her chair and paced the room apart from him, their hope of love was killed. Only a very powerful magnet, only indeed the magnet of the past, the past which was her other self, could have drawn her from his arms in that first hour. And it was his own fault that it had done so. His mistake had been to ask desire to wait upon the long delights of tenderness. Had he but known it, a mortal sin would have secured him Caroline. The full oblivion of passion would have been a sea between her and her yesterdays that she could not easily have crossed, and would have made her his, at a greater price to herself than he in his deepest love could ever understand, but yet irrevocably his. But he was a stranger to mortal sin and to the Catholic mind, and looked upon Caroline not as a beautiful woman to be played for guilefully, but as love, that must give itself or not without a clamour.

"What am I to do?" she muttered as she passed him. "Oh, father, haven't I endured enough, haven't all these years been long enough for you?" And as she turned and came towards him again she wrung her hands.

"I'm not hard-hearted, I'm not, I say! It's he who's hard, I tell you, he and the rest of them! Oh, Richard, what are we to do?"

He sprang to her then.

"What is this torture, Caroline? I tell you love makes nothing of these things."

She peered at him, for the changeful firelight made their faces strange.

"That isn't true," she said in a tired voice.

"It is! It is!"

"A minute ago it was. But now——"

Her words half revealed his mistake to him, as her gesturing hands seemed to indicate all the presences that she, permitted by his folly, had raised and could not lay.

His arms went round her.

"Come, sweet," he murmured.

"Light the candles, Richard."

"We don't need light." His voice was heavy with dream, and she answered its tone before its words.

"It's too late," she said, without being aware of what she meant. "Light the candles, Richard."

He lighted six candles on the mantelpiece and Caroline, watching each little point of light awake and climb unsteadily to fullness, thought of the acolytes in the Jesuit Church at Mellick preparing the High Altar for Benediction.

Richard threw his taper on the fire and turned to her. In the new light his face seemed suddenly invincible to Caroline. She covered up her eyes.

"I wanted to love you," she cried. "I wanted to love you, and remember nothing else!"

"Then love me, as I love you and remember nothing else."

"I can't."

"A minute ago you could."

"A minute ago you were the only living thing in this wide world." Her voice pondered this statement as if bewildered by it while she made it.

"And now?"

"Ah, now! How did it happen, Richard? Oh, Richard, why did you let it happen?"

"My sweet, my dear——"

"All the people I've ever known in these twenty years—you've let them come between us! Oh, it's no use. I'm crushed by them, Richard. I'm owned by them. I think my heart is dead. My father—listen—he died the night I—the night—ah, well, he said to me, 'Be good, you silly bit of silk, you!' Oh, father, father! And it isn't only him. I have six children, Richard! And I'm forty-two! And poor Jim's hair is grey. I took him for better, for worse! Oh, isn't that terrible?—for better, for worse! Isn't it terrible how there's no getting away from that?"

Her voice had climbed high in this speech, but dropped again to hopelessness at the end of it. "You see, my darling, those twenty years are me. If only they had never been—ah, Richard!"

"If they had never been, perhaps I shouldn't have loved you, Caroline."

"That proves that they are me. I am those twenty years, and would be nothing without them. They can only die when I die, Richard."

"Love, when I kissed you they died."

He gathered her to his breast. His embrace was fierce now, his mouth imperious, but there was no answering urgency in her. The ghosts had chained her back in her own place where wives are faithful.

"You see, it was a dream we had," she said, "a kind of madness, Richard. Let me go."

"Go where?"

"Anywhere. Away from you. I'm going home to-morrow."

"You're not, Caroline. You're never leaving me again."

"I'm leaving you for ever."

"How can you dare then to pretend you love me?"

"I do love you. And I shall never forget to-day. That's something, anyhow," she added dreamily, as if talking to herself.

"Something?" he cried in anger.

"Ah, love, it's everything! It's all I've ever had and to the end of my days I'll thank you for it."

"Fine talk! And what about me?"

"You!" She stared at him, tears brimming from her eyes. "Ah, darling, I am old. Look at me!"

"You're all I want, Caroline."

She gave him a small, unhappy smile, then raised her hand, her emerald-bearing hand, and lightly touched his face.

"I'll—I'll remember you," she said, "but we've no choice. We never had." She turned away from him.

"Where are you going?"

"To bed."

"Love, give me one more hour! Only one! One half-hour, Caroline!"

She shook her head and made a little helpless gesture with her hand.

"Don't leave me like this, Caroline! You can't do this to me!"

She was by her bedroom door now and he went to her and took her by the wrists and coaxed her.

"You've had no dinner, my dear, foolish love."

"Neither have you."

"We'll drink champagne together, Caroline, and begin our love all over again."

"No one can do that," she said, as if she were very wise in love. Then she flung his hands from her and took on the stature and the voice of a fate.

"I'm old, I'm old!" she cried. "And I have sons as tall as men, as tall as you! I must go home to them!"

Richard threw back his head in anger.

"You have a husband, too? Are you going home to him?"

"To everything. There is no way to get rid of a whole life. I thought there was. Oh, love, I thought there was!"

A swish of silk, the sound of a door that opened and closed, and she was gone. She had been saved for the Considines, not by any Considine strength within herself but by the sentimental weakness of her lover.

§ 2

RICHARD sat in the winged chair and watched the fire die down, the candles gutter. He heard the clock of St. James's strike twelve, and then strike one.

At last a door opened and there were soft steps in the room.

"Ted, is that you?"

"Yes. Where is Caro?"

"Gone to bed."

"The management of this respectable hotel will be perplexed at us."

Richard did not seem to hear these words.

"May I light a lamp?" Eddy went on matter-of-factly.

"Don't."

Eddy came and leant his elbows on the back of the winged chair, staring at what was left of the fire. Two candles still flared wildly in the pallid, shapeless flames of their last agony. In their light Eddy's face seemed even more tired than Richard's, but the younger man did not move to look at him.

"I thought by staying out to make you happy," Eddy said.

He got no answer. He cupped his chin in his hands and

began to talk softly, as if unaware of the other's sadness and to ease some burden of his own.

"When we were young at home she was so beautiful that sometimes I couldn't bear to look at her, and sometimes I held my breath for fear I'd miss the least small flicker of her face. Ah, if I could show you what she was like at her first ball, in her first white evening gown!"

Richard stirred uneasily and there was silence for a moment.

"She did me a great harm," said Eddy. "She made it impossible for me to look at other women without measuring them against her, and that always made them seem absurd. Their faces never could bear scrutiny as hers could. Or if it seemed as if they could, that made me angry. She turned me against women, except when adventure with them could be cheap as cheap. And I only discovered what she had done when it was too late. Well, you know my life. I've told you much of it. I've never loved a woman except Caroline; and you love her, and I love her more perhaps than I love you, more even than I love myself. And these loves of ours are out of order and can come to no good."

One candle guttered out at last and then the other. But still Eddy leant on the back of the winged chair, and still Richard crouched unmoving within its darkness.

THE TENTH CHAPTER

JIM LANIGAN went to Mellick Station to meet the Dublin
train on a wet, cold evening.

The stationmaster bowed to him with respect as he walked
onto the platform, then gimletted his rigid back with curious
eyes. Old Mrs. Fahy and her son returned his bow, and wondered to each other what brought him to meet the Dublin train.
So did Dr. Ewers, who held the record for being the most
talkative man in Mellick. He would have tried a conversation
now with Jim were he not already conducting one with a more
important personage, John Aloysius Hennessy.

"That was Lanigan you bowed to?" said this austere, white-
bearded man, staring shortsightedly along the platform after
the figure of Caroline's husband.

"Yes, oh, yes, that was Lanigan all right—couldn't mistake
him—even in this light—know him anywhere. Oh yes, yes."

Dr. Ewers always talked like that. That was how he held
his record—on sheer words—because he never had anything
to say.

John Aloysius Hennessy went on peering after Lanigan.

"Ha!" he said.

Dr. Ewers itched to gossip and wondered if he dared. John
Aloysius Hennessy was a hard man to converse with. But the
doctor did just as well to spare his pains, for the old miller
knew everything that happened or was said to happen in the
town without any help of his.

The train came in.

Mrs. Fahy's daughter and son-in-law descended from a
second-class carriage. Dr. Ewer's talkative aunt descended

from another. Gerard Aloysius Hennessy, the miller's magnificent third son, sprang from the first-class coach. And from
the further end of it appeared Eddy Considine, who turned
and gave a helping hand to Mrs. Lanigan. As he did so, he
waved to Jim, a beautifully casual brother-in-law's wave. Then
he plunged back into the carriage. This meeting between husband and wife he could not help and would not witness.

Jim came to Caroline, smiling at her, his quiet lawyer's
smile.

They managed their meeting very well. Twenty years of
automatic association stood them in good stead. Caroline held
up her cheek and her husband's mouth touched it. Even in that
second neither felt the trembling of the other, so well were
they suppressing themselves under the skin and clothes of the
law by which they lived.

They passed down the platform with Eddy, bowing right
and left—to Mrs. Fahy—"How very well you're looking, Mrs.
Lanigan"—to Dr. Ewers—"Delighted to see you back,
Mrs. Lanigan, delighted, yes, yes, delighted—and so is my
aunt—but you don't remember my aunt, of course not—how
could you?"—to John Aloysius Hennessy, whose smile and
hat-flourish were very cordial, and to Gerard Aloysius, the
third son, who spoke with bright self-confidence—"Oh, Mrs.
Lanigan, how do you do?"

The Lanigans drove home through the rain with Eddy sitting opposite them in the closed carriage. Caroline stared at
the wet, quiet streets with the eyes of one who had been absent
from them many years. The two men talked, with an ease that
surprised them both, of the journey and the weather.

§ 2

IN HER bedroom Caroline stood before the long mirror and
removed her toque. A fire was burning and the room was
brightly lighted. The little blue lamp before Our Lady of Victories was full of oil and burning with a new wick. All her
bric-à-brac was as it had been, shining, dusted, and well-cared
for. The bed was made for two.

Caroline clutched her jewelled hands together and drew a
hissing breath.

"Oh, Richard, what have I done! Oh, Richard, Richard!"

There was a knock and Jim came in. He was carrying her dressing-case.

"I thought you might be wanting this."

She turned to acknowledge it. He had shut the door. He was staring at her.

"Thank you, Jim."

"I see they've brought you hot water. I expect you're hungry."

He looked wolfish in the· strong light, not a bit like a wounded bird. He kept on staring at her out of comfortless eyes. His staring made her afraid. She moved her hands in a little half-made gesture of entreaty, and as if he understood he shifted his stare from her to her reflection in the mirror. All that he could see there was the tall, clear line of her back, a raven's wing of hair, her little ear, a scrap of her white neck.

She moved to the dressing-table. She drew in her breath as if to speak. He looked attentive. but she had nothing to say after all.

"Well, I'll go down. Dinner whenever you're ready, my dear."

His hand was on the doorknob.

She wheeled on him. The frenzied swish of her silk apparel commanded him to pause. Her blue eyes swept him up and down, and after him swept over their bed, and Our Lady of Victories and the little blue lamp, and so swept back to him again—a wild and wheeling look, such as her face had never worn to him before—a look in which some crazy question shouted. "What are you all?" she was saying in that look to her husband and her furnishings—"what are you all? Are you the numb, dumb things of a dream that I feel you to be, things that I'm only remembering out of years ago, that I see behind glass, behind folds and folds of memory, things that aren't there at all, that I can't touch, that I never knew—is that what you are? Or are you me, a bit of me that can never die while I'm alive? Have I come home—am I real here, are you real, do you want me, do you know me? Are you going to come alive in a minute, are you going to break the glass and come up close to me—are you the real me? Are you going to shake me out of this place I'm caught in, this dull and speech-less place, this despair, this cage? Oh, are you going to master me—am I to grow stupid and warm and peaceful here—at last, at last—are you at peace?"

Her wheeling, snapping nerves, her hunting eyes said in-coherent things like that. Her lips said nothing.

She wrung her hands.

"Jim, oh, Jim!"

Her husband cleared his throat.

"My dear," he said and took a step towards her. Then he drew back as if pulled in spite of himself, drew back and left the room.

The wrung hands fell apart and Caroline's blue eyes moved without any frenzy now, but slowly and with indifference, over the solid objects that surrounded her. They came to rest before Our Lady of Victories. Friendly, smiling figure, set to watch twenty years ago over Caroline's bed, still watching, noncom-mittal; Mother of God, under whose shadow she had shed so many tears, of whom she had asked so many favours, great and little, whom she had thanked so often, coaxed so often; immaculate Mary, riding the little world, the winds of space against her skirts, her Son in her arms, her crown on her head, the silver emblem of her own heart slung on a silver chain about her neck—Comforter of the afflicted, Help of Christians, Queen of Angels—ah, she at least was home and memory and reality.

"I think I'll say a prayer," said Caroline.

She dropped into the old blue priedieu that took her knees kindly to its velvet hollow. She bent her head before the little lamp.

"I'll say a prayer."

She knelt a long time with her face in her hands.

"Richard, Richard, Richard," she prayed to Our Lady of Victories, "Oh, Richard, Richard, Richard, Richard!"

§ 3

ANTHONY came home on Thursday, two days after Caro-line. The very next Sunday all the family came out to River

Hill to eat roast lamb and rhubarb tart, and for the deeper purpose of behaving to Caroline as if she had not just given them
all the fright of their lives.

Ten years ago when the paint was new in River Hill they
had sat down twelve to their first lunch in Anthony's big
dining-room. Now Honest John was missing and Molly's
chair was Agnes's. But Reggie and Alice Mulqueen were of
the grown-up party and so was Millicent Considine. So were it
not for Denis they would have been thirteen, a state of affairs
which Sophia could not have faced, she said.

The party went beautifully. The three long windows were
open and sunlight wreathed itself about the Considines. The
year's first daffodils swayed as gaily from the epergne as if
Molly's long-closed eyes were still there to flatter them. The
cry of the river clamoured into the house, but the Considines
hardly heard it nowadays any more than they heard their own
jaws masticating. For years it had been crying to them; while
the last generation was passing and the next was being born,
while the silver plumes were spreading in Anthony's dark
head, while Sophia's neck was sagging, and Danny's paunch
was rising, and Tom was picking his careful way to parish
priesthood, while Reggie was learning to break maidens'
hearts, while whiskers thickened on Agnes's lips and chin, while
Denis planted cypresses and roses—in all that time the river
had not ceased to cry to River Hill. No wonder River Hill had
given up listening.

Everyone was very nice to Caroline—nice without ostenta-
tion, and with that strange tactfulness that often visited this
downright family.

She sat between Eddy and her lively nephew Reginald.

Anthony, from the head of the table, steered all the talk
with his quick drives of impudence; his wits chased after
everyone. He chivvied Joe for a tip for the Munster Plate
and warned Teresa that this second son of hers, Reggie, was
the Don Juan of the town. He made sly jokes about the Hennessys and caught a blush from Millicent; he invited Agnes to
seek the family's support for her wrath over the banished
Chinese temple; he contradicted Jim about Mr. Gladstone's
Land Bill, he swapped a proverb or two with Danny and
dropped alarming hints as to Eddy's London life; he mimicked

the Bishop for Tom's benefit; he winked several times at Denis and kept Sophia's glass unwisely full.

But his smile was flashed most often to Caroline and his best jokes seemed to ask for her especial laugh. So Denis thought at least, who observed him as no other did, and who was also watching his Aunt Caroline.

She managed well, gave Anthony smile for smile and every laugh he coaxed for, talked to Eddy too in soft asides and took what points there were in Reggie's pleasantries, met each pair of eyes as they were turned to her—each, that is, except two pairs that were nearly opposite: Denis's, full of anguished question, and her husband's that were comfortless. Only twice during the long meal did she seek escape with her glance, which sped then through the gap that Denis's smallness made in the family phalanx and rested on the sunlit, happy garden. Perhaps, hearing the cry of the river in those pauses that enclosed her, she saw again the winding Thames. But Ted's voice pulled her back each time—Ted's tender voice safeguarding her:

"Want to hear a good joke, Caro?" or "Caro, you've taken all the cream!"

Afterwards the fourteen poured out over the garden and paced and strode about, cigars and arguments and voices just as strong, it seemed, as on that first Sunday that they had discussed the house and view, and their possessiveness in it heartier than ever, though each of them was ten years nearer to relinquishment of all things.

When Caroline walked presently along the river-path, it was Tom who walked beside her. The family saw him with satisfaction as he escorted her gravely down the slope of the little birchwood.

What the two talked of, there is no guessing. No doubt the priest was very kind. Here by this water ten years ago Caroline had told Ted of her only love. Now she had two loves to boast of, but the chances are all the same that she let Tom do most of the talking.

Reggie played bits of Chopin in the drawing-room during tea, flippantly, as if he were making jokes to himself against the tide of talk that never paused for him. His mother sat and listened, her dark face turned in rapture on the loose, handsome face of this son, her especial darling. Denis hurried politely to and fro with dishes of toast and cups of tea. Uncle Jim had given him Tony's last letter to read. Tony was in the second eleven this year! Denis was eager to ply his aunts with food, so that then there might be a little peace for Tony's letter. Danny didn't notice that his son was playing the piano, so he wound up the musical box. But no one minded. Caroline sat at the tea-table with Agnes and heard the latest news of Mary and of Sister Attracta at St. Joseph's Convent. Joe boasted to Anthony of his plans for Victor's coming-of-age; Alice Mulqueen talked to her Cousin Millicent and both of them tried not to hear, and tried to hear, what Sophia was whispering to Tom about Gerard Hennessy. Eddy sat alone by the fire, half-listening to the lazy bits of Chopin.

One by one the carriages rolled up through the tunnel of the lime trees and gathered grotesquely together on the gravel sweep, until they blotted the west out of the windows. Chopin dropped away, and the tide of voices surged into the hall. The musical box had the drawing-room to itself.

The family broke apart, drove home. How beautifully the whole thing had passed off!

THE ELEVENTH CHAPTER

THE Summer of 1870 was eventful and alarming for the world. For the Considines it blossomed with warm, fulfilling peace. In June Charles Dickens died and Millicent's betrothal to Gerard Hennessy was announced. In July France and Prussia went to war and Anthony made a brilliant deal with North Sea ports to supply forage to the Prussian Army. In August guns growled over Paris, and Mr. Gladstone got his Irish Land Bill through. Victor Considine came of age that month and there was a brilliant dance in Finlay Square at which all the Hennessys attended. In September Sedan, Eugénie's flight, the Marseillaise—in September too, Millicent's marriage at St. Peter's with a hundred guests and three hundred wedding presents, bridesmaids and Mellick lace, rice, silver slippers and orange blossom, a honeymoon among the English Lakes. In October Pio Nono lost the temporal power of his old dynasty; in the same month Considine's half-yearly dividends were large enough to satisfy Joe. In November Anthony was elected mayor of Mellick. So the gold leaves fell to shroud a golden summer.

Golden for Denis as for the other Considines. Looking back to it from winter it seemed to him as if he had spent it all, without a pause, among the burning splendours of his garden.

How it flowered for him that year! From the last day of April when, trembling for pride, he had led Tony across the croquet lawn and down a flight of mossy steps to look at a long blaze of anemones, marvellously come to life as he had dreamt them, until he stood in October rain among dahlias and bright-tossing Michaelmas to gather his last, brave rose, the garden sang and shone and trumpeted to delight him.

§ 2

HIS fourteenth birthday, at the end of June, was a garden feast.

His brothers and sisters were home from school for it, and so were all the younger cousins, Mulqueens and Lanigans, and Finlay Square Considines. These, the eight River Hill children, stray cronies of theirs from other families, as well as Denis's odd assortment of school friends, Mickey Cogan, Dan O'Reilly, "Ratty" Madden, Jack Keogh, Wally Mullens, Mr. Devoy, and Father Dowson, made up a lively gathering. But the older cousins came too, and all the aunts and uncles called in to pay their respects.

No joke for Aunt Agnes—no wonder she was bad-tempered that day.

Tables under the elm trees, tables on the lower lawn, sun-blinds on the big red house, carriages driving up and driving away, new voices every second, presents for Denis, wrappings from presents scattered on the grass, all the best silver out, maids, with their caps askew, run off their feet, a mighty iced cake melting in the sun, two Spode cups broken in the first half-hour; Considines streaming from house to lawn, from lawn to house; strawberries mountained in silver dishes; children careering in hide-and-seek, children falling and cutting their knees, children playing croquet, children refusing to say "how-do-you-do?"; children eating cream-buns, children wetting their drawers, children quarrelling and turning somersaults; grown-ups everywhere in the thick of it, prohibiting, scolding, teasing, advising, adoring, contradicting; flowers to blind you, Denis's ridiculous unorthodox, far-stretching flower-beds, tulips, roses, lupins, poppies, larkspur, violas, parasols brighter than all these put together—boater hats and garden chairs, and a blinding glare flung up on it all from the river. The entire responsibility on one pair of shoulders too! Aunt Agnes could hardly have been expected to be in good humour.

Silvery-bearded Jehovah helped himself to strawberries and

was reminded of one of his own best jokes. He never forgot his own jokes. He told this one now, under the elm trees, to a group that had already heard it twenty times.

He had been walking with Anthony in the kitchen garden one autumn day and had found Denis busy with a gardener at the strawberry beds.

"New plants, he was bedding, he told us. 'Look, father,' says he, 'I'm putting St. Anthony of Padua here, and British Queen in the other side of the bed.' 'Indeed, my boy?' says I, and then—this'll amuse you, Jim"—he caught his brother-in-law's eye—"and then, 'If I know anything, Denis,' says I, 'that's a bit of matchmaking that'll please neither party!' Got that, Danny? St. Anthony of Padua! Ho, ho—there's my brother Tom walking off in a huff. Come back here, Tom, and have a glass of wine!"

He saw Denis far-off then—he had already been drinking long life to the boy in iced champagne.

"Hi, Denis!" He lifted his plate of strawberries. "Are these the result of St. Anthony and British Queen?" They were, it seemed.

"Well, well," said Joe, with a wink that was anyone's who wanted it, "it only shows you what the most unlikely unions will do!"

"That's right," said Danny, who was sometimes a thought too eager in his waggishness. "That's true for you. Isn't it, Millicent, my girl?"

An unlucky apostrophe.

"Tch, tch!" said Sophia in a fury. And the newly betrothed Gerard Hennessy hoped that he looked as annoyed by all this vulgarity as a young man should be who is accustomed to Anglo-Indian life. But he had also been drinking to Denis in iced champagne. It was a thirsty day.

§ 3

CROSSING the lawn, Anthony paused for a second near his excited eldest son.

"How's the birthday going, my son?"

Denis caught his breath. How to say "thank you" for a day

like this, for all the laughing, happy faces, for light and flowers and presents, for dear familiar things and people gathered together in the sun? Oh, kindly world! Oh, happy birthday! Oh, rapturous business of growing old!

"It's simply splendid, father!"

Eight-year-old Tess flung herself at Anthony's coat-tails.

"I won the race! Did you hear, father? I won the race!"

Tess was a terror for winning races. He caught her up on his arm.

"And where were your manners, miss—to go beating your visitors?"

"Aunt Caroline! Aunt Caroline!"

Denis flew down an alley of roses to a yellow gown and yellow parasol.

"Aunt Caroline! I was looking for you all over the place! Don't you want some flowers to wear? Special ones, Aunt Caroline?"

"Have you got special ones for me?"

"Come and I'll show you. Gloire de Dijon. Look!"

He pointed to a bush of golden flames.

"Oh, Aunt Caroline—with that gold dress of yours——"

He cut three young and perfect flowers.

"That'll be heaps, Denis."

"I think so. You can see them better then." He pulled a piece of bast from his pocket, which always bulged with gardener's odds and ends.

"Look! Look how different the three of them are from each other—just like people!"

Caroline took them in her hand.

"Smell them, Aunt Caroline!"

His voice coaxed and besought her. It had been doing so in every word he said. It always did that now, every time it spoke to her—had formed the habit of doing so since the day she cried under the yew tree. She heard its plea with terror always but quite distinctly. She loved it and wondered how she suffered it. It was the one voice in Mellick that seemed for ever now to be reassuring her; it was like the steadying voice of one who flings a rope to the drowning or a voice from a window entreating the lost to come in where there were fire and light.

Denis didn't know that he said these unsaid things to Aunt Caroline. He didn't know that she was an uneasiness now at the base of his heart, or that he would not be happy, even to-day, unless he could wheedle her into being happy. He didn't know that he was always subtly flattering her, or that his flatteries were hard for her to bear. He didn't notice at all his perpetual compulsion to console Aunt Caroline.

"Ah, Denis—they're lovely!"

She pinned them to her breast with a topaz brooch.

"You're all gold now—oh, lovely you look!"

He beamed on her.

"You're always reminding me of Uncle Eddy, Denis."

"Am I? Wasn't it lucky you wore this colour? Of course, I've lots of other roses"—he waved a princely hand—"but you look glorious with those ones!"

"Such a boy you are! Are you enjoying to-day?"

"Yes, yes. Aren't you?"

He waited in anxiety until she answered. His eyes searched hers.

She smiled as if the day were June for her too and a happy birthday.

"Well, you haven't given me any strawberries yet."

He took her hand.

"Come with me, Aunt Caroline. There are lots and lots."

§ 4

DENIS was talking to Mr. Devoy and Uncle Jim when two of the Lanigan boys, John and Tony, appeared far off in the lime tunnel of the avenue. They had come home from Downside the night before. Denis sped in their direction as if on wings. Martin Devoy looked puzzled. Jim laughed.

"He's seen my son Tony in the distance, I think. They're devoted to each other."

"Oh, of course, I'd forgotten. I believe I met Tony last summer."

The scholastic turned to look at the trio who were crossing the upper lawn.

All the Lanigan boys were tall and dark and ruddy, with

large, beautifully made heads and clean-cut features. In the distance John and Tony looked extraordinarily alike, except that the former, who was seventeen, was taller and more matured. A nearer view would show that he, like the eldest son, Peter, and like young Jimmy, had grey, noncommittal eyes and dimly forecast, like them, the legal aquilinity of their father. But Tony was the masculine version of his mother; virile, merry, full of life and lightness and muscle and fun —but Caroline for all that, with her blue eyes and radiant, childish smile, Caroline renewed and set free.

Denis seized plates of strawberries and rushed Tony away from all his relatives to sit on a distant bank in the sun.

"Tony, Tony—why are you so late?"

"You keep on growing, young Denis. I'm afraid you're as tall as me now!"

"Oh, but look at the shoulders you've got! Don't play cricket all the vac., for heaven's sake!"

"Well, don't you dig and weed all the vac., for heaven's sake!"

"What was your average? Uncle Jim told me you carried your bat against Marlborough!"

"Yes. What a crowd you've got here! I must go round and greet the family, you know."

"In a minute. Eat your strawberries first."

"The garden's a marvel, of course. Now don't tell me you planted every flower I see!"

"Pretty nearly. But don't look at it—it's hideous still— except for the flowers—you wait awhile! You wait five years at least before you look at this garden!"

"Oh, I brought you this, young fellow. Many happy returns!"

He thrust a parcel on Denis. It was *Great Expectations*.

"That's the one you haven't got, isn't it?"

"Yes. Oh, Tony—I was dying to have it!"

"It's one of his best." Tony was crazed on Dickens. "Awful that he's dead, isn't it?"

"Terrible. Don't know what you'll do for books to read."

"I don't know either."

Tony stared in front of him, his face full of honest mourning.

"Here, eat your strawberries!"

"Rather! Huge fellows too! You grew them, I suppose, you lunatic?"

§ 5

TOM thought Teresa was looking bothered about something.

" 'Tisn't Reggie you're worrying over, is it?" asked Caroline.

"It is then," said Teresa.

Reggie Mulqueen had gone to Dublin a few days ago to see a specialist and was coming home that evening. He had seemed queer and worried about himself for the past three weeks— ever since he came back from his holiday, in fact. Usually, the family smiled at Reggie's complaints. He had been a notorious "micher" from school with this and that symptom, when it was clear that there was nothing wrong with him but dislike of work. Joe never put a tooth in it when reassuring his mother:

"All that's wrong with that fellow is that he has too much to eat and too little to do."

When he went into Considine's Anthony diagnosed him.

"Oh, yes—an organic disease, and incurable. Laziness. He's so delicate that one hour's hard work would finish him."

But Teresa thought it was kidney trouble. The Mulqueen grandfather had died of that.

The family liked Reggie. He was large and loose, handsome in a coarse way, and had inherited some of his mother's horse sense. He was self-indulgent, an amusing, lazy gossip and something of a connoisseur of food and drink. A connoisseur of women too, maybe, in a small way, though Teresa knew nothing of that. Reggie's smoke-room stories would have been quite incomprehensible to his mother. He was good-natured and could have been a tolerable musician had he had even average desire to work. A commonplace and common young man, and not the most promising Mulqueen—but for some reason, probably because he possessed in a small measure the two gifts which most of all she herself would have coveted from life, the gifts of personal beauty and of music-making. he had grown up to be out of all her children the sun and centre of Teresa's heart, her darling, the light of her eyes, much dearer to her than her edifying eldest boy, Ignatius, who was now a Redemptorist priest, and much, much dearer than any of her daughters.

In May of this year he had begun to fuss about needing a holiday, and though Anthony was ready to swear that there was nothing whatever amiss with him, he let him go away for a month chiefly in order to humour Teresa, who had been so much depressed by Caroline's adventure. But the holiday seemed to have done more harm than good, for certainly Reggie was in a very jumpy and listless state when he returned from it.

"It's his kidneys," said Teresa now. "He isn't strong, that boy—they can say what they like."

"He's gone to a very good man anyhow," Tom reassured her. "You can put absolute faith in Dr. Clancy."

They were sitting under an elm tree watching a game of musical chairs that was being played out passionately—for prizes—on the lawn. The musical box was providing tunes, with Danny in charge of it, to turn it on and off. He was enjoying this important office and was very clever at catching the players off their guard.

"Tired of playing, Aggie?" said Caroline to the youngest Mulqueen girl who was leaning rather forlornly against a tree. Aggie was fifteen and self-conscious. She felt too large and plain for her own peace of mind, and she hated having to run about with small, light-footed children, under the critical eyes of her elders. She was temperamentally what her mother had been at her age. She got on Teresa's nerves.

"Yes, Aunt Caroline."

"You've no business moping round at your age!" said Teresa. "Run on and play, like a good child!"

Aggie's feet shuffled reluctantly.

"Why don't you do as your mother wishes, Aggie?" Tom asked her gently.

"Join in, can't you?"

"I'd hate to, mother."

"You'd hate to! For pity's sake will you tell me why you'd hate to play musical chairs? Run on at once, miss, and play! We want no 'notions' from a child of your age!"

Aggie ran on, red-faced and unwilling.

Teresa glared after her and forgot her as she glared.

"What time is it that Dublin train gets in?"

Jack Considine, brown and sturdy, lost his chair at that minute and came over to them.

"Hard lines, Jack, old man!" said Father Tom.

"Oh, Aunt Teresa, is Reggie coming out to-day?"

Teresa smiled at him.

"I'm sorry to say he isn't, Jack. He's coming home from Dublin to-night. I'll tell him you were asking for him."

"Do. Tell him to come out soon."

Norrie Lanigan won the musical chairs.

"I've won it! I've won it! Oh, where's my prize?"

Like a leaf in the wind she was, whirling round Danny and Agnes.

Caroline bent her head until her mouth touched Denis's roses.

"Richard!" an irrepressible voice was crying in her. "Oh, Richard, Richard!"

§ 6

WHILE Sophia sipped an afternoon glass of port, she gave Martin Devoy her reasons for this practice. He accepted them without a murmur. He was only just aware of the faded and richly dressed lady who took such pleasure in the discovery that he had been born in Rutland Street—not a stone's throw from Mountjoy Square, and quite as highly thought of in the old days—oh, yes, quite!

His eyes were on the hills beyond the river, hills where he had trudged so often and whose colours and lines he had learnt by heart in his three years in Mellick. With what an austere grace they took the summer day! He leant his spirit on them now; guiltily he drank their quietism. He was tired; he was discouraged. The last weeks of the teaching year had scarcely been endurable and now that they were over he felt himself even further off from ordination than he had been twelve months before. All the strain of prayer and humility seemed wasted. He was still unconquerably impatient; still fretful and proud, still antipathetic to his rector. He was sick of himself and his high dreams, tired of the subtle and measured rebukes of his superiors.

He was a failure—externally, at his work a failure. So he insisted to himself to-day, trying not to see his real trouble. The fact was that he was exaggerating his superficial depression and its causes, by way of escape from a deeper confusion. He had not got through the duties of the term as unsuccessfully as he pretended now, nor was his rector particularly displeased with him. The mischief lay deeper in Martin Devoy, deeper than his subtle superior had yet probed, deeper than he could allow himself to seek it.

"O God! What is it? What's coming over me, my God?" He leant forward in his garden chair and stared at the quiet hills.

Whatever the disturbance was that had lain this while back unexamined below his consciousness, it was rising more insistently to-day than ever before, rising coldly and creepily, like a heavy tide. "But what is it, what is it?" he asked himself, and would only admit that it was a sick heaviness, something made of fear and uneasiness and shame. But fear and uneasiness and shame for what cause?

He lay back again in his chair. Whatever it was, it seemed to be at its worst in this lovely, friendly garden. He had noticed that before.

". . . and so my husband says—you know Dr. Considine, of course?—that I *must drink* port—just one small glass of good port every afternoon. Have *you* ever been troubled with palpitations, Mr. Devoy?"

Martin Devoy didn't remind Dr. Considine's wife that she was then sipping her second small glass of good port for that afternoon.

His eyes still turned to the hills as if they held some boon for him. He wished he were among them, tramping up that valley that from here seemed like a deep blue pencil mark across the green and brown—up it and over the Gap of Storm to the western side, where the winds came clean from the Atlantic and only the call of plover or snipe would break the silence.

James Lanigan passed before him, deeply and surprisingly in conversation with Father Dowson.

". . . I doubt if he knows himself what his plebiscite

means. Meanwhile, he is extremely important to the Church, who can't do without her Eldest Daughter at this juncture . . ."

Ecclesiastical politics! How they sickened Martin Devoy! All this feeble, temporal, transparent plotting in the name of one who would neither scheme with men nor defend himself against their schemes!

"Have you seen Denis, sir?"

Jack Keogh and Wally Mullens stood before him, hot and sweaty, full of hilarity.

Martin Devoy had seen him.

"He's over there—look, Jack!—against those azalea bushes, with Cogan and Tony Lanigan!"

"Oh, yes, I see—thank you, sir."

They ran off, bowing uneasily first to Sophia.

"Who was that common-looking boy who spoke to you, Mr. Devoy? I've wondered more than once to-day how he got here."

"He's one of Denis's school friends. Jack Keogh."

"Ah, a veterinary surgeon's son. Of course, we all know that the Holy Name is a delightful school, delightful—all the same I shouldn't have thought that that boy—Keogh, you call him? —would be a suitable companion for Denis?"

"Social niceties aren't troubling Denis, Mrs. Considine. I doubt if they ever will."

"Dear me! What a dreadful thing to say of the child, Mr. Devoy! My own boys are at Beaumont, of course, which makes me perhaps a little over-particular. But I don't think one can be that. Do you? As my poor, dear father used to say . . ."

Jack Keogh and Wally Mullens had reached the azalea bushes and now the five were lolling on the grass.

Martin closed his eyes. This bright and overpeopled world of Denis's—he had no business in it—he had given it up, it wasn't his world. It tired him, bothered him, stirred this unnameable sickness in his heart! Ah, to be quit of it all, to be a monk in a cell, a humble lay brother, scrubbing stone floors for the good God!

"Those were the days for garden fêtes, Mr. Devoy—they have nothing like them in this part of the world—no elegance!

I wish you had known the Dublin that I knew, the Dublin of twenty years ago!"

Far up the lawn Martin could hear Anthony Considine's ringing laugh. Proud and self-confident it sounded, even from here. How Denis loved that man!

Martin turned towards where the proud laugh came from.

"He's in his element to-day," he reflected grudgingly. "Extraordinary the pride he takes in Denis—as if he were solely responsible for his every move and thought."

Anthony was talking to Mrs. Dominic Hennessy and to her eldest daughter Anna, a slender, uneasy-looking child. Mrs. Dominic, flowery, cool, and parasoled, seemed to enjoy the cool flattery of Anthony's eyes. Martin, watching them, let his thoughts run.

"He should have married again. That would have been kinder to his son in the end than the thing he's done. He has no right to load Denis with affection as he does—making chains round him, making himself adored beyond all reason, as Denis adores him! It would have been kinder to have been less kind. Denis won't want what that man wants for him, and is determined to have. Denis won't want the smug and ready-made world of the Considines, all mapped and tidy, with every opinion hall-marked and every action clear-cut in advance! Ah, Denis will want to find life for himself, out of the workings of his own mind, out of his own personality —in reaction from all shades of life. They can't trap Denis— except by loving him too much, by loving him too much.— O God, what's this to do with me?"

He looked away from Anthony and Mrs. Hennessy.

He wished he had gone to the hills and walked this crazy mood into subjection—to the quiet hills instead of this silly, old women's party. Came to please Denis? Well, Denis didn't want him. Denis had all these chattering relatives, Denis had his father, Denis had Tony Lanigan.

"If I could pray to You, my God—if I could pray and escape from all this noise!"

He stared down at the river and presently forgot himself as he appraised for the thousandth time the noble look it wore just here, and the glorious curve it took to the south for Mellick. It was running fast between its rocks; no doubt there was many a salmon leaping in it. Its cry was hushed to a mere breath like the voice of an old woman humming out of tune. But the summer air was full of sound, and quivering with light. And a happy discord floated out already from Mellick's chiming spires. To-morrow was the feast of SS. Peter and Paul. Martin thought how the confessional boxes would be murmurous soon with the tales of stragglers hurrying to catch their Easter duty by the heel. He smiled at the thought of all these laggards and wished he were at priest's work among them instead of mooning here.

He was looking at this scene with hunger, he perceived, as if he were never to see it again. That was strange. He would see it so many times again. So far as he knew, his work for another year at least would be in Mellick. He had had no warning of removal. The rector would not oppose such a move with any zeal, but so far he had not heard that it was mooted. Going away, unless for the final steps to ordination, had somehow never suggested itself to him. Now for the first time he stared at the idea with unwilling interest. And it occurred to him that maybe, if he gave acknowledgment to that which had been swirling under his mind all day, maybe he never would behold this scene again. Maybe this was farewell to Denis's garden.

Cautiously now he allowed himself to look on at least the surface of his dark trouble. Cautiously he told himself that his interest in this boy Denis had been misplaced, that the friendship he had given him was far more needed by a hundred boys less fortunate. As things were in this world, Denis had too much, love, beauty, wealth, intelligence, charm, an adoring father. In justice to others what need had he of unsought solicitude?

Martin called up, as sometimes on sleepless nights he did, a vision of the misery that moment being wrought upon the earth; brothels and tenements and hospitals he saw, prisons, morgues, and open graves, doss houses, padded cells, penitentiaries, leper colonies—all the dark work of man against himself. Deliberately then before this vision of pain he stood small, unimportant, well-protected Denis, stood him there and forced himself to smile at the juxtaposition. But even as he smiled the point of the contrast escaped him, and he hurried from it, back to accusation of himself.

"That notion you've bluffed yourself with that you were somehow necessary and helpful to him—what was that, admit it, but an inversion of the truth, that he was helpful and necessary to you? Wasn't he? Wasn't he? Would you have borne this drudging year one quarter as well without him, without his brightness and grace—and his hero-worship of you? And your notion of changing and influencing him, of giving him strength and self-assurance? Nonsense, egotism, an excuse to seek him out. His love for his father too? What do you know of it? Why should you dare to foresee danger in it for him? Oh, admit, admit that you were jealous of Anthony, always, from the beginning—admit that you're jealous now—this very minute and all this day! Why, you're jealous of Tony Lanigan—you know you are—jealous, jealous!"

Martin Devoy threw up the sponge.

Afraid that he might groan aloud, he covered his face with his hands. Then, forgetting that he was engaged in conversation with the wife of Dr. Considine, he rose and went striding down the lawns towards the quiet river.

§ 7

COUSIN ROSIE ambled up through the lime trees when the day was beginning to cool. A small child walked on either side of her, Charlie, aged seven, and Nora, aged five and a half. All three looked the worse for their walk. Charlie's nose needed wiping, Nora could hardly keep still for wanting to "go somewhere," and Rosie's varicose veins were hurting her. Charlie clutched a small parcel in his dirty paw. All three pairs of feet were white with dust.

Anthony hurried to them, shouting vociferous welcome. He had clean forgotten to ask them to the party.

"Rosie! You're a heroine! Two miles in this heat!"

" 'Twas only and I looking at the paper after dinner that I noticed the date! It's well I didn't faint! Sure, you'd have my life if I forgot his lordship's birthday!"

"Hallo, Charlie! And how's my friend Nora these times?"

He lifted the little girl onto his shoulder. The change of position was a relief to her. "It'd serve me right, Rosie, if you forgot us altogether—seeing the way we forgot you to-day. Your own fault though—you never seem to remind us of your existence these days. Come on to tea, you must be dead! Room in there for birthday cake, Nora?"

He poked the child in the pinafore. Her face became scarlet; she kicked him frenziedly.

"Put her down, Anthony. Run over there, Nora, to that servant that's going into the house. She'll show you the way!"

Nora flew as directed.

Anthony sat the dusty pilgrims in the shade and made a great fuss of them. Servants were sent flying for fresh tea.

"Here, Paddy, where's your brother, where's Denis? Go and find him—look sharp! Tell him his Cousin Rosie's here and that I'm inclined to think Charlie Barry has a fine present for him, what's more. But don't let on to Charlie that I said that!"

This sally and the wink that went with it gave Charlie Barry the giggles.

Teresa came across the lawn.

"Well, Rosie, I declare it's like seeing a white blackbird to lay an eye on you! And Charlie too! Growing into a big boy, isn't he? How's your leg keeping?"

"It's at me a bit now—but that's only the walk."

"You walked out? Well, what next? You must put it up now and rest—it's very bad to have a leg like that under you."

Rosie's bad leg was propped on a chair then with a cushion under it. Miss Wadding poured out her tea.

"Two lumps, Miss Wadding—and cream—oh, thank you."

"Like a drop of rum in it?" said Anthony.

"I would not indeed. What do you take me for?"

"Oh! For a bit of a fly-by-night, my dear—what you always were!"

She chuckled delightedly. Neither he nor she knew what he meant.

Nora came back, looking calm now, and escorted by Agnes.

"Say your grace first, Charlie, like a good boy. No, wipe your nose. Oh, I see—take mine."

Rosie handed a grubby lace handkerchief to her son.

Denis came running up, scarlet with confusion.

"Oh, Cousin Rosie—I'm glad to see you—oh, hello Nora, hello Charlie!"

"Happy birthday, Denis!" The two shabby little children beamed as they thrust their parcel at him.

It was a blue silk square ornamented with horseshoes in three colours. Denis's eyes shone as he shook it out and so did the eyes of the givers.

"It's simply beautiful! Isn't it, father? Oh, you are kind! Thank you a million times! It's a lovely present!"

"Well," said Rosie, "we thought as you're such a horsey character——"

Anthony looked on with gentle eyes.

This cousin of his, whom he remembered beautiful and rich and full of hope, was a seedy, fat drudge now with varicose veins. Her children had nothing and she had nothing but her love for a drunkard of a man. And she had spent five shillings at least and walked two miles in the sun out of sheer good nature to greet her kin who had forgotten her. He knew well enough too that it was all done with no faintest underthought of currying favour. Simply it was Denis's birthday.

He turned and walked a little way off.

Denis ran after him.

"Look, father—the lovely thing they brought me!" And then, in anguished tone: "Oh, father, I forgot them for the party! Oh, how hideous of me, father!"

"Ssh, my son. That's all right. I made a joke of it to Rosie. She didn't mind."

"But it isn't a joke! Father, I'm a pig! I'm a pig!"

There were tears in his remorseful eyes.

Anthony laughed at him gently.

"Run back and be nice to them. It's a lovely scarf. You'll look a masher in it, all right."

"You'd like some strawberries and cream wouldn't you, Nora?" said Aunt Agnes.

"Oh, Nora, why didn't you bring Willy?" said Denis.

"Ah, poor old Willy's legs wouldn't stretch to it, Denis. He's only four." Cousin Rosie laughed. "He roared when we came out without him."

"Oh! Will we send the trap for him now, Cousin Rosie?"

"You will not then, if you've any consideration for his mother. He'll be quite happy with Baby Tom and the little nurse-girl. It's an ease to me to be out of the place from the two of them. Such a pair of roarers you never knew!"

Cousin Rosie luxuriated under the tree.

"Could I take off my hat for a while, Agnes?"

"Anything you like, my dear," said Joe, coming up behind. "Anything you like. But I warn you there are three clerical gentlemen on the premises."

This had always been Rosie's dream of the good life—to sit under trees beside a large red house, to sit under trees and regard a summer scene, with one's feet up, and noise and talk going on all round, ladies and gentlemen dressed in the height of fashion passing to and fro; and port wine and strawberries and cream being for ever handed round by servants about whose conduct or wages one didn't have to trouble for a moment. It was the life that went on in novels, life at its zenith, a dream.

She sat and wondered at it now, with pleasure that was only faintly sad. Here, as it was going forward, it wasn't exactly what she dreamt, it wasn't quite perfection. Maybe it was the familiarity of the faces that moved in it that made her feel that; maybe it was the preponderance of children in the scene. For children aren't restful. Wherever they are, it may be necessary to desist at any moment from having one's feet up. There's no knowing when you'll have to run to a child, or slap it or get it a drink. And, of course, in the ideal scene, the sitter, the dreamer, did not have painful varicose veins. All these things made faint differences between the ideal and the real.

Caroline came and sat at the other side of the tea-table, between the two children.

"Ages since I've seen any of this family! How are you, Rosie?"

The Gloire de Dijon roses were drooping on Caroline's breast.

"Ah, Caroline, you're a sight for sore eyes this minute!"

Rosie's smile was generous with flattery.

"So are you," said Caroline. It was a family mannerism to

talk as if Rosie's good looks were a present-day fact and not a dimming legend.

"How's that husband of yours?" said Joe. "I hope he's minding the advice I gave him a month ago."

"I suppose I can guess the advice you gave him, and faith he isn't minding it."

"I saw him at Nenagh Races last week. Any luck?"

"No, then. But if Belle of Kilboy had only won the Visitors' Plate, sure he'd have brought off the finest thing you ever heard of in a double."

"I'll believe you," said Anthony. "Tom Barry's the most unlucky fellow that ever lost a race!"

"Ah, can't you leave him alone to-day, Mister Clever? Sure, if that double came off we were made, I tell you."

"I'd leave him alone with pleasure, Rosie, if he'd leave your money alone and gamble with his own, my dear!"

"Well, well—we're not managing too badly these times, thank God."

"Whatever your troubles are, Rosie, you conceal them well. Your cheeks are like a young girl's this minute," said Joe. "It's the likes of you that's ruining my profession."

"Had enough, Charlie?" Caroline beckoned to Jimmy, her youngest son.

"Jimmy, my pet, take Charlie and Nora down for a ride on the pony now—or p'raps they'd like to fish in that pond thing for a prize."

"Very well, mother."

"Ah, they're too small for Jimmy, Caroline: he couldn't be bothered. Wipe your mouth nicely, Nora, my pet."

The three children went off together in silence.

"Nora's going to be a beauty," said Caroline.

"I hope so, poor child," said Rosie. "Is that Peter I see over there, your eldest, Caroline?"

"Yes. Isn't he tall?"

"And the very image of Jim. They're all home now, I suppose?"

"Yes, he came down from the University ten days ago. The others got back last night. We're a rowdy house, I can tell you."

Her blue eyes searched the sunset.

"Where is he now?" she was thinking. "What is he doing, is he thinking of me? Is he comforted yet? Has he forgotten? Oh, Richard, where are you? Richard, am I going to be able to go on living?"

Cousin Rosie watched the sunset too.

"It's beautiful up here. I always loved nice surroundings," she was thinking. "I wonder will Tom be in at all to-night to his tea? He'll be shouting and blaspheming about the place if I'm not there. Well, there's no rest for the wicked. Anthony's a bit hard on him—I don't care what he says. It's easy for his lordship to talk, that was never short of a halfpenny, and had his own way from the cradle upwards. I don't know is there anything tasty in the house for the poor fellow's tea—he'll be tired out from the long drive. . . ."

§ 8

THE shade grew deeper under the elm trees. The party thinned. Groups of children were bundled into pony traps and driven away, protesting, weeping, clutching the afternoon's spoils; carriages assembled for the elders. Miss Wadding made weary efforts to collect Tess and Joey and Floss and Jimmy and march them up to bed. Father Tom departed on foot down the shadowy lime tunnel; he would read his office walking home, he said.

Father Dowson made to follow him.

"You coming, Devoy?" But Martin muttered some excuse. He felt he must walk home alone.

Aunt Agnes entreated Tess to set a good example to her little brothers and sisters by going up to bed obediently. Tess dashed like a squirrel into the birchwood.

Teresa was giving Cousin Rosie a lift home.

"It's taking me out of my way—I wouldn't mind any night but to-night—only Reggie'll be anxious, waiting to tell me his news, poor child."

Sophia was very sympathetic. Unfortunately, with Millicent and Gerard, there was no room in her carriage.

"It's an act of charity, anyway," Teresa soothed herself. "The creature's varicose veins are terrible."

Teresa was right in thinking that Reggie was anxious. He

was pacing the garden at Roseholm in a sweat of anxiety and shame. He could find no satisfactory formula in which to tell his mother what his illness was.

"Good-night, Denis," said Teresa. "We had a lovely day. Many happy returns of it to us all."

Caroline stood with one foot on the step of her carriage.

"Ah, Denis," said she, "my poor roses are dead!"

"Put them in water, Aunt Caroline. Anyway, I'll bring you more to-morrow."

"Have you your shawl, my dear?" asked Jim. "The dew is falling."

"Good-night, Denis; happy returns!"

Peter and John drove with their parents, but Tony chose to walk home with Cogan and Keogh and the rest. He was in no hurry.

Sophia's face was extremely flushed.

"Where have Millicent and Gerard gone? Really, Joe, you might have been more careful. It isn't right to let them wander off like this. Oh, I know Gerard's a perfect gentleman—still, I don't like it. . . ."

Anthony strode to the wood in pursuit of Tess.

"Come out of that at once, young lady!"

He stood waiting for her by the path that led down to the river. Gerard and Millicent were ascending it, framed in silvery trees with sky and river for back-cloth. They were walking virtuously uphill, side by side. Sophia need not have had a qualm. But Millicent's head was dreamily bent and there was something strong and submissive, some new dignity of love, in the lines of her. She appeared to Anthony in that minute as if she were ready for marriage and would find peace and grace in it. Perhaps it was some trick of light, some irony of the tender hour, but Anthony thought as he looked at the unsuspecting two that maybe a great wisdom had guided the young man's desire.

Miss Wadding's troupe were got off to bed at last.

§ 9

HARNESS and carriage wheels on the gravel.

"Good-bye, Millicent! Good-bye, Aunt Sophia!"

"Long life to you, Denis, my boy!" growled Jehovah.

The Joe Considines drove away.

"Mr. Devoy, a penny for your thoughts!"

Arms linked and shining in young beauty, Denis and Tony stood before Martin Devoy on the upper lawn.

"Why, you're not ill, are you?"

Denis searched his master's face with anxious eyes. It seemed suddenly old and was scarred in heavy lines.

"No, Denis, I'm not ill."

"Then let's all sit here for a while. Come over, you chaps."

Jack Keogh and Mickey and Wally Mullens and Ratty Madden came and flung themselves about the grass. Martin Devoy dropped into a garden chair.

"There's Venus coming up," said Tony.

Yes, there she was, sailing the green harbour of the evening.

Martin rested his troubled eyes on her and yielded to the spurious calm that her remote, imperturbable beauty can shed on the tormented heart. What a fuss! What drama! He had done no harm and would do none. He had only to begin again to work for God. He would empty his heart of all these earthly things and begin again to master himself. Surely that would be possible? Now that he knew the worst of himself, he could be watchful, now he could pray and be made strong. Ah, Venus, lovely star!

"It was hereabouts you had the anemones in April, wasn't it, Denis?"

"Yes, sir, below the steps. What put them into your head?"

"I don't know."

The blinding flowers had flashed into his mind, like a phrase of music, as he looked at the climbing star. Some shade in the sky had suggested them maybe, but he felt now that it was improbable that they would ever pass from among remembered things. He had told Denis one April day that they were supposed to be the lilies of the field that Christ had pointed out, and that on Mount Tabor they grew like buttercups.

"Will you grow them there next April?"

"I expect so, sir."

Martin Devoy was unaware that he was taking notes of Denis's garden as one might who was going into exile.

"Sing, Wally," said Mickey Cogan. "Give us a song."

Wally Mullens was the chief soloist of the Holy Name choir.

"Oh, no!" said he.

"Yes, do. Go on," said Jack Keogh.

"But I don't know anything properly, except holy things."

"What better could you sing than a holy thing, Wally?" said Aunt Agnes's voice from the gravel.

"Come on," said Tony, "give us a holy thing."

Wally, leaning against an elm tree, broke into a simple "Benedictus."

"Benedictus qui venit in nomine Domini . . ." Silver music, holy, unselfconscious, undefiled, a chalice lifted to the Lord, a monstrance raised in evening benediction.

While Martin Devoy listened to it he looked at Denis's dreaming profile, and saw at last what it was necessary for him to do.

"Benedictus qui venit . . ." Wally's innocent falsetto soared into the evening and then dropped shyly back to silence.

"Thank you," said Aunt Agnes's voice. "That was beautiful, Wally."

"Good old Wally!" said Denis.

"Who's coming home? Come on, you fellows!"

The troupe of them trailed away, fooling and laughing, over the grass and into the dark tunnel of the limes.

Martin Devoy stood up and followed them slowly. They broke into a race, and disappeared.

At the edge of the lime tunnel he met Denis, coming back alone.

"Going too, Mr. Devoy?"

"Yes. Good-night, Denis. And good-bye too, I think."

His voice was light.

"How, good-bye?"

"Well, they're changing me—I won't be there next term."

"Oh, but why?"

"Ask the Provincial of the Society—not me!"

"But it's hateful—oh, why must they do that? And why are you saying good-bye now anyway?"

"Well, I don't think I'll be seeing you again. May be off any day."

"Oh, but I'll see you again. I must. Come to tea to-morrow?"

"No, thanks. Truly. Good-bye, Denis."

He hadn't wanted to shake hands, so foolishly was he afraid of himself, but Denis's outstretched hand was not to be denied. It clung to Martin's angrily.

"You mustn't go."

"I must."

"I'll hate whoever comes instead of you."

"Oh, no, you won't. Good-bye."

Martin raced into the dark lime tunnel as if to catch up with the vanished boys. But hidden in it he slackened and took a breath of coolness from the trees. His own soft steps were the only sound that broke his deep retreat. Then Anthony's voice, far off outside it:

"Where are you, my son? It's dinner-time."

BOOK III

1874–1877

Denis

THE FIRST CHAPTER

DENIS celebrated his eighteenth birthday in Antwerp with Anthony. The latter, having a long business tour to make, had snatched his son from his last term's work at school, and borne him off to Europe. London, Paris, Bordeaux, Marseilles, Paris again, then Antwerp and Amsterdam and Haarlem, then Hamburg and Copenhagen, then Brussels, then Antwerp again, then London, then home. They were absent from Mellick for three months.

On a night of their homeward stay in London, Uncle Eddy asked Denis to dine with him, and, eyeing him reflectively as they settled down in the restaurant, wondered what the young man had made of his first, kaleidoscopic view of Europe.

Denis looked more a young man than a boy now, Uncle Eddy thought. He was tall, and of a meditative appearance, and he wore his clothes with a certain studied, untidy grace that amused Uncle Eddy. It was clear that he had not yet made up his mind between being a stupendous masher and a dreaming, heedless poet. The present compromise—expensive elegance donned with care and then forgotten—was agreeable.

§ 2

DENIS had two reputations to uphold in the family nowadays —that of being "extremely handsome"—indeed, ridiculously handsome for a boy, Aunt Agnes said—and of being a "terrible bookworm." He enjoyed both reputations and lived up to them.

He was an intelligent young man—arrogant at school, where

the wide-flung net of his general reading gave him a dangerous advantage even over some of his masters; at home alternately irritable and abstracted, inclined to wild fits of ill-humour against Aunt Agnes, casual with his brothers and sisters, radiantly happy when his cousin Tony was about—but always, whatever his mood for the rest of the world, gracious and humorous, his best and most alluring self, to his father. Some people said he was a prig, some that he was a fool, some that he was an insufferable young cock-o'-the-walk. He was laughed at for the poetic flop of his pale, fair hair, for the light buffs and greys of his clothes in an age of black broadcloth, for his habit of carrying learned tomes about with him—"for fear we wouldn't know he was clever, the marvel!"—for his trick of riding through the town with bunches of tulips or bunches of roses on his arm for his Aunt Caroline. Aunt Agnes said "he'd try the patience of an archangel"; Victor Considine said he was a milksop; Reggie Mulqueen called him "by a long shot the nicest youngster in the family." Tony Lanigan spent every day of his vacations with him—and Anthony, with an unnamed anxiety rising higher in his breast every passing year, pampered and indulged and more and more deeply loved him.

The outer Denis was therefore, during adolescence, a vain, moody, annoying, attractive young person. The inner Denis was preoccupied and lonely.

The slow changes of his body in these years exacted much of him. He had thought that the putting on of manliness would be an exalting process, but he found it instead both wearisome and frightening—a long-drawn business of sudden fevers and sudden languors, of nightmares and unlovely fantasies and bitter self-disgust and a helpless sense of sin. This last he resented angrily, finding it absurd that guilt should oppress him about a physical state which he could not help and did not enjoy. To relieve his sense of exasperation he talked a good deal, obscenely with Mickey Cogan and other school fellows, and more seriously, on a shy, impersonal note, with Tony, of physical and sensual matters. He read of them too, in Fielding and Sterne and Defoe and Rabelais, and Ovid and Suetonius. But he read enormously at this time in every kind of book, as much to escape as to seek the oppressions of sensuality—Milton and Pope and the Elizabethan playwrights, and Dr. Johnson's *Lives of the Poets* and Boswell's *Dr. Johnson,* and Renan's *Vie de Jésus,* and Stendhal and George Sand and Hazlitt's *Essays,* and Prescott's *Conquest of Mexico,* and Plato's *Symposium,* and Mark Twain and *Moby Dick* and the novels of Charles Reade. He bought new books lavishly, becoming acquainted with writers that had emerged in the last decade—bought *The Dream of Gerontius* and *Poems and Ballads,* and Fitzgerald's *Omar Khayyam,* and *Modern Love,* and *In Memoriam,* and *The Ring and the Book* and *The Angel in the House* and *Goblin Market,* and *Desperate Remedies.* He did not appreciate equally each one of these works, but he read the greater part of all of them.

Meantime he thought he saw a vocation rising out of the vigorous confusion of his brain. He would be a gardener, he told himself, an architect of gardens.

He had become enamoured of the history of gardening and saw, with mixed anger and delight, that the great art which in one form or another had decorated every civilisation of the world had fallen into an evil slovenliness in the nineteenth century. He would restore it, give it new formulas, new philosophic and æsthetic significances, emergent from the old, but fresh and living in their own expression. He would restore to their proper, functional grace the gardens, orchards, pleasaunces, the parks and squares and cemeteries and playing fields of the uglified modern world. In tremendous, secret moods of excitement he created this ambition, and pursued it through books and day-dreams.

In revolt against landscape gardening, he laughed with ferocity when he read of the far-spread works of William Kent and his followers in England. His youthful trend was all to formalism—an individual formalism, more monastic than mannered—hesitating, as Uncle Eddy noticed his style of dressing did, between two very different severities.

By the time he was eighteen he had crammed his father's library with books, most of which, whether strictly technical works, or volumes of history, travel, æsthetic criticism or philosophy, bore on the ambition that consumed him. His reading led him on many a wild-goose chase, but the further he explored garden history and the more it sidetracked and perplexed him, the more patient and concentrated did he become in studying it. Soon he began, for all the weight of details and fake theories that impeded him, to have a glimpse of what he was after; he began to see the history of gardens as a strand twisted through the intricate growth and rise and fall of man, to see that everywhere and in all times a garden was the outcome of a particular culture, an outward sign maybe of an inward grace, a shot at giving permanence to some essential quality of a mind, and through it, of a race and period. It was an issue of man's antagonism to Nature and his subjection to her, a complicated outcome of his need to make his soul not only in spite of her but through her. And as with excitement he followed the theme of a garden, from Spain and the Arabs to the Muslim's Garden of Paradise; through Japan and China to India's sacred water gardens, from Renaissance palaces and college quads back to cloistered lily gardens where only altar flowers might grow—with always the road of history leading, he noticed, to the spirit's heavenly hunting-ground—as he pursued these bewildering paths, he saw too, cloudily, uncertainly, but with immense desire, the gardens he would plant.

He was very humble before his visions but quite undaunted.

He piled up knowledge, accurate and inaccurate, of gardens in Assyria and Thebes and Egypt, in Greece and Rome, in Renaissance Italy and Moorish Spain, in England and Holland and Peru, in seventeenth-century France and eleventh-century Japan. The achievements of Montorsoti and Le Nôtre and Rikyu and the Chevalier Algardi were as full of stimulus for him as the lives of Dante and Goethe for a young poet. He told himself with proud pleasure that garden architecture as he ambitiously and thoroughly conceived it was no joke, that it implied not merely knowledge of architecture, horticulture, hydraulics, forestry, geology, and other exact sciences, but just as insistently an appreciation of all the liberal arts, a sense of history and period, a wide and adaptable taste, an understanding of how to blend feeling with restraint; it would require him to be trained in observation of men and manners, to be accurate in emotion, to be precise and sensitive in comprehending spiritual things. A tall order, but not an inch too tall for the rapt and excited Denis.

"I'll thank you not to glare at me, Denis. I mean something very different from those great cold things anyway. Pretty little steps, made of logs of wood. So that you wouldn't know they were there at all. They have the very thing I mean at Mrs. Tim Dooley's."

"Mrs. Tim Dooley is welcome to them," said Denis. "What's the reason for having steps at all if you don't know they're there? Look here, Aunt Agnes,"—he threw up his head in conceited fashion—"get this into your noddle—a flight of steps is a most beautiful thing—a lovely, plain, sensible, graceful thing—that needs no hiding whatever. Little logs of wood! I only hope Mrs. Tim Dooley doesn't trip on the top one and smash that remarkable nose of hers!"

"There is nothing in the least remarkable about Mrs. Tim Dooley's nose. You're a most impertinent boy, Denis!"

"Ah, you're always saying that—I'm sick of it. For heaven's sake don't say another word about rustic steps! Rustic! Rustic your grandmother!"

"Well, of course, if you're going to blaspheme——" Aunt Agnes's notions of blasphemy were her own.

Denis was satisfied that he had found his vocation. But he spoke of it to no one, not even to Tony, nor did he allow himself to consider the reason of this reticence. It was hidden in the mists of his great love for his father.

§ 3

In his second year of widowerhood, Anthony had considered the pros and cons of marrying again. The idea suggested itself in almost everything—in his sensual restlessness and the unaccustomed masculine loneliness of his bedroom, in the boredom of evenings spent alone with his sister Agnes, in the new cordiality towards him of the mothers of daughters, and in the angry expectancy of such a thing in his relatives' eyes. "You needn't put it past that fellow to insult poor Molly's children with some flibbertigibbet of a stepmother!"

Only Joe, a uxorious man, had looked sympathetically on a possible second marriage.

"Well, what's the poor fellow to do, if he doesn't marry?

Will you tell me that?" Jehovah asked with indecent mirth in mixed company.

Anthony himself had only one argument to set in the scale against re-marriage. That argument was Denis.

If he took a wife, he must somewhat lose touch with Denis, or at least bring a difficulty into their harmonious relationship. That in itself would be bad enough, but its effect would be more serious, for it would decide Denis's future. Anthony's intuitions had told him early in his preoccupation with his eldest son that that son was not gregarious by temperament or likely to be ruled by family feeling or stimulated by the traditions and excitements of commerce. These discoveries shocked him, but did not temper his headstrong, uneasy love. He weighed them against Denis's love for him, and as he watched the scales, reminded himself of the wish of Honest John that Denis John Mary should be third chairman of Considine's. He allowed himself to inflate this wish until it assumed the solemn proportions of a patriarch's command. But behind its false barrage he was well aware that it was his own ruthless and already anxiously dependent love that must bind his son to Mellick. So he threw it into the scales, with Denis's love for him, against the personality of the son. He abandoned marriage, and undertook so to companion and charm and indulge the child as to make himself indispensable, and make that familiar, traditional life that might have seemed a prison the only possible life because he was the centre of it. Even when it occurred to him that his own marriage, by dividing them and lessening their interdependent love, would remove the element of struggle between them and so set Denis free without pain to either of them, he dismissed it with impatience. His love for Denis was untouchable from without —he chose rather to have it on any terms, however difficult, than to seek even a pleasant way of lessening it.

It did not occur to him that his line of decision, which was not so much thoughtful as a series of half-veiled sensations and intuitions, was cruelly immoral, any more than it would have occurred to him to regard his absorbing passion for Denis as dangerous or unnatural.

So it came about that he did not take a second wife, and

accordingly kept Denis at home to be his companion when the younger boys were sent to boarding school. So it also came about that a beautiful woman of Amsterdam became more or less the permanent mistress of Anthony Considine, meeting him on his travels now not only in Holland, but in Paris and Hamburg and London. And if Joe or Eddy or Jim suspected anything of her existence, they made no comment in the hearing of the ladies of the family.

But if Anthony was as steeped in his dream of keeping Denis with him in Mellick all his life as Denis was in his of leaving it to wander over the world in search of his own knowledge for his own work, they were a match for each other in reticence. Anthony had sworn to himself, making a kind of bargain with the future, that he would use every weapon except that of the spoken wish or command to get Denis into Considine's. He would not even hint at his desire, he told himself, until the moment of decision came. And then his son must speak for himself and speak freely.

So, in Denis's last year at school, the silence that lay between father and son on the subject of the future was marked, and struck everyone in the family as strange and foreboding. But the issue seemed clear. Everyone knew Honest John's wish, and how overwhelmingly it had become Anthony's. And everyone thought it plain that Denis had no wish at all for anything so sensible as the Charles Street office.

So, with that which most concerned them still ignored, Denis and Anthony went abroad together.

§ 4

ONE night in Paris they were dining in the garden of a restaurant of the Champs Elysées. Very handsome and well contrasted they looked, and the eyes of many a woman rested kindly on them.

Denis was dreamy and tired. He had spent a day of exquisite excitement in the Little Trianon. His head was full of eighteenth-century graces; the crescent moon was up, and chestnut blossom rained softly here and there about him. He lifted his wine-glass with a smile to toast his father.

Anthony's eyes were very bright. He looked as if he too had had a happy day. Denis wondered with amusement where he'd spent it, and even as he wondered guessed what must have been. His glass halted halfway to his lips. He was conscious of faint shock, but as he looked with more attention at Anthony, lost this sensation. "He must be very attractive to women," he found himself thinking.

"Versailles again, I suppose?" said Anthony.

"Yes. Petit Trianon. The loveliest ghost of a place."

"You made more notes, I suppose?"

Anthony tapped the notebook lying near him on a chair.

Denis smiled. Suddenly his father took a breath of courage.

"But you can't want all that information to apply to our thirty acres?"

Denis measured his face with a grave look.

"No," he said.

Anthony saw his own cue. He had led up to it on an impulse of generosity. Here it was now. All he had to say in answer to that long, waiting glance was, "What is it, my son?" All he had to say was, "Go ahead, what are you going to do with it?"

He didn't say either. He turned away from Denis's expectant face. He murmured something about a theatre.

If he mustn't ask Denis to stay with him, no more could he give him the word that he might go. Surely that was only fair? Surely he might be allowed his full neutrality?

They stood up and went to their theatre. Anthony felt ashamed, but of what he hardly knew. He felt happy also.

§ 5

So, on their return to London, Uncle Eddy took his nephew to dine with him.

They settled in their chairs in the quiet, expensive, masculine place that Uncle Eddy had chosen.

Uncle Eddy was quite grey now, and very thin. His sunken blue eyes had caverns of shadow about them.

"Sherry, Denis? And then a good Heidsieck, I think. I hope you are hungry. What about hors d'œuvres and a salmon mayonnaise, then chicken breasts grilled—and then asparagus?"

So it was agreed. The waiters hummed about them.

"You've grown up. I don't like it, this business of playing uncle to a tall young man. I wish you hadn't grown up, you wretched boy."

"Do you feel very old nowadays, Uncle Eddy?"

"Oh, yes, go on. Ask me to what I attribute my extraordinarily long life!"

Laughing at the boy across the table, Eddy was also indulging himself with a taste of that sweet melancholy that was his foible. To have a son such as this, blue-eyed, dreaming, beautiful—ah, what a strange, precarious happiness! What a risk men took who had sons, but what a miser's store they laid up too against these winter-quiet fifties. Eddy gave himself a moment of envying Anthony, but the moment stretched against his will and took on unsought sincerity. He noticed that often nowadays. His sins were finding him out. His old, fastidious love of dropping the exquisite bitter into every sweet was taking a revenge. For nowadays there were moods when he could hardly see beauty for its blinding sadness, and when he slipped into his old trick of seeking melancholy, it sprang to take him by the heart.

He wrestled now against his stupid, sentimental pain. Life couldn't be everything to every man, and if Anthony had this son and the bright hopes of his manhood to look out at, well, he had known ranges of dream and passion unguessed by Anthony. He had had the life he chose, and it had been good and deep and full. He had a memory now for every hope of Anthony's. Ah, but memories, what are they?

"You like this wine, Denis?"

"Very much. You must know London awfully well."

"I've lived here since I was twenty-nine. Twenty-one years. Clever boy! He's guessed my age!"

"Have you liked living here?"

"I've liked living, and for people who do, London is the place. Now if, on the other hand, I had loved life, it wouldn't have mattered where I lived."

"You like splitting hairs too, don't you?"

"Lately, yes. An old man's hobby. But it's about you we should be talking."

"Why?"

"Because you're a young man with the world at your feet. What are you going to do with it?"

A veil, a very thin veil seemed to drop over Denis, between his eyes and Eddy's.

"I'm afraid this salmon is Scotch, Denis, a terrible insult to you and me. What are you going to do with the world, now it's yours?"

"How is it mine?"

"Well, your father's a rich man. You're young and—let's flatter you!—you're presentable. They tell me you have a brain. Surely you see what all those things can mean?"

"Grandfather said I was to go into Considine's, didn't he?"

"Who told you that?"

"Aunt Agnes."

"He made no rule about it. He was too wise a man to want to rule living people from the grave. He expressed a pious wish that Anthony's eldest son, Denis John Mary, should follow Anthony in the chairmanship. But that was only sentiment. He knew you very well and was fond of you. You were a pretty baby. But your father has three other sons. Grandfather was never a man to let sentiment stand in the way of common-sense."

Eddy didn't seem to notice how this talk was agitating Denis. He went on with it imperturbably:

"Why did you mention this wish of Grandfather's? Your father hasn't spoken to you about Considine's, has he?"

"No."

"I thought not. I've never heard him speak of you in connection with it."

Denis twisted about on his chair.

"No, thank you, I don't want any chicken."

"Truly? But Denis, they do this dish so well here?"

"I—I couldn't eat any more."

"Very good," said Eddy, "but I'm afraid you must watch me doing so."

Denis's eyes ranged rebelliously over the quiet restaurant. To judge by his moody face, it might have been a dungeon into which he had just been flung.

Eddy's next remark seemed like a change of subject.

"Tell me how you liked the continent of Europe," he said. Denis's face lightened as if a beam of sun had struck it.

"As much as that?" said Uncle Eddy.

"Oh, I saw almost nothing, I know, but——"

"How did you like Paris?"

"Well, funnily enough, in the first day or two it—it disappointed me."

"And then?"

Ah, how to explain? A tempest of words and emotions swept over Denis—for in Paris he knew that he had found himself—found his own ghost, his own projection of himself, his own future, his own unchained, unchallenged, unclaimed personality—waiting for him, as a dream-self waits for every imaginative egoist in Paris. He had felt then as if some nostalgia of years had gone from him, as if he were back in a place known a long time ago. He had hurried about the quiet streets as if identifying them out of things remembered. He had been fantastically, obliviously happy. He had felt at home. How explain that?

He moved his hands nervously.

"I—well, I felt at home there."

"Exactly," said Uncle Eddy with soft emphasis.

Silence fell.

"Oh," said Denis suddenly. "how could I get a look at Knole or Penshurst, do you know—or Sutton Place? Do I get a permit? And whom should I write to, Uncle Eddy? There's Stowe too, of course, and Blenheim and Chatsworth——"

"Good Lord! I'll find out for you." Eddy laid his knife and fork together with precision, leant an elbow on the table and looked straight at Denis.

"What are you chasing after in all these gardens and places? What are the notes about that you take at Hampton Court and Kew?"

"Why, nothing. You know I'm half-mad about the garden at home—and all gardens interest me a bit. It's a hobby—like splitting hairs."

"I see. Don't spill your wine. Uncles—those who aren't fathers anyway—are inclined to think that they have a special part to play, for which heaven particularly designed them. That's to say, I do. I had only one real Uncle myself—Uncle

Thady, now with God. Do you remember Uncle Thady? He took up his share of the earth's space, poor old chap, but I must say he had no views about himself as an uncle. It was Aunt Judy who had views in that family. I'm the Aunt Judy of this generation maybe. Anyhow, I have views—views about you, Denis."

Denis wouldn't smile at him. His heart was hard against the intruder.

"One of my views is that you have views about yourself, secret views. Another of my views is that you aren't a Considine at all, except by the narrowest accident. Some streak that ran thinly in your mother has come out with a vengeance in you. You don't look like a Considine. You lack some qualities that we have, and you have qualities of your own that are foreign to us, and that we distrust. No, no, listen to me!"

"Look here!"

"I won't look here, I tell you. Don't speak to the man at the wheel. You aren't a Considine—mind you, it's only my opinion—except about once in every two years, when a queer, dark, noncommittal look comes into your eyes, that reminds me of your grandfather of all people. And when I see that look, I wonder at my cocksure views. Still, Considine or not, you were born among us and you haven't escaped any more than the rest of us our terrible family affection, our cowardly inability to do without each other. Why, our whole strength is simply in our instinct to be large and populous and united. We cover all our secret misgivings by mass formation. In every crisis we steady ourselves by getting together and having a bit of a squabble, and if anyone of us ever sits apart for a while to ponder on the terrible mystery of being oneself—as Aunt Teresa does sometimes, I shouldn't wonder—we can always escape from that dark meditation in the nick of time by remembering that we aren't ourselves, really—we're Considines. Aunt Caroline even had to go back to that, miserable as her subjection makes her."

"Aunt Caroline?"

"Yes. How is she?"

"Well, you saw her at Christmas. She's getting grey now." Eddy winced.

"Yes. Once it seemed as if she couldn't wither." His eyes lost Denis awhile.

"But where was I?" he went on. "I won't be sidetracked. If you live among Considines, making their life and interest yours, you'll do so out of unconvinced affection—your personality will be wounded, exasperated, and insulted even, every week of the year—all the more so because the family feel this sort of hiatus between you and them and resent it—and resent too that they are fond of you in spite of it. Just as you will resent your affection for them and your sudden, unlawful sympathies with them."

"Uncle Eddy, I don't understand all this!"

"You do. You understand—already you are living among your uncles and cousins on a kind of compromise, you respect them only by compromise. The compromise that will be required of you in all your years in Mellick will be a long one. You have some idea growing in you, Denis, that would take you away from the Considine world and give you to the one that so much of you belongs to. It may be a foolish idea, it may be a complete misdirection of your talents—it may be your inevitable job. I don't care which or whether—if it's symphonies you want to compose or cathedrals you want to build or epics you want to write. It seems to me you're about as fit to do one as another at present—and it's a complete toss-up if you could ever attempt anything genuinely creative. What I'm trying to say is merely this—that success may or may not count in the end, and the right choosing of a career will count, I suppose, sooner or later—but the most important thing for you is not the end, but the means—not fame or success, but the kind of life you have while you're meditating on them. Mellick isn't your life—by which I don't mean to say, young man, that you're too talented for Mellick. Your father is a gifted man—maybe more gifted than you—but he's in his right spot. You won't be—if you stay in Mellick. That's why I say—whatever this crackbrained ambition is—wrong or right—pursue it. You have money. Even if Anthony cut you off with a shilling, your grandfather left you over two thousand pounds, and that sum has been well nursed for you meantime. There's no reason why you shouldn't take possession of that money to-morrow. Have a go at this ambition that's burning you!—simply because if you don't—drink your coffee, like a good boy—if you don't the hiatus will widen, the resentment will grow into a living sense of wrong, the family——"

"Oh, damn the family—they've nothing whatever to do with it!"

"Damn the family. I agree. I used them as a covering term really, for Anthony, your father. Anthony stands for all the best things that the Considines are. He is the head and centre, both in type and because of his position. He carries the family along; they are his concern and his pride and his life. He loves them, in our ridiculous way, simply because they are himself and he can't escape them. And it's only through him really that you love them or can understand them at all. Wait—let me have my peroration—I don't care how you resent it. You love your father quixotically, Denis, absurdly. That's your great danger. You love him for better, for worse, and all the rest of it. Well, you shouldn't. He shouldn't let you. But then he doesn't understand you. And you, I'm afraid, do understand him. That's a disadvantage. In fact, at your age, it's ridiculous. At your age, young man, you should be free and selfish and quite blind. You should be trampling over this and that and everything to reach yourself—you should tolerate no cramping, masterful, enduring love—oh, God!—and if I were to preach as long and as flowerily as my brother Tom you wouldn't even hear me if Anthony flicked his little finger! Come on, come out and look at a few chorus-girls!"

As Denis followed Eddy's erect and graceful figure out of the restaurant he thought that everyone in the room must hear the unhappy thumping of his heart.

Eddy argued with himself:

"I did it because I had to. Oh, I daresay I've done more harm than good—what business is it of mine? The thing's between the two of them, and I've only made him furious. What do I want him to do anyway—leave Anthony and forge ahead alone? Am I so sure then that that's right? Is all that he'd be leaving so little a thing, and the pursuit of oneself so great or so important? Who is happy anyway? And do I want him above all things to be happy? Oh, hell, does it matter what I want?"

§ 6

IN THE train going home to Mellick Denis pondered the debate
on his future that could not now be far ahead. "Well," he
told himself, "it's got to be faced."

No doubt he was grossly exaggerating his own importance.
No doubt his father would be amused at what he'd call a "rum
notion"—no doubt it would somehow be arranged. It must
be—that was all.

He looked across at Anthony—looked coldly, with resentment. How right Uncle Eddy had been! And how ridiculous
to make so much of denying one small wish to a man who
got his way in everything and was, in fact, outrageously
spoilt. Ridiculous!

And then Anthony turned and smiled at him, and Denis,
who was in a sulk and saw no reason at all for smiling, could
not even deny that eager face so small a thing as an answering
smile.

Ah! Here it was, the Vale of Honey. There northward,
tipped into the shrouding sky, were St. Phelim's mountains,
and away to the south, through Anthony's window, the outlines of Ardcolum and Knockbride. Soon, if he craned forward, the blue, low hills of Bearnagh would be visible and
maybe a silver flash of the long-winding river.

They stood together at the window as landmarks crowded
up to them.

The day was fair and soft. There had been rain and more
was coming on a warm west breeze. But now the sun was
filtering through from a sky of milky blueness. The light it
shed was temperate, just an aureole to rim the fields, enough
to bless and warm. Quietness everywhere, even in movement,
in the stirrings of overfed cows or the spiring of a lark, or
the somnambulant motion of a donkey cart. No hurry, no
hurry at all—it would be all the same in a hundred years.
Richness, unused, untroubled, oozed out of pastures and bogs;
colours were dim and subtle but beyond all counting. A
familiar exhalation of piety and sadness drifted up even to
the rushing train and filled and captured Denis.

Yes, there was Mellick at last, grey drift of roofs and smoke—there St. James's spire, still storming the quiet heaven, and there the river, far-off and voiceless, in a gap of Kildrumman wood.

Denis stared when Anthony pointed, first at one symbol, then at another. He let them take him for the moment. Afraid, unwilling, tired, he let them catch his heart. They were enemies, all these—they were tradition, conformity, conservatism—they were values that were not his, they were pride and funny pomp and the will of others—but they were home too, his history and his guardians. They were his enemies and he loved them. And the strongest enemy among them stood here beside him, singing and laughing, and he loved him above them all.

"Look, look, my son! There's River Hill—just the south corner—do you see that bit of red?"

THE SECOND CHAPTER

O N THE first Saturday that he was at home, Denis went
for a walk up the Gap of Storm with Tony.

Tony had only just got back to Mellick, for he had gone
to stay with an English school friend at the end of the Downside term. He was seven months older than Denis, and like him
had now finished with school. There was an immense amount
to be said between the two, and yet, for once in their long
friendship, they were nervous of each other.

The day was cloudy and fitful, but of a perfect temperature
for climbing hills.

"We used to come up here a lot with 'Flasher' Devoy. Do
you remember 'Flasher'?"

"Yes. Decent chap he seemed."

"Decentest master we ever had at Holy Name."

"Where is he now?"

"Don't know. He was moved very suddenly—and he never
wrote. They said he was at Belvedere for a bit. I expect he's
ordained now and gone abroad. He was wild to be off to the
farthest-away and most dangerous missions that could be
found. He was an awfully good chap; a bit of a saint really, in
his way."

They reached the top of the Gap and dropped over the other
side, where the wind was salty and where stony downs rolled
away for miles, with scarcely a tree on them, to meet the
Atlantic.

"Cricket all the time at Warrenders', I suppose?"

"Yes. Marvellous fun. They had their cricket week while
I was there."

"What else did you do?"

"Oh, danced at night, and had picnics and things. Warrender has swarms of sisters and cousins."

"Ah!"

In the last year or two Tony had developed an enviable talent with girls. Denis knew on the philanderer's own confession that he had already kissed a good many of them, though he would never disclose the exact number of these salutes or the names of the fortunate fair.

"Ah!" mimicked Tony, who was blushing, "you and your 'Ah!' You're like an old maid at a tea-party!"

He threw a clump of heather at Denis.

"Well," said that young man imperturbably, "did you like any of them?"

"Yes," was the slow answer. "I liked one of them. Oh, for God's sake!" He jumped up.—"I'll beat you to that forked bit of rock."

But it was Denis who beat him to the forked bit of rock.

Funny chap, Tony. Seemed to have something on his mind to-day. Couldn't have proposed, surely, to Warrender's sister or cousin or whatever she was?

Denis stood to consider this. Could Tony actually be engaged this minute, or wanting to be? Heaven knew, he was good-looking enough for any girl in the world to say "yes" to him!

So he was. He had grown tall and deep-chested without losing a glint of his bright charm. His cheeks were ruddy and his hair curled thick and childishly. His blue eyes were full of generosity and fire. It would indeed go hard with all the girls that he'd make love to.

Denis wondered, unable to hold back the darkness of his own anxiety that the thought poured over him, what Tony had decided to be. Two or three years ago they used to talk very much of their careers, but Denis, though full of wild and far-flung suggestions, had never ventured to uncover even a corner of the real idea that was shaping in him. He had often wondered if Tony too was holding something back. But lately, by that freemasonry that was between them, they never said to each other, "What are you going to be?"

One day in the winter Anthony had said to Jim in Denis's presence:

"What are your ideas for that fellow Tony?"

And Jim answered that he was waiting for Tony to speak his mind.

"Well," said Anthony, "I'd like him in Considine's if that seems to suit his lordship when the time comes."

Denis noticed a quick light of pleasure in Uncle Jim's face.

"That would be entirely satisfactory to me, Anthony," he had said in his stiff way.

It had occurred to Denis that this idea of going into Considine's would probably appeal to Tony. Even so he had not mentioned it to him—he hardly knew why. But in moments afterwards when some premonition stirred that he refused to listen to he would hear a voice—a consoling, placating voice that said:

"If Tony were there it would be easier. If you had Tony with you—if Tony were there . . ."

Perhaps Tony would say something to-day. Denis could not ask him a direct question, because in return for its answer he would have to be prepared to expose his own intention. And just as he couldn't reveal it to Uncle Eddy, when so hard-driven, so neither could he tell it even to Tony until Anthony knew it first. That was a fetish with him now.

They tramped ten miles along the ridges of the hills; they talked and sang and teased each other; they were hardly quiet for twenty consecutive seconds. But when they turned their faces towards Mellick again in the sunset, neither had said anything of what was filling his mind.

As they dropped back at dusk onto the sheltered east side of the Gap, the clouds that had been hesitating all day came together with a rush and broke into teaming cataracts. Denis and Tony were soaked and blinded. They lost their path and trudged about uncertainly. Their boots grew heavy with water. They were cold. They began to long for great cups of stewed tea.

"Speak of an angel," said Tony, and there, sure enough, straight in their way, was a thatched cabin with a light in it.

"God save all here," said they, and the old woman welcomed them.

They sat on straw-bottomed chairs before the fire of turf and watched the big black kettle swaying from its chain. They hung their coats and boots to dry. They listened to the ticking clock and the rain spitting down on the flames, and the broken voice of the old woman. They drank great cups of stewed tea. They ate eggs and thick slices from a hot new soda loaf. They turned to the fire again to toast their toes.

The old woman went cackling off through the easing storm "to get the pig home out of that from the bog field." They heard her calling and praying as she crossed the yard.

Denis took the cat on his lap and scratched it behind its ears.

"I never heard a clock tick so loud," he said. Tick, tock, tick, tock, it seemed to fill the lonely world.

"Your coat'll never dry that way, Tony. Spread it out more."

Tony spread it out.

"The rain is over now, I think."

Tick, tock.

"Denis." Tony's voice rang queerly. Denis's heart gave a sickening leap.

"Yes?"

"Denis, oh, Denis!"

"Tell me, can't you?"

"Why, it's nothing terrible." Tick, tock. "I don't know why I'm going on like this. It's—it's only that I'm going to be a monk."

Tick, tock.

"A monk?"

"Yes." Tick, tock.

"A Benedictine?"

"Well, a kind of one. A Cistercian—at Mount Melleray."

A plover cried above the chimney shaft.

"Mount Melleray. A kind of Trappists, aren't they?"

"Yes."

"You can't mean it! You can't, Tony!"

"I do. I'm going to do it."

"But why?"

"It seems a thing worth doing—the hardest thing. Don't ask me to explain."

All the girls that Tony had kissed were trooping past

Denis, a lovely, bright procession, muslin and flowers and little lace handkerchiefs—Warrender's sister or cousin, or whatever she was, at the head of the long file.

"Do you remember, Denis, we saw Mount Melleray last summer, when I played in that match at Waterford? Up there on the hills behind the pine trees."

"But why? Tell me why. Couldn't you be any other sort of priest?"

"I could. But I'd like this best. It's the hardest thing I could find to do."

The plover was crying still, quite near the house.

"Uncle Jim?"

"Oh—father. I don't know how to tell him."

"He won't let you do it."

"No one can stop me. I'd do anything I could for father—but this—this I must do, Denis."

"I can't see why!"

"If you were in me you'd see. I want to get out of mischief. I want to do hard work, chop down trees and dig potatoes and—and pray. I—I thought you'd understand a bit better."

Denis stood up and walked about the kitchen. He thought that to move might ease the sick, hollow feeling that he had.

"In a way, I do. But it isn't you who should go, Tony. There's no need for you to run away from things. Oh, God! You're just the very one who should stay in the world—and do you know why?" He wheeled on his cousin excitedly. "Because you have the courage to give it up! That's why! It's people like me, Tony—people like me who should run away and hide on the tops of mountains! Oh, Tony, don't go! What mischief could you do, you silly ass?"

"I'm the best judge of that."

A sod of turf fell over from the fire and scattered a dust of sparks. Denis watched them go out one by one on the gray flagstone. Tony wouldn't be there now, Tony wouldn't be going into Considine's . . . Tony was going away, as far as if to death.

"It's preposterous! It's—it's simply crazy."

"But you can't say that? If you're a Catholic, you can't say that! Don't you believe some way or other in the soul, Denis?"

Denis laughed angrily.

"Whether I do or not, it seems to assert itself."

"But you go to Mass."

"Yes."

Denis stared into the fire. He went to Mass. That was true, but nevertheless his church had gradually become to him no more than a set of symbols for the unexplainable, a fantastic and half-satisfying dramatisation of an unquiet legend in the heart. He went to Mass because his sensuous imagination found rest there, because something in his blood responded to the ancient prayers and mysteries while his mind remained detached from them, and because he could not insult in his own people an ancient necessity which he understood. He went to Mass, not because he believed in it, but because he believed in the impenetrable mystery of life and felt that mystery heightened and enlarged in his own breast by such phrases as *"Quoniam tu Solus sanctus, tu solus altissimus"*—*"benedictus qui venit in nomine Domini"*—*"sanctus, sanctus, sanctus"*—*"Agnus Dei, qui tollis peccata mundi . . ."* He could not think why it satisfied him to repeat such phrases to the unknown, the impersonal, the unknowable, for he knew that his only intellectual belief was in man's powerlessness to explain life and death.

He stared into the fire.

"I—I thought you loved the world, Tony."

"I do. Too much. If I were a genius of some kind, or else a complete fool—I'd love the world. A genius can do as he likes with all the rules and instincts. And a complete fool must just obey them. Either way would be fine. But I'm neither one thing nor the other. I'd be an excellent professional man or business man—and a good cricketer. I'd be beautifully mediocre—just like my poor, intelligent, unhappy father! But I couldn't stand it, I tell you! I couldn't last! I'd have to play old Harry with it all—and I'd have no excuse for doing that —no justification. But I can't do things by halves—and that's all I'm fit for—in the world. So I'm giving it up. I'm going to boss myself, Denis—do you hear? I'm going to thrash this damned restlessness into subjection—and get to understand— understand——"

"Understand what?"

"Well, God, I suppose."

"But what sort of God do you believe in?"

"I don't know."

"You see! What'll a master of novices say to that answer?"

"I don't know. Does it matter to him?"

"He'll say it does."

"Well, obedience is part of the process. I'll work it out."

Tick, tock. A cavernous, lonely sound, filling the world.

Tony bent forward suddenly and covered his face with his hands. "Ah, Denis, Denis!"

But Denis was huddled in desolation.

". . . He won't be there. . . ." Tick, tock. ". . . He won't be there. . . ." Tick, tock. ". . . Up there on the hill behind the pine trees. . . ." Tick, tock. ". . . Warrender's sister, poor Warrender's sister. He won't be there. . . ." Tick, tock.

"No, Puss, get down."

The old woman was cackling and praying in the yard; the pig was grunting.

"I'm not mad, Denis. Honestly, I'm not. But Melleray's tormented me ever since I saw it. I'd give a lot to stay with you——"

"Oh, stop it, Tony, please!"

"Here, are those things dry yet?"

They dressed. They put a handful of silver on the table. They lifted the latch and went out from the little room and the ticking clock.

The rain was over, the moon shone on their path. During the nine miles home they did not speak nine sentences; Denis could find no words at all with which to bridge his lonely, tender, useless thoughts of Tony.

§ 2

NEXT day, the uncles and aunts lunched at River Hill, to welcome the travellers home.

Denis sat towards Aunt Agnes's end of the table, next to Aunt Teresa. Aunt Teresa was ageing. Her hair would never turn grey, but her face had hard lines running down it now, and she had a double chin. She often went into deep fits of absent-mindedness.

"And how is Reggie keeping, Teresa?" Agnes asked her.

Four years ago Reggie had spent nine months in a nursing home in England, having treatment for what Agnes understood was kidney trouble. As she knew the kidneys to be an indelicate part of the body, she never asked for detailed information, but she guessed that Reggie must have been very ill, because every now and then since he'd come back he had to go away for another longish spell of treatment.

"He's very well indeed, thank you, Agnes. Won't need to go away from us at all this year, thank God."

"Ah, that's good," said Father Tom with kind eyes on Teresa.

It was an excellent lunch, and everyone was pleased with the presents that had been brought home to them from the Continent.

"Oh, Denis, I didn't know there were such pretty fans in the world!" said Aunt Caroline.

Over dessert, the clatter was lulled in the dining-room. It was a warm day and Anthony's Moselle had flowed liberally.

Father Tom leant towards Denis across the table.

"I suppose by now you've learnt all that the Jesuits have to teach you, young man?" he said with gentle irony.

The indolent relatives bent to listen to this bit of dialogue.

"And now your father has shown you life. A regular man of the world, I suppose we must call you. What's the next move?"

"How do you mean, Uncle?" said Denis.

"Why, you're over eighteen. What are you going to be?"

Anthony was sitting at the end of the table, a good way from Denis and Father Tom. But like everyone else he was listening to their talk. Denis had twisted in his chair in order to face the priest, so that his back was to Anthony, but he could see his father and the whole family group in the console mirror at the end of the room. He could see them brightly and clearly reflected, as they sat in the revealing sun.

When the priest put his question, "What are you going to be?" the silence that had been indolent round him was suddenly a purposeful, deliberate hush. Everyone was interested in

the question—eager for the reply. There had been specula-
tion about Denis's future. Anthony's silence on the subject
had annoyed and mystified his brothers and sisters. Obviously
it was Denis's duty to fulfil his grandfather's wish and enter
Considine's; still more obviously it was the darling hope of
Anthony's heart to have him do so. But Denis was queer. There
was no telling what he'd be up to and the way he was spoilt,
too—treated like a young prince, you might say! Oh, you
might be sure he'd give trouble. You might be sure poor
Anthony was going to get his punishment now for the way he
had brought Denis up.

"What are you going to be?"

It was almost a certainty that the answer would be against
all Anthony's wishes. And if it was—what about their own
father's wish, they wanted to know? Why was that to be
trampled on by a slip of a boy? Excitement hung on the next
second, a family scene, and maybe a hurt to this cocksure,
invulnerable Anthony. Tom, Teresa, Agnes, Joe, Sophia, Jim
—they all kept very still.

Denis hadn't expected this public opening of the most difficult of all subjects. Neither had Anthony.

They did not look at each other now. Anthony kept his chin
in his hand just as it had been when Tom began to speak, and
stared at his own wineglass. Denis looked past Father Tom to
the reflection in the console mirror. He looked at his father
there.

He knew exactly then what Anthony was saying to him in
the crowded stillness of the second. He was saying, "Do what
you like, my son—answer what you like. You're free, you're
absolutely free." He saw the self-control that was keeping his
father statuesque—but he saw beyond it, too, to the appeal
that he was trying to hide under it. He saw almost the words
of the prayer that Anthony was making and he knew why he
wouldn't lift his eyes. Denis would see panic in them—it
would be unfair.

But Denis saw this panic, without meeting Anthony's eyes,
saw clearly at last that he was stronger than his father and
could do as he willed with him, saw with a leap of his senses
that the world was his to ask for now, that what he said in
the next second would stand, that because the antagonistic

world of relatives was ready to attack him, his father would defend and uphold—scatter all his own desires to champion him and set him free. He saw that Anthony's love was helpless, must bear whatever he chose to set on it. Ah, God! The air of Paris blew divinely over Denis, and Uncle Eddy's words came trembling through his brain—"if it's symphonies you want to compose, or cathedrals you want to build or epics you want to write . . ." Ah, he was free! He had only to say the word, after all. How simple it was proving, this decision he had dreaded! He had only to say the word and that man over there, that dark-haired man in the mirror, bent so intently above his glass of wine, would listen and consent— because he must, because he loved him too much even to raise his head and watch his own brief now. He was free! He went on staring at the dark, motionless man in the mirror. So he would sit, motionless, when he heard what was about to be said. So he would sit often in the future, when there was no one here to notice his sad immobility. Denis stared, and the divine air of Paris subsided, the words of Uncle Eddy died away. Oh, what was this power his father had, a power so great that he didn't even trouble to use it? Denis smiled towards the unmoving figure in the glass and then he smiled at Father Tom.

"But I'm going into Considine's, naturally."

"Indeed? I'm glad to hear that."

The hush was broken. The exquisite family moment was safely past. Anthony had got his wish, as usual.

Denis turned in his chair and looked at his real father, no motionless reflection now, but a living man with tear-bright eyes. They lifted their glasses gravely to each other.

The wine burnt Denis's throat. He felt as if on fire inside. Had it meant so much, then, his staying at home, that even Anthony, his father, so forthright, couldn't raise his eyes when the moment came and ask for it? Had it meant so much? Denis shuddered. What was this love he was given that was even more pitiable and dependent than the love he gave? His power had been revealed to him, but revealed so that he couldn't use it.

"Oh, yes, Aunt Teresa—oh, yes, I always meant to."

He pushed his chair back, stood up, and smiled at his father, the slow, casual smile of a good actor. Then he walked across the dining-room and vaulted out of the window.

"I'm going into Considine's. Of course—oh, yes, Aunt Teresa. Tony won't be there—ah! up there on the hill behind the pine trees—Tony won't be there—oh, father, father . . ."

As he cleared the window he heard Uncle Danny telling the table that what's bred in the bone comes out in the flesh.

THE THIRD CHAPTER

Tony Lanigan went to Mount Melleray in September. A week after his departure Denis entered Considine's, as a modestly paid junior clerk. On the day of this event Anthony opened a banking account for his son and gave him control of his inheritance from Honest John, which, soundly invested, had now more than doubled itself. It was with feelings more exasperated than placated that Denis assumed the new sensation of being a comparatively rich young man.

For his first six months he worked in the receiving office under Flannery and was too much confused and too anxious to be dutiful to know what he thought of his occupation. But even then, as he filled in dockets, counted up loads, and shook hands with farmers, there were black minutes of misgiving. The next six months had been relieved by the excellent fun of observing Uncle Danny qua omniscient business man. Arguments with railway clerks, the checking of carters' books, and the writing of Uncle Danny's curiously worded letters in a hand that would reproduce as nearly as might be Uncle Danny's idea of copperplate—all these were nearly made worth-while by the sport of watching the flustered man tie knots in every transaction and look ponderous and cryptic about matters that were as clear to the chuckling novice as the soapy shine on his uncle's face. It certainly wasn't Uncle Danny's fault that the bartering of hay and straw remained a comparatively simple thing.

In those days Denis used to stroll up to the chairman's room when his own work was done and wait for his father, lounging on the leather window-seat near the desk until Anthony was ready to walk home with him.

This habit of his son's was precious to Anthony, and no matter how busy he was, or what important personage was closeted with him, he would call "Come in!" almost impatiently to the particular treble knock, and then beam at Denis through the smoky lamplight.

"Mind waiting over there, my son?"

And Denis would wait on the leather seat, as he had sometimes waited in his schooldays.

Merchants, bargainers, petitioners, whoever they might be who sat with Anthony at these times, were flurried maybe or put off their argument by the sense of a shadowy third behind them. Anthony knew this, but he didn't care. Not for anything that a customer could bring him would he have checked the filial friendliness of his son, or made him think that he could ever be unwelcome.

The customers needn't have troubled. The window of Anthony's office gave on the dock-road and the river, and at this hour of evening, even in winter darkness when the west was emptied long ago of its brief splendour, when the hills and woods across the water were only an added gloom and there was no glimpse at all of Aunt Teresa's garden, even then Denis found uneasy dreams on the leather seat. The river would be loud and full perhaps and cars would be jingling to and fro on Wellington bridge. There would be a ship getting under way from Vereker's or Hennessy's or Considine's, or perhaps a ship casting anchor. Dockmen were trudging lazily home as a rule, and a woman in a shawl might be singing outside O'Malley's pub. Voices would shout from riggings in unknown languages; there would be lights on the buoys; downstream the old dredger might be coughing. There might even be a fight on the water-steps, or a cheer and a siren as a ship got under way. Denis watched it all without stirring. Away at the ends of the roads those clumsy ships were taking lay the world he had wanted, away where they went were the knowledge he lacked and the life and the hopes and the freedom.

Anthony had sometimes to call his name twice before he turned to go home with him.

§ 2

DENIS did his work honestly and put his brains into it. The result was that his immediate superiors reported favourably of him to headquarters. A further result was that Anthony, talking over general business questions with him, found the fruits of observation in his comments and thought them lively and to the point.

Denis knew therefore that he was giving satisfaction and that was not unpleasant. He was finding interest too in the rough life of an office and the company of all sorts of men. As Aunt Sophia had spotted long ago, there was an odd attraction for him in coarse and lively fellows, of whom he found plenty on Considine's office stools.

The reason why he liked rough diamonds was probably simple enough. He answered the flicker of originality wherever he caught it. He had found it in vulgar Jack Keogh; he found it and liked it in his coarse-grained Cousin Reggie.

Tony had been dear to him chiefly because of that streak of oddity that had driven him at last into the Trappist silence, and his father attracted him so much probably because, though normal, he was normal brilliantly and to the point of eccentricity. Now in the office he found cronies among the loosertongued and less exemplary clerks because they were, as a rule, more original fellows than the sobersides.

All these things were good, but they were compensations. A central zest was missing. He was not doing his own work, he was doing another man's and doing it as another man wished it done. He was a part of someone else's machine— and he was not made to find satisfaction in such a rôle. He needed to be making his own machine. Buying and selling forage might be glorious fun—it was for his father, who was spinning the intricacies of it out of his own mind—but it wasn't his particular job. To do it well, to earn money, to make amusing friends, to laugh at Uncle Danny—all these, and above them all, the satisfaction in his father's eyes—all these made Considine's endurable. But he wasn't twenty yet and he wanted to do more with his days than be able to bear them. There was a dragging awareness in his brain that only half of him was functioning—the less important half.

§ 3

HE HAD sickened lately of his garden. One winter morning he looked up from the orchard at his father's house and his heart sickened.

The ugliness of the River Hill mansion had long been visible to him, almost as long as he had been aware of his father's great pride in it.

He had done what he could to temper its effusiveness. He had had the conservatory removed, and the woodwork painted an inoffensive green instead of imitation wood-grain. He had replaced the fanciful white-painted handrails of the front doorsteps by plain stone balustrades. One day he might manage to have the lucarnes in the top story replaced by simple windows; he might also get the fussy stone fretwork cut away from the gable edges. Meantime, fifteen years might have done a scarcely perceptible something in toning the bright red bricks —fifteen more might do a little more. Short of covering the good-natured, unembarrassed façade with ivy, which he loathed, or with stucco, which Anthony would never hear of, there was nothing to be done to River Hill except ignore it or pull it down.

When Denis was fifteen the latter remedy had once commended itself seriously to him for two complete minutes, until it occurred to him that it wasn't his house and that its owner admired it passionately. Since then he had looked away from it when scheming at his garden.

Now, however, he looked back to it again. Oh, God!

He dropped onto a pile of flagstones and stared in weary boredom at his inchoate terraces.

After that morning he couldn't shake off a feeling of hopelessness about the garden. He continued the operations he had begun, for order's sake, but his heart was sluggish. What was the good? He was wasting money, time, and passion on something that had been spoilt before it was begun. He was sick of gardening anyhow—let it all go to blazes.

He turned about for some other interest. What he really wanted was companionship. The men he yarned and gossiped with at Kilmoney Street all seemed to have wives or similar pursuits out of office hours. Besides none of them wished to appear over-friendly with the chairman's son, knowing well that such uppishness would be frowned upon by authorities over his head. Young Jack was still at school, but even if he had been at home, he could talk of nothing nowadays but race-horses and his ambition to breed them at the Curragh. Mickey Cogan was studying medicine in Dublin; Jack Keogh was trying to be made into a vet by some kind of cheating process somewhere in England. And Tony—ah, Tony, best of boon companions, what was he at now? Chanting in Latin, or digging potatoes or looking northwestward to the hills behind which Mellick lay forgetting him?

In December Denis was moved into a department of Considine's called the Map Room, where, Anthony told him, his knowledge of French would be an advantage. Denis smiled broadly at this optimistic notion, but he had no objection to the added liveliness of struggling with a foreign tongue. The Map Room, called after one small dingy chart that hung there, dealt, like the North Sea Room, with Considine's European export trade.

The Map Room was a lively place, chiefly because Don José worked in it. Not that he was Don José until Denis named him so. His real name was Joe Duggan. He was a great striding fellow with a throaty laugh and the shoulders of a bull. He was going grey and there were creases round his small, bright eyes, but he was very handsome, matador fashion, and wore three rings on his fine strong hands and a red cummerbund inside his waistcoat. He was a boaster and a liar. A stranger to Mellick, he had drifted in on some recent ship and picked up a job in Considine's because of his colloquial acquaintance with the tongues of Spain and Portugal. He was the very fellow to interest Denis, and interest him he did with his fantastic tales and flourishes and his rattling *"Qué tal?"* and *"Jesús!"* and *"Muy buenas!"* Don José was a lucky find just when everything was falling flat.

He was born in Dublin, but according to himself his native land had been honoured with very little of his company, which had been freely and adventurously bestowed on every other country of the globe. Why, when still in full health and manhood, he had condescended to sail up-river to such an unimportant port as Mellick and take a dull safe job in a mere forage merchant's office, Denis was never so tactless as to ask. José had clearly been no saint in his heroic past, and an adventurer must be allowed his lapses into oblivion.

José really did know about ships and a great deal too about the Eastern and Southern worlds. He could spin yarns that might or might not have been true for all Denis cared but that passed the time for the two of them as well as they could wish. The temples and palaces, the jails and opium dens that man had seen or could invent, the trees and cactuses and orchids and strange unimaginable lilies, the panthers and the snakes he'd tackled, the women who had made love to him, the women he had made love to, the fakirs he had shown up, the Chinks who had never quite managed to swindle him! For the re-creation of all these novelties, Don José had epithets from at least ten languages.

He was great fun. In the teeth of January winds Denis and he would sail a light wag down to the river's mouth on Sunday mornings, and come back at midnight to the sleeping town, frozen, exhausted, and with bleeding hands, but full of pleasure in their day of duress and in each other. Or Denis would force him out to River Hill, to play strange games of cards and to drink tea—poor, subdued José—with a bitterly disapproving Aunt Agnes and a half-amused but unenthusiastic Anthony. Or, with Reggie Mulqueen perhaps, they would tramp across the Vale of Honey towards Ardcolum, eating and drinking at public-houses and falling into talk with other playboys who would try a hand at swapping boasts with Don José. On these occasions Denis noticed awkward contradictions in the narratives of his friend and that towards the end of the day, when the halts had been many, his stories gave up all attempt at hanging together. He soon became expert at helping the matador out of the entanglements of memory and at snubbing any doubter in the company who might cast aspersions on his truth.

One night, coming back into Mellick by the Dublin road, they had the misfortune to meet Father Tom at a very awkward moment. They had fallen into company with a tramp, a fine, unshod, unshaven man of the road who said that he remembered meeting José twelve years before in Sacramento. José knew nothing of that, but was sure that he had once blackened the other fellow's eye in Tokio. The other fellow couldn't remember ever having been in Tokio, and as they went the road, José was proving to him, with oaths and flourishes and some slight staggering, that he had most certainly been in Tokio.

"Why not, señor? Why wouldn't you have been in Tokio? What's to stop you going to Tokio? What's to stop you, señor? *Nada, nada, por Jesús!* That's Spanish for nothing, señores— Spanish for nothing at all!"

It was then that Father Tom passed. He didn't know Spanish, and so did not identify the Holy Name in its foreign disguise. But he identified his intoxicated, laughing nephew and the disreputable clerk who was his constant associate nowadays. The tramp was a new horror. Father Tom went straight back to Mellick, to take counsel with Teresa about Denis's behaviour.

The family had been muttering for some weeks—now they thundered. They lectured Anthony, and he laughed, though secretly he wished José at the bottom of the sea. They lectured Denis and he smiled.

"I hear you were drunk on the Dublin road last Sunday night," said Anthony to him.

"I suppose I was pretty drunk," said Denis. "José was drunk, all right, and so was the other artist."

"You're a cool customer," said Anthony. "And that chap Duggan—José is it you call him? What do you see in him?"

"Oh, he's a great fellow—a marvellous liar."

The Map Room continued to echo Denis's *"Buenos días"* to José and José's uproarious *"Muy buenas!"*

Work went well, he grew interested in trying to improve his French, he forgot the garden, forgot Tony, even forgot sometimes that he didn't care for forage-selling.

One night he turned out of the office with José onto the dock-road, and strolled along it with the river's flow. It was very dark, with a thin rain falling. The two halted at a cross-

ing under a street lamp, while José fumbled in his pocket for
some treasure of the East he wanted to show Denis.

"Está Duggán! Por Jesús y Maria. Duggán!"

Denis wheeled to the new, wild voice, and saw a dark face
that had murder in it rushing into their small zone of light
and at José. As it came, however, José's face vanished, vanished as a lightning change swept over it from swaggering
amiability to terror. The stranger flashed up and simultaneously José was gone—nothing left of him but the wild, flying
thud of his feet.

Denis did a very sensible thing then. He sprang at the throat
below this wild, new face. He threw all his weight into his
hands, and brought the stranger down with him into the mud.
There he rolled and rolled in the other's demented grip, rolled
and kicked and swore—he didn't care how long—all the more
time for José to make his get-away.

The dock gathered round in delighted amazement. There
were cheers and oaths and guesses at who in God's name the
two were that were rolling together in the dirt. Carters
brought their lamps to illumine the ring, women shrieked
"Murder!" and "Mother of God!" Men laughed and cursed
and flung advice out gratis: "Easy there, easy!" "Let me at
them, will you—let me at the two of them!" "Keep back out
of that—they'd whip a knife at you!" "Is it in the rats they
are, do you know?"

A peeler bent down at last, very cautiously, and in wheedling
tones implored the two to fall apart before he had to force
them to. They did so out of exhaustion. They stood up. The
Spaniard began to shout again and tried to run for it, but the
biggest labourer in Mellick dock had a grip of his collar. He
jabbered and screamed and the dockers and their women
laughed at him. Sergeant Rooney wagged his ponderous head.
The first mate of a newly docked boat strolled on the scene
and recognised the shouting dago. In the twinkling of an eye
the enemy of Don José was marched back to his ship under
arrest.

Denis wiped the mud from his face and the peeler and
carters stared as if at a miraculous statue when Mr. Considine's eldest son revealed his pleasant features to them.
Sergeant Rooney gasped.

"Be cripes, if it isn't Mr. Dinis!"

"Holy Mother, who'll be fighting next?"

"Well now, Mr. Dinis, sir, I'm astonished at you. Sure that's no way at all to be acting, sir—if I may take a liberty."

"You may, Sergeant, you may," said Denis, who was feeling extremely pleased with himself.

Before he washed he went up to Anthony's office. He had an idea that his father would enjoy the sight of him—and he did. He enjoyed the story too.

But Don José was never seen again in Mellick. And the Map Room lapsed thereafter into being a very dull place indeed.

§ *4*

THE next excitement at Charles Street was an outbreak of trades unionism. It was no novelty. In Honest John's time a few of the dockers of Mellick had attempted more than once to form a union. No employer who used the dock took the slightest notice of these attempts—Honest John least of anyone. There was no need to. Mellick was very far west of the English midlands where this new-fangled crime had been giving trouble off and on for forty years. Employment was scarce in Irish towns and those who gave could be contemptuous of those who needed it, who must have it on the giver's terms or leave it for the next man. Honest John and John Aloysius Hennessy had between them set an example of tranquil indifference which other employers had imitated with varying success according to their temperaments. But all had praised it.

Now, in March 1876, a union had actually been formed at last by a few of the toughest characters on the dock. Rumour had it that there were twenty or thirty members in the union, and that it had a secretary and a place of meeting. Four or five men who had regular work from Anthony's ships were said to be the ringleaders of the thing. There was much scandalised talk about it among the black-coated clerks with whom Denis worked.

One day one of these five ringleaders had a dispute with the chief loading-clerk of Considine's. The dispute was reported and he was sacked. On the evening that he left the remaining four trades unionists marched into the general office at Charles Street and demanded to have a paper that they handed in sent up to the "boss." They said that they would wait for his answer.

The paper went up. The general office twittered and wriggled. The four big, dirty men stood by the wall in silence. Denis came out of the Map Room and was told what was afoot. He waited too, in silence, like the trades unionists.

They had not to wait long. Anthony came down the stairs, pausing midway on it, while fifteen pairs of eyes from below were riveted on him, to call back some amused instruction to O'Halloran. He had the paper in his hand but his backward smile was beautifully unconnected with it.

After this easy-going pause, he came down the remaining steps briskly, giving his attention once more to the paper in his hand.

"Ha! These are the men who wanted me, Hayes?"

He crossed the room and stood with his back to the clerks. Very straight and fine he looked, active figure, silvering hair, and well-made clothes, against the row of sweaty, sullen giants that confronted him.

"I've read this paper of yours. Which of you wrote it out so tidily?"

"None of us," said the man nearest the door—he was the spokesman. "None of us, but the secretary for us—the secretary of the Mellick Dockers' Union."

"I see. The gentleman is unknown to me."

"Well, did you understand what he said in it, anyway?"

"I did. I'll read it out now, for fear there's any mistake."

He read it out, turning sideways for the whole room to hear. It was a short and ungrammatical protest against the unlawful dismissal of Thomas Molloy, dock labourer, and announcing that until he was reinstated no member of the Mellick Union of Dock Labourers would work for Considine & Company.

Anthony paused at the end of the reading, and said in an effectively soft voice:

"That'll be inconvenient for us."

The clerks giggled appreciatively.

"It means," said the spokesman of the dockers—"it means that we're going on strike, I'd have you know."

He pointed to his allies along the wall. Their eyes, like his own, were troubled and angry.

"It does not," said Anthony amusedly. "It means that you're going—for good, like Thomas Molloy. Line up for your wages and good-bye to you."

He turned on his heel, flicked the paper across the room over the heads of his clerks, and walked upstairs at a leisurely pace.

The dockers filed out, their four pairs of eyes more troubled and angry than ever. The clerks gave a titter of relief and scrambled for a look at the famous paper. Denis went back into the Map Room without opening his lips.

The story of the little episode flew round the town. The Hennessys had it, the Verekers, the O'Donoghues, the O'Currys, the Devlins, all the important employers, every Considine household, and every small, admiring shop and parlour in the town. The dockers' secretary had it too, no doubt, and the members of his little union. The Mellick *Sentinel* gave an approving paragraph to it next morning, a paragraph which was telegraphed to the Dublin evening paper. Anthony was a hero in his own town, and he took his hero-worshipping with an agreeable air of contemptuousness. So did he take the stone that was flung at him as he drove up King Street. It knocked his hat off and cut him on the temple. He went on driving, waving a hand and flinging a smile back to where the stone had come from. He only pulled up his horse when William Hennessy ran after him to return his hat. Then he remembered his bleeding forehead, and went into a chemist's shop to have it plastered. He wore his plaster like a plume all day, but gave no other sign of being the man of the hour.

Nevertheless he was pleased with himself. He knew far better than he pretended that these small mutterings of insubordinate labour were not so small now as they had been ten years before. He knew they would grow louder, and he was glad that he had been given the first chance in Mellick to face them. The idea that anyone, least of all a few illiterate hooligans, should attempt to tell an employer when to sack

or when not to sack his employees, or to say what they should
be paid or for what hours they should work, was simply an
insane conception, in Anthony's view. That summed up his
position. The Considines owned Considine's and no one but
they should say what was or was not to be done there. So he
felt, and so, as a man of feeling, he acted towards the four
audacious dockers, who would be workless now for months
through their own fault. God help their wives, that was all!

Anthony felt he had carried the thing off excellently, and
had given the lesson of their lives to all his witnesses. He
didn't know that his son was one of them.

At dinner on the day after the sacking of the men, the
day the stone hit him, his sister Agnes was all solicitude and
prayers and abjurations against the wickedness of ignorant
men.

"Tch, tch, Agnes—hold your tongue. They're not worth
talking about. I'm sorry for them, to tell you the truth."

"That hurting you?" said Denis, jerking his head in the
direction of the sticking plaster.

"Not it."

Anthony smiled at him, coaxingly. He had had everyone's
good word to-day, except this boy's whom he hadn't seen, and
who had stayed out late the evening before. He wanted his
applause now, the last and best of all.

"He's like a baby, wanting to be told he's a good boy,"
thought Denis miserably. But he couldn't say what was expected and went on eating chocolate pudding.

He had been distressed by the scene in the office the night
before. The issue itself, perplexing as it was, did not engage
him half as deeply as his father's reaction to it. He was disinclined to think that the wounds of the world could be ap-
preciably staunched or deepened by any gesture made in
Mellick. But he had seen the pathos and significance of the
four dirty men as they waited for his father, he had seen the
perplexing questions that they stood for reaching out beyond
them to the future and to all men, and had seen also the bewildered personal struggle and anxiety in their eyes. They had
seemed full of tragic dignity to him, they and their bit of
paper. He had waited excitedly for his father to match that
dignity with his own. It was as if he watched a play in which

his favourite actor was to play a great part. And his favourite actor had come on, and had seemed to Denis to miss the whole meaning of his part. He had played for himself, and let the play down.

Denis didn't know what he had expected his father to do. Certainly he hadn't looked for sentimentality or softness; anything so uncharacteristic would have been bitterly offensive to him. But he knew better than Anthony's loudest admirers how real and quick his intelligence was, and in the silence of waiting it had occurred to him that now in this moment, so important and perplexing for Mellick, that intelligence might spring a surprise, not by solving the issue, but by facing it in some new way, some subtle and maybe unpopular way. Denis thought that Anthony might take the thing slowly, impersonally—even with a touch of statesmanship.

Instead, there had been a gesture, any man's gesture, imperious, picturesque, theatrical, cheap. The easy, popular way out, from someone fit to take any other. Denis had despised his favourite actor's performance—despised the speed and impudence of it, its facile victory over lumbering, dirty misery. He had been ashamed in every nerve as he saw his father stroll upstairs and the four heavy labourers plod out. This was not any way at all to meet an important moment. His favourite actor had thrown a big chance over the moon.

Denis had gone for a long walk then. He could not go home and dine with Anthony with disappointment so hot in his heart. And through this day of plaudits he had avoided him. But now, he knew how it would be; the man would coax and worry till he got what simply wasn't in Denis for him tonight. For once in his life he could not admire his father, but he thought that probably he had never loved him so much as in this baby's mood of vanity, with his silly sticking plaster over his eye.

Aunt Agnes got up presently and left the dining-room.

"How's the day been, my son?"

"Oh, all right, I think."

"H'm. You heard about the little scene I had with my trades unionists, as they call themselves. last night?"

"I saw it."

"Saw it?"

"Yes. I was in the outer office when you came down to them."

"Well, I'm damned! You're a cool card! Never even mentioned that!" Pause. "Didn't you think I handled them well?"

Denis walked to the fireplace. He stood and stared at the flames.

"You were very quick about it."

"That all, my son?"

Denis didn't turn round.

Anthony's face, had he seen it then, might have made him laugh. It was blank from the shock of not being admired.

"Quick? How do you mean? Didn't you think it funny? I was thinking all the time, 'Pity Denis isn't here to see this joke!'"

Denis turned round.

"I didn't think it funny, father. I didn't see the joke a bit. I thought it serious and difficult."

It occurred to Denis that perhaps now, for the first time in their lives, Anthony would shout at him and act the parent. He didn't.

"Serious and difficult! Oh, I suppose it is, in one way. No use getting lugubrious over these things just yet, though."

"Those four men——"

"Those four men are blackguards, I may tell you!"

"If you're calling them blackguards simply on the strength of last night's business—well, it's ridiculous. They've a far greater right to call you a blackguard, father." This was said with every alleviation of gentleness, but it startled Anthony.

"Denis!"

"Listen! You have every advantage over them—every advantage in the blessed world! And you used them all without mercy, father, in the easiest possible way, and made a pack of snivelling clerks laugh at the poor devils into the bargain. I—I simply couldn't see the joke. I'm sorry."

Denis was trembling. He could only just endure this wounding and disappointing of Anthony. He could only just endure the hurt perplexity in his father's face. He hurried his words as if to race them against his longing to keep silence.

"They've a perfect right to form trade unions—it's only silly to pretend they haven't. You didn't think yesterday, father—you play-acted. They're perfectly free to say whether they'll work for you or not—at least as free as you are to say that they won't. They're free souls, after all."

He bent and clattered the shovel against the coal.

"It's very cold to-night," he said.

Anthony gave a little gasping laugh.

"So it's a Chartist I've got for a son, is it? Or a—what do you call 'em—a Socialist?"

He crossed the room and laid his hand on Denis.

"We've never had a row, the two of us," he said, "and in the name of God don't fight with me now about a few old dockers. I must run Considine's my way, my son. Your turn will come, and your times won't be as easy as these, by the look of things. But you'll have fair play from me then, because I won't be there to trouble you. Let me have fair play now, will you?"

Denis knew that the argument was false but the manner of its setting forth was one he could not resist. He smiled into Anthony's brilliant eyes.

"For heaven's sake, father, don't cry in the heel of the hunt. You're a worse cry-baby than Flossie."

THE FOURTH CHAPTER

Denis took a notion for trout fishing in that Spring of 1876.

The way it came to him was this:

One Sunday in April Father Tom was entertaining his relatives to lunch at his fine house in Glenwilliam, five miles from Mellick, where he was now parish priest. Denis arrived at his host's at noon and took a stroll over the broad sweet pastures of the parish.

He was nervy and bored and ashamed of himself these days. Everything seemed to be going wrong. There was a cloud between him and Anthony. It was nothing, no more than the mist that had blown up on them the night he spoke his mind about the dockers. Still, there it was. They two, who never had to dodge any other subject whatever, went warily now about trades unionists. That they did so exasperated Denis, all the more as he had no illusions whatever about himself as a social reformer. He knew very well that he had neither talent nor inclination for putting the world right; but he had both talent and inclination for living at ease with his father. The latter he desired to do by almost any means, the former by none at all. And here was this silly business—this bit of nothing—making something like anxiety between them!

The fatuous talk of his colleagues at the office on this subject of unions and strikers was another weariness to him. He listened in amazement to their quite meaningless lawgiving and sensation-mongering.

He was new to the sycophancy and cowardice of men; their inability to think alone appalled him as much as did their need to get together and reassure themselves with windy words. He was new also to the pathetic shifts of their respectable, shabby lives, and to their hundred frets and worries and gallant economies, of which he was now always learning. It frightened him to realise that they, so many of them, and their worried little firesides, depended uneasily for everything on his remote, impetuous, indifferent father. But he wished they were less uneasy. He wished too that Uncle Joe and Uncle Tom would find less to say about the criminal tendencies of the "lower orders," a theme they were very hot on since the historic small stone had been flung at Anthony.

God! he wasn't looking forward to this luncheon-party! Father Tom, flushed and self-confident from his sermon on the Gospel of the day, and Uncle Joe, making sly inquiries of him about "the girls," and Aunt Sophia getting drunk for the sake of her palpitations, and Aunt Caroline, with her beautiful mouth sinking in a little and her chin coming forward, Aunt Caroline incredibly nagging and scolding at Uncle Jim, and Uncle Jim being informative about Cardinal Manning and the Bashi-Bazouks and whether or not the Queen should be called Empress of India, and Aunt Agnes, bleating over her latest craze in nuns, and Uncle Danny telling him what the business wouldn't stand, and Aunt Teresa, snubbing everyone and looking at redfaced Reggie as if he were God, and Reggie, poor decent unlucky chap, making silly jokes— and Anthony his father, riding the scene with arrogance, not even perceptibly uneasy when the crimes of the lower orders were being dealt with—but uneasy nevertheless.

Denis was in no mood for that energetic host. He wanted Don José, he wanted Tony. He scanned the lovely sky and wondered vaguely where "Flasher" Devoy had got to by this time. Poor old "Flasher"! Missionising away for all he was worth in the East or the West, oh, some uncomfortable spot you might be sure! Well, he'd got his wish anyhow. Lucky fellow, "Flasher." How far off Mellick looked to-day! Much more than five miles you'd say.

He pulled himself through an unpromising gap in a hazel

hedge, and dropped, a startlingly deep drop, into the next meadow.

It was a queer, sunken place, quite two feet below the level of the field he had left. It was large and triangular in shape and bounded on its western side by a quick brown trout stream. To the south lay a little wood of willow and ash and Spanish chestnut. The hazel hedge grew from a deep embankment that was luminous with primroses. A splendid oak tree threw its arms out wide above the water, and made a grove of shadow about its own roots. The grass was rich and vigorous already. The white scut of a rabbit flashed here and there against its green, but Denis could detect no other movement anywhere save from the stream and from some fussy nest-makers in the wood. An unremarkable piece of landscape except in its sunken remoteness from the surrounding scene and the heightening of silence that this gave it. Its only window on the world was across the span of water to another meadow, another belt of wood, a slow-rising hill, a dim farm gable, a twist of smoke.

As quiet as a chapel on Monday evening it seemed, as utterly forsaken by men.

At lunch he asked Father Tom about the trout stream.

"It's the Taigue, you ignoramus. The bit you mean is on Sir George Lewis's land, I imagine. Very good fishing and well preserved. Might be a let just now."

Five days later Denis became the tenant for that season of the half-mile of trout stream that flowed past the triangular meadow and the little wood.

Afterwards there were not many evenings of the week that he didn't escape from Considine's while at least two hours of light could still be counted on. The mare under his gig had to be brisk then covering the five miles to the Keener's Cross where she was stabled. Three quarters of a mile on foot across the fields and he was through the hazel hedge and under the shadow of the oak tree.

It wasn't the trout he was after so hungrily, though he caught enough of them for honour, enough indeed to exasperate his relatives, who regarded fish as penitential food and were loth to put a second Friday into the week. It was himself that he sought in the triangular meadow.

§ 2

THE evenings lengthened and grew warmer. Denis spread books about him under the oak tree and life gradually became a less and less precarious thing for the trout that swam in the Taigue.

His absorption in gardening and garden history had taken much of his attention of late from his father's miscellaneous shelves, but he was a subscriber to the *Cornhill* and *Fraser's*, and under their guidance was still a zealous buyer of books, many of which still lay unread. He turned to them eagerly now, filled the well of his gig with them and exposed them to all the chances of Spring weather.

They made a still deeper refuge for him within his green chapel-of-ease; through them he could forsake that smaller, discontented, irritable self and its circumstantial accidents that were fretting him, to find his own humanity in widest commonalty spread. A sense of proportion came to him out of his books. Reading under the oak tree he somehow discovered the unimportance of circumstances when weighed against the divine importance of life on any terms.

He read *Esmond* and *Elia* and *Imaginary Conversations,* and *Persuasion* and *Modern Love* and *Don Quixote.* He read here and there in Spenser, here and there in *The Canterbury Tales,* here and there in *The Anatomy of Melancholy.* He read the *Compleat Angler* with piety and pleasure. He read a few of Shelley's essays; he read *Prometheus Unbound.* He read Keats very much as the poet himself had read Chapman's Homer, read and re-read with flushed cheeks and catching breath, read his letters and laughed and groaned over them —"My dearest girl . . . sweet Fanny . . ." and often sat under the oak tree when the light was gone and bats were wheeling, mourning Adonais with personal sorrow, as the young must ever do. He read Shakespeare's sonnets, some of them four or five times without a pause, something like consternation quickening him for their packed and knotted passion of experience.

He read Edgar Allan Poe. "I was a child and she was a

child in that kingdom by the sea . . . " haunted him until
Anthony caught it.

"Were you indeed?" said he. "And what happened then?"
Denis told him, reading the poem.

"That's good," said Anthony, "that's mighty good."

Throughout all this reading he disciplined himself by reading French too. He had been ashamed in Paris and now in
the office was ashamed of his schoolboy inefficiency with it. He
took a great dictionary out to Glenwilliam therefore every
day, and began heroically to read *Les Misérables,* looking up
every word. It bored him. On the fifth day he pitched it into
his basket among the trout and turned back contentedly to
The Gold Bug.

Next day he tried *Candide.* He finished it, playing absolutely fair and finding the meaning of every word. When he
had finished he began it again. The third time he read it with
ease and passion, marred only by a regret that was deso-
latingly strong. He wanted Tony to share this book, of all
books in the world. How Tony would have purred over it!
*"N'êtes-vous pas bien étonné, continua Candide, de l'amour
que ces deux filles du pays des Oreillons avaient pour ces deux
singes, et dont je vous ai conté l'aventure?—Point du tout, dit
Martin, je ne vois pas ce que cette passion a d'étrange."* How
Tony would have argued about that book! How he'd have
laughed and grown excited!

Denis bought *Zadig* and the *Siécle de Louis Quatorze* and
Essai sur les Mœurs. He wrote to Paris too for the works
of a man called Flaubert and of a writer called De Maupassant
of whom he had just heard.

May passed. He grew very happy. He found his work hardly
a burden, so lively and stimulated was his mind and so was
it detaching itself from impatience and from the windy arguments and debates of the elder Considines.

Always he stayed under his oak tree until the sky was given
over to night. When the light was too thin for reading, he
would lie at peace, remembering what he had read. The quiet
of the field was never broken, for he counted a part of it the
children who trailed by sometimes, going home from
primrose-gathering, and who would only stare and wriggle
when he spoke to them. The poacher who grudged him his

long twilight thoughts was as much a part of the evening as
the little white owl on the withered tree across the stream, or
the cough of a sheep on the hill.

Always in this peace he had a sense of tranquil waiting—
for he knew not what.

§ 3

ONE evening of long-drawn light a swan came sweeping up
the stream, going northwards, past him, with the gentle tide.
Denis leant out to watch her, holding himself very quiet as if
she were music that he heard. The water curved ahead of her
in a long, slow sweep. She took it on its crest, the track she
knew. Two oars of water streamed behind her, wide and
noiseless, from her folded wings. Her unstained whiteness
blazed against the light that it was fleeing from, then dropped
with distance into a gradual merging with the silver stream,
then vanished. It was as if a ghost had passed, or was still
passing. It seemed to Denis that the water that her movement had scarcely troubled held something of her now though
she was gone—an echo, a trail of decoration. Where she had
been was made more lovely for ever because of her sailing
past. Denis stared and saw her still, beyond his sight, taking
her dreamy course to where her rest and purpose lay, her
motion heavy with rest even now, her lines sharp cut in isolation, and yet the whole of her at one with the warm splendour
of the evening. She was alone, a northward-faring ship, but
she knew her path and had turned to it because of a command in the changing light. Where was her nest? Had she
found it yet, or was she still at her drowsed, unhurried navi-
gating?

A twig snapped at the edge of the wood. He turned his
head. A farm girl was standing a few feet away, standing
as if she had been there some minutes. She carried a bundle
of firing-twigs under her arm.

"Did you see the swan?" said Denis.

"I did. She's nesting beyond in Farrell's reeds."

"Where's her mate?"

"Gone from her. She's alone with the young now."

Denis stood up.

He had forgotten the home-faring bird. The beauty of the girl before him, which did not blaze or startle, came out in slow waves of revelation with each word she said. She was tall, and might be his own age or more. She was slender too, but the lines of her womanhood were clear and lovely. Her brown hair was parted in the middle and looped low upon her neck; the sleeves of her dark cotton dress were rolled back from white forearms, her hands were rough with hardship. But in her face, her white, deep brow, on her slow-smiling mouth, in her innocent, sane, unflurried eyes, fold after fold of unconscious beauty seemed to have been laid away and then forgotten. Denis thought that he had never looked on a face so strong and pure.

"Are there swans here every year?"

"Yes, sir." Denis started at the epithet. "There were four of them this time last year."

She moved to cross the field. He sought a strategy to detain her, and then abandoned the search with a feeling of shame. He stood aside, staring at her in hunger and perplexity. She passed him, giving a slow smile.

"Good-night," said Denis.

"Good-night, sir."

She crossed the field to the dim corner, where the gap was in the hazel hedge.

THE FIFTH CHAPTER

D ENIS killed no fish the next evening. He lay on the grass and read, and then abandoned reading. He fretted and fidgeted; the fair, cool hour seemed a heavy slab of time for which he had no use! For once, he felt lonely in the triangular meadow. He wished and yet only half-wished that there was someone to talk to—Mickey Cogan, or Jack Keogh, or Quirk from the office, that oily-haired giggler. He wondered in what hemisphere Don José was now, and ranging the world with his thought to pursue him came, not on him, but as so often he did, on "Flasher" Devoy. "Flasher" preaching under the Mexican sun or in some frozen twilight of the snow, clearly to be seen against a red-baked land, or through a mist of Arctic blizzard—clear-voiced always, preaching with cool, unstaying passion to any and every kind of man, preaching with like fidelity to ignorance and cynicism all that he knew or dreamt or desired of the Son of Man. "Flasher" had gone the way of his own will about his business, and so had Don José and so had Tony, while he still lingered alone in the fields of childhood where they would never come again. He only mooned among unnecessary things, in a sleepy place of rules and ties, while all his desires and powers drummed through him still, uneasy and untried.

He twisted from his right hip to his left on the gnarled ground, and shivered petulantly against the rising breeze. He flung a clod of earth across the stream towards a cow that stared offensively.

"You'll know me the next time, anyway," he muttered at

her. What the blazes was he doing in Considine's that couldn't be done ten times as well by Quirk or any other giggling ass? Why was he on his stool day in, day out, painstaking and polite, when all the pains and politeness were only the thin, uppermost skin of him, a skin that hid a million rusting, hopeless, but unquiet energies—all the real him that lived in his dumb mind and had no outward showing? Why was he here in Mellick, fretting under an oak tree, staring at a staring cow, while Paris, Rome, Heidelberg were only three days away, with their books and learned men and their free familiarity with beauty's progress and tradition? That was what he wanted to be busy at—the march of beauty down the years, across the world—to map and memorise and somehow compass it—and here he was nevertheless, of his own choice, of his own will, in an office where men took account of life in terms of prosperity or expediency, where all they sought was comfort and uniformity and to become in some small way perhaps the envy of other men. He had committed himself to all this for life, for the long, sweet years of life, because of a father to whom he could not say "no."

Denis wriggled again from his left hip to his right. He turned away from the hypnotising cow. That wasn't fair. He couldn't fool round with a legend of his own generosity.

"If you thought you could be happy without him, you'd be gone like a shot," he accused himself. "It's because you could no more face going away from him than he could face your going away that you're still here. You know that—right well you know it. It's six of one and half a dozen of the other. And in the name of Christ what does it matter in the end where you are or what you do? Of all the whingeing-whiners I ever met you take the biscuit!"

So he scolded himself, disenchanted to-night in his green solitude. It seemed a tame place now in which to sit alone. He wanted companionship and teased his depression with memories of lost friends. And yet he knew that had anyone of them come suddenly through the gap in the hedge, he would still have been dissatisfied. It was some unknown befriending that he longed for, something he had never had before.

He gathered himself up, sick of the chilling breeze, indifferent to night's oncoming glory. He flung another piece of

turf at the cow and without even a glance at the edge of the
wood, the new significance of which he had not so much forgotten as submerged in his egotistical mood, he strode across
the field to the gap.

The chestnut mare had to clatter home without a pause
under his irritable command. The sweet-smelling lanes that
on every other night had pleased him with their shadowy
changefulness were tame and monotonous now, and the lovers
murmuring in the hawthorn, by whom he never passed without a troubled, envious curiosity, were silly fools to-night,
whom Father Tom had every right to chase home to their
beds. But as he fumed against himself and them and clacked
his tongue at his willing horse, as he appraised the climbing
stars and wondered what there was for supper, as he lifted his
hat in King Street to belated, moonstruck citizens, and let
his nerves relax to the spell of lamplit windows and the clear-
heard cry of the river coming up from behind the grey mass
of Considine's, he had a sense of having mislaid some new
important fact, and was aware that the back of his mind was
dancing round a bright preoccupation, to which the rest of him
could not find its lost way back. The rest of him was tangled
up in peevishness and in lonely contemplation of familiar,
forefront things.

The Old Town slept with a grave and sad demeanour under
the moon. Denis felt the reproof of its poised resignation and
compunctiously allowed his imagination to salute its broken
monasteries and looms and wine-vats, its decaying panelled
parlours, its walls broken in siege, its humpy old bridges
linking canalled and rivered islands—all, all of the past, their
purpose and glory done and only the grey beauty of patience
left in them to face the unclean end. But what a beauty, Denis
thought, as the moon washed tenderly over the crumbling,
weary heap—like the beauty of an old woman at prayer.

His grandfather had come out of that poor, dying heap
of stone—Honest John, dim, half-remembered figure of
legend, ugly old man in the dining-room portrait, so beloved
of all the elder Considines, so strangely, wordlessly venerated
by his youngest son, Honest John who had raised up the
family structure and flung them all without ruth for good or
ill into its inescapable labyrinth—Honest John had dragged

his pride and blood out of that place of death into new roads and tides of life. Kilmoney Street was crumbling away without a protest, but wasn't its business done after all, thought Denis with a smile—weren't the Considines a mighty spawn to have flung up out of reach of its own corruption?

Anthony waited for him on the steps of the house, from whose open door and windows lamp-streams poured in golden overlapping of the moonlight. The garden scarcely sighed in its tranquillity, which only deepened to the trot and jingle of the chestnut mare. Denis's eyes searched into the lowest-valleyed terrace for the sober lines of cypresses and beyond them to the thinning, scattering snow of his monkish orchard. The steel curve of the river was clear and cold, the hills lay waveringly, as if they breathed, against the sky.

Anthony called to him: "Welcome home, my son."

The last of his petulance fell from Denis then, and pleasure in what lay before his eyes broke over him like a wave of the sea. His senses purred irrepressibly in gratitude for the garden's hidden green and sap and flowery earth; his father's voice was warm; the lamplight beckoned; he was hungry for the good food and drink of River Hill. He leapt from the dog-cart. Home-coming had suddenly a taste of ecstasy.

"Hello, father! What's for supper?"

§ 2

FOUR days later the farm girl came again to the triangular meadow.

Denis, stretched on the roots of the oak and happy with *Consuelo,* lifted his eyes and saw her thirty yards away at the edge of the wood.

He rose in a glow of complacency, as one who feels himself in good time and mood for an appointment.

He had not been thinking of her.

Indeed for three days now his thoughts had not slackened perceptibly if they brushed by her; she seemed to have taken an unobtrusive place in that film of chance and routine associations that is the smudgy back-cloth of the mind; he had more than half forgotten her, he would have said. But now

as he stood up to greet her, he was aware of a click and satisfactory coming together of pieces in his mind. The important
fact that had been eluding him and that he had grown tired
of chasing—here it was—clear and stock-still before him—
why, here it was—and it was only this girl all the time!

Denis smiled, at her and at the relief of **having** cleared up
that small confusion.

But even as he smiled, disappointment was slipping over
his mood of welcome and satisfaction. Was she only this after
all—just a graceful, upstanding young peasant, with no distinction but her tidiness? Why then had he so enhaloed her?

She answered the question in her own movement. For as
she drew nearer veils seemed to fall from her and Denis saw,
and remembered then that he had seen before, that distance
was the cloak of her enchantments. All that she gave the long
vista was her slow, ripe grace. She had no far-flinging colour
in her hair or cheeks, nor any dance in her footsteps. She
wore the dark cotton dress of her class, unrelieved by ornament or by escaping gleam of breast or arm; fine ladies' tricks
for heralding beauty were unknown to her. Her step had
weariness in it, for she was working before last night's stars
had set, and would be working when they rose to-night—but
she walked with contentment and pride—at the pace of the
pavane indeed. And as if in time to such a tune this second
revelation of her beauty crept upon the watching boy, somewhat as a rose reveals its structure leaf by leaf to those that
pause for it, so that he appraised once more as separate discoveries the intelligent forehead and soft, well-balanced
triangle of this face, with its secretive mouth, straight nose
and straight-set, indeterminable eyes, and had time to marvel
why the assemblage in one person of unremarkable qualities
such as simplicity, brown hair, white skin, should be so deeply
pleasant to behold, before she was within addressing distance.

When she got there, and halted with a half-smile, superla-
tives were jumping in his brain to praise her, and he was in
a blaze of shyness.

"The loveliest, loveliest face—oh, God, how beautiful she
is—I'd clean forgotten——"

But he must speak; she was half-smiling.

He had no hat with which to salute, and so he bowed,

nervously, pompously, bending his head low down on his chest until she had only the fall of his gold hair to look at and the bright tips of his ears. And it was with an effort that he pulled himself up again from this ridiculous position.

"Good-evening," he said.

"Good-evening, sir," she answered, fully and graciously smiling, as Denis realised she would on any civil passer-by. Her voice was like her, unselfconscious, and in the inflection of these three words there was neither harsh finality nor the coaxing, on-coming "your-turn-next" intonation of femininity. The absence of this would have embarrassed most of Denis's male cousins. The Mulqueen and Lanigan boys and Victor and Hubert Considine were only at ease with girls when the glove of coquetry had been flung down; if the other sex spoke to them they listened for challenge and timidity. But Denis, as they all admitted, was unskilful with coquettes, so now, instead of being flustered, as they would have been, by this uncoquettish voice, he was disarmed and set at ease.

But to make her pause and talk was still a delicate problem. How was he to do it and not seem importunate?

"I haven't laid an eye on that swan ever since."

"Ah, 'tisn't often she'd come down from her nest as far as this. Last year, and I coming home this way from McIlroy's I only saw her once below this meadow."

"Are you coming from McIlroy's now?"

"No. I came to the wood to see were there maybe a few bluebells for the chapel. But the children have them trampled."

"There weren't any children here all the week. There's been no one next or near me since you came four days ago."

"Do you mean to tell me you're here every day?"

He nodded. "Every evening."

She smiled ironically at his empty basket.

"God bless the work," she said.

The mockery was faint.

Indeed, she barely allowed it a legitimate gleam, but the more direct and quickened smile that marked it lit up another aspect of her face, an aristocratic fineness which somehow contrived not to contradict but to glorify all her manifest signs of simple stock. Denis marvelled. A nerve of delight began to tremble in his breast.

"That's all very fine, but I haven't cast a single fly this evening. You ought to have seen that basket yesterday!"

"Is it trout you're catching?"

"Yes. Look at these for lovely flies!"

He turned the leaves of his flybook feverishly. Any fool's chatter must do, so long as it delayed her.

She fingered a Red Spinner.

"I never saw a creature like that on the top of the water," she told him with amusement.

"Ah, but the trout see them!"

"Christy catches loads of them every night with his hands only."

"Is that the poacher?"

"Yes."

She spread her right hand against the trunk of the oak tree and leant on it, arm's length away. It was an attitude of relaxation. Heaven be praised, there wasn't such a great hurry on her to-night. Denis wondered greatly at her friendliness. It didn't occur to him that she might be finding it seductive to stay awhile and look at him.

But as he stood below the girl on the strip of bank between tree and water, with western meadows and evening sky to set him off, he must have seemed charming enough to make any pair of eyes incline to linger. Perhaps from much walking with Anthony, he had caught an unselfconscious poise of bravery into his slight, tall body, and though his shoulders sat less arrogantly than his father's, they had a firm sculptural beauty to define them. Now in his twentieth year his face was neither babyish nor unsubtle, but at this moment, suffused with mingled shyness and delight, it shone with a strange, enhancing light of innocence.

"I don't know how Christy does it," the girl said. "He's a perfect terror. He can catch any mortal thing in the night."

Her talk seemed as aimless as Denis's. She laughed a little now at some remembered tale of Christy's exploits and there was a chance to note the controlled curve of her lips about two rows of teeth that, although white and even, were too strong to be called beautiful. "Sailor's teeth," said Denis to himself, "buccaneer's teeth," for inexplicably the flash of them recalled Don José's wild stories.

"Where do you live?" he asked, taking courage.

She jerked her head towards the east behind her.

"A good mile from here, sir—by the fields." Why was she calling him "sir" again? "My aunt has a bit of a farm over beyond Blackwell and I live with her. The widow Danagher she is."

"I think I've heard my uncle say that the parish is full of Danaghers."

"True for him. The parish priest is your uncle, isn't he, sir?"

"How did you know that?"

"Well, my cousin was saying that he heard at the Keener's Cross that young Mr. Considine of Mellick had this bit of fishing from Sir George."

"Is Sir George your landlord too?"

So they slipped into question and answer, and lost some shyness in satisfying their curiosity.

§ 3

CHRISTINA was this girl's name—Christina Roche. She was twenty-one and the only child of her mother, who died giving birth to her. This dead mother had got into trouble when in service in a big house in the west, and Christina was illegitimate. Her aunt, Mrs. Danagher, had fetched her here to Glenwilliam when she was a week old, and had brought her up with her own children.

Denis gathered that the Danaghers were extremely poor, and that Christina's aunt was for ever fighting a half-lost battle against starvation. He gathered too that although the girl spoke with courteous gratitude of this aunt, she had no real love for her but indeed a kind of dread which she covered up, even maybe from herself, in decent bandages of platitude.

All this came out in casual, dislocated sentences, replies to questions. Its essentials were stated as euphemistically as might be, its commonplace points with greater ease. And as Denis pieced the story, the broken bits of circumstance seemed to him to indicate a logical background for Christina.

If he had known more of her story, bits of it which she did not know herself and which even her aunt only suspected, she would have been even more fully explained.

Denis was without snobbery, as the word is ordinarily interpreted. He was also only theoretically and in fantasy interested in young women. He read and talked about them a good deal, and liked to hear the views and experiences of others in regard to femininity. He had erotic day-dreams and vast ambitions for the conquest of the fair. But so far girls, in their habit as they lived, left him cold. He was not attracted by any of the soft young misses of his acquaintance in Mellick, and such prostitutes as had attempted him had not so much frightened as chilled and repelled him. And certainly it would never have crossed his mind to look for amorous excitement in what his relations called "the lower orders." It was not that he was bothered about whether people belonged to lower orders or to high. Simply his nature was selective and fastidious; he was at present exaggeratedly concerned, in all things, with form and grace and manner. No one could be more absurdly contemptuous than he, in certain moods, about a voice or a hand, or a smile. He once told Aunt Agnes that a very good-looking nun with whom she was then infatuated had "deplorably vulgar nostrils." This was both rude and silly of him, and Aunt Teresa told him so—but he was often rude and silly, and even when he wasn't he was fussy about details, in persons and things. When he made arrogant comments on the intonations and mannerisms of their perfectly respectable friends, his relations were wont to fling his own disreputable cronies in his face. Jack Keogh for instance, or Don José. "But you don't see my point," he would retort witheringly. "I'm not *talking* about being disreputable! I *like* disreputable people!"

That kind of thing was one of his juvenile poses, but intrinsic in him nevertheless was a certain accuracy of fastidiousness, and his love fantasies always took him into the company of great ladies, women much older than himself, whose witty and sceptical minds bewildered him and whose personal exquisiteness was an extravagant fairy-tale. It had never occurred to him that a peasant girl in a cheap, stained cotton dress would move him to desire.

Christina did not know that her father had been the second son of the great house in the west where her mother was a housemaid. This young man was the descendant of a strain that was conventionally aristocratic in all its members and ordinary customs, and had a claim also to intellectual aristocracy. The barons of Mask were not only masters of foxhounds and members of White's, but had won some supremacy in the universities as well. There had been a great archæologist among them and two good mathematicians; one of them, even now, wandered like a lost soul about Oxford, white-haired, senile, for ever mumbling bits of Meleager and Theocritus; a gifted young musician of their house had fallen in the Peninsular War. Christina's father was both spirited and intelligent, of a lonely, passionate, courageous turn of mind. But when he returned from a brief stay at Mask to the Embassy where he was attached, it is unlikely that he then or ever again, in the course of a long and brilliant life—he was now a dilettante middle-aged philosopher—gave half a thought to the beautiful peasant girl from whom he had taken some hours of mixed, uncertain pleasure, and to whom he had seemed as a god. Certainly he had no idea that a daughter of his, inheriting as much of her beauty from him as from her mother, wandered about Irish fields burdened not only by her own bastardy but by a considerable and unnourished share of his lonely, aristocratic, passionate mind.

Denis felt abashed and uncomfortable. How ridiculously he had dreamt of great ladies, when here in utter simplicity lay such a terrifying hoard of beauty.

§ *4*

CHRISTINA leant her whole body now against the tree, and talked, with every word she said, a little less as one who pauses by the way to gossip, and a little more in the manner of having reached a destination. Her eyes were filled with sunset, but she did not turn her head or trouble to move from where she stood. Her mood was passive—only now and then, as she talked, she would look long at Denis, keeping her dazzled eyes on him until she could see him accurately.

Her speech was the speech of Mellick fields and shops to which Denis's, overtoned by wealth and Jesuit training, was still allied; she had the large vocabulary of Irish country people and spoke in completed sentences, as it is their habit to do. But she seemed less impelled to talk than the average of her kind, using words as if, on the whole, she preferred silence; she interjected few of the customary peasant prayers into what she said and had no extravagance of phrase; strangely too, for an Irish talker, she seemed shy of the subject of herself.

But this was the subject to which Denis pointed every question.

"Are all your cousins at home?"

No. Julia was married in the County Cork, and Paddy, aged seventeen, was in Australia. Michael was just out of school and helping John on the farm, and Nora was only a little bit of a thing, aged eleven, always dancing about the place. Christina herself had been in service in a big house nearby from the time she was fifteen until her aunt was taken sick a year ago. Now the aunt was as well as ever, and Christina must be finding another place. There were relations of the Danaghers in Australia and America, and an uncle in Liverpool, who were asking to have her sent out to them and saying that they could start her well in a good place with good wages. Her aunt was always telling her that it was to one of those countries she should go.

"Would you like to?" said Denis.

"I'd sooner die," she answered gravely.

Always hope died in Christina before the glamorous hopes of exile; always she was frightened beyond reason when her aunt spoke coaxingly of the fairy gift of emigration. She was affectionate and shy. There hadn't been much use for affection in the farm beyond Blackwell—but she had given a share of hers to her nearly half-witted good-natured cousin John, and to Nora, the little bit of a thing. The rest of her undemanding heart found ease in the quiet ways and places of her childhood. Nothing could be worth having, it seemed to her, if it had to be fought for out of reach of everything she knew, among strangers, in the confusion of a town. So

long as she was at home, either about the harsh business of
the farm, or scrubbing floors in some great house of the Vale
of Honey, she carried with her, delicately and consciously, an
idea that this condition in itself was happiness and to be
cherished. Her notion of New York was of an unending grey-
white pavement over which dust and rubbish swirled on a
hot, wild wind. Night never fell on this pavement, and men
and women tore up and down it in packs, like wolves—and
screamed and fought and fell, and had trains and cabs run
over them—and the wind never dropped and there was no
catching a word of all the twanging chatter of the wolves.
Melbourne and Liverpool were variations of this vision, which
would have shocked the boastful returned emigrants from
whose reports it sprang. From their reports, and from the
sight of the emigrant train, taking desolate young men and
women, her friends, away from all that was native to them,
to hopes that she only saw as hopeless. The vision would
descend on her sometimes in the night, if maybe her aunt
had been talking of these far-off places, and would drive sleep
from her in the same definite way that the throb of a fester-
ing sore might do. And she would lie and contemplate it,
patiently, refusing to twist away and cry out, as if afraid that
any movement might stretch the nightmare wider. She let it
move before her and would neither encourage nor deny it—
only stared without a word, as the superstitious do into a
crystal.

Christina had no particular ambitions, which was well,
considering her handicaps. Illegitimate and without a halfpenny of a fortune, her chances of marriage among the small,
respectable farmers round about were non-existent. Her aunt
had explained this to her, and had never attempted to make
her a match. The effort would have been regarded as comic
throughout the baronies. Not that Christina wasn't well liked.
She was. There wasn't a man or woman in Glenwilliam that
hadn't a good word for the quiet, good-looking girl, but it
was understood that even a common labouring man or a
man going the roads with the tinkers would look for a girl
with five pounds maybe, or a cow, before he'd court Christina.

She didn't look forward to marriage, therefore, nor had

she other fantasies to put in its place. The religious life had attracted her once and she had thought very much of going to be a lay sister with the nuns of the Good Shepherd, but her aunt's bad health had come in the way of that, and now the wish was not so clear. On the other hand she had no hankering after what are called the pleasures of life. Knowing nothing of them, she was uncertain how to dream of them—but they were of the town, and towns, even gentle Mellick, smoky and spired, a dreamy smudge to the north of the saucer-plain, seemed no way glamorous to her. Her natural place was in the country, and her instinct was to treat each day as if it were her life, and not as a bit of prologue—she regarded its work as what she was there to do, and took her compensations from the peace of the fields and in tenderness for foolish John and little, dancing Nora. She was unlearned and intelligent, and took pleasure in the mild, secret use of her own intelligence. Nothing that came her way, actually or by hearsay, escaped from her unconsidered. She liked the taste of irony, and the unevenness, cruelty, and malice of life were not hidden from her. Almost as rigorously as she examined her own conscience on Saturday nights outside the confessional, she would examine the multiple soul of men as it was shown to her in her restricted day—and it seemed to her as complicated and unjudgeable as her own. She knew her world well enough to be reputed a sensible girl—too well, that is, to ask the impossible of it, either impersonally or for herself. But she had no quarrel with it. Her religion sufficiently explained it. This earth was a place of imperfection and trial, a place of error and suffering, for the making of souls. It seemed to Christina to be adequate for that. She was willing to try and make her soul, out of hard work and poverty, among the sights and sounds that long knowing had made very dear. And it was only when exile from these was threatened, or when her private vision of New York or Liverpool or Melbourne descended on her hard poor bed, that terror took her by the heart.

Even so, she embarrassed herself now by the extravagance of her reply to Denis's question.

"Would you like to?"

"I'd sooner die."

Was that true? And it seemed to her, though she tried
to laugh at herself, that it was nothing less. In that minute
anyhow, life in which a sea must flow between this sungilt
meadow and herself, between these friendly eyes of a stranger
and her own dazzled ones, would have been as unwished-for
and incomprehensible as death. Yes, she admitted to herself,
it was true. She'd sooner die.

Her words rang so gravely for Denis that he attempted no
reply to them. He jerked his head in vague acknowledgment
and turned to fidget with his rod.

Christina went on looking at him a few seconds in silence.
Then she straightened and stepped away from the tree.

"I'm due at home long ago," she said. "I'll have to hurry
myself."

"It's early yet."

"That all depends on what you have to do."

He began to unscrew his rod.

"May I go a bit of the road with you?"

Her eyes seemed amused as they took his straight inquiry,
but the amusement was a blind. She was really debating something important with herself while she replied to him.

"Indeed you may not. What would my aunt say if she met
the two of us?"

She had decided for once in her life to have a secret.

"Would she be cross with you for talking to me?"

"She'd think I'd gone out of my mind," said Christina with
a soft unexpected chuckle.

She turned to the field-path.

"Good-night, sir," she said.

Denis's cheeks burned red again. "Don't call me 'sir' in
that silly way. Please don't. Why do you do it all of a sudden
like that?"

She seemed at a loss for an answer.

"Well, I ought to do it, oughtn't I? And it's the way I
forget when I'm talking. And then I remember and do it
again."

"You see! It isn't natural. It's a peculiar notion you have
that you ought to do it."

"No, it isn't. We're different classes, after all. What's the
harm in admitting it?"

Denis was miserably uncomfortable.

"Look here—there are about fifty good answers to what you've said, but will you, just for friendliness' sake, drop out that idiotic 'sir'?"

His fear was that he might be misunderstood as making "advances" to her, playing the condescending young lord to the village maiden, and as he spoke he blasphemed in his heart against a fatuous world which had made the necessity for so ungainly a request. But she did not misunderstand. She smiled with candour at him, as if she saw the whole anxiety of his mind.

"I'll drop it," she said. "I don't care at all for saying it."

His heart praised her then for her easy way with him and for the promise, implicit in what she said, that she would come this way again to talk to him. He had not dared and would not dare to ask her that. She was going from him now without a word of second meeting—and he might never see her again, though she carried in her all the bright meaning of the hour, and the reason for this pounding of his heart. She was going, and must come again or not, as she pleased. For the moment it was enough, it was almost too much to bear, that he was thus surrendered to her will.

"Good-night now," she said, with a promise in her voice again.

He felt solemn and small, as he watched her go across the field from him; he felt oppressed, weighed down and saddened by some new-stirring element within; but his eyes strained after Christina, fussily observant. The grass was tall and flowering for hay, and Denis watched how it brushed against her knees and scattered its gold and white dust upon her dress that displeased him with its shabby dullness. The long, deep path she cut stretched back to him as if still linking them, and her shadow went gauntly ahead; shadow and track, and the girl, drab-clothed, dark-haired—a black, significant curve they flung across the evening peace; impatiently, intently, Denis watched the distance fold her in commonplace again, shroud her fine subtlety.

"Good-night," he heard in his own voice as her drab olive-green became a part of the hedge of hazel; but the word may only have been thought, not said, for she did not look back.

§ 5

THEY met the next evening.

Christina came through the hedge and across the meadow without making pretext of having other business but to seek Denis out.

She leant against the oak tree again; she refused to squat on its roots.

"I'd stay too long then, maybe. And you'd never know who'd come by and make talk."

"Are you afraid of your aunt?"

"I don't know that I'd say I'm exactly afraid of anyone," said Christina in the measured, reflective tone that distinguished her. "But if I was to annoy her now—well, it's the toss of a halfpenny till she'd pack me off across the water. And small blame to her either! Hasn't she been good to me long enough?"

"You earn your keep from her, I imagine," said Denis, noting the stains and darns on the ugly cotton frock, and the roughness of the sinewy hands.

Christina laughed.

"Well, it's a pity I wouldn't sit with my arms folded," she said.

"My uncle's the boy that'd give it to you if he caught you talking to a strange man. He's a holy terror about the way girls should conduct themselves."

"And 'tis we that know it in Glenwilliam parish, I can tell you!"

"Do you like him?—you, I mean—not the parish——"

"He's a very holy man."

"That isn't what I was asking you."

"Aunt Bridget thinks the moon and stars shine out of Father Considine."

"Funny!" said Denis. "That's the very last thing that would occur to me about him. Well, I'm thankful that it's not me but your Aunt Bridget that has to listen to him every Sunday. 'Fifthly and lastly, dearly beloved, let us bear away in our hearts this morning the words of our dear blessed Lord . . .'"

It was a pretty good rendering of the manly and solemn tones of Father Tom. Christina chuckled generously.

"It's the dead image of him—but oughtn't you to be ashamed of yourself? Anyway, what he says is always right, isn't it?"

"I don't know. I never listen to him."

"But he's a priest. He must be right."

"Are you holy, Christina?"

"I'm not. But I'd like to be."

"Rather be holy than anything else?"

"I think so. 'Tis the most peaceful thing to be."

"I have a cousin who thought that. Oh, I had a cousin, I mean. He went to be a monk at Mount Melleray."

Denis looked east and west across the evening, deep-stricken in his heart. Ah, Tony! What praises was he chanting now? What earthly distraction was he driving back?

"It was a good thing to do," said Christina.

"I'd give my right hand to have him back," Denis cried. "Oh, I think I mean that literally."

"Well, you won't get him. Anyone that once went there would most likely have the sense to stay."

"Are you frightened of the world, like he was?"

"Some things frighten me. America and those far-off places."

"But when they're far off, why let them frighten you?"

"Ah, I don't know." She looked about her, at the meadow and the stream and the green hill asleep against the brilliant west.

"I'd like to live and die in these parts," she said.

There was something in her voice that forbade Denis to reassure her.

"Do sit down, won't you?" he asked. "Let your aunt go hang for once."

She laughed softly and agreed to sit awhile among the gnarled roots of the oak tree.

Denis, stretched beside her, leaning on his elbow, beat gnats away and began to talk sixteen to the dozen, as was his manner when confused or very happy. He talked of his father now, for Anthony was a theme that often captured his attention. Christina had already noticed this, with a faint jealousy.

"You must have thousands of those creatures slaughtered," she said, "your arm is like a windmill."

"But you *have* seen him," Denis went on without heeding her, "you must have seen my father in the streets of Mellick. Anthony Considine. I'm sure he was pointed out to you."

"I don't go into Mellick twice in the year, I tell you."

"Even so, you couldn't miss him in Charles Street or King Street. He's the handsomest man in the town—easily!"

"Handsomer than you?" Christina teased him gently.

"Oh, Lord, yes—quite different."

"Don't be bothering me about what he's like. All I know is that he's the terror of the farmers round here, if they aren't in to him up to the minute with their crops—and he's a mighty hard bargainer, they say."

"He is that. He leads the farmers a dance, all right."

"He's rich and proud, and so are you. And I've no business at all to be sitting talking like this with my betters."

There was neither sting nor purpose in her words. Her eyes laughed sweetly at him.

"Oh, Christina—I simply have to say it—I've never seen so beautiful a face."

For the first time in their friendship she was visibly embarrassed now. She looked as if she had an answer to make; indeed her lips moved to make it, but then she turned away, and fumbled with the pages of a book.

Denis felt that he had made a terrible fool of himself.

"Do you ever have time to read—anything besides your prayerbook, Christina?"

"I've no books anyway."

"Do you think you'd like to read?"

"I don't know. I don't know anything about what's in books."

She had begun to read the book she fumbled with. Denis leant across and saw that her eyes were scanning the verse: "though one were strong as seven, he too with death shall swell . . ."

"I don't think that fellow would appeal to you much," he said.

Christina read the verse through.

"Singsong," she said then, with a little wondering smile.

But her eyes were sad as they turned back to Denis's face. They talked this evening for a longer time than usual. She seemed gradually to forget that her aunt would be looking for her, or that Christy the poacher might go by. It rained soon in the dark, and they crouched under Denis's waterproof cape, talking softly and childishly, hush-hushing each other sometimes if they heard a water-rat stir, or the white owl's cry or the cough of a far-away sheep. Shoulder touching shoulder, arm against arm, they talked and groped their way to each other's love. They told odds and ends of their child-hood, stories about Aunt Agnes and Aunt Bridget. They re-peated things said before—about "Flasher" Devoy, a great Jesuit now, away in the snow or the sun somewhere, and about Christina's uncle that had a newspaper shop in Liver-pool. And Denis talked of his brother Jack, who was wanting to have a racing-stable at the Curragh, and of Tony, the monk at Melleray, and always his refrain, of Anthony, his father. Christina told him about the great house where she had scrubbed floors for five years and of how Nora, the little cousin, had all but died a while back of a fever, and how John, that wasn't quite right in his head, could do any mortal thing that he liked with a horse or a cow or a dog. They spoke of the swan that they had not seen again and of the hay-saving that soon would be in the triangular meadow and of the christening of her cousin Julia's new baby in the County Cork.

But often their voices fell away, and they sat bemused in the cold dark, without moving arm or shoulder that touched so lightly under the waterproof cape, talking suddenly again at random, because they had become aware of their fantastic wish—that this awkward, happy companioning could last for ever and the rainy night have no dawn.

A frog jumped onto Christina's hand.

She started and laughed. Their elbows jerked together. She rose to her feet.

"I'll catch it this time from Aunt Bridget."

"Oh, Christina—let me come with you."

"Indeed then I won't. Is it make bad worse? Anyway John

will let me in—and if she is about, I'll make up some lie."

"I'll bet you a sovereign you won't be much good at that."

"That's why she'll believe me. She knows I don't tell lies. Good-night to you now."

"No, no, Christina. Not yet, I say!"

The mood between them had changed, was no longer restful. Imperious, frightened, Denis caught at the girl's hands.

"No, not good-night, I tell you!"

Her fingers received his so simply as to make his nervy snatching seem ridiculous. Humble and trembling now, he gave up his hands to the terrible, clear message hers were giving of a tenderness no longer easy to endure.

They stood very quietly for ten seconds under the dripping tree, their joined hands making a bar between their hearts.

"Good-night now. Do you hear me—good-night! Oh, Denis —I can't stay any longer!"

It was the first time that he heard her say his name—and he cried out on it. But with the ceasing of their two voices she was gone.

THE SIXTH CHAPTER

IT WAS eight days before he saw her again.

For seven of these the film that she had been gently raising between him and the world was so heavy about him that he was only barely able to keep up his pretence that it wasn't there. The days were golden—the hours at the office were hot and flurried—the world was in flower; and of these things he took only such cognisance as if he had read of them in a newspaper. Four things alone concerned him and wore the outline of reality. The first of these was terror lest he should never again find Christina at the oak tree; the second, which shocked him with its intermittent domination, was a weary sensation of relief when evening succeeded to evening and she did not come, an easing of tension because this ordeal of Christina was perhaps not to be, after all; the third thing that kept its zone clear of mists and shadows was his father's self-confident, observing face; and the fourth thing that swept and sang through him and was never quiet and never subdued to any of the other three was his desire for Christina, desire for his first love.

How he got through the lonely, expectant evenings by the stream he could not remember afterwards. On the sixth of them he left his rod and wandered about the fields, spying north and south for a glimpse of her. He could not keep still; his whole body was in pain; his eyes ached with watchfulness.

"Christina! Christina!" he sobbed as he beat his way among the shadows.

He went back to his rod and gathered it up.

"It's no use," he said to the cow across the water, "she'll never come again. Oh, love, Christina!"

On the seventh night he went farther over the fields and down the lane until he found the Danaghers' farm, the poor, clean cottage-farm where Christina lived. He prowled about it without caution; he watched its back and front doors—both were shut. He crept up to peer through the one window where there was a light, but pots of geraniums filled it and he could see nothing. He looked into outhouses; he patted a calf on the nose. He leant on a gate and stared at the small green door, so blankly shut against him. He whispered the name, "Christina!"

He wandered away and up the lane again. A hundred yards from the Danaghers' gate he met his Uncle Tom, breviary open, eyebrows raised in affable surprise.

"Do I see you here, Denis?"

"Oh, no," said Denis, "your eyes deceive you."

"Come, come, young fellow, that's no way to talk."

The priest's laugh was good-natured and disarmed his nephew.

"I'm sorry, Uncle Tom. I'm afraid I've picked up my manners from father."

Father Tom thought this an odd sort of apology, but he could see by Denis's smile that it was well-intentioned. He appreciated too that one had to be always making allowances for Anthony's spoilt darling.

"That's all right. I didn't expect to find you so far up from your trout. Taking a bit of a stroll?"

Denis nodded.

"Well, come in and have supper with me. I'm late going home to it, you see. We'll open some champagne to celebrate so rare a visitor."

Champagne with Father Tom, while there was one hope in a million that Christina would be coming to the oak tree!

"No, thank you, sir. I must get my rod before it's dark. And the mare's a bit fresh. I don't want to keep her too long at the Keener's to-night."

"Very good, my boy—as you please. But any time you're sick of your bit of river, you know, run up and see me. Indeed, I ought to be insulted to think that you're in my parish so much these times and never come next or near me!"

"Oh, well—good-night, Uncle Tom."

"Good-night, Denis."

But Christina didn't come to the oak tree, though he waited for her there until midnight.

§ 2

HE WOKE at five the next day, crying her name. His windows were wide open and morning blazed in them. He sprang from his bed and leant far out of the nearest one, running his hot hands along the dewy sill. Birds were in wild session; Denis listened to a pandemonium of blackbirds and of chaffinches. Through a gap in the trees he watched a lark shake its wet wings in the heavy paddock grass and mount its long spiral to the sky. The elm-tops were misted in gold; heaven, very luminously blue, seemed of the texture of a bubble; the wine-coloured hills shone like wine held against a light. Denis bent out farther above the garden he had half made and then forsaken. How justly, with what grace it took its slow descent! Wide lawns, dipping to wider, short lacy shadows on the turf, grey, noble, northward-going steps, lavender embanked with scarlet gillyflowers, and fuchsia breaking over from the north like a wave of tempest. Lower down, the long, massed cypresses, piercingly tall, fantastic, vigilant, like gaunt monks at their matins above the monkish orchard. And the river gathering it all in at last, into its bright embrace that had the sweep of a Spanish sword. Denis could hear the water-music now against the shouting of the birds, and he marvelled that noise and light, so riotously scattered, could fall together into such a holy peace. For that was what the exuberant morning was, holy and peaceful, as if this garden were the very Paradise, with every flower and blade of grass deep-washed in man's first innocence.

Denis breathed the smell of roses. He leant against the window-sash and took another long, slow breath.

"Are you awake, Christina?"

He smiled to think how that question would amuse her who had been at her work this hour.

"Christina, come back to-day—do you hear, Christina?"

Cobwebs glittered on the gable end. Beauty's most mysterious joke they always seemed to him, these summer-morning cobwebs.

"A cobweb! Ah! That's a good sign!" He invented the superstition with delight. "I'm positive that's a good sign. Oh, Christina, Christina, to-day!"

He flung off his nightshirt and raced across the room. He was as beautiful as the morning and as innocently unconscious of his beauty.

§ 3

HE RODE until breakfast-time. At breakfast he talked full pelt until Aunt Agnes, who was suffering from what Paris-trained Doctor Joe diagnosed as "tick doolaroo," screamed at him to hold his tongue.

During the walk with his father to the office, along the green Carberry Road and over the humpy bridges of the Old Town, a silence fell on him. The face that had been so wildly gay when it exasperated Aunt Agnes became locked in gravity and his eyes searched far into the sky.

"What is it, Denis? What is it, my son?"

These words kept forming in the back of Anthony's mind, and falling apart and reforming, the whole way in to Charles Street. But when the two reached the door of Considine's he had not said them, and he passed through the general office with a look of preoccupation on his face that frightened the wits out of Mr. Flannery.

§ 4

AT HALF-PAST five Denis lay down under his oak tree, whose shadow, unrolled eastward on the scented field, was like a Mussulman's praying carpet, he idly thought.

Golden light flowed all about him; peace, after the high stresses of the day, lay golden and glowing in his heart. His rod was idle on the grass, his basket empty of fish. The river hardly whispered. He had turned his face away from it, to watch the corner of the hazel hedge, but he could hear the whirr of dragonflies above it and knew when a water-hen's wings dishevelled it with a homeward rush.

The cow lowed sadly from the western bank; voices of birds were few and tender; the grass was over-sweet for mowing. The hazel hedge had grown so high that even by climbing on its bank Denis could not see over it now to where Mellick lay in the dip of the saucer-plain.

He did not want to see over it or think of climbing on its bank. He had made Mellick to be a vaguer image in his mind just now than its smoke-shroud was upon the evening landscape; he had left it behind and would not be aware of it. He was not even aware of his father now. He had only room for one certainty at last, and the hedge, cutting off his view of Mellick's spires, cut off his past and future too, his traditions and affections and perplexities, his panics and duties and inescapable Considine destiny, all that dead or unborn Denis who had no life in this radiant, living hour that he would not forego, this here-and-now, this slowly moving, green-encircled dream.

The lovely, uncompanioned hour was made perfect by an unnamable expectancy, and he rested in it with the patience of such a deep impatience as he had never known. Christina would come to him, and here was her hour at last, the last hour of the sun. She would come across the meadow, deep-trailing through the buttercups, whose dust would stain her fingertips and scatter on her dress. She would break through the pattern of the Mussulman's carpet and stand upright among its dapples, half-smiling back to his smile.

As he thought of her coming she came. He saw her suddenly, a grey-green shadow, like a young willow tree against the hazel branches. But now she was moving forward in the sunlight, her fingers feathering the grass, a dark track curving behind her where she had trodden on the buttercups. She wore a ·dress of green-printed cotton, clean, cheap and clumsily made, the sort of dress she always wore; her hair was drawn harshly as ever back from her brow to the nape of her neck. Her step was the slow, familiar one that Denis had watched so often. But to the staring boy she moved now as under a foreign and more searching sun, whose light gave strangeness to her dearly known face by simply lighting it more clearly. Her simple and unconscious gravity was like a mighty banner held above her, so that when she halted in the carpet of the oak tree Denis saw not only Christina in a cotton dress, the farm girl of his native county, but another Christina too, someone older and wiser than he had guessed, in whom a habit of courage and purity had called up aristocratic grace to meet this hour.

"Christina! It's eight days!"

They came near to each other.

"Yes, I know," said Christina.

Her eyes flickered over him hungrily and a flame of delight rose in them for this refreshment after abstinence. He did not touch her, although the movements of his heart were shaking him so that to stand before her without swaying was not easy. But he pondered her face once more for what seemed a long stretch of time, letting himself become amazed all over again by the vast and stormy nobleness of her brows and the reserve of darkness, for all their light, in her generously shining eyes. Her lips were closed in gravity so that he could not see her splendid teeth, "sailor's teeth, buccaneer's teeth," as he called them; but he saw how the veins in her throat were pounding and that her breasts were being stormed by the heart between them as wildly as his heart was shaking him.

"How could you stay away so long, Christina?"

"Ah, I don't know," she said, as if she truly did not know, now she was restored to him, how she had suffered separation. "I thought maybe we'd better try and have sense, the two of us."

Her voice trailed off on the last light words and as it dropped away the evening clanged loud and terrible in Denis's ears. There seemed a storm about him; some sea was roaring in his ears. No buttercup field remained, or hedge or shadowing oak tree. He was caught up, enmisted and illumined, in the country of his own desire, and all that was familiar there was her assenting face. He could not stand apart from her another breath.

"Christina! Oh, love, Christina!"

He saw her arms open wide, as if for crucifixion, and it

seemed to him that he had to run to them from a long way off, across a perilous plain. But when he reached them, suddenly there was no more noise, and no light except the long shaft of the sun; earth came back, sweet and mortal, when he stood in Christina's arms; buttercup field and stream of trout and shadowy tree, the little bright world that they had shared this month long lay quiet round them as they took their first embrace.

Neither had ever loved before and their surrender now was to a power of which they still knew nothing, but when, by an unworded instinct, they turned aside together from the still searching sun, and took the cool, protecting wood for shelter, it was as if the ghosts of dead amourists were stirring from every tree-trunk to breathe knowledge of good and evil on these babes; it seemed as if Angus himself, the love-god of these old fields, were hovering instructively about them, for they cried each other's names with a new insistence amid the green shadows, and their hands and mouths clung in immediate, undeniable demand. Wading through pools of fern they went, as Angus may have led them, to a still greener, quieter place, where, canopied by long, satiny leaves of chestnut, their bed of wood sorrel was laid.

A word from Christina now, from that chaste, Catholic Christina, whose wish it was to serve God and be holy, would have brought Denis back, quick as an arrow, from his uncalculating, passionate purpose. A word from Christina would have saved the flower that was in danger.

Strangely, she did not say that word. Her eyes, though reflective still, were the eyes of one who has come to the end of thinking and, having decided on a course, has pledged herself to deal with whatever perils it may bring. Thus, wiser and more fatalistic than he, no dreamer or loser of the world as he so often was, no heedless girl in the sense in which he was heedless boy, but conscious, as a well-trained Catholic, that she was gambling an eternal heaven for a fleeting one, and newly aware with a shock that made her smile that it was possible to commit what priests call mortal sin without the faintest sense of guilt, she gave herself up, with the catechism's "perfect knowledge and full consent," to her desire for Denis.

So the two innocents learnt and taught the art of love, and when they had reached its last secret and cried out and sobbed in startled revelation, they lay a long while as if asleep in each other's arms. But they were not asleep, as their hearts knew that clashed together, as their lips knew that sought each other still in drowsy thirst, as all their nerves and flesh knew, humming with wild wakefulness.

"Christina, why did you come back to me to-day?"

"Ah, when I woke this morning I knew I'd have to."

"I knew it then too. You stayed away eight days!"

" 'Twas a long time."

"Longer for me than you."

His soft, laughing breath blew over her face. She stared at his near-bending beauty with a brief anguish, as if she were never to see it again.

"Why did you stay away so long, will you tell me?" he scolded.

"I told you, child. I did it for the best. I thought we wouldn't be able to be good any longer."

"And then you came back, and we weren't."

"So you tell me," she teased him.

"Christina," he spoke delicately, perplexed for her orthodox conscience, "we've committed a mortal sin—according to your way of thinking—I have, at least."

She smiled at the generous modification.

"Why you?"

"Oh, well, I'm a man," he said vaguely, and smiled again.

"A terrible villain you look this minute," said her tender voice, while her hands made a frame for his fair young face. And then she drew his head down to her breast and crooned to him as she held it there.

"Don't talk about sins, let you, since it's plain enough you don't believe in them, you sinner, you! Maybe you're right —and maybe you're wrong. Maybe our two souls are blackened now, but it's hard to believe that, I admit. How could God put the like of you in hell, my darling? Sure, doesn't He love you more than I do, and if that's true, there isn't a hair of your head will ever come to harm."

"And you, Christina, you! What terrible nonsense they talk, these holy men!"

She stared up dreamily at the long, glossy chestnut leaves. "Do you think they know rightly what they're saying about it all?"

He laughed.

"I don't, if you want to know. But I suppose they have to try and keep order some way, God help them!"

"But what harm are we doing this minute, will you tell me?"

"Ah, Christina—there's the rub! If we were only just ourselves, not bits and pieces in a scheme of someone else's——" He bent to search her eyes. "But if you're happy just this minute—if only you're happy, Christina!"

"I didn't know there was such happiness in the wide world," she said, "as I'm having now in the sight of your face."

Physical love it was that they gave each other, the bright, clear, sensual love of the young, never again to be so fresh and sweet with the sweet surprises of the flesh. Never after this first love would the body's passion be enough to wash the spirit too, and the hot, restless, lonely mind; never again would easing of the senses seem the whole man's panacea or the end of isolation. Denis and Christina were lucky in their hour and in each other. There was nothing stale or evil in either of them nor any calculating thought, nor wish to plague the other with hypocrisy or blame. Each saw, however dimly, that religion and society waited behind this forbidden joy for a grave reckoning, and Denis in especial saw how the world might hound Christina for it; but meanwhile, ah, meanwhile they would have the wit to trust themselves to love and let the hourglass run.

It ran unheeded now until Christina noticed that the quiet of the wood had sunk to night's absolute stillness and that Denis's face was only its own shadow to her peering eyes.

"Denis, it's very late. I simply must go home!"

"I'll go with you."

"Indeed you will not. Is it to ruin everything? You won't stir from this spot till I'm over the field and across the lane."

"Over the field and across the lane!" He played with the words indolently, anxious to prolong the time before she left him.

"How'll I know when you're gone that far, Christina?"

She kissed him.

"Guess it, Mr. Clever."

"Why must I stay here without you? Why can't I come halfway?"

"Because there's no telling who'd be abroad. Christy the poacher maybe, or Eily Ronan after some boy——"

"Like yourself."

"True for you."

They lay still again, as still as if no word had been said of parting.

"I love you. I love you for ever."

"Ah, no, child, don't say that."

"But I do. I love you and love you and love you—for ever, Christina."

"Say you love me—that's enough."

"Well, I won't say even that unless you say it back."

"Ah, child, you know I love you."

He laid his head in her breast again and for a long minute she stroked his hair.

"Good-night to you now; I'm going."

"What'll you say to your aunt when you get in?"

She gave a perplexed little sigh.

"Oh, another lie, I suppose. I'm getting to be a marvel at lies. Let me get up now, Denis—there's a good boy."

They stood on the crushed sorrel; the glossy chestnut leaves brushed their shoulders with a ghostly sound.

"To-morrow, Christina?"

"Yes, I'll come to you to-morrow."

"I wish I could fall asleep here until then."

"Oh, Denis—if we could!"

Anguish overweighted her voice. The last words were a sob.

"Good-night, Christina—good-night!"

Simultaneously they were flung forward to the moment that waited for them beyond this parting, the moment in which incredibly they would be bereft of each other's comfort, alone with their second thoughts. The wood about them was voiceless, as dark and still as that moment would be that they now looked to. Paradoxically, as they faced its isolation they pressed once more together. But this embrace was to console, not to enrapture. Their hands were gentle on each other. "Hush, hush," they seemed to be saying, as if they heard a sob in their own and the wood's silence. Maybe they did. Maybe some sprite was weeping among the trees because innocence had had to die again. An old tale, surely, over which tears and to spare have been shed. But to this boy and girl it seemed of a sudden a sober story—a piece of bad news, half understood, half disbelieved. Each had to put out courage to accept it and tenderness to ease it for the other. So they embraced now with little passion and great love, with hands and lips that reassured and fumbled to reassure again, and clung, imploring for love's reassurance. Resignedly at last they held each other, agreeing without a word to take this bitterness in what had seemed a moment ago all sweet. So Love made them his in everything.

"To-morrow?"

"To-morrow."

The swish and soft crackle of Christina's going troubled the wood awhile. When they were over Denis sank face-downwards on the sorrel and waited in some wonder for his second thoughts. But they were only of Christina's face when she had opened her arms to him beneath the oak tree, of Christina creeping alone this minute across the moonlit meadow, of Christina's voice when she had said, "Ah, child, you know I love you." Her face shone for a flash, as a saint's might in a vision, against his dropped eyelids. It was pale as ivory—no, it was ruddy now, and laughing—it was Tony's face. And he was saying—no, no, not Tony—who was saying, "Welcome home, my son"? . . . "Ah, Christina, I love you. . . . To-morrow, Christina."

He fell asleep.

THE SEVENTH CHAPTER

"HOLY MOTHER!" prayed Mr. Flannery in distress. "Holy Mother Mary!"

He pushed his steel-rimmed glasses to the tip of his nose and peered across the room.

"Mr. Denis, will you come here a minute, sir? Will you come here, Mr. Denis, in the name of God?"

Denis was at the door of Considine's receiving office, hat in hand. Shafts of summer-evening brightness cut across the dusty room and divided him from Mr. Flannery.

"Well, if you put it like that——"

He crossed to the desk with a smile.

"What's the matter now, will you tell me?"

"Yerrah, what'd be the matter, sir, only that you have the affairs of this office in a meelsthrim——"

"In a what, Flannery?"

"In a meelsthrim, Mr. Denis—in a doodah, sir. Look at this, if you please"—he pointed at a daybook that had been in Denis's recent charge, pointed dramatically with a steel pen and threw a blot.

"Yes, indeed, look at this," said Denis and fussed indignantly with blotting paper.

"Yah, what's a blot," said Mr. Flannery—"in the thick of this confusion, what's a blot here or there?" He waved his pen and flung three more of them.

"Flannery," said Denis, "will you please mind what you're doing!"

"The same to you, sir—and many of them," snapped Flannery. "If I was to be sitting on this stool until the Angel Gabriel sounds his bugle I couldn't find rhyme or reason in these figurings of yours, sir!"

"Oh, Flannery, not even a bit of a rhyme?"

"Your work is a disgrace this month past, a holy and sacred disgrace, if I may make so bold—but in the last five days, God help us all, it's gone to ballyhoo entirely! You're no better than a hindrance in the place, sir—and pardon to you!"

He glared at Denis. His little, weary, irritable face was touching.

"I'm dead sorry, Flannery. I swear it. But put the old mess away now in heaven's name. I'll straighten it out for you in the morning."

"You'll straighten it out now, sir!"

"In the morning, Flannery. *La nuit porte conseil.* That's French for 'I'll sleep on it.' "

"Ah, French indeed! And I suppose it's in French you're keeping this daybook!"

"Put the old thing away, Flannery. You're so tired this minute that you'll only make bad worse!"

Flannery bounced on the stool.

"I'd have you remember, sir, that I'm a ledger clerk of forty years' experience!"

"That's right. That's why you're tired. Forty years of ledger-clerking would addle anyone, Flannery!"

"It isn't like you, Mr. Denis, to be impertinent to me."

"I didn't mean to be impertinent, honestly." He smiled and took up his hat again. "Good-night to you now. I'm off."

"Oho, so you're off! Sure, of course you're off. You're hardly on these times before you're off! Are you aware that it isn't half-past five of the evening yet?"

"I am not." Denis pulled out his watch with a virtuous flourish. "I'm aware instead that it's twenty to six."

"And if it is that same—what call have you to leave the job when it suits you—without as much as by-your-leave? And we in the height of the busiest hay-harvest that's been for years—with every other unfortunate fool in the place putting in extra time—grand evenings and all that's in it! Oh, isn't it well you know you're the chairman's son!"

"Shut up, Flannery!"

Denis swung out of the office in a fine fluster of rage.

"Holy Mother," prayed Mr. Flannery, "what's coming over him at all, at all?"

"What's coming over him?" said Quirk of the oily hair—"what would be coming over him, you old gazebo, but some bit of a girl?"

§ 2

THE ordeal of Christina, not having been diverted, was working tempestuously in Denis. Since he had taken her and lost his boyhood, life, that is, his daily life of habit and familiar scenes, had lost all definition. On the other hand, he was alive with a new kind of life that stung, delighted, and alarmed him. His mental processes, which normally were nimble and easily applied to things as they came, were now so much engrossed in one proposition, that he was capable of treating a daybook even as Flannery said he treated it, and without feeling any regret. But within the orbit of that proposition his activity was endless and not altogether happy. It was as if his brain were sealed against every thought and impression that did not bear upon Christina, and as if further that brain had become disintegrated into a hive of smaller brains, each cell an independent functionary, and as if, so sealed up together with only one thesis, these functionaries held perpetual and loud debate.

Christina, Christina—over and about and round her thoughts, dreams, and apprehensions clashed. Love was inebriation and he was at that stage of it wherein reason is active but light-footed. Arguments moved about within him, clearly seen, but none paused long enough for him to master or be mastered by it.

He loved Christina in a fashion that his relations would have called pagan. That is to say, in all the days of their acquaintance, until he took her, she never once appeared to him in the guise of wife and mother of his children. It is true that it had not been his habit to think with enthusiasm of a future wife and child and fireside or dreamily to prefigure them, but he had vaguely believed that with the coming of love they would be an irresistible suggestion. Now love was here, sweet, clandestine, unbridled, and certainly at its heels, on its fulfilment, came the question of its afterwards. But not in such terms as convention would have demanded. Not on the current of desire, but with perplexity, sometimes in detachment, sometimes in bitter tenderness, Denis faced it. As a member of society he looked at the problem of Christina which Christina's lover had created, and he was alarmed to find that it was a problem for him and not a matter of one inevitable destiny. But though alarmed he could not feel dishonoured by his own unexpected attitude of indecision. He felt no more dishonoured by it than he could feel that his illicit love dishonoured her, as inevitably the world would say it did.

The world would have had a very great deal to say about the business. The world would say that he had brought his love to the old, classic situation. It would say that there were only two roads ahead of him, that he must either disgrace himself by deserting his love—no great novelty in that—or amend his wrong by marrying her. And it would conclude by reminding him of the laws of God and man of which he should have thought more timely.

All this Denis knew without having to ask the world to say it—and it contributed nothing to him.

That he should desert Christina—as the phrase would run —was the same sort of proposition as that he should make a square circle. It was talking in self-cancelling terms. One did not desert love, since love was now a part of oneself. On the other hand, must one lay a load on it that it had not asked and that would look like crushing it—ring and name and house and bed, cradles, midwives, visiting cards, dinner-parties, a carriage-and-pair? Did every love need these things to complete it? Was there no other way of imprisoning the elusive guest, or must Christina truly and really become a Considine for her sins? Because he loved her? To one at least of the debating entities in Denis's brain this progressional link between love and marriage which was the world's routine, and which he had only contemplated now and then with mild surprise in the affairs of others, seemed suddenly fantastic. But even while this faction chuckled another was springing up to question it.

"It's right," this other said. "At any rate, it has the sanction of all history that marriage and housekeeping should be a fruit of love. And anyway, who are you, young fellow-me-lad, to jib at so venerable an impulse? Badly as they manage it, the home-making and home-going inclination is one of the gentlest and least harmful things in men. Besides, there are more needs and aspects in love than you have found; what do you know of it yet, you whippersnapper? What do you know of your own demands on it, or of Christina's? And even if it's only physical passion——"

"It isn't!" he thundered to his restive parliament.

"Well, even if it were only physical passion, that force between a man and woman is not only their affair, irritating as that may seem; it's society's business and must be either admitted or not to concern the next generation. Mere hedging won't do and neither will anti-social petulance. Love isn't easily bought!"

And then a more cynical voice spoke.

"If you could remain virginal no longer," it said, "don't pretend that you've never heard of other ways to manhood besides this difficult business of falling in love. You have money, and the wise world would have looked the other way. That's what your father is doing, even now—looking the other way, being wise. And even the Church, which is the wisest of all worldly institutions, would have only pretended to grudge you your fling."

"Oh, my fling! I haven't been thinking of flings!"

"No, no. Of course you haven't. You've only been mooning by rivers and fields, fretting about this and blaming that, and swearing at the other thing. You've only been sunset-gazing, and sighing for departed friends, and reading Rousseau and reading Keats and reading Mr. Swinburne."

"But what's the point of all that now? I love Christina."

"Well, what's your plan? How are you to go on loving her?"

Simply go on. That seemed to be his plan. And when the world found out that he was Christina's lover? Why, he and Christina would tell the world that so it was. And then?

These were the battles that blazed between him and his daybook, between him and his sleep, between him and his father's face. But the promise and the memory of his evenings gleamed above them, like a serene sky roofing and dwarfing a noisy world. For whatever was to come, and however his mind might belittle and harry itself with its misgivings, his body was at peace. An animal ecstasy controlled him, that brightened his eyes with new knowledge, even when they longed for sleep, and gave arrogance to his limbs, weary though they sometimes were from love's excess. It was physical well-being that made him impertinent to Mr. Flannery, as it was the spring in his feet and the light in his eyes that gave up his secret to young Quirk of the oily hair.

§ 3

HE HURRIED from them now towards where Christina would be waiting, six miles away. He was angry at Flannery's taunt about "the chairman's son," because he knew it to be accurate. For a month now, and more than ever in this week, he had been meanly using that advantage in order to leave the office before the other clerks. Well enough he knew that no one would dare stop him, and he was ashamed of himself for playing on that knowledge. But in his present mood he could even brush away shame without really feeling it. He shook it off now with the last houses of the town.

"Tch, tch," he urged the chestnut mare, who sped under his hand as if she saw his desires like colts outstripping her.

§ 4

CHRISTINA waited on the far side of the wood, for the haymakers were about the oak tree now. It was their sixth meeting since they had given each other love. Denis searched her welcoming eyes but could read no deeper in them than their deep-shining gaiety of tenderness.

"Have you been waiting long?"

"Oh, I don't know. A minute or so, I think."

She sat on a log just within the wood, from which, unseen, they could see a green corner of the world and a flash of the stream.

"Christina, when are we going to be married?"

His own question surprised Denis. He had not known that he was going to ask it or that, if he did, it would be on so breathless a voice.

As he ended it he felt Christina's hands gently trying to withdraw from his. He tightened his hold on them.

"Please, Christina, when will you marry me?"

"Why are you saying that?"

"Why else but because we love each other—don't we?"

"Yes, we do—I'm sure of that."

"Well, then——"

Laughing at him, she put a hand over his mouth.

"Don't say it any more, child. You're a bad hand at proposing."

He freed his mouth from her fingers.

"Proposing? I'm not proposing! I'm simply saying that you love me and have got to marry me!"

He was excited. He swung from the log and stood before her gesticulating.

"I'm not proposing to you, young lady. And if I am, who has a better right, will you tell me that? Oh, come on, Christina, don't be a tease. When will you marry me?"

"Stop waving your hands, like a good boy. Here, give them to me. No one could talk with those things whirling in front of them."

He gave her his hands and dropped on his knees before her. He stared into her face and coaxed her.

"What is it, darling? Oh, darling, darling, darling—what's up with you this evening? Why won't you talk sense, Christina?"

"Because I'm afraid to, I think."

"Afraid to?"

She took his head into her hands.

By now Denis roughly understood the idiom of Christina's fingers. She had a contrary trick of overcharging them with wild, dumb expression of her love when on the point of seeming to belittle it in words. So now that their light touch burnt his hair and face with an especial warning tenderness, he waited in perplexity for her to speak.

"I'll never marry you, my darling, and so please don't say another word about it."

The moment was here for which Christina had been watching. She knew that if Denis asked her to marry him her whole inclination would be to say "yes" and take the consequences. Her love was simple and had been further simplified by her surrender to it, desire's confusion clarified into a straightforward longing to share her lover's life. Whereas, before she had given herself to Denis, the thought that he should ever touch or kiss her had seemed enough for every need, now their caresses, though paramount still and wildly sweet to her, were revealed as a part of love instead of the complete thing she had intended them to be. Her hot young passion was only a beginning of emotion, not the end in itself she had coaxed herself to wish it. What should have been, to be manageable, a madness, had grown sane and strong in her heart—against her will.

A distinction in Christina was her natural, untutored sanity. This was so much a part of her as even to heighten her beauty by subduing it. Now, entering her love, it compelled her to look honestly ahead.

Denis was going to ask her, sooner or later, to marry him. She knew that before he did, saw the question flit across his eyes with all the enemy questions in pursuit of it, many and many a time when he was scarcely conscious of their whirling in his head. Beyond the happy "yes" that leapt in her to answer him the world was waiting with its intricate regulations, the pompous, watchful, self-sufficient world that she, ignorant and unworldly, understood well enough for the purpose of her debate. She saw how that world would receive her as affianced wife of Denis Considine—that in fact it would not receive her at all, that it would rave and thunder, cry out and denounce, as if in choosing her this one of themselves had done an unnatural deed—that it would fling itself together in great crowds to stare at her, to obliterate and mock and wound her. Indeed for one who was a stranger to the proud middle class, she formed a surprisingly accurate picture of how that class would regard her tentative of entering it. Beyond the first storms and the first piercing humiliations, she saw the long array of years that she would have to live at the centre of that great, possessive horde, unforgiven by them, unaccepted, but forever hemmed in; felt their contemptuous eyes on her as she fumbled to learn their superficial tricks, not for their sakes but for Denis's, fumbled and failed because of them standing by; saw their resentment if she made Denis happy, their sagacious head-wagging if she didn't; heard their anxious comments on Denis's children, tainted with her lowliness; felt her own gnawing terror of them that would never lie easy in her to the end of her days.

These things unsteadied her. Again and again she had to admit herself terror-stricken, almost beaten by them. Could any love outweigh them? Even the near presence of his beauty, his faith and cherishing and tenderness? Even the pride of bearing his children, the consolation of being always his consoler?

And then across the blackness of these questions Denis's face would shine and tatter them as morning tatters the east, so that she knew her love could look a million Considines in the face. It became clear to her that these people with their habits, prejudices, and exactions, these people who would be a great part of her future life, would still be nothing of it, since they would be its externals only, its coat put on from without. She could not disbelieve in the impregnability of the inner life, or see how the irrelevant winds of the outside world could quench the sheltered lamp within her heart. So, though she was afraid of the Considines, she knew that she could face them for love's sake.

But she saw now that love could differ, root and branch, from love.

Denis and she had been impelled into passion by similar causes. Each had been overcome by the personal beauty of the other and the other's superficial strangeness, by the eternal harmony of youth, by the adornments of hour and place that framed their meetings and by commonplace, complementary urgencies in their blood. Both needed an escape, she from a fear of exile that was growing morbid, he from his own sense of futility and waste. These things had given an immeasurable passion to their first embrace, a deceptive finality that seemed to say that here was an end of hungering and asking, and that this moment was time's crowning gift which would neither fade nor change.

This passion had not stayed long with Christina without suffering change. If she was passionately happy now, that came from observing the happiness she gave her lover far more than from taking what he gave.

When she committed herself to Denis, she did so, as has been seen, with eyes wide open, solemnly brave and asking no quarter from the great law of her church. Because she desired him beyond the strength of her strong religious sense, she took him and risked damnation, keeping her own counsel about what that dark and perplexing idea meant to her. Sin would be punished hereafter. She accepted that, being too honest to assure herself that there would be time to do penance between now and death; indeed, on the contrary, she told herself that retribution would be all the harsher because her audacity had been great and cool. But leaving eternal justice to its own time, Christina had noticed that pleasure rarely comes to men without leaving them some immediate aftermath of responsibility or sorrow. The mighty pleasure of love would not surprise her if it showed that characteristic, and if it did, she would not protest.

So as the hours of love revealed to her that her love was changing, she schooled herself for what she recognised as pleasure's aftermath. Passion was putting out undreamt-of flowers: tenderness, loneliness, jealousy, curiosity, the desire to make a familiar thing of love, to set up house with it, to have it near her by the fire at night and at the morning's waking, to eat and drink with it and work and rest. Christina let herself dream of sharing twenty-four hours of the day with Denis. She thought of how it would be to walk through streets of people on his arm, or to be tired and sit alone with him, or to answer his sudden shouts or make his tea or fold his clothes or light the lamps against his coming home—and all these everyday doings shone for her in that blessed, tremulous light that only dreams can radiate. To have the daily custom of such nothings would turn the great Considine enmity into a very pitiful affair.

But Denis wasn't dreaming as she dreamt. She knew that. She knew that for him love remained what he had first required it to be—an escape, a refuge from all that life of commonplace towards which her eyes were looking covetously now. He did not want those intimacies that she wanted. He wanted this that he had found, this hidden, summer ecstasy that explained and illuminated life, this initiation that was an end in itself and needed nothing more to sustain or justify it. He had found an evening secret that was unacquainted with the rest of the dusty day. He had no instinct to domesticate it.

No instinct. But the rational part of him was perplexed for all that, and for twenty external or uppermost reasons that Christina knew or guessed would insist on taking charge of his irresponsible love, so as to take away that which made it perfect for him.

The rational part of him reckoned without Christina, whose intention it was to give him in this love only that which he truly wanted, and not one iota more. Whatever became of her or however she was to bear her own overburdened heart, she was fixed in this that she would not misunderstand his true demand on her, or spoil what she had given by overgiving.

"I'll never marry you, my darling, so please don't say another word about it."

"I'll say a thousand words about it—I'll say a million words! Christina, when will you marry me?"

She bent over him, taking his face into the hollow of her shoulder so as to escape his staring eyes.

"Denis, don't you know yet that I'm one of those people that mean what they say?"

"There's more than you in this world can mean what they say. Don't you see—oh, surely you see that you've got to marry me?" Still keeping his arms round her, he drew himself up again onto the log. "Christina, listen to me. Leave love out of it for a minute. We can't go on like this. You, who're so holy and good—you can't go on committing sins for me. I should never have let you, Christina, knowing what it costs you—knowing what it means—it was all my fault from beginning to end, but oh, my sweet, my darling——"

Their faces, pressed together, burnt each other. Ecstasy was surging up to defeat their talk.

Christina laughed very softly.

"You see," she said, "you don't mean a word of all that you're saying. You're just as bad this minute as ever you were."

"I know I am. Sit farther off, you terrible woman, sit away off there at the end of the log." He slithered to his end of it and waved her to hers. "I mean it. Good-bye, Christina— keep your distance, if you please, until I tell you you can move."

She sat obediently at the extreme end of the log.

"You'll have to shout now," she commented drily, "and the whole parish will hear you."

"They're welcome. They could hear worse than a man proposing marriage to a girl."

They stared at each other, smiling uncertainly. There was something forlorn in both faces.

"What do you mean?" Denis asked her. "Tell me what you mean when you say you'll never marry me."

"Only that I won't."

He leant along the log, and whispered.

"Do you want to go on committing mortal sins?"

"Leave that alone. I know my catechism, child, without any instructions from you."

"Ye-es—but—and anyhow, how am I to go on meeting you all through the year—when it's raining, Christina?"

She chuckled.

"You have a fine waterproof cape."

"Don't be silly. In the winter, when it's cold——"

"If you still want me in the winter, when it's cold——"

"Christina, how can you talk to me like that?"

"Ah, don't look that way, my darling!" She stretched her hand to him in pleading—forgetfully they drew together again. "I'm not doubting your love, Denis—indeed, indeed I'm not. But what age are you—nineteen?"

"I'll be twenty in a fortnight."

"Well, and if you were twenty-five, what matter? The day will come when you won't want me."

"What right have you to say that?"

"I don't mean it unkindly. Anyway, if you still want me in the winter, and I'm still here——"

"How, still here?"

"Oh, my aunt is talking from morning to night now of—
of Australia and America—and the money I'll be sending
home to her next year!"

He gathered her up with violence to his heart.

"No, I say! No! Do you hear? By God, you're not her
slave, or to be frightened away by fifty aunts out of your
own country! My love, my dear, I'll have to marry you by
force!"

Christina nestled awhile to this strong, sweet comforting.
Why not give way and marry him, and so end for ever this
unbearable threat of exile? Why not take a chance on her
power to keep him happy, in spite of his own wilfulness? To
live here quietly in this green plain that was all of the world
she asked to see, to be his without expecting him to be too
much hers, to let him come and go and have his way . . . Ah,
lightly as with silk she'd harness him, or indeed not harness
him at all!

"Besides, you know, Christina, that that's all nonsense about
wanting you in the winter. I love you. I've never loved any
girl before—and I never, before I saw you, looked twice at
one of them. That's a fact, and you know it. I don't run
after girls—and so it doesn't matter about my being young.
I'll be faithful, Christina—I know I will, if you'll marry me."

She believed that. She had an idea that he would take his
marriage seriously. She did not know if perpetual fidelity
would be possible for him, but only that to ignore or offend
her love would not come easy to his sensitiveness. It was odd,
considering the lawlessness with which he had taken her, that
Christina should have been so sure of the will and power of
this boy to cleave to her. But she was more or less right, for
all that. Profligacy was not what she would have to fear, any
more than she feared, so far as he was concerned, the difference in their stations. With regard to the difficulties and
embarrassments that that would make in their marriage she
trusted him implicitly, and in this she made no mistake. In
matters that called for delicacy of feeling, Denis was reliable.
He seemed to Christina to have an odd, unboyish, two-edged
understanding of the littleness of little things and of the great
discomfort they can cause. So, she felt, he would neither ignore
the thousand chances of humiliation for her among his rich,

proud relatives, nor, should all those chances descend on her at once, believe that they really humiliated. She didn't know that he inherited this trick, which was no more than inability to be pompous, from an old, rough grandfather called Honest John of whom she had heard the farmers round about tell tales. She thought that his common-sense in human values was her lover's own especial gift, but where he got it from was neither here nor there. She only knew that if she married him, it would be, far more than her own courage, her talisman against his world. It was indeed a heavy argument for giving up her silly struggle against happiness.

"Christina, I don't see what we're to do if you won't marry me. We can't go on like this—it's wrong. That sounds ridiculous to me, I admit—but you do believe it to be wrong, don't you, Christina? And if you do, it can't go on, do you hear? And listen, love." He gathered her up again into the consoling darkness of embrace. "Listen—supposing you have a child——" She stirred as if she wanted to speak, but he held her head to his breast and hurried on: "If you have a child! How do you suppose I would consent to have you unmarried then? Don't you know the world even that much, Christina? And after all, you'll admit that I too would have some right in the child, don't you?"

She raised her head.

"Denis—that's true. If I were to have a child I'd be afraid. I know the way they treated my mother—and the way they sometimes treat me. If I were having a child, Denis, I'd be terrified, and I'd want your help. But if you stood by me——"

"Stood by you! Christina, will you stop talking like a lunatic? I love you, I tell you, I love you! I'm your husband whether you like it or no—I'm yours, do you hear? You can't escape me!"

The wood was dark now and the last brightness gone from the flash of stream and wisp of field outside it. Love had been patient with the lovers' talk and could wait no longer. So, with nothing settled of their argument, they kissed and let it be. For this hour at least they were together—wasn't that enough? Maybe they'd die now in each other's arms. Maybe the end of the world would come to-morrow.

Thus love carried them again from all their moorings.

THE EIGHTH CHAPTER

Two days after Flannery's lament on the daybook, Anthony sent word to Denis that he wanted him in his office.

Denis went to him and crossed the desk to sit on the leather window-seat.

"Yes, father?"

"Aha!" said Anthony. "So you're making yourself at home, are you? Maybe you're thinking that I sent for you for the sake of your beautiful eyes?"

He smiled very tenderly on his waiting, smiling son, for fear his next remark should be taken seriously.

"I suppose you're not even aware that I'm having you on the mat this time?"

"I wondered when you would, to tell the truth, father."

"And disapproved of my unjust leniency, I suppose?"

"Go on," said Denis. "What is it?"

He knew that these heavy preliminaries meant that his father loathed going on and would have to be pushed to it.

"Go on, man alive! Is it the sack?"

"Flannery's right, by God," said Anthony amusedly. "You're getting to be a very impudent fellow. No, it isn't the sack. How can the second chairman sack the third? But look here, you're getting me into a fix. In the first place, such work as you're doing, you're doing badly. You'll admit that it must be pretty bad when Flannery finds the gumption to report you to me?"

"I do. I admit I'm working rottenly."

"And in the second place you're hardly working at all. No, my son—I'm not asking you to tell me why. I know why."

Denis opened wide eyes at him.

"Oh, I can't give you chapter and verse, or the name the young lady took at Confirmation. I don't know a word about your goings-on, as a matter of fact, except that they're going on. All I want to point out to you is that while you are carrying your head in the clouds, we're having here in this place an extremely busy hay season. Though you don't seem to be aware of it, you're the only clerk in my employment who has done no overtime at all during this rush."

"I am aware of it. And I'm sorry, father. I'll start tomorrow, if that's what you want."

"It is and it isn't."

"How do you mean?"

"You know me. You know that, as far as I'm concerned myself, I don't give a row of pins for what the whole shoot of those fellows below say or don't say about the way I favour you."

"You ought to give a row of pins."

"Well, I don't. But for your sake, I mustn't give them the chance to throw mud at us both. You'll have the handling of them sooner or later."

"That's not the point, father. I've been feeling an absolute hound about not staying in late—only——"

"Why should you feel a hound? If they work late, they're paid for it."

"I should hope so."

"Well, I'm not grumbling at that—and they needn't either. I pay through the nose, so I do."

Denis laughed at him.

"Not through the nose, father. Not if I know you. There's no one in this place gets a halfpenny more than he's worth."

"With the possible exception of the Mulqueens, father and son."

"That's right. What are you going to pay me for overtime?"

"You should know that better than I do, Mr. Karl Marx!"

"Will it do if I begin next week?"

"Of course it'll do. At the end of that week the rush will be over anyway."

"All right. I'll tell Flannery that I start on Monday—that

is," he twinkled, "if I approve of the rate of remuneration."

He got up from the leather seat. "Is that all, father?"

"That's all, my son."

A long pause swung between them which Anthony broke at last with an anxious, hurried voice.

"No, Denis," he said. "Don't tell me anything."

He leant back in his chair, and went on speaking slowly, with his eyes turned to the ceiling. "I'm not a fool, and don't want you to think that you must dot every *i* and cross every *t* for me. I know the world, and if I do, maybe I ought to have talked to you about it some time or other—but no one did me that doubtful service when I was young and yet I managed to grow up without becoming exactly a byword among the nations. And so it seemed to me that what I could manage between myself and my confessor you could manage ten times better."

"Father——"

"I suppose no man grows as old as I am without wondering why the world is made the way it is, and why all its toughest bits are handed out to youngsters. But I honestly don't see that we old fellows are likely to do any good by butting in and talking. I didn't want a haloed saint for a son, and, heaven be praised, I haven't got one. Only,"—here Anthony turned his glance from the ceiling to Denis's face— "for a first love-affair, this seems to be serious."

"It is very serious, father."

"Well, of course, they all are—the first ones. 'Serious' isn't perhaps exactly the word I mean this time. Oh, damn it—all that I mean is that, for some reason or other I feel fussy about you—like an old hen after a chicken that's too spry for her. But it isn't a bit of good. I know I must leave you alone. So long as you can manage things yourself——"

Anthony looked gravely at Denis, who flung up his head with sudden petulance.

"Of course I can manage things myself."

"That's good, my son."

"Oh, I didn't mean it that way! Father, I'll tell you all about it in a few days—when everything's settled."

"Settled? How do you mean?"

"When she's said that she'll marry me."

"Marry you? At nineteen—marry some stray acquaintance of the countryside?"

"Ah, you wait!"

"It's you who ought to wait, my son. Are you in earnest with me?"

"Father, do you think I'd play the fool about such a thing?"

"No, I don't—and that's the worst of it. It's some trap you've got into—some designing hussy——"

"That's so ridiculous that it doesn't even make me feel cross. Listen, father—I was never more in earnest in my life. I'm going to marry her. I've money enough of my own to do it, and start some other kind of life if you don't keep me here. You know that I'm not saying that to hurt you, but only to prove that I'm in earnest. And anyhow when you see her—oh, father, I'd love to tell you all about her now, but she'd be angry if I did—and she's still saying she won't marry me."

"Good girl! If she means it."

"She seems to. I can't understand it, because I know she—she's fond of me."

"God!" said Anthony, staring at his son's illumined face. "God! I should think she would be!"

He moved from his desk and paced the room.

"At nineteen! Great heaven!"

"Just twenty."

"Some obscure country bumpkin, I suppose! Oh, Denis!"

"Wait till you see her." Then, yearning over the trouble in his father's eyes, he tried to lighten it with a word of tribal vanity. "Even if she's obscure now," he said, "she'll soon be a Considine."

The coaxing fell flat.

Anthony strode to and fro and clacked his tongue in distress.

"To be tied up at nineteen! No love could stand it!"

Denis had a bitter thought of how love had tied him up at eighteen to a forage merchant's ledger.

"If she's refused you, Denis, isn't that enough? Can't you leave it at that?"

With a sinking heart Denis realised that the question did not seem unreasonable. But marriage, which did not attract him, seemed to have become an obsession in his brain.

"I'm in love with her, father. I must persuade her to marry me."

The truth of the first of these sentences lifted Denis's heart again, and made the second ring inevitably.

Anthony stopped in his walk.

"I'd give my soul," he said, "I'd give all I have on earth to prevent this thing; I believe it to be madness."

"You haven't tried very hard—have you? Why don't you roar and shout and curse at me, like Uncle Joe would, or Uncle Tom? What sort of a parent are you at all?"

That was his way of thanking Anthony for being true even in this difficult thing to their special harmony. It was understood. The older man's eyes brightened, half with humour and half tearfully.

"Now you mention those gentlemen," he said, "what do you think they'll say to this? How in the name of God could I face them with it, Denis? They'll murder me! They'll have my life!"

"Bosh! What would you be doing, will you tell me, while they were murdering you?"

They stood together at the window, their knees against the leather seat. They stared across the busy river, at the leafy, sedate, suburban road, whose only traffic was one slow baby-carriage. They stared at the proud chimney pots that loomed up here and there out of the green seclusion. They stared at Aunt Teresa's bright azaleas.

"My greatest wish has always been to keep you happy," said Anthony brokenly.

Denis did not turn his head, but he put his arm along his father's shoulder.

"Don't cry, man alive. Oh, you great baby of a man, don't cry."

The office door opened.

"Excuse me, sir," said O'Halloran's voice.

Denis crossed the room and went out.

§ 2

WHEN Denis and Christina parted on the following Sunday night, not to meet again for six successive periods of twenty-four hours, they were filled, as only the exaggerating young can be, with a sense of infinite farewell.

Denis had argued that while he was doing overtime they should meet at nine o'clock instead of half-past six, but this was impossible for Christina.

"If I can't slip out after tea, at twenty-past six," she said, "I've no chance of getting out at all these times, the suspicious way Aunt Bridget is. Anyhow, it'll be no bad thing, maybe it'll quieten her down for a while, if I stay in for six solid nights."

So it was settled that they would meet again at half-past six on that day week here where they were now on the log at the entrance to their wood.

"Can I write to you, Christina?"

"If you attempt it, I'll never speak to you again," she threatened him tenderly.

"Why can't I?"

"Aunt Bridget is why. If you knew her, you'd have more sense."

"Listen to me then. I won't bother you again to-night with talking about our marriage." Already he had squandered an hour in trying to coax a promise from her. "But you'll have seven whole days now in which to see my point. And you'll give in to me next Sunday—won't you?

"Oh, Denis—please don't talk like that!"

"Listen!"

"No!" She laid her hand on his mouth. "Don't spoil this last minute, let you. Say good-night to me instead and let me go."

"Love!"

"Oh, love, oh, Denis!"

There had to be seven "good-nights" to-night, Denis said, and they took a long time, and sweet as it was to say them, with hand and mouth and voice, these lovers seemed troubled by the sweetness that nevertheless they sought and sought again.

They stood at the edge of the little wood and scanned each other's faces in the moonlight, blue eyes searching into blue eyes as if into the hiding place of all earthly hope.

"It won't be long," said Denis. "Six days are nothing, after all."

"When I'm away from you, Denis, and try to remember your face, I never can get it to come clear! Why can't I remember it as I see it now?"

Tenderness was weighing on them dreamily, a heavier load than passion. What they were aching for was to be melted and sealed together in spiritual peace, to communicate once and for all somehow their incommunicable sense of gratitude and understanding and completion, each in each. The insistence to say what can never be said was making them half delirious.

" 'No love could stand it'—that's what father said. Ah, he little knows."

Christina shivered, faintly jealous that he should remember Anthony now.

"You're cold, my darling!"

"It's got a sad sound, that breeze."

"Oh, why are we sad like this—when there was never before so great a love as ours?"

"Good-night, love—good-bye!"

"I'll go a bit of the way with you, Christina. It must be eleven o'clock; there's no one stirring in this respectable parish."

"Is it safe, I wonder? Ah, well, to the top of the field anyway."

Leaning together they trod the dewy grass. The stars were a pale dust above them, dimmed by the proud-riding moon. Denis thought of Tony. Was Tony looking at the same sky now, was he praying to it through the window of his cell?

"Are you frightened of the stars, Christina?"

"Yes. But there's comfort in them, the way they remind you of how silly and small you are. It's like as if they blessed you."

They had been walking by the hedge that separated the field from a cart-track that would take Christina a short cut home. The hedge was thinning and broken in one or two places near the gap where they must part.

"Good-night in earnest this time."

There was a skirmish of frightened wings behind them.

"Oh, Christina, we've wakened up some bird."

"Sh, talk easy, my darling."

They took their last kiss now, but as if the stars had quieted, or blessed them as Christina said, there was no anguish in it but only a pure and happy tenderness. This kiss seemed indeed almost to succeed in saying all those best things of love that can never be said. It reassured the boy and girl.

"God bless you, Denis."

"Good-night, Christina."

She ran from him then, through the gap and along the cart-track. When she was out of sight he went slowly back across the dewy field.

§ 3

DENIS was wrong when he said that no one would be stirring at eleven o'clock in his uncle's respectable parish.

The parish priest was stirring.

Father Tom had one of his bad headaches that Sunday night, and knowing sleep to be impossible, went out to cool his burning forehead under the stars.

He wandered far among the lanes and byways of his quiet cure of souls.

The thoughts he took with him were jumbled by his pain. The Confirmation class was bothering him, and he was sad for his sister Teresa, from whom he had heard to-day that Reggie would have to go away for another spell of treatment. And the handsome new bay hack that he'd paid forty guineas for was broken-winded after all.

Father Tom sighed sometimes as he walked, and pressed his hand against his burning head. Sometimes he halted and looked up into the noble night, invoking its Creator; blinking through his headache at the pale dust of stars and the high, tormenting, lovely moon, he lifted his heart, and prayed for all the sons of men, sleeping and waking, living and dying, in that hour. He offered his headache to God for whatever soul stood most in need of divine assistance then. And so his thoughts strayed back to Reggie and the new bay hack and the Bishop and the Confirmation class.

The cart-track was soft under his feet. He passed by a gap in it that led into a dewy field. Beyond he could see the curling brightness of the Taigue. Passing on by the broken hedge he could still see the little river.

He heard a woman's voice, liquid with tenderness.

"Good-night in earnest this time."

He heard a skirmish of frightened wings.

"Oh, Christina, we've wakened some bird."

That was his nephew's voice, and that which he saw through the broken hedge his nephew's form.

"Sh, talk easy, my darling."

Father Tom looked down then on the last good-night kiss of Denis and Christina. What he would have thought of it had his mood been detached there's no knowing. He who preached so often and so eloquently against the seductions of the flesh had never before permitted himself to observe a caress of love.

Denis, Anthony's son, Denis, his nephew, aged nineteen, kissing a peasant girl, an illegitimate charity child, one who had been in service as a scullery maid! And kissing her like any ploughboy, under a hedge by moonlight!

The nerves that were aching in Father Tom's tired head leapt up and beat a tattoo against his skin. Did he truly have to believe this preposterous thing? And then he remembered his meeting with Denis in the lane, a Denis hasty and disgruntled, in the lane that led only to the Danaghers' farm.

Father Tom held his breath and wondered frantically what he must do, with what words he must leap on these offenders, with what penalty he must drive them for ever apart.

"God bless you, Denis."

"Good-night, Christina."

The voices were muted strings, tuned to a softness Father Tom had never heard. And now the embracing forms were loosed apart, and the girl was speeding through the gap and along the cart-track the way that he had come. Denis, his nephew, went straying across the dewy field to the river.

Father Tom held his throbbing head and tried to think, tried to pray. He would know how to deal with this audacity —he would end this trifling with the laws of God and men. But he must have time, he must think. Anthony's son, Anthony's darling—oh, God! Rage swirled in Father Tom as he stood with bowed head beside the hedge. He thought his rage was justifiable—he thought that it ravaged him only because he saw the fanaticism of a lifetime flaunted by one of his own blood. He thought that his anger was all for God and the chastity God exacts—or maybe he would have admitted that some of it was for the insult that a Considine was offering to Considines. But what he did not know was that a part of his violence was envy. Long fought and long controlled, buried now, as he thought, past all temptation or disturbance, the emotional fire in Father Tom was still awake, and had flickered piteously in spite of him, when he looked at last, unwillingly, on love. Rage as he might, he had been not altogether blind to the beauty of Denis and Christina as they kissed, nor deaf to the strange music of their voices. This flickering, unrecognised recognition was a part of his bewildered anger now.

He looked up to the sky, and fumbled to-pray to its Creator. Nobility still rode the night, but he could no longer find it. Pity for the sons of men, sleeping and waking, living and dying, was shivered to pieces in the priest's heart. He couldn't even turn his thoughts to Reggie or the bay hack or the Bishop.

It was long after midnight when he went to bed, with a far worse headache than he had had when setting out for his walk.

THE NINTH CHAPTER

THE seven days that were nothing came to an end at last. On Sunday evening at ten minutes past six Denis reached the log at the entrance to the little wood. It was a thundery evening and he had brought his waterproof cape in which to protect Christina should the hovering showers come down. He laughed very tenderly as he flung it on the log, remembering how she had said that it could be their shelter in the winter.

"She thinks it's as good as a house, my old rag of a cape!"

There was no use in watching for her yet.

He strolled down the field to the river-bank. Caddis-flies swarmed on the water; the trout seemed hungry and were leaping with great self-confidence.

"Aha!" said Denis to them. "I've been letting you off mighty easy, haven't I? We must have another battle one of these fine evenings."

He looked at his watch and wandered farther by the bank, but kept a vigilant eye on the gap across the field through which Christina would come.

A pair of mallards rose with a cry from the water-weeds. He watched them sweep westward against the pale, descending sun, and marvelled at the great beauty of their ungainliness.

"If she doesn't come soon she'll get drenched," he said, and went back to the log to roll up his cape and hide it in a tree-hollow, so that it would be dry when Christina came. A few drops of rain were splashing about already.

"I hope she's started now anyway, because if it comes on

to pour I don't know what excuse she'll make to go out for a walk."

He looked at his watch again. It was twenty-nine minutes past six. He moved a few paces deeper into the wood, then stood and listened for a rustle of footsteps. She might be coming from the other side, by the oak tree. There was no sound louder than one brief whirr of small wings. He went back to the opening of the wood and stared towards the gap. No sign of her yet.

Thirty minutes past six. She was very punctual—she must be just beyond the gap this second. She always told him that if she wasn't out of the house by twenty-past six her chance of getting away was small. That meant she had started ten minutes ago, and it wasn't much more than half a mile.

The raindrops were still few but they were large and spoke of a downpour.

"Christina, child, come on! What's keeping you?"

There was a wild orchid at his feet. He gathered it and pulled it through his buttonhole.

"There!" he said, pulling his waistcoat down and straightening himself. "Now I really look like a fellow that's going courting."

He went back into the wood.

"Where the dickens did I hide the cape? Nice thing if I can't find it when she comes! Oh, I know—there it is."

He listened again. Only a cuckoo answered his rigid sense.

"Blast you!" he muttered to it. "It isn't you I'm troubling about."

He sat on the log and kicked his heels.

"Oh, Christina!" And then: "Don't be so damned impatient," he told himself. "Don't be so idiotically impatient. It isn't a quarter to seven yet."

"Cuckoo!" he called back to the persistent bird, and then, still kicking his heels, and leaning out to peer at the distant gap where there was no one yet, he sang very softly but with a queer, firm cheerfulness:

> *"When Pat came over the hill*
> *His Colleen fair to se-ee—*
> *The wind was whistling shrill——"*

Uncle Joe's old song. He wondered what put it into his head. He sprang up in the middle of the verse and strode out into the field.

"Christina, I implore you! Oh, Christina, my dear—what's the matter?"

The empty field had no answer for him. The hedge-gap yawned stupidly. He paced about, keeping his eyes on the ground.

"I'll count twenty-five before I look again."

He counted twenty-five and still she didn't come.

"Ah, well, a watched pot never boils. I'll go back to the log and shut my eyes."

While he sat in imposed darkness he heard the rain get earnestly to work. First a sharp tattoo on the dry upper leaves of the chestnuts—like the irritable tapping of a conductor's baton to assemble the attention of an orchestra. Then a pause. Then a rush of pure, steely sound, full strength against the expectant quietude.

Denis did not open his eyes. He had persuaded himself that there is no boiling a watched pot. He sat very quietly and noted how the first harsh motif of the rain became interthreaded little by little with sudden music-patterns of drip and suck and gurgle, heard a small wind creep into place in it, like a muted 'cello, caught a harp arpeggio of furry feet.

"Christina, you'll be drowned, you silly child! Oh, what the mischief's happened you?"

Maybe she was crossing the field that very minute, drenched and careless. He could wait no longer behind closed lids. He opened his eyes and rushed outside the wood. It was startling to see how in a minute the storm had swept the landscape from uneasy bright to grey. The sky was stone-coloured, the field a smudge of drab; the far-away gap was blurred, but not too blurred to show its dreary emptiness.

"Where is she, the wicked child?"

Could she conceivably be waiting at the oak tree by mistake? Or was it his mistake? Was she over there all the time, and getting angry with him?

He wouldn't go by the woodpath, which was too circuitous. He sped down the field to the river and along its path that skirted the little copse, the wild rain pouring on him.

He got to the oak tree, but there was no one under it. Rain lashed it, rain streamed about its naked roots where he and his love had sat so often. The triangular meadow, mowed into haystacks now, was unfamiliar and unfriendly. He stared at every corner of it.

"Christina! Christina!" he called.

Christy the poacher might be out, but he didn't care. The dreadful Aunt Bridget herself might be hiding in the oak tree, like King Charles. Ah, if she was, let her come down and answer him! Where was Christina? He peered and strained into the gathering gloom, pushing his blown hair back from his face, sweeping the rain out of his blinded eyes. But she was nowhere—no violence or prayer could summon her.

How could she, oh, how could she have failed to come to-night? To-night of all nights! She who was so sure and steady and unfailing. How had she come to do a thing like this?

He blamed her only to seek escape that way from his irrational panic. But he could not escape it.

Might she be coming even now? Was she at the log this minute?

He skimmed once more along the river-path and up the soaking field. He might just as well have saved his breath and strolled. She wasn't there.

Ridiculous! What could there be?

He sat on the log again and forced himself to think quietly. What was best to do? Would he go to her aunt's farm now and knock on the door and ask to see Christina? But meantime she might turn up here, and then be unhappy at his having presented himself before Aunt Bridget. She was always so sincerely distressed when he mentioned going to her house that he knew he must not do it now until every other chance of seeing her was quite used up. And after all, why shouldn't she stay in to-night—this terrible night—if she liked? Perhaps she had a headache, perhaps she was ill—oh, perhaps she was at the oak tree now, the stupid child!

Three times in the next hour he made a desolate journey over the slippery, dark path between their two meeting places. Three times he came back alone. He kept forcing a laugh at his own anxiety, telling himself that she'd come to-morrow and explain it all and that it was unkind of him to make a mountain of a molehill. And yet he knew that this night's meeting had indeed been a mountain for them both, a high, sweet eminence towards which she had longed as he did, and that like him she would have come to it radiantly through danger. Never lightly would she have laid this woe of disappointment on him.

"Dear, darling Christina! I'll hear all about it from her to-morrow. God! Won't I lecture you, Christina! Oh, why aren't you here to-night? My love, why are you so unkind?"

It hurt him, who knew the infinitude of her kindness, to scold her thus. But such a hurt was more bearable than that he should let himself think that impossible malevolence from outside withheld and tortured her.

The rain poured on as if it could never lash enough the beaten, sobbing earth. Darkness was complete now except where the steely river cut its way. The far-away hedge-gap had long since folded itself out of Denis's sight. His clothes were soaked, his boots squelched when he moved; rain poured inside his collar from his hair and from the bending trees. His matches were so wet that he could not strike one to look at his watch, but by all the signs it must be nearing ten o'clock. There was no hope whatever now. She hadn't come; he wouldn't see her. Their lovely, glittering, beckoning Sunday night had come and gone like this. It was a stranger thing than any dream.

He sat and shivered; the shivers turned to sobs. He covered his face with his hands and let the sobbing have its way with him.

§2

THE next evening he came to the meeting place, full of sweet reasonableness and more than a little ashamed of his outburst of the night before. How Christina would scold him when she heard of the scene he made, running about in the rain and calling her name and crying! Well she might scold him indeed! But for all that he'd have a word or two to say to her. If he was repentant she must do penance too.

"Darling, I won't scold you much, though—I think, in fact, that I won't scold you at all, you absolute darling of a Christina, you!"

He turned a cartwheel along the muddy field, dirtying his hands and spilling money out of his pockets.

"I'd better leave it there for luck," he said. "The children will think it's fairy gold. Pity it's only silver!"

There was no storm to-night. The breeze was chilly, the sky grey-white and characterless; the little wood was sodden and sweet-smelling.

"Come on, Christina—you've only five minutes to go, and I'm not standing any nonsense to-night, my girl!"

At half-past six she did not appear. Nor at seven, nor at fifteen minutes after seven.

At twenty-five minutes past seven Denis was still trying to stand her nonsense. Hardly moving at all, he kept his place at the edge of the wood. He didn't sing or gather buttonholes; he didn't run about or call "Christina!" He was in fact most admirably behaved. But at the expiration of these fifty-five minutes his face was very pale and there was a dew of sweat round his lips and nostrils. Hardly a flicker of expression disturbed his features that were usually so mobile; his jaws were set with uncharacteristic stolidity, his eyes burnt sombrely like Honest John's.

At fifty-seven minutes past six he had not moved except to look at his watch.

His heartbeats were by now so thick and eccentric that he heard them with curiosity; his throat ached as if he had been running at full speed for a mile. The field and its far-away gap took on for his hypnotised sight the strangeness of familiar things rediscovered in a dream.

§ 3

AT HALF-PAST seven he had done with standing Christina's nonsense.

He moved away from the edge of the wood and crossed the field to the gap with long, slow strides. This way he had walked with her eight nights ago, under the blessing of the stars.

Here by this broken hedge they had kissed good-night, and through this gap she had gone hurrying out of his sight.

He strode down the cart-track, swung over a gate halfway along it, and into another field. From here he could see the thatched roof of the Danagher's poor farm, lying below him in the valley. Smoke was rising from its chimney.

"Christina," he said, life coming back into his face as he looked at her house, "Christina, I'm sorry to have to do what will make you angry, but it's your own fault, my darling. Who's your Aunt Bridget, anyway, that she can bully us like this? If she's God Almighty, it's news to me."

This soliloquy warmed him, and he ran down the sloping field, clearing the low stone wall at the bottom of it, and landing airily in Mrs. Danagher's potato patch. He skirted this and hurried past the cowhouse into the front yard. The half-door of the little dwelling-house was closed. He leant over it as he knocked, and smiled into the dim, clean kitchen.

"God save all here," he said.

"And you too, sir," came back to him from over by the hearth, in a hard voice that had still in depth and gravity a kinship with Christina's.

Denis unlatched the door and entered.

"May I come in a minute?" he asked politely as he closed it.

The woman by the hearth had risen now and came a few steps across the earthen floor.

"What is your business with us, sir?"

Denis could have taken his oath that she knew his business. He had therefore to admire the cool diplomacy with which the question was intoned.

As his eyes grew accustomed to the dimness he studied his interlocutor. Tall, thin, emaciated, ageing, but not so old as he had pictured her, Mrs. Danagher was the wreck of a great beauty and held herself still with that poise of imperturbability that beauty, having given, does not take away. Her features did not resemble Christina's; she had brighter, more passionate eyes, and her mouth was hard and frugal—a peasant's mouth. But as in her voice, which was not exactly like Christina's, so in the shape of her head and set of her shoulders there was a hurtful reminder of the girl.

"Yes," thought Denis, as he took this woman's measure

and told himself that, striking though she was, she was still the shrewd and haggling farmer type which he met every day in the receiving office. "Yes, Christina's right; she's a tough customer."

"I want to see Miss Christina Roche, if you please. Is she at home?"

As he said this, he looked round the kitchen, knowing well Christina wasn't in it, but seeking to identify the shadowy forms that were. That wild-eyed, nervous-looking boy who stood in the doorway behind the woman—that must be John, who wasn't quite right in his mind. He stared at Denis fixedly, with some deep anxiety upon his face.

A stolid younger boy had been eating potatoes at the table, and now stood up from them politely and leant against the dresser. That would be Michael. Ah, and there in the chimney-corner on a stool, was a small, unhappy-looking, barelegged child with wide blue eyes. Little dancing Nora. Where was Christina from the midst of them?

"What do you want with Miss Christina Roche, may I ask?"

The woman's voice was embattled. Denis looked at her gravely and gave a little bow.

"I'll be happy to tell you that, Mrs. Danagher, after I've seen her."

"Then I'll have to go without knowing it."

Denis's heart leapt again with the thick, eccentric rhythm that he had allayed, but though his voice was not quite steady when he spoke again, he kept it courteous.

"How do you mean? Is she not at home to-night?"

The woman ignored his question. She was looking at him with attention.

"Your name is Considine?"

"Yes. Denis Considine."

"Ah! Well, I'm sorry you had the trouble of calling in." She indicated the half-door with the merest flicker of a hand. "My niece isn't here, sir. Good-evening to you."

"No, we're not saying 'good-evening' yet. Where is your niece, if she isn't here?"

The wild-eyed boy at the door behind the woman was signalling to Denis in unintelligible frenzy.

"Is it your business, where she is?" asked Mrs. Danagher.
"Much more my business than yours."

"Why so?"

"Because I love her—and have asked her to marry me."

He watched his opponent closely as he said this, and saw
a flicker of surprise cross her face at the last words. But it
was gone before she spoke again.

"So you asked her, did you? Faith, that was handsomely
done, and you knowing well there isn't one of your great
relatives, from your proud father himself to the last and
lowest of the Considines, that'd let you within ten mile of
her if they had the wind of your goings-on, or that'd give
you a penny piece, or a hand or a word till the day you die, if
you married her! Small blame to them either! I'd be the same
myself. Is it let the like of you marry a girl out of a thatched
cottage, without portion or schooling? Is it let you marry a
charity child that hasn't even a name? Why wouldn't they
come between ye? It's little I'd understand them if they didn't.
Oh, a grand marriage you offered her, my fine whippersnapper, and you knowing well that the skies would fall down on
us the day it came to pass!"

Denis's whole body shook as he listened to this address. His
cheeks burnt him. Veins rose and knotted in his forehead.
Were these the terms in which he must talk of his love to this
old peasant? He struggled to get control of his voice before
answering her and the effort was useful to him, for during it
he had time to remind himself that this insolence, even the
insolence to Christina, was of no account, that his business
here was solely to find his lost one, and that thereto he must
be wily.

Deliberately then he loosened his clenched nerves and took
a long breath. When he spoke, he spoke with cunning.

"You've got it all wrong, Mrs. Danagher. In the first place,
Christina has so far refused to marry me. But I still hope to
persuade her, because she has said she loves me. If she does so,
I can make her comfortable. I am not dependent on either the
least or the greatest of the Considines and have enough money
of my own to make whatever life Christina and I may choose.
More than that, the only member of my family whose friend-

ship really matters to me is my 'proud father,' and he knows of this desire of mine."

He had the satisfaction of seeing that she was taken aback. He had guessed that her hostility was simply because of her conviction that the game could never be worth the candle. Her bright eyes narrowed as they searched his face. She was trying to gauge the amount of probability in his last speech. He, on the other hand, raked through his mind for the source whence all this trouble of revelation might have sprung. Not from Christina—that was sure—and not from him. Outside of them, there was only his father who had any hint at all of how things were with him, and even if Anthony had known Christina's name it would never have occurred to Denis, not for the smallest fraction of a second, to associate him with this sinister turn that things had taken. Who, then, had come gossiping to the old woman? Was it that wild-eyed boy with the strange, nervous face? Or had she spied on them herself? What was her game anyway? Where had she hidden Christina?

She gave a sudden laugh and jerked back her head. Evidently her calculations were over—she had come to some conclusion.

"It's lies you're telling me, young man, black lies. Sure aren't the Considines known to the twelve winds of Ireland for the big notion that they have of themselves? And didn't your own uncle tell me, and he a holy priest——"

"My uncle?"

"Your uncle. Who else? Is Father Considine your uncle, or will you tell me another lie?"

"He's my uncle, all right." Denis's voice was low and smooth. "Go on—what did he tell you?"

"What else would he tell me but what I know, that your father would rather see you dead in your coffin than married to the likes of my niece—and that what's more, he wouldn't have it, and that you could go against him in nothing."

"Ah, I see. And if he is so sure of that, what need was there to come here and say it? If the marriage is impossible, what's my uncle exciting himself about?"

"He's exciting himself because he's a good and saintly man that has charge of the souls of this parish. He won't see bad come where good can't, if you want to know. There's only two ends to love-making in the hedges, young man, and if the one end can't be, it's right to see that the other can't either. Father Considine is exciting himself to prevent a great sin, and will have no one, not his grand nephew no more than any other, bring a girl to shame!"

The boy who leant against the dresser stirred uneasily, as one does who fears he may have to listen once more to what he has often heard. Mrs. Danagher swept on relentlessly.

"Neither will I. I've had enough of that. Her mother brought blushes enough to the Roches in her time—and what is the child herself, as a result, but a living blot of sin before us all, though that's no fault of hers, God help her! I'm not saying she isn't a good girl. She always was, and whatever's between you, I've never known her anything but good. But so was her mother good, until the temptation came to her. What happened once can happen twice. If her father is the man I think he is, there's strange blood in Christina, and I won't stand here and see her in the path of danger. I want no more nameless brats put on my hands either; I've had enough of that. I've done enough for her—and I'll do no more. Not another hand's turn. There's no more to do, thank God. She's out of harm's way—and whatever's in your proposals, lies or truth, you can keep them, my fine gentleman. The Roches were ever proud, and want no condescension. What his reverence and I agreed to do is done—and Christina isn't here for you. Good-evening."

The room was dark now, with only the dull turf glow to lighten it and the dim patch of evening sky through the half-door. The four faces that watched him seemed like gargoyles to Denis, staring effigies round a black labyrinth in which he had lost Christina. Fear, hatred, anger, anguish, love, all these were drumming in his heart and in all the surrounding air. Where was Christina? With what trap of cruelty had they ensnared her? Was she weeping this minute in her hiding place? Oh, how they would have wounded and humiliated her, this old woman and—oh, Christ!—his holy uncle! But steady, steady. The thing was to find her—not to rave or rant, simply to find her. She couldn't be far. She was in this spot a week ago.

He fastened his eyes on the chief gargoyle.

"You and his reverence, what did you agree to do?"

"What we thought best."

"And that was?"

"What you're not going to hear from me."

"Why? How much did his reverence pay you for your complicity? I have money, Mrs. Danagher, believe me. I'll spend it more freely too, for less return than my uncle would."

There was a pause. He saw her smile grotesquely, almost kindly, in the shadows.

"You can keep your money, you bit of a child. I wouldn't take it because what I could tell in exchange for it would be no comfort to you. What's done is done, and she's out of harm's way. We acted for the best. Go home now, let you, because I'll say no more."

Denis closed his eyes, to shut out the gargoyles and the shadows. "What I could tell would be no comfort to you . . . what's done is done . . . we acted for the best." What were these sentences of death, what did they mean? What was the beat of mourning in them?

Strength was gone from him. He stood in darkness, without will or purpose, in this house that had been Christina's home and that had driven her out because of him. He didn't know what to do. He could catch onto no steadying thought —too many swirled in him, and all were nightmarish, fantastic. Let them swirl awhile—he didn't care. He was defeated. Yes, yes, but while he stood here helplessly, how was it with Christina? In what distress was she? What misery was she enduring?

He straightened himself and looked again at the four gargoyles, the little goblin one of dancing Nora, the weary mask of Michael, the twitching, signalling face of the boy in the doorway; last of all, he looked into the bright and passionate eyes of Mrs. Danagher, the skeleton of beauty, etched now by the dusk into a terrible face of avenging fate. Clearly there was no hope here, and nothing to be done for Christina. He must go elsewhere. At least he knew now where to find the mischief-maker.

He crossed the room to the half-door. When he had opened it, he looked back at Christina's aunt, noticing idly as he did so that John's twitching face had vanished from behind her.

"I'm going to his reverence," he said. "He'll tell me what I want to know, and if he doesn't tell me, he'll tell my father."

He closed the half-door gently and crossed the yard into the lane.

Before he had gone ten paces from the gate he was aware of swift feet following him. He turned to meet John Danagher.

The wild-eyed boy had a letter in his hand, which he thrust at Denis.

"I was to take this to you last night—and I tried every way —but me mother was watching me like a tiger; I'd no means at all of dodging her! I was making another thry for it to-night when you came in below."

Denis snatched the letter, but as the boy made to run off again, he caught him by the arm.

"Please! One minute only! Where is Christina? What has happened?"

"I don't know at all. By God and his blessed saints, sir, I swear there's none of us in that house knows but my mother."

"Tell me what happened."

The boy looked timidly down the lane towards the farm.

"I mustn't stop, I tell you. She has me killed with fright. All I know is the parish priest came in to her of a Monday, and they went into the room, and they were talking inside, as soft as fairies, for two hours by the clock. Thin they called in Christina, and after about another half-hour the three of them came out to us, and not a word between them about what wint on inside. Christina looked as if the sorrow of the world was on her—oh, Holy Mary, I must be running back!"

"I beg of you——" said Denis.

"That's all I know. From something I heard my mother say-ıng I don't think Christina answered a word to whatever the priest said to her. And then on Tuesday morning my mother and Christina went off, and Christina's box in the car with them. My mother wasn't back till the Thursday night. Some-where by train they went. We don't know what to think, the three of us. Christina didn't cry a tear, sir, but 'twas terrible to look at her face. It comes to me sometimes in my sleep——"

The boy began to sob.

"Thank you very much," said Denis. "I hope you'll get in

without being missed. Don't cry. I'll find Christina—stop crying, I tell you."

The hard, grave voice of a woman called suddenly from the yard.

"Where are you, John? Come in to me this instant!"

On the first note of the sentence the wild-eyed boy sped down the lane and over the gate.

§ 4

DENIS stood and fingered the poor, thin envelope that covered Christina's first letter to him. "Denis Considine" was all the address it bore and the two words were written in the careful, unformed writing of one who is bent on doing as well as possible something that does not come easily.

Having scrutinised the writing, Denis turned the envelope and stared with the same appearance of interest at the wafers with which it was sealed. While he stared, he pushed the tip of an index finger under the corner of the flap, and then withdrew it.

"Open it, can't you?" he said to himself. "Open her letter."

But instead of opening it he walked up the lane, still feeling the poor, thin envelope, still looking at the wafers and the careful, unformed handwriting.

He turned into the high road and, suddenly conscious of great weariness, sat down on a heap of road-mender's stones.

"There's still enough light to read it by," he told himself. "You must read it before the light goes."

He fumbled a fingertip under the flap again, and again withdrew it. Then with great deliberation he took a penknife from his pocket and slit the envelope across very neatly, very slowly. That done, he put the knife away.

There was still a pause in which he stared dully at the letter on his knee without making any movement to unfold it. He was afraid, not for what it would tell him of his own loss, since that was no longer hidden from him, but because it must be the story of how two wiseacres had misused Christina.

He picked it up at last and took the folded sheets from the

envelope. The paper crackled in his quivering hand, and he held it a second against his mouth.

"What are you going to tell me, love?" he whispered.

Then he straightened himself, unfolded the sheets and read:

MY DARLING:

Your uncle saw us together last night. He came and saw Aunt Bridget, and then they both spoke to me. Your uncle wasn't unkind at all. Indeed in all he said I suppose there was no more than the truth, but he was upset because I wouldn't answer all his questions. I could not speak about you to them. The end of it is that they are sending me away. Your uncle is paying all the expenses, and Aunt Bridget is taking me to Queenstown to-morrow. We don't know till we get there if it is to Australia or America I am going. It depends on what way the ships are. I am to go on the first that leaves. I think Aunt Bridget is glad I am being made to go off at last. She always wanted it, and now she is getting me off without any expense to herself.

I could have refused to go, and I could have sent a letter to you to Mellick to-day, but I didn't do either. The reason is that I think it right for me to go. Not to please Aunt Bridget, or because of what the priest says. I'm going away, my darling, behind your back like this, as the chance has turned up, because you'll never be easy with me now until I say I'll marry you, and that's the last thing on this earth I want to do. I'm not afraid of your relations, the priest or any of them. It is you I would be marrying, not them. But I won't marry you because if you are to be happy, my darling, you must be free for many a long day yet, and maybe always. I'd sooner know that you are happy than be married to you. Another reason why I am going is because when I'm with you I can see no sin in either of us, and even this minute I cannot feel sorry for what we did. Maybe when I am far from you and can say my prayers again, I will be able to believe that we offended God. Anyway, it had to end some day, and maybe this is the best time. We could never love each other more than we do now if we were together a hundred years.

I am not used to writing letters, and I never wrote so long a one in my life before. So you must not mind the mistakes and my bad writing. You will be very unhappy when you are reading it, I know, and for a long time afterwards maybe, my darling. But I must not think of that, because I cannot bear it. I will never be sorry I gave you love, whatever the sin of it was. Every day of my life I will ask God to protect you. Good-bye, my darling.

CHRISTINA.

It was no wonder that Denis had feared to read that letter. Holding it now he stared beyond it at the darkening sky, where some of its sentences seemed to be written indelibly. "Your uncle was not unkind at all . . . we don't know till we get there if it is to Australia or America I'm going . . . you must not mind the mistakes . . . good-bye, my darling."

He stared at these words that swept about the sky, and beyond them deep into fathoms of suffering that the letter had not mentioned. All that Christina had borne he looked at now and bore again. He saw her stand before his uncle who was not unkind at all, and knew what her dumbness covered when the holy man poked at her love. Australia or America; it wouldn't matter a fig to her what way the ships were. The dread that had hung over all her youth was here at last. Australia or America—what matter did either make to her home-keeping heart? Out of the eyes of her sorrow Denis looked now on the gentle fields that were all she had asked to know of the wide world—with her farewell tenderness he saw them.

The letter crackled madly as he held it against his heart. He knew that it was the shaking and twitching of his hand that caused the din, his hand that could not hold back this outlet of his rage.

But that must wait. Those devils and fools, there would be a time for them, and it was very near—but not the first moment, when Christina's authentic voice had spoken these terrible things of her own woe and courage to him—this first moment was not for her persecutors but for her.

"Be quiet, will you!" he whispered insanely to the crackling paper, and then turned back to staring at the fields and sky that knew her no more. He must find her this instant with his spirit. His heart and soul must crack their boundaries now and get to her wherever she was, wherever the grey sea dandled her. This love that strained and overweighted him, oh, surely now it could fly out and find her, and lay its consolation on her heart, and tell her that he was coming, and that she was all wrong, and that not even she nor the sea itself had power over their great love? Oh, surely, wherever she was, crying or praying or sleeping, this force of his pain and tenderness would get to her for consolation?

Still his hand shook with the rage that he was trying to delay. Still a great hatred of the blundering world held back the tears that burnt behind his eyes for Christina.

"My darling," he whispered, "oh, my Christina, oh, my dear, dear love," and as he groped, and even as he thought he saw her, grey-eyed, tear-blinded, hardness and sorrow swept him back again to the world that had driven her off.

"Devils! Devils!" he heard his own voice shout and found that he was standing up and shaking from head to foot.

He ran down the high road then at full speed, her letter still crackling in his hand. He never slackened pace until he came to his uncle's white house, with its glass porch and its yew trees.

"Father Considine isn't at home, I'm afraid, Mr. Dinis. But what's on you at all, sir? What's on you in the name of God! Come in and sit down, child, till I give you a dhrop of brandy!"

"Where is he?"

"God help us, Mr. Dinis, don't ate us! I believe he said that most likely he'd be dining with your auntie, Mrs. Mulqueen."

Back to the Keener's Cross then to harness the mare and drive her, savagely, inconsiderately, as she was never driven, along the hawthorn-scented lanes, down Mellick's bland wide central street, over Wellington Bridge and in at last past the white gate and the evening-veiled azaleas to Aunt Teresa's placid house.

"Your auntie and your uncle are after dhriving out the gate five minutes ago, sir—with his reverence, your Uncle Tom. Over to River Hill I think they were going. Anyway, I heard the misthress saying that the best thing was to see Mr. Anthony at once. They seemed a bit throubled in themselves."

Back past the azaleas like a flash and up the quiet riverside road and over Wellington Bridge again and through the noisy Old Town and on to the Carberry Road.

"Over to River Hill I think they were going."

Ah! And wasn't it to-night that his father was having the Lanigans to dinner, and Uncle Joe and Aunt Sophia? So they would all be there, all standing round his reverence. Very well then, let them stand round.

He flicked his whip violently through the air, and even as he did so, saw Christina's face, a vision of lost heaven, filling the darkness.

"Oh, help me, my love—oh, Christina, tell me how to find you!"

His whip fell from him into the road; his cruel rein slackened on the mare's hot mouth.

"Christina, you had no right to do this thing—darling, there was no sense in putting this trouble on us."

He swung into the tunnel of the lime trees—he could hear the river calling now, and could see the lights of his father's house, that was full of Christina's enemies.

He drove the gig straight to the stables, where he found that the Mulqueen carriage and coachman had just arrived.

THE TENTH CHAPTER

D<small>R</small>. J<small>OE</small> had enjoyed his dinner and was in good mood for treating his relatives to a song. He paced about the River Hill drawing-room, beaming good temper. Pausing by the piano, he beat out the tune of "Nelly Bly" with an index finger.

"June and all as it is, it's nice to see a fire," said Caroline.

"What about giving us a bar of Tom Moore, Anthony?" said Joe by way of giving the evening a lead in the musical direction.

But Sophia, Jim, and Agnes were for whist, and already the table was being unfolded.

"You can sing away to yourself, Mr. Sims Reeves," said Anthony, airily. "Your wife and I are going to rob our friend the lawyer of every halfpenny he has before he goes home."

"And I suppose there's nothing for me to do but listen to him," said Caroline. "Where's Denis, Anthony?"

"Ask no questions," said Joe, "and you'll hear no lies. When I was nineteen I wasn't often to be found sitting with my aunts of a June evening."

Very pleasantly then he trolled in his big voice:

> *"The time I've lost in wooing,*
> *In chasing and pursuing,*
> *The light that lies*
> *In women's eyes,*
> *Has been my heart's undoing—*
> *Though Wisdom oft has sought me . . ."*

"Are they shuffled, Sophia?" said Jim.

"Oh, Jim! Don't drum your fingers like that!" Caroline snapped at him.

Carriage wheels crunched the gravel.

"That's Teresa's fool of a coachman," said Anthony. "I'd know the commotion his horses make anywhere."

"You might have told us you were expecting them, Anthony," grumbled Agnes. "Really, in this place, you never know where you are."

"I might have, and I mightn't, if I'd been expecting them," said Anthony, and he swung out of the room to welcome the Mulqueens.

"Tom seems to be with them," said Jim, irritably.

"Tch, tch, tch," clucked Sophia, "this really is too bad. We won't get as much as a rubber now."

She was flushed with wine for a great night of battle.

"Ah, Anthony," said Tom, as if perplexed, "I see you have the others here."

"Well, and why not? Come on, Teresa—come over to the fire. 'Twas nice of you all to drive round."

"How are you, Teresa?" "How are you, Danny!" "Well, Tom, how's the parish?" "Is Reggie at home these times?" "Has Millicent settled a name for the new baby yet, Sophia?" "That's all right, Agnes, don't you stir!" "A grand night now —nice and cool after the storm." "Sit down, let some of you."

The room was a babel of greeting, but Tom and Teresa looked perplexed still in the midst of the familiar noise, and Danny kept hissing uneasily through his teeth.

"You're looking tired, Tom."

Tom was feeling dead tired, and had a headache.

"Oh, nothing. A bit worried, that's all."

Caroline made room for Teresa on the sofa.

"I'll ring for more cups," said Anthony. "You'll have some coffee, won't you?"

"But go on with what you were telling me at dinner about Eddy," said Caroline to Anthony.

"Isn't he due over this way soon?" asked Joe, breaking off his lively humming.

Anthony laughed. "He says he's too old now to be always hopping across."

"Ah," said Caroline to the fire, "is Ted really talking about being old?"

"Rubbish!" said Teresa. "The nonsense that fellow talks! Looking for notice, that's what he is! Why doesn't he get married? Then he'd have something to think of besides his age!"

"Cream in yours, Teresa?"

"Black for me, Agnes, if you please," said Tom.

"Brandy, your reverence?" Anthony called out.

Danny chatted with Sophia.

"And how is Victor finding life on the Continong?" he asked playfully.

"Delightful, Danny, delightful. Vienna of course was made for Victor! Such gaiety, such elegance! I remember that Lady Drumstick once said of Victor . . ."

"We wanted to talk about something rather serious, Anthony," said Tom, sipping his brandy as if he needed it.

"Well, talk away. There's no reason why all the rest of them shouldn't have the benefit of your solemnity, is there?"

Tom looked at Teresa.

"No, really—no, I suppose not," he said. "They'll hear it all wrong if they don't hear it now."

"Go on, man. Have you been excommunicated, or what?" Joe was still set on singing.

" . . . *My only books were women's looks,*
And Folly's all——"

"For God's sake stop that tune, Joe," said Tom.

"Sorry, Saint Thomas," said Jehovah, salaaming. "It won't occur again."

"Are we playing whist to-night or are we not?" said Jim.

"That's what I'm wanting to know," said Sophia.

"Is Denis at home, Anthony?" Teresa's voice was as grave as Tom's.

Anthony looked sharply at her.

"No, why?"

"Perhaps it's as well," said Tom. "It's something about Denis that I want to tell you."

The whole room became quiet. This family always felt a dramatic moment accurately.

Anthony looked from Tom's to all the other watching faces, then back again to Tom.

"Well, you can keep it," he said. "I hear all I want to know about Denis from himself."

"Not this, I think."

Anthony was frightened.

"Mind what you're about, Mr. Infallible," he warned the priest.

"Let it be, Tom, let it be," said Danny suddenly, his face very red and uneasy.

Tom set down his empty liqueur glass.

"When I am in need of your advice, Danny, I shall ask for it."

Sophia pushed the cards mournfully across the table and folded her hands. Evidently there was no hope of whist.

"You're in the right to speak of it, Tom," said Teresa. "God knows no one wants to be hard on the boy, but he needs a sharp lesson."

"Indeed?" said Anthony. "And since when has he appointed the lot of you his instructors?"

§ 2

AT THIS moment Denis entered the drawing-room. The Considines turned and stared at him.

They saw a beautiful young man who was breathing hard as if in physical distress, a young man with a death-pale face and yellow hair that fell untidily across his forehead, who wore a modish sack coat of buff and trousers checked in buff and whose boots were mud-stained. The eyes of this young man burnt sombrely, reminding some of the starers of their dead father, Honest John. And Anthony thought that he looked on someone made strange to him by a flight of years, for Denis seemed to have aged a decade since breakfast.

The young man for his part swept a quick attention over the group confronting him. Every senior member of the family, except Uncle Eddy, was present. And every one of them had been thinking of him when he entered, and was excited now to see him. Uncle Joe, hands in pockets, leant against the piano and gave him a quizzical, Jehovan look; Aunt Agnes dropped a coffee-spoon with a clatter when she saw him; Aunt Sophia peered through her lorgnette—oh, yes, they were all there, and in the midst of them, half hiding Aunt Caroline so that Denis could only see her soft green skirts and one white hand, stood Uncle Tom. Tall, superb, a trifle heavy the priest looked in his irreproachable black clothes, his weary face lifted and one strong, pink hand arpeggioing lightly on the white marble mantelpiece. But where was his father? Ah, there, near the centre window, stepping out of the shadow of it into full lamplight, his face turned eagerly to the threshold, and if troubled with the general trouble of the room, still radiating the old, unchanging, welcoming delight that he kept for Denis's homecomings.

"Hullo, father."

"Hello, my son. You're nice and early."

Denis closed the door then, and gave his assembled relatives that nervous, courteous bow of his that half amused and half annoyed them by its "Frenchiness." Then he crossed the room to within three feet of Father Tom, who never took his eyes from him.

"I've been looking for you for more than an hour," he said to the priest in a voice of calm, hard insolence.

"Indeed? May I ask why?"

"Whether you ask or not you're going to be told."

The Considines made wonderful audiences for one another. They were so quiet and attentive now that they heard the usually unheard voice of the river with that impatience with which playgoers at the climactic hush of the play hear the passing jingle of a cab.

"First of all," Denis went on, "would you rather I spoke to you alone—in another room?"

Father Tom's strong, pink hand ceased to arpeggio on the mantelpiece.

"What do you mean, you insolent boy?"

Denis was not lacking in the family sense of drama and just now believed himself to be in the presence of a spirit of evil. Also, the tension in the room was playing on his nerves. A savage excitement stabbed into his voice.

"I mean that I have things to say to you, about yourself, that you might prefer to hear in private."

Father Tom laughed.

"Say them here, Denis. And if you do ruin my character, well, you warned me anyhow!"

"How can I ruin your character, you smug, self-confident prig, you?" A ripple stirred across the audience. "What's it matter to you if I say that, priest and all as you are, you're a brute as well, a cruel, crafty, unimaginative blind brute, a kind of a devil!"

Uproar in the audience, but Father Tom turned to it, and raised a hand in gentle deprecation, miraculously winning silence.

"It matters nothing at all to me, Denis. Nothing matters that you say in this heat. Now, if you were to speak like this in cold blood——"

"Cold blood!" Denis had lost even such self-control as he commanded on entering the room and was handling the scene disastrously. "How dare you talk to me about cold blood? If all our blood was as cold as yours, your job would be an easy one, you—you frog!"

Sophia screamed. Agnes pressed her fingers frantically into her ears.

"Steady, steady," said Joe, in his best medical-cum-theocratic tone. "Steady, young fellow. Here, have a drop of brandy!"

"By no means!" said Jim, springing from his chair. "You're a dangerous sort of a doctor, Joe!"

Tom had turned his back on Denis and was staring very quietly into the fire. It seemed to Teresa that he was praying. She prayed herself as she looked at him, in sudden dark acknowledgment of man's helplessness in passion. Pity moved in her, who had a son for ever blighted by lust, pity for this boy now frenzied by it, and for her good priest-brother who hated it with a grim and dangerous hatred. "God help us all," Teresa prayed, "God help us to see what we're doing."

Anthony had put his arm round Denis's twitching shoulders.

"Couldn't we leave this business till the morning, my son? Perhaps if you were to tell me about it first——"

"I'd have liked to, father, but there isn't a minute to lose—besides, I don't care what I say to him!"

"Well, I do. I don't like to see you throwing your case away to them all like this."

Denis sprang from Anthony's touch.

"Case! What case! I'm pleading no case! I want nothing from any of these people, father! I've nothing to gain or lose by telling his reverence what I think of him!"

Father Tom turned round. He looked even more weary than when he had entered the room.

"Isn't it time we made it plain what we're talking about, Denis?"

"It is," said Denis. "Where have you sent Christina Roche?"

The audience hummed again.

"Aha!" said Joe. "Churchy la fem. I thought so."

"Brilliant fellow, Joe," said Anthony.

"Where is Christina?" Denis asked again.

"Before I deal with that question," said Father Tom, "may I explain certain things to the people in this room, Denis—and without interruption from you?"

Denis jerked out a small, dry laugh. Then without a word he slouched wearily away to the middle window.

§ *3*

FATHER TOM turned to address his sibilantly attentive relations. He directed his glance to the left side of the room as he spoke, past Caroline to the card-table, and beyond it to where Teresa and Joe and Danny were grouped, thus avoiding not only Denis, who faced him from the window, but Anthony also, who leant over an armchair close at his right side and whose eyes, Tom knew, were flinty with uneasiness.

At about eleven o'clock in the evening of yesterday week," he said, "I had a headache and went for a walk about the parish of Glenwilliam. In a gap of a hedge in a very lonely part, I came on a young man and woman parting from each other with every mark of affection. I recognised their forms and voices but almost as I did so the young woman had disappeared, and the young man was disappearing in an opposite direction. I let them go. Maybe you'll think when you hear the rest of it that I oughtn't to have done so, but I was severely shocked, and needed time to think. The young man was my nephew, Denis. The young woman was a parishioner of mine —a girl called Christina Roche, the niece of an unfortunate widow called Danagher, who rents a miserable few acres from Sir George Lewis, and can hardly keep body and soul together. This woman very charitably brought up her niece along with her own children. Christina is illegitimate, poor child—her mother was an unfortunate servant girl that got into trouble somewhere in the west. She died a week after Christina was born. Christina herself is a good, steady sort of a girl. For four years she was scullery maid at Lord Dunwhitty's place and she was due very soon to go to Australia or America to relations, and go into service out there, where they'd place her."

Father Tom paused. He was telling his story with truth and skill and he saw that his listeners were already as painfully shocked as he had wished them to be. He even gauged, with blood sensitiveness, that Anthony, outwardly motionless, was wincing and writhing under his skin. Anthony, most Considine of the Considines, had not expected anything quite so indefensible as an illegitimate scullery maid.

"I don't understand," Sophia was wailing. "You can't mean that you saw Denis, Denis, with Lord Dunwhitty's scullery maid?"

"An illegitimate girl! Oh, Tom, will you mind what you're saying!" Agnes begged him.

"Denis, are you out of your mind?" gasped Caroline.

"A bad business," said Jehovah. "A bad business, by God!"

"Go on," said Anthony. "What did you do when you were over the shock, you poor fellow?"

"He's not over the shock yet," said Teresa. "And would you blame him?"

Tom waved aside this sympathy.

"I went to see Mrs. Danagher next day. I pointed out to her that there could be no more meetings between her niece and my nephew. I told her that I would deal with Denis myself, and that she must handle Christina. She was perfectly agreeable about it. I pointed out too that, her niece's history being what it was, however admirable her character, it wasn't right to let her run into danger. In saying that, I intended no slur on Denis. We all know him to be a gentleman and have perfect confidence in him, I'm sure. But no one is proof against temptation, and as I am responsible for the souls in my parish I can take no risks. I believe in keeping young people out of danger—however they may resent it. And as of course there could be no question of honourable courtship between Denis and a girl of Christina's class, I wished to protect her from something that could only grow difficult for both of them."

"Did you speak to the girl?" Jim asked.

"I'm coming to that. Mrs. Danagher told me then—what I already knew—that she was anxious for a long time past to get Christina off to either of her aunts, in Sydney or New York, and was only waiting for the passage money to come— as she could afford to keep her no longer. Christina was against going always, she said, and wished to stay in service in Ireland—but Mrs. Danagher very naturally wanted her to be where she'll get big wages and could send home something, after all her years of living on charity. Well, I told the woman then that I'd speak to Christina, and if she had no serious objection, and I could see no strong reason against it, I'd pay the expenses, and she could get her off at once. It seemed to me a sensible way of ending a silly business—seeing that Christina had to go in any case, she might as well go before harm was done."

The narrative was broken here by a mighty sigh from Joe, towards whom the priest glanced inquiringly.

"Yes, Joe?"

But it seemed that Joe had only another sigh to contribute and a deific shake of the head.

"Get on," snapped Anthony. "When you saw the girl?"

"What was she like?" said Caroline.

"Like? Oh, I don't know. Quiet and unremarkable. But I must say there was nothing about her manner or appearance to suggest, to suggest——" Tom hesitated.

"To suggest what?" guffawed Joe, coming unexpectedly out of his cloud.

The priest stared at him in disgust.

"As I say, she was quiet and unremarkable. Not at all the sort of person to inspire calf love, one would have thought."

"Keep your impressions to yourself," snarled Anthony, who alone of the company during this narration had eyes for Denis, or pity for the tears that were racing each other down his face.

"She could hardly speak to me," said Tom. "Indeed, from time to time I wondered if she understood my questions, simply as I framed them for her. All we could get out of her was that she would go wherever her aunt sent her. Fortunately, her acquiescence made it plain that there was no reason —you know what I mean—no reason at all why she shouldn't be sent away. I did in fact ask her point-blank"—Father Tom flushed uneasily—"if, if she had any—any sort of claim on Denis. And she said 'No,' quite clearly and politely."

"Ha!" said Jim. "You're sure she understood you?"

"Perfectly. And if she didn't her aunt did. I know the Danagher breed. If they have a claim to make they make it, I can tell you."

"Lord Dunwhitty's scullery maid!" murmured Sophia, still lost in the earlier mazes of the story.

"Everything being clear, I arranged for Mrs. Danagher to have what money she needed to go to Queenstown next day, and get the girl onto whatever boat was available—either one for Liverpool or London, to link up with Australian sailings, or a White Star direct to New York. She was to be well provided for——"

"Ah, we can be sure of that!" chimed in Teresa. "You were ever generous, Tom!"

"—and would have the addresses of her relatives at either end. Moreover, she is a steady girl, and can look after herself. That is all. I presume you agree that I acted judiciously, in Denis's interests as well as the girl's?"

"Ahem!" said Jim. "You were a trifle precipitate."

Tom had had enough of his ordeal, and never liked criticism.

"I don't understand, Jim," he said icily. "Do you mind explaining?"

"He needn't," said Anthony. "He's hit the nail on the head. You were in the hell of a hurry, weren't you? In such a hurry, by God, that the very fact of Denis's existence on the map escaped your notice! Who are you, will you tell me, that you have the right to handle the private affairs of every living being in this godalmighty-style?"

"Now, Anthony, now, Anthony!" expostulated Joe. "That's no way to talk to the poor man!"

"You acted like a saint, Tom," said Agnes. " 'Twas God Himself was guiding you for us all!"

Danny fussed about the far end of the room, hissing through his teeth. He felt very unhappy.

"Let sleeping dogs lie," he was saying. "Let sleeping dogs lie!"

§ 4

DENIS moved out of the shadows into the centre of the room. He was calm. Tears were drying on his face, which was composed and weary.

"I didn't interrupt you, did I?" he said to Father Tom. "Be so good now as to let me speak awhile."

It was Anthony's turn to move out of the lamplight.

He was in deep perplexity. His outburst against Tom's method of interference was not genuine, but only a means of signalling his love to Denis. Beyond the fact of that love he could at present see nothing. He did not know what he was going to do, or what he wished to emerge from this terrible situation. Everything in him except his love for his son was with his brothers and sisters in judgment, and agreed with their condemnation of this love affair of the fields. And much as Father Tom was infuriating him, he knew that a part of his nature applauded the swift and ruthless cunning with which a source of folly had been removed from a Considine path. He was not the easier in his mind because he alone had seen in this month that Denis was in love, and had been too wise, as he thought, to interfere, or further, that having at last had his son's confidence that the emotion, mad as it was, was serious and final in his eyes, he had still done nothing—out of sheer love, and for fear of spoiling his son's love for him by showing haste or arrogance. Tom's news of the girl's class and origin had been a blinding shock. Somehow, in his deep

confidence in Denis, and with an odd, humble belief in his
superiority to himself that always remained with Anthony,
he had believed that this girl, though doubtless not of the class
in which he would have had Denis choose a wife, must still,
since his son loved her, be rare and strange and beautiful in
some dazzling, eccentric way that would redeem all disappointment. He had clung to that, in all his anxiety—that if
Denis must marry her, that surely was proof enough that she
was of exceptional intelligence and loveliness. But a scullery
maid, the bastard of a scullery maid—stupid, quiet, unremarkable, out of a thatched cottage; illiterate, spiritless, rough with
farm slavery and starvation, the usual helpless cargo of the
emigrant ship! This, such a one, for Denis! This for the beautiful son of lovely, finicking, fastidious Molly! Tom was right
indeed to gauge that Anthony writhed and winced under his
skin! And right too to guess, as he was guessing now, that the
head of Considine's, however he might storm against him, and
however Denis's anger might distress him, was secretly glad
that the harsh step had been taken in this swift way, without
his knowledge but irrevocably.

Anthony knew as he waited for Denis to speak that in such
circumstances he would have permitted no other young man of
the family to open his mouth in self-defence. Hot and hard
would have been his jibes at any young Mulqueen or Lanigan,
or at his own sons, Jack or Paddy, if they stood now in
Denis's shoes. There was nothing at the moment between him
and all the traditions and instincts that he represented save an
untraditional, uncharacteristic mania of love. If he could only
hold that in abeyance for the next five minutes he would become master of this scene, and so discover with racing wits
not only how to reassure the family but even how to console
and rehabilitate his dear and foolish son.

He went aside so that he might listen to that strangely
steady voice without betraying his own conflicts.

Denis had reached calm out of sheer exhaustion. During
Father Tom's speech so many moods had stormed over him
that he was stupefied now. Rage had been overtaken by a
multiple bewilderment to hear outsiders giving tongue in the
secret covert of his heart; he was amused at their false scents,
and in his amusement curled up deep into his hidden place of

love. The sweet, unstained, unhardened friendliness of passion that he and Christina had found was a fortification for
him now and, sheltered in it while his uncle prated, he almost
laughed out loud to think that it, of all unguessable, lovely
things, was the cause of this ridiculous parliament of know-
alls. He hardly knew which was funnier, this incongruity or
the self-revealed stupidity of his uncle when in the presence
of Christina. He thought that he might have laughed a great
deal at both were it not that tears kept on drowning his eyes.

He listened quietly therefore and took in all that was said
without laughing. But sentences that no one spoke kept twisting through the priest's eloquence. ". . . Your uncle wasn't
unkind at all . . . what way the ships are . . . you must not
mind the mistakes and my bad writing . . ."—phrases that
drooped like funeral plumes about Father Tom's grave
periods.

But now he must speak—speak to this fool who understood
nothing. In what language did one explain his own folly to a
fool?

"I haven't much to say, Uncle Tom. I thought I would
have, but you've been so stupid that I don't know how to talk
to you. You missed the point of Christina from beginning to
end."

The priest's eyes were unnerving Denis. It wasn't the anger
in them that perturbed him—for that was straightforward
enough. Maybe it was superficial too. This moment was the
first since entering the room in which Denis had been able to
look calmly into his enemy's face. It startled him now to find
in it not the incarnation of calculating evil, but a more easily
read expression. Father Tom looked more stupid than evil,
Denis thought, but not so stupid as to be unaware of the possibility of his own stupidity. His was the face of a vain, hasty,
strong-principled man in the clutch of a secret consternation.
The eyes with which he held Denis were angry, challenging,
arrogant, but was it possible they were pathetic too? Were
they trying to veil fluster? Was some kind of appeal to pity
exposed in them? The paradox amused Denis, but he did not
see how to grant pity to the pitiless.

"Didn't you ever look at her face, Uncle Tom?" he asked.
"Didn't it occur to you to listen to her voice?" With genuine

enquiry Denis searched the priest's confused, defiant eyes. "But you were too busy, of course. And if you were I suppose it's no great wonder that you forgot that she is a human being with a few rights of her own—not so many as you or Mrs. Danagher of course—but one or two. The right, for instance, to stay in her own country, in which, as you know well, she has always more than earned the wretched living she was given."

"She said quite calmly, Denis, that she would go wherever her aunt sent her."

"When did she say that? Wasn't it after she had listened to a few speeches from you and her aunt? And when she did say it, I suppose it never crossed your mind to search into the reasons for such strange docility. Did it ever strike you to wonder if she had any feelings about being whistled off at your nod—three thousand or nine thousand miles from where she had always lived and always hoped to live? Or do you honestly think that transportation is a natural, happy sort of thing? And if you're concerned for keeping people out of danger, are New York and Melbourne inhabited only by such saints as yourself? Are steerage ships full of nuns and angels? Oh, Uncle Tom,"—Denis's voice vibrated now with a rising strength—"you're not nearly such a fool as you'd like to be! If you'd never seen Christina in your life before, you had time and to spare that day to see how divinely beautiful she is! And if she said no more than 'Yes' or 'No' to you, don't try to tell me you were deaf to the kind of voice she said it in—because you weren't! And it's plain in your eyes this minute that you weren't! It would be better, easier, more comfortable to believe that she was nothing, oh, nothing at all—quite unremarkable—someone dull and gross whom your dullness and grossness couldn't hurt, because she wouldn't see them! A bit of wood, a piece of lumber that was in your way and Mrs. Danagher's, and to whom, most conveniently, America or Ireland or Australia are all one! Ship her off since she says she'll go! But let it be on the very first ship—no matter where—for fear she wakes up before she's out of sight! Oh, Uncle Tom, if only you'd been as blind and dull as you wanted to be—how much easier you'd be feeling now! But you can't fool yourself any more than you can fool me! You saw that she was

most astonishingly beautiful and quick-witted and brave, and
that she saw through you and despised you! And what's more,
you saw that she not only understood your highly intellectual
conversation that you were so kind as to simplify for her, but
that she followed every twist and turn that lay behind it in
your brain! Most of all, you knew when you were looking at
her, and you know now, and you'll always know that the real
Christina is hidden from you and your like for ever, and that
you'd never be allowed to guess one iota of what she might
think or feel—never, not if you split her heart in pieces!"

The family sat absolutely still, spellbound more than
alarmed by what they were hearing. Even Agnes had forgotten to cry out or hold her ears. They were beginning to
think that the scene in which they sat was a dream, from
which they would presently awake with an immense start of
relief.

All but Anthony. He was alert in every nerve. But for the
moment anxiety had left him, and the sense of conflict was
numb. He had almost forgotten that the situation must have
an issue and that he waited to direct it. He stood immobile
in the shadowed window and kept his eyes on Denis. The
beauty, passion, and mad young exaltation of his son had
lighted in him too an exaltation that he could not check. Perhaps it was nonsense that the child was talking, perhaps all
these wild, unreasoned words were false and crazy, but how
torrentially they rattled through the shrinking room, how
vibrant and moving was this voice, how strangely the young
lunatic seemed irradiated from within, by some inner flame of
passion and compassion! Let this moment be! Let him rave
and rant and ease his foolish heart! Afterwards, there would
be a time for duller talk, for wrangle and indignation and reproof—no doubt they would come thick and fast from this
outraged crowd that just now believed itself asleep! No doubt
he would himself have wise, crafty, worldly things to say—
oh, there was cold water in plenty at hand to pour on this
outrageous youthfulness, this crazy, insolent extravagance!
But meantime, how fine and strange the youngster was—and,
God help him, wasn't he right? Wasn't the wildest of his
exaggerations, the worst of his unjust insults to the priest, a
better, more honourable, more worth-while thing than all their

craft and moderation put together? Was there one of these mesmerised starers that wouldn't give half his earthly hopes to be able to feel once again as this boy was feeling?

"Go on, my son," Anthony's heart prompted, "go on, and make the most of this! Your time won't be long now! Every manjack of us is waiting to destroy you! Oh, my son, if only the world were what I'd have it for you!"

Denis had forgotten his father, or that there was anyone in the room with him but Father Tom.

The priest moved a step towards him, lifting a hand as if he wished to speak.

"No, no!" said Denis. "I've more to say. I wish to God I could let you alone! I wish I could feel sorry for you, because I think you're a person to be pitied. It's easier to be a fool than to be cruel—but you thought it best to be cruel while pretending to be only a fool. You saw what you were at—you saw that in doing what you did to Christina you were acting savagely towards someone of whom you only knew this, that she saw through your savagery and that it had power, oh hellish power to hurt her! You saw all that, and then you told yourself you didn't see it! For reasons of policy, for the sake of some silly bit of pomp that you've made a god of, you said that you wouldn't see what Christina is, and what you did to her! No, no—you told yourself what you have been repeating ever since—that she was unremarkable, quiet, willing—a scullery maid, the illegitimate daughter of a scullery maid—as if that had anything to do with the argument, you holy man, you preacher of the Gospel, you! But let all that be. I'm almost sorry for you. But there is this one very important thing still to say—one point about Christina I believe you did not see. I believe you were sincere in thinking that she and you might mean the same thing by the word 'claim.' I believe that when you asked her if she had any 'claim' on me, and she said 'No,' you thought that she and you understood each other! Oh, Christ! There, I grant, you were merely stupid! There, I grant, you and Christina were speaking different languages. I don't blame you for not understanding her reply. She said 'No,' Uncle Tom, only because she thought the question irrelevant. Christina doesn't see what love has to do with claims and claiming. She has loved me—I know that she loves

me still—and as far as she is concerned that is all that there
is to be said about that. She doesn't see what you mean by
'claim' on me! But I do—and acknowledge your meaning. Listen to me, Uncle Tom! Listen, all of you!" He flung a sudden
hand of recognition to the hypnotised outsiders. "Christina
has every possible claim on me, and I on her! I am her lover,
do you hear? Oh, do you understand? Her lover in the sense
that you call sinful! And I have asked her to be my wife—and
she has refused! But I'm going to find her! I'll find her and
ask her again—Christina!"

His moment was over. The audience had come out of its
dream with a great start of horror. And he, who had held
them so long with the rattling fire of his rage, forgot them
now. Though his head was still high, he was sobbing again,
and between closed lids he let his tears have way. With whatever strength of feeling now remained to him, his heart was
ranging the grey waters of the world, that held somewhere his
banished love. His concern with these outsiders had shrivelled
as utterly as a wisp of tissue paper in a candle-flame.

§ 5

FROM the noises which the ladies in the room had been making in steady crescendo since Denis said "I am her lover, do
you hear?" it was to be gathered that they were suffering
severely from shock.

Sophia went into straightforward hysterics and swayed back
and forth on her chair, giving out a staccato series of gasps
and giggles.

Agnes's face was buried in her hands. She sobbed and
prayed aloud with violence. That she should see such wickedness and live seemed like a miracle. In one hour sacrilege had
been revealed to her—for was it not sacrilege to call a priest
a frog?—and insolence to authority and, and—— Agnes did
not know how to name the most terrible sin of all. All these
from one of her own blood, a boy of nineteen who dwelt in
this very house with her!

Teresa's murmurings were contralto.

"God help us, this is a pretty business. Oh, the poor girl,

God pity her! But wasn't she the obstinate hussy—oh, how was poor Tom to know things were gone that far?"

She talked more to herself than to anyone else. She did not sob, but tears shone in her eyes. The only great love that Teresa had known was the maternal. Passion for a man, though she could have felt it, had never come her way—and now growing older she was at a loss among the extremities to which lust of the flesh could drive the young. Her blighted son Reggie was never far from the sorrowing pity of her heart, and now here was this strip of a child, Denis—half out of his mind, and deep in sin, for some impossible girl that seemed as crazed with love as he was. Teresa was bewildered.

Caroline had sprung to her feet, her body arrow-straight, one hand with its great emerald lying, white as the marble itself, on the edge of the mantelpiece; fugitive red, whipped high in her cheeks to signal a strange excitement, brought back the illusion of summer to her face, so that Jim marvelled as he often did at beauty's persistent haunting of his wife.

Love, that Caroline had so long foregone, then found and flung aside and wept for, had now become a thing she hated to consider. It was only with mock-kindness that she looked on the legitimate pairs of young lovers who were for ever cropping up in these days in the young generation of the family. But for the kind of love she had now been hearing of she had no endurance at all. The legend of it never reached her in gossip or novel or play, without encountering her cruel jibe. Only thus could she bear the disturbance which such news still made among nerves and desires that she wished to regard as dead.

"Young fool!" she said out loud, even while she remembered Denis's sweet courtesies to her when she had been sick with folly—"theatrical and scandalous young fool!"

But no one was paying heed to the ladies. This was an affair for males.

Jim drummed his long fingers on the card-table.

"You see, Tom," he said, "you were precipitate. It's unwise in these cases to assume that people are gentlemen."

Father Tom, though no one might guess it from his face, was in great distress of soul. So far from being the preposterous evil-doer that Denis just now believed him to be, he was in fact a man earnest to practise the kind of charity he understood, and he was generous both of time and money to help the helpless. Had Christina let him understand that she had given herself to Denis, he would then have regarded her with terrified pity as an "unfortunate woman," a "fallen woman," and clumsily, earnestly, he would have applied himself to the business of her protection and reformation. Had he suspected her danger of pregnancy, he would not have hustled her away on an emigrant ship, even though the temptation to do so would have been trebled. He was by no means savage or cruel, but indeed sentimental to a dangerous degree. The wilful, wordy timidity with which it was his habit to approach sexual questions was a part of this sentimentality and had now played a trick on him. He would have been kinder to the accomplished sin, because of his constitutional terror of it, than to what he saw merely as temptation and a dangerous slur on Considine pride. He was confounded now by this declaration of Denis's that he was the girl's lover. It gave him too a slight feeling of sickness to look at this nephew and know him deep-soaked in sin of the flesh.

"Indeed it seems that you were right, Jim," he said, and then, with a look at Denis that had something like revulsion in it: "I must ask you all to forgive me my simplicity."

He need not ask. He certainly had the majority of the room in sympathy with him, however they might carp about a trifling matter of procedure.

A tremendous family mood was afoot—mixed up of disgust, excitement, indecision, curiosity, faint pleasure in the disgraceful exposure of Anthony's paragon, faint pity for Anthony, faint sympathy with the intemperance of youth, traditional fear of the Sixth Commandment, traditional shyness of facing it in this open manner, determination to yield nothing to Mellick gossip of the family repute of rectitude and pride, determination likewise to behave with Christian decency, determination to punish heavily this iniquitous Denis and determination to let the world see no cause for punishment in the conduct of any Considine. He must lie on the bed he'd made—of course he must! But what a bed for the chairman's eldest son! Must he indeed lie on it to humiliate them all? Must all the town see him married in haste to a housemaid he had wronged?

Oh, heavy confusion of Considines!

Painfully stirred in every one of them the temptation to let well alone. The girl had chosen emigration—hadn't she? Well, she had a tongue in her head, hadn't she? And if she didn't have a child after all—what more about it? Denis could be punished by all their subtle ways of punishment and still the world could see him proud and free. If he had made his bed, hadn't the girl done likewise—and hadn't she had her chance fair and square from Tom?

But no. That wouldn't do. The Considine moral sense was limited by the conventions of its period, but it was honest. That a girl might be in trouble and maybe in danger of death at the other end of the world through the fault of one of them, and because of their notion of themselves, was a risk their consciences could not accommodate. But heaven, heaven—what price would they have to pay to be free of it? Receive a bastard maidservant as one of themselves? Hear the giggles and whispers of Mellick? See Denis publicly degraded, and so be degraded with him?

They twisted and turned about the room. They sighed and coughed and hissed through their teeth, and snapped in fury at one another. From Anthony downwards, even to Danny and Sophia, they were in real pain of mind and almost of body. It must be remembered that their idea of their own importance was slightly fantastic—a part of their power to dramatise themselves.

"It's terrible, terrible!"

"There's no knowing what'll happen next these times."

"I always said you'd ruin him, Anthony—I always said . . ."

"But what on earth are we to do?"

"Lord Dunwhitty's housemaid!"

"Will you stop that screeching, Agnes, in the name of God?"

"We'll be the mock of the town—our high and mighty Denis, if you please!"

"Ah, what would the old man have said to this?"

"At the same time,"—this from Joe in professional voice—"there's no knowing. I'd want to have a private word with Denis. Often these young people jump to conclusions. There may be no need at all—in any case, he may have had the sense . . ."

Many of the family faces were turned to him in uncertain hope. But Agnes replaced her fingers in her ears.

Denis looked at Jehovah and smiled very faintly.

"I've nothing to talk to you about, Uncle Joe."

He turned to Anthony.

"Father, don't you think they might be asked to go home? They've got all my private concerns out of me, and all I want in return is simply to know where Christina is. Where have you sent her, Uncle Tom?"

The priest looked slowly round the room, and let his eyes dwell for one last question on his favourite counsellor, Teresa. Each saw in the other's face that there was nothing for it, that decency was more to them, a little more, than pride. Indeed, remembering their father, perhaps they realised that it was the rock on which all their claims to civic eminence stood.

"I have sent her to New York, on the *Germanic*—to her aunt. The address I must obtain from Mrs. Danagher."

Denis bowed.

"Thank you. I want it to-morrow, if you will be so good."

The bow was too much for Tom's patience.

"Well, Anthony," he said, and pointed a finger, rigid with a passion of contempt, at Denis—"well, Anthony, I hope you're proud of him now—now that he has ruined you—your son and heir!"

Anthony, moved by Denis's crazy eloquence, had been filled at its ceasing, as he knew he would be, with the characteristic worldly questionings of the family, and had found himself incompetent and vague at the end of the long debate. Only one thing seemed clear to him—that Denis's love affair was deplorable, and its serious character a blow at all that was important and permanent. But while the others groaned and voiced their feelings, he had been silent, for Denis's sake, and because he felt the pleasure of the others in his disappointment and their less endurable pity. He was silent also because he was aware that his son had a point of view about the thing which was as much hidden from him as from all the others. As he stood waiting to make the speech of dismissal that everyone expected from him, he was in sore distress be-

cause the only words that would come to him were those which
would satisfy the family—the sincere words that he felt—that
the thing was deplorable and a bitter disappointment, but that
there it was and Denis and the girl must do as they thought
right, and least said now soonest mended. Such words about
Denis, to Denis's face, in the presence of all these who were
triumphing over him, seemed unspeakable, but Anthony could
find no others on his tongue.

Now Tom, pointing his finger in mockery, gave him such
words as he had never thought to say. Tom ought to have
known better. It was the crowning blunder in a chain of
blunders, that pointing finger and contemptuous voice.

Anthony sprang to the centre of the room, his head flung
back, fury and adoration in his eyes.

"I shall be proud of him always," he cried—"always, do
you hear, till my last breath! And whether I am or not is
neither here nor there to him just now. The question might be
—is he proud of us—of you and me, Tom, and all of us,
trampling like bullocks over his most personal concerns? Ah,
that's a question we'd better far not ask! But here's one none
of you put to me this evening, and I'll answer it for you all
the same. None of you, gasping and spluttering over his
reverence's great bit of detective work, thought of inquiring if
by any chance the story he brought was news to me or not?
Did you now? Well, here's my answer, free, gratis, and for
nothing. It wasn't."

Trust Anthony to take the wind out of other men's sails.
The family gasped, one large, well-synchronised, slow-dying
gasp. The priest's eyes stared in ludicrous doubt and exasperation. This indeed was a bitter joke on him.

Anthony went on with his revenge, which he certainly had
not planned, and which was an unfair one, founded on a half-
lie.

"It was no news at all, you poor old windbags, you. As
stale as last week's loaf, my poor, clever Tom!"

"You're telling a lie, Anthony," said Teresa, who was terribly shrewd.

"A ridiculous lie," said Tom, who could have taken oath
that his information about the illegitimate housemaid was an
icy shock to Anthony.

"Sure, of course you'd say that!" Anthony laughed magnificently. "What else could you say, now you're all feeling such
fools, God help you? And I say in return that you're wrong.
Denis, for no reason that I can guess, thought it best to tell
me of this love of his, and of his serious intentions in it. And
I, regarding it as his business, not mine, let it go at that. But
of course, I admit I'm not a priest, and it's no job of mine to
lead the souls of Glenwilliam parish in at heaven's gate one of
these fine days. It was easy for me to take a boy's love affair
easy. But Tom, my earnest poor fellow, next time you're onto
a bit of detective work, make sure before you kill yourself
over it that it really needs detecting! Good-night now to the
lot of you—you've had a great night of it—far better than
whist—not to say better than a few songs from Joe! Good-
night!"

He crossed the room and opened the drawing-room door.

The departure of the family was confused and inglorious.
Exclaiming, snarling, protesting, denying, they fussed about
the hall and down the steps and into their carriages. Nothing
specific could be said with coachmen and open doors on every
hand—and anyhow they knew that, justly or unjustly, Anthony had had the last word and had defeated their attack on
his son. That the attack could now be made directly on himself because of his scandalous laxity in dealing or not dealing
with Denis's confidence, mattered nothing, as they all knew,
to their self-confident brother. Besides, it was all too late. He
had flung the matter out of court, unsolved and unsavoury
just as it was, and somehow in doing so had made fools of
them all, saved his own dignity and most unscrupulously
glorified his erring son. That some of them had been moved
by his cry of pride in that son made matters no better. Ah,
well! They bundled themselves off.

Denis, standing alone at the drawing-room window, saw
Aunt Caroline looking out of her carriage at him as she rolled
by. He waved to her, a little anxiously, but the only answer
from her lovely face was an angry, contemptuous lifting of
her brows.

He turned back towards the room and found his father
crossing it.

"They're all gone now, my son," said Anthony coaxingly.

"Where's Aunt Agnes?"

"Gone up to bed. She's learnt so much about life to-night, poor woman, that it's brought on flatulence. That reminds me, you've had no dinner. Come and eat."

"I couldn't, father. I couldn't eat."

"Even a little? I want to drink Christina's health with you, my son."

Denis swayed where he stood and tried to smile. But this simple, tender joke of his father's was the last straw. It sent all the dead passions of the day upwhirling through him again in hot confusion. He was too tired for such a renewal, too hungry.

"Christina's health?" he questioned, as if something in the words puzzled him. As he said them, the voice of the river seemed to leap up and thunder in the room; his father's face grew shadowy, his form gigantic, a gigantic priest he seemed to become. "You mustn't mind the mistakes and my bad writing . . ." Who was saying that? The words had a crackling sound, like paper.

The room swam about Denis. He tumbled forward into Anthony's arms.

THE ELEVENTH CHAPTER

THE New York address of Christina's aunt, Mrs. Conroy, which Father Tom had given Denis, proved to be a dark and stinking "rookery," the top floor of a tenement house in a court off Christie Street, downtown. When Denis found it, it was inhabited by two Swedish families who seemed to have as little English speech as they had worldly comfort, and that was little enough. With extreme difficulty he discovered from their uncertain syllables that they had reached this new country of hope three weeks ago, and had been somehow installed in these rooms which were then empty. They had never heard of or seen any Mrs. Conroy. Here their powers of interpretation came to a standstill, and when the questioner tried to find out if a young woman had called within the last fortnight, looking for Mrs. Conroy, they could only shake all their sad, fair heads and shout, "No Connaroy—Thraalsen. No Connaroy—Thraalsen!"

He tackled the dwellers on the floor below—but they were Poles, and all either under five years old or over eighty. They recognised the name "Conroy," and smiled and pointed to the upper floor, then shook their heads and waved their hands to indicate departure.

As he passed through the entry, Denis heard a drunken contralto voice singing:

> *"Near Castleblaney*
> *Lived Big Dan Delaney,*
> *And pure as chaney was Meg McCann——"*

379

He knocked on an open door and passed through it, without waiting for an answer, into a dark room that was strewn with unwashed underlinen. A large-girthed woman, the contralto singer, was pouring water into a wooden tub. A whisky bottle stood conveniently near her on the mantelpiece.

Yes, she had known Mrs. Conroy of the top floor, and wasn't ashamed to say so. A bloody, fine decent woman too, the misfortunate creature! With that auld sod of a husband making her black and blue every night of his filthy life. Faith, she, Mrs. McNulty, would black and blue him if she had him! Lay him stiff, more likely, wid wan steady blow of an iron. But Mrs. Conroy was soft, the creature, and her dhrink was always disagreeing with the poor sthreal. Did her no good at all, at all! Oh, yes—they were gone this month and more, and what business was that of his, she'd be greatly obliged to know? If he was a cop—and he didn't look it—let him get away to hell out of that! Mrs. Conroy owed the speaker two dollars and a fine double blanket, but that was no reason at all for setting the law on a misfortunate neighbour!

But no; Denis was not an instrument of the law, and, reassured by the crisping music of greenbacks, Mrs. McNulty found herself able to part with the information that the Conroys, who were ten in family, had departed a month ago to Pittsburgh, after some job or other that Conroy had hopes of there, the dirty blackguard. No, the divil an address did they leave behind them, faith, and how could they, God help them, and they not knowing the name of a street or a house from wan ind of Pittsburgh to the other?

And had a young woman called lately, looking for Mrs. Conroy?

Mrs. McNulty scratched her head and took a drink out of the whisky bottle.

Aye, things were coming back to her! A young woman had called. To be sure she had! A nice decent young woman too, with a fine, solemn face on her that'd put the fear of God into a herd of elephants. What was this her name was at all, at all?

Was it Roche? Denis suggested.

Cripes, but so it was. Roche, Roche—look at that now, that he should know her name and all! The story crept back to

Mrs. McNulty, bit by bit. She remembered that she was very low in herself that day—the same as she was to-day in fact, if not worse—and her memory was never very clear after her attacks.

She took another drink.

Yes, the young woman had only come up that minute from Castle Garden, straight off the Queenstown boat—oh, it must be three weeks ago and more, Mrs. McNulty reckoned. She was troubled at not finding her auntie, and Mrs. McNulty went so far in friendliness as to offer the immigrant half her bed for a night or two. But this had been declined. The young woman said she'd find a lodging somewhere round. She seemed to have money enough. Anyway, Mrs. McNulty didn't mind who knew that the young woman had been free and generous with her.

And was that all? Would she please try to remember?

No, that wasn't all. The young woman had called back two days later, to ask if there had been any news of her aunt's whereabouts. She told Mrs. McNulty then that she had a lodging—but Mrs. McNulty had long forgotten where, except that it was round the Bowery. It seemed that the poor young creature had found work too——

"Oh, where? Please, Mrs. McNulty—where?"

But Mrs. McNulty could only recall that it was in an eating-house near the waterside, between the North River and Washington Market.

And that was all. Not all the greenbacks in Denis's wallet could make more out of this information of the friendly and regretful Mrs. McNulty. Having made her swear therefore that, if the young woman called again, she would take down all particulars about her in writing, and having made it plain that more greenbacks could be earned in the affair, Denis departed from among the piles of unwashed, verminous shirts and pants.

§ 2

MANY weeks passed. Denis was assiduous in revisiting Mrs. McNulty; he made enquiries too, that he knew in advance to be futile, from the immigration officers at Castle Garden; he invoked the help of the English Consulate; he made himself ill with eating innumerable plates of coarse food in every dive and bar that he could find in Greenwich Street, Washington Street, Canal Street, and all the swarming lanes of the "Market Wagon;" he paced for hours of every day between the Bowery and Broadway, between Broadway and North River, and down the wharves to the Battery, and so back again zigzag to his starting point, and in all these days and journeyings he added no fraction of a clue to Mrs. McNulty's story.

During his dismal and monotonous walks his nerves were either on a painful stretch of attention or stupefied by boredom into uselessness; his eyes ached alternately with watchfulness or with non-seeing. Sometimes he searched shops, doorways, and courtyards with a thoroughness that alarmed observers, and peered into the faces of young women as if his demented purpose were immediately to rape them; sometimes he stumbled through bad-smelling crowds as though his strained blue eyes were sightless. And always the unpitying sun lashed him, the fierce, tyrannical sun of New York's midsummer, scorching, shouting, blaring over a mad strange congeries of streets in which, for ever caught, as it seemed to him sometimes, for ever trapped, he sought dementedly, not for a lost reality but for some dream that had never had substance.

The fields of Mellick seemed now much more than three thousand miles away, much farther off than the evening star. Such quiet as theirs, sweet-watered, murmurous with the small sounds of silence, seemed to Denis more a lost habit of mind than the every-evening fact of a June barely sped. That he had lately walked on unsequestered grass with his Christina and with her watched the daylight slip reluctantly from pious, unprotesting hill and field, that he had lain at peace in a green shade, to take in heedless happiness all the happily given beauty of her love, that they had been used to whisper and laugh together long after the last thrush was still, and to peer each into the other's ghostlily-peering eyes when all was dark and asleep but their two near-yearning faces, that it had been their way to part in dew-drenched, soundless midnight under the royal moon, and meet again as tenderly, as quietly, when the low-lying sun pointed cool fingers on their oak tree—that such things once had been or, having been, could play so wild a trick on two who had trusted to them, turning them out from that dewy paradise to this—ah, what could such an overthrow be but some sick dementia, or what could so fair a memory be but jibing fantasy? Either this was reality or that—but both could not exist. Two states of being so unrelated, so self-cancelling could not have fallen on Christina and on him. And then, shaking himself from thoughts that revealed the silliness of exhaustion, he would unfold again her first, last letter, and with its innocently stabbing sentences restore blank reason to himself. She was here, near him in this place that would craze her home-keeping, quiet heart, and he was failing to find her. Her heart was grieving somewhere in this wild confusion, and she didn't know he was at hand. Ah, God, what was there he could do, what was he leaving undone, how was he to crack this pandemonium asunder and tear his darling out of it?

That was one mood, and as he grew exhausted by days and nights of vain fatigue it possessed him more and more, stupefying him by its alternating dreaminess and frenzy, and thereby keeping a darker discouragement more or less at bay.

This came from his knowledge that love, the delicate thing, had been shivered to pieces in him. Darkly, unwillingly, in cold sweats of shame he had to reveal to himself that there was no more inevitable desire in him for his dear, dear Christina. He was searching for her and must and would find her because she had been whipped and hounded for his love and because the thought of her present grief and exile was intolerable. What had been done to her was unbearable to him. Every generous instinct flamed towards her. Gratitude, tenderness, pity, devotion, understanding of what exile meant to her, the impulse to heal and restore and reassure, the brotherly and even husbandly instinct to protect and reëstablish, to obliterate what crudity had inflicted—all these, and mixed in them a desire for full revenge on his unforgiven uncle, were the impulse that kept Denis prowling night and day about downtown New York. But desire—he had to face it—desire, most unjustly and irrationally, was gone. He might beat away this knowledge or, briefly facing it, call himself cold, shallow, faithless, incomprehensible, but saying so made no difference.

Christina was still Christina, wasn't she—still beautiful and
brave and generous beyond all women, and what change was
there but the endearing, binding change of grief and parting? Well, then, how could it be but that he loved her more,
not less, because of this? Ah, perhaps in a way he did. He was
hers anyhow, for better, for worse, to do with as she desired.
The weight of his tenderness for her would outweigh all the
years of life, he insisted to himself—but magic was gone, and
he knew it. Cruel and unlooked-for loss! How was it to be
explained, and how to be concealed in their hour of meeting
from Christina's searching eyes?

"I love you for ever, Christina!"

"Say you love me—that's enough."

These echoes came back to him now as from another life,
and mocked him with their ghostliness. Wild hours of green-
lapped sweet forgetfulness, in thrall to them he had indeed felt
and meant his vow—to love her for ever. He *had* then loved
her for ever, maybe. Maybe in some timeless moment then
their sense of union had transcended natural laws and swung
them for a breath into eternity. There had been then no death
or change, no ache or hunger left in body or mind. That must
have been eternal love, however time returning, and his own
unaccountable weak nature and the black, trampling ignorance
of others might since have darkened it. But darkened it they
had, and mists lay heavy between him and that June-quiet
wood to which he had for ever lost the pathway back. He
would love Christina now with every other love but that which
sang between them in those magic and magically vanished
days.

In his first week he had stayed uptown at 46th Street on
Fifth Avenue, in the new and expensive Windsor Hotel, but
soon, urged by a desire to be near Christina's haunts, he moved
down to the Merchants'. Here he endeavoured to live only
in the dreary problem of his search and as if the clambering,
clattering, impressive and ridiculous town all round him were
as insignificant as Ballyhooley. But he was impressionable,
with little in him of the hard-and-fast stuff of resolution. New
York disturbed him, not with love as Paris had done, or with
a sense of having come home, but with curiosity, fear, amusement, wonder, delight, disgust. In spite of himself he observed

the place and groped to know it better; in spite of himself he frequented theatres, beer-gardens and concert-saloons, talked here and there, shyly and almost guiltily, with all kinds of citizens. At the Windsor he had exchanged civilities with millionaires and the lively sons of millionaires and had evaded their desires to take him coaching, or down to Long Branch or up to Saratoga, with a consciousness of virtue in himself that afterwards amused him. At the Merchants' he met pseudo and would-be millionaires, touts, drummers, stockjobbers, boosters, politicians, men who amused him and whom he despised, not understanding yet the terrific strength of their get-rich-quick purpose or that they were the very pith of America, the fathers of a particular and important race of men one day to be called Babbitts. In the cafés and cellar concerts of Broadway, against which a street preacher took much pains to warn him, he swam among cross-tides of type and race. He met Jews here and shrill, ingratiating dagos, and noble-looking Scandinavians who could outdrink every race, and Negroes with voices like deep bells, and Tammany men with Irish names, who wounded that pride of race in him which he had never till now believed himself to possess—clerks, waiters, actors, dancers, brokers, shoeshiners, prizefighters, seamstresses, shopgirls, ladies of the town—among all these he moved and talked every other night, his mind aflame with interest, his heart very troubled, and his conscience calling him back perpetually to where Christina must be looked for.

The talk of these people was nearly all of money, Denis found. This was the year of the Centennial Exhibition at Philadelphia. It was also the last year of Grant's presidency, and the Tilden-Hayes election campaign was in full blast. The talk of graft and corruption arising from these two topics was a new language to Denis, as were the wistfully or cynically told stories of the new alchemy—petroleum. The name of a young man called John D. Rockefeller fell from American tongues as awesomely as long ago the Trojans may have named their Hector, or the Franks Roland; there were stories too, told not without admiration, of a man called Tweed then in prison, who appeared to have been a demigod of superb dishonesty; there were hero-worshipping tales of the "Commodore" and of John Jacob Astor. These people were gods—

they had wrenched life's only gift from between its grudging teeth—they had money.

Denis marvelled. And often he escaped from his weary self into moods of tremendous sympathetic excitement with the life about him. This country had what was left of time before it, and all the sins and warnings of a hundred fallen empires and jaded cultures to point its way. It was naïve now, it was comical. Its architecture was a hideous joke, its painting ludicrous, its literature hardly to be found. It believed implicitly in money; gold was its first principle and holy grail. But it would grow beyond that first position—it was a child, and the days before it were great and terrible and long and dangerous. It had need of more than gold, and would find that out and have the lusty strength to kick and grab for other necessities. Sentimentalising, he exulted sometimes above the cradle of this Hercules to which so sad a chance had brought him, or dreamt of how imagination, loose-reined, might ride in this uncharted land to a new Periclean glory. And then embarrassed by his own comic enthusiasm, he would remind himself that he was a stranger, here to-day and gone to-morrow, and that these things mattered nothing to him, and that he must go up from his Broadway cellar to hunt the dark streets for Christina.

Sometimes he went uptown to Martinelli's, or into the eating-houses of Greenwich Village, to sit among the velvet-coated men who played so wistfully at the game of being in Europe and in the "quartier" that most of them had never seen and would never see. He talked with these, and learnt from each, as one often does from painters and writers, that no one then alive, with one modestly unnamed exception, had any talent at all or the least right to live. Whitman was an exploded windbag, Denis learnt and was half-inclined to concede, but it surprised him to hear from the velvet-coats that in their pontifical opinion he had never been anything else. Mark Twain was a vulgarian, they said, but here Denis jibbed, if for no better motive than loyalty to Tony who had loved him; that swashbuckling fellow Whistler was bluffing old Europe that he could paint, and an upstart called Henry James—oh, Denis actually liked *Roderick Hudson?* Then he'd probably like this new thing *The American,* too—an appalling, bloodless novelist. Pernicious anæmia. Now they, the talkers, were at this moment working out an absolutely new technique . . .

So they talked. All except one shabby, grey-haired man, who said he was a sculptor, and who, though he always came to sit at Denis's table in Martinelli's, said little else. He stared at Denis strangely, sipping absinthe, smoking and fidgeting. Once, as the young man leant in weariness above a glass of bad Chianti, the grey-haired sculptor found husky voice. "God, but you sure are beautiful! A model for Dionysius, a miracle!" He put a hand on Denis. "Come to the studio, young Considine—oh, God, come now!"

Denis looked into the tired, debauched eyes, and was not pitiless to their exposed desire. But always he left Martinelli's alone, while the velvet-coats were still talking, and only the grey-haired sculptor saw him go.

§ 3

STILL the hot days passed in fruitlessness, and with every one of them Denis tried some new, vain method to trace Christina, avoiding all but the briefest conversations with strangers, and devoting himself wearily to his disheartening task.

He paced about. He questioned restaurant keepers and lodging-house keepers, Catholic priests, nuns in convents, post-office clerks, policemen, children, newspaper-sellers. He watched the entries to courts and lanes and tenements. He went to Mass in every Catholic church that he could find and stared throughout the service at each devout and kneeling woman. But he saw no Christina—no ghost or shadow of her.

He was growing so tired now, so enervated by his sense of helplessness and by this wild heat for which his rearing in the soft Vale of Honey had been the worst possible preparation, that sometimes he would sit and laugh in a hysterical way at the pitiful business.

He was not only tired; he was desperately lonely.

One night he felt a craving to drink good wine and sped in search of it.

He went to Delmonico's. As it was August, the famous

restaurant was almost empty, but Denis cared nothing for that, believing his only desires to be for champagne and quietude.

Facing him, three tables away, a beautiful painted woman sat alone. After Denis had spent half an hour avoiding her amused brown eyes, she laughed and beckoned to him as if she had known him all her life. He went in some excitement to her table.

They held then the conversation that most young men hold at least once in a lifetime with a shrewd and charming adventuress. There is no need to chronicle it here word for word. Its wisdom was worldly, and perhaps not so wise even within its limitations as its dispenser thought. But the Anglo-Frenchwoman, who called herself Cécile and talked agreeably, seemed to know Europe as well as New York. She was merry, and managed withal to keep that sweet vein of sadness in her talk which is essential to a woman of experience when seducing a young man. Though her coming into life, she lightly implied, had been an unwelcome accident, it seemed to Denis that she was well bred. He gathered too—since business was always business with Cécile—that for all her silky and jewelled splendour she was at present down on her luck. Someone whose duty it was to be with her here was at that moment being unfaithful among respectable circles at Long Branch.

Denis, though shy, was not awkward, and he found subtle ways of making his companion aware that he had money and could spend it. Such innuendoes were not wasted, he observed. They brightened the lady's bright eyes and quickened her laugh.

During this conversation the boy learnt many things and forgot many more. The things he learnt were trivial; cheap mysteries of flattery and desire, of invitation and suggestion, all the old and overrated shoddy of man-and-woman lore, the fleshly vanities and titillations that he knew well enough were the whole world's commonplace, his to-day and the next man's to-morrow. The things he forgot had been his own and unsharable—a bed of sorrel, a sleeping wood, Christina's yielded eyes, Christina's breast of gentleness.

"You're making me forget so many things," Cécile was murmuring.

Shabby talk, but she was growing a little cold and sad within. For all her habit of it, her head for champagne was not first-rate, and now she was beginning to like Denis's face more than she had bargained for—and so to envy him. But he did not care how foolishly she talked so long as she bent as now she was bending towards him above the vase of roses, lifting her face so that he could stare his fill at the radiant brown and clear blue-white of her eyes in their startling frame of long black lashes.

"I wonder how I ever dared to cross the room and speak to you," said Denis.

"Irish voice. I've never known an Irishman before! I wonder what they're like?"

They drove in a growler to her apartment. She inhabited one of the new French flats that were springing up all over New York and becoming so popular as to be losing their pleasant association with impropriety.

The drive was slow from 26th Street to the now fashionable 50's. The cab was musty, but when both windows were opened a precious little draught stole into it. Denis leant back and looked out at Fifth Avenue. He was very quiet.

"What are you thinking of?"

When she spoke he felt her breath on his neck. He turned and looked deep again into her clear, bright eyes, so brown and white and black-ringed.

"Of you," he lied dreamily. He had in fact been thinking of his father.

She kissed him then—a quick but by no means a shy kiss—a darting, skilful kiss of violence, like a bee-sting—a kiss for which, had Denis but known it, she was famous.

It stung him wide awake. He drew himself up into rigidity and Cécile may have been preparing herself with good-natured tolerance to suffer the first crude embrace of a very young Irishman, when the growler stopped.

In Cécile's luxurious apartment house there was an elevator, the first that Denis had seen in a private building. But as it swung him to the fourth floor, he had no thought for its glittering efficiency. The bee-sting was still troubling him, though not exactly in the way the bee had meant.

In her little drawing-room, while Cécile hummed and fluttered about the room, removing her cloak and pouting and prinking in the mirror, in fact being perfectly tactful so as to give inexperience all the time that it might need, Denis stood and stared despondently at a blue rose patterned on a pink carpet. He was concerned, most desperately concerned, with an unusual point of etiquette.

He wanted to be gone out of this place—not because he had no desire to stay, or because there would be no immediate solace in taking whatever this lovely, painted lady might be so gracious as to give—but only because that terrible, darting kiss had most fantastically awakened memory of very different kisses taken from love in the quiet wood at home. The memory did not check this new and cheap desire—rather embittered and enhanced it, and placed it out of reach. He wanted with all his senses now to embrace Cécile, but how was he to do it with Christina weeping in his heart?

Well, it was easy to bow and withdraw. But here the point of etiquette came in. He had wasted an evening of this kind and gracious lady, who made no secret of the fact that time was money. Though many grades removed in her profession from the ladies of the street, she clearly made an honest living by being kind, fastidiously, here and there. She had expected to do so to-night. How then, how in the name of all the crazy gods, did one compensate a lovely and quite cynical lady for a favour that one must decline? How indeed, in any circumstances, by what fantastic piece of tactfulness did one present money in return for physical pleasure?—and money, straightforward money, he knew to be in this case the needed thing. Passionately Denis stared at the blue rose on the pink carpet—and heard Christina talking to him, "Child, don't you know I love you?"—and beat round his mind for a formula.

Cécile turned from the mirror and surveyed with a certain tenderness his bent, fair head. He was being overlong in pulling himself together. She crossed the room to him and took his hand, covering it with her pretty, manicured one.

Denis's eyes turned from the blue rose to that little pink and white toy.

"Christina," he said to himself, "your hand was more beautiful than this pretty little claw."

He used the past tense, for he felt himself turning backward from one world to another.

"What are you so shy about, you darling boy?"

Denis took a leap then at his problem of etiquette, tackling it exactly as his father would have done, only that he was diffident where Anthony would have been cool. He put his situation honestly to the woman who had not bluffed over-much with him.

"Listen," he said, looking once more into the bright brown and clear white of eyes that promised such sophisticated rapture—"listen, and don't misunderstand. I must go away—now. I'm terribly sorry—oh, I'd be glad enough to stay, I can tell you—but, well, think what you like. I can't explain. You've been most awfully kind to me—but I'm sure you're bored with me now. You must be. No, please don't interrupt. The trouble is that I've squandered a whole evening of yours—and you've been so extraordinarily friendly, I'd—I'd like you to let me be friendly in return——"

"Sit down," said Cécile, caressingly. "Sit down, darling child, and don't be silly."

They moved a little way towards the sofa.

"No," said Denis. "Honestly I must go—but, well, you said you were a bit hard up just now. I hate to think of that, and, if there were any particular bill I could pay, or anything—you've been so marvellous."

He was in a sweat. He could say no more.

Cécile ran her pretty little claw over his hair. There was a look of concentration in her eyes, behind which many ideas were conflicting. Hope and greed—for she was in fact in a very bad mess—were fighting with compassion for his youth-fulness. Also she was wondering how much she dared to ask of him.

"Bills you could pay, darling child? That desk is bursting with them—far more than you could ever manage——"

"I wish I could pay them all," said Denis, breathing more easily now.

"So do I," she answered merrily. "But—well, one has no idea what you can afford, but if you did happen to have five hundred dollars lying about"—she gasped a little—"they'd be most amazingly useful."

Five hundred dollars. The figure was a shock to Denis, but he behaved with perfect calm.

"It's more than good of you," he said, "to let me give them to you."

He crossed to her desk, took one of her ridiculous gilded pens and wrote a cheque, which, in the best manner of French novelettes, he left in the blotter without further comment.

The greedy, worried part of Cécile wondered regretfully if she could have had more; the generous part was ashamed and troubled.

"I must say good-night to you now," said Denis. He took up the pretty little claw and kissed it.

"Stay with me, silly—we could be very happy!"

"Happy—yes," he said with new bitterness—"but not very happy."

"That's rather rude."

"You know it isn't meant rudely; thank you a million times. I don't suppose I'll ever forget you."

"Oh, these farewells! Come and see me again—I shan't foist any more of my debts on you, I promise!"

"Good-bye—no, no, let me go!"

He made his hackman drive him downtown at racing speed.

§ 4

*"Kennst du es wohl? Dahin, dahin
Möcht' ich mit dir, o mein Geliebter, zieh'n."*

The vast wave of song was listless, bedraggled by beer and heat. Denis knew no German but, even had he known much, might not easily have detached the words from the big sad burr of singing in which they were embedded.

The Atlantic Garden was full this midnight. German immigrants had poured into it after the performance of "Oberon" at the Bowery Theatre next door. Denis had come in because it was a place of rest on his unchanging beat and was growing familiar to him, and because it was probably no hotter here at this minute than anywhere else in New York.

"A large Pilsener," he said to the waiter, "and when you've brought it you can start bringing a second, and when you've brought that"—the waiter was gone but Denis was too tired

and lonely to stop talking—"you can start bringing a third—
und so weiter," he persisted, proud of a phrase he had learnt
in this very Atlantic Garden.

"*Dahin! dahin!*"

How they dragged the sad word, whatever it meant.

It was that hour at the end of a hot day when the only sure
manner of keeping the peace is to be maudlin, the hour when
men must sing themselves rather than listen to others singing.
Sit still and smile and sing and dim the immediate world with
smoke in which to body out a dream. That is what two thousand Germans were doing as they trailed their "dahins" across
the Atlantic Garden in an untidy sigh, not for the poet's Italy,
but for their own lost Oder and Elbe and Rhein.

"*Dahin, dahin!*" What on earth were they all sighing over
with such earnestness?

How cool it would be at River Hill to-night—under the
cypresses where one could watch one's shadow crisscrossing
the patterned shadows of the trees on the moon-whitened
grass! The orchard would be green and thick below, but there
were gaps in it, down its narrow paths, through which the
river shone—its eternal cry making no more wound in the
quiet than the thudding of bats' wings did about one's head,
or the stray laughs from the far-away lighted house. The
lavender walk must be past its glory now and already in the
heart-rending sweetness of decline; gillyflowers would be
drooping too and the La France roses perilously open-hearted;
the tang of early dahlias must be on the air and the sweet
verbena tipped with gold. A few dropped leaves were surely
sighing already in the pathways. What glory September would
bring to River Hill! Denis closed his eyes and ransacked
memory for details of his garden. They wouldn't come. A
host of people crowded over his thoughts instead—Aunt Teresa
calmly blocking the view, Jack Keogh, Aunt Agnes, Tony
vaulting towards him across a gate. With an effort he swept
them aside, and conjured up the wide green sweeps of River
Hill. But they came to him under the night shadow again,
and tiger-striped by the moon, so that all he could see clearly
was **the** glow of a cigar end moving up the long stone stairs
and all he could hear besides the river was his father's footsteps.

"Dominic, have the biscuits come?" he heard his own voice chanting through those quiet shadows—but here where he sat in blare and noise the Germans were still tugging wearily at their monotonous word—*"dahin!"* What did they mean, those dejected syllables?

An oppression of craving to see his father's face descended over Denis. It dropped on him like a heavy shroud and, hiding him from all this new and strange America, possessed and smothered him. It seemed in this moment that, very strangely, all the adventures, changes, and fatigues of eight hot weeks had left him now with only one real desire—to see again his father's brilliant and self-confident eyes. All the new faces and figures of this country where he was were suddenly dead—the coaching, uptown millionaires, the Wall Street know-alls, the sailors and stevedores of the waterfront, the desirable Céciles, the silly and pitiful velvet-coats, the Tammany men, the melancholy Negroes, the little anxious, quarrelsome dancers of the cellar-cafés—all the passionate, urgent, clean-driven streets of this tumultuously evolving city, all its vigorous, immediate movement between its rushing rivers, and the rivers themselves and the clear, hot, foreign sky that overtopped the whole —all these that were so suggestively exciting to the mind, and that seemed a very fountain of that life of freedom and individual effort that he had always longed for—were gone in a flash and had no more to do with him. And the purpose that had brought him here—why, that was just as far away. What had it been, anyhow? A stupid chasing of the past, a stampede for vengeance, a desire to mend that which, having once been perfect, could never now be restored by the superficial remedies he had to bring. Yes, everything was dead in him, it seemed, except his loneliness for Anthony.

He rose and left the Atlantic Garden, still followed by the Germans' burbling cry—*"dahin!"* He moved with a hurrying step. He had a fantastic idea that he was going home at once.

He went south along the wild Bowery in which life never seemed to close its eyes. Traffic, movement, and backchat were as lively now at one a.m. under the unsteady gasjets as they would be at one p.m. to-morrow—more lively than then indeed, since now the hour was almost cool. A babble of languages swirled about Denis, but he did not hear the jabber that had now grown familiar to him. There was a breeze coming up from the sea towards which he had set his face. It blew the dead day's leavings of straw and rags and paper hither and thither over the broad pavements; jocosely it filled the pants and shifts of all nations, pegged out to dry from window to window; it touched the indifferent faces of men asleep in the gutter; it flicked the petticoats of loafing girls.

Denis took off his hat and lifted his head eagerly into the breeze.

The gaunt lewd face of a woman thrust itself before him.

"I'll do you for half a dollar, dear," she whispered in a cracked, despairing voice.

"Not just now, thank you," said Denis automatically, hardly aware of her interruption as he thrust some money into her hand. He swept along the mighty street as if a home-going steamer waited for him at the end of it, entering comparative quiet at last in Battery Park.

Here the blessed wind had freer play, and eyes might be rested by the sight of moving waters, over which, however she might load them with her eager ships and ferries, New York had still no power to spread her greater fever. Here, however many masts and funnels might assemble, there would always be an underdepth of peace. No hustle can hustle the sea, which will suffer but not accept it; no greed or fuss can deflect it from its long routine. So this corner of the waterfront, given over in the small hours to the down-and-outs, the lost and homeless who like to huddle where tides ebb and flow and where they may stare at the heart-lifting movements of great ships, laid a sudden slackening peace on Denis's mood of urgency.

He crossed to the water's very edge and leant upon a parapet.

Lights were everywhere, but they only pricked to emphasize the darkness—lights eastward on Brooklyn, westward on New Jersey, and all about the great breast of the waters, from the sterns of ships that marched out to the Narrows and the bows of ships that trundled in, from darting river police and anchored clippers, from fishing fleets asleep and easy-going coalers, lights that served little men their little turn but made no deeper rent in the night's curtain. The last of the ferries was home from Coney Island, and the sailboats of pleasure had done with scudding for to-night, but a bar of song would float across the water sometimes from some happy waterboy; an occasional splash, an occasional oath, a brief murmur of talk between two watchmen, a scurrying up East River of the night patrol—but over all these noises peace.

"Glug, glug," went the water against the wall.

A fire bell clanged remotely in the town.

"I'll meet her when the sun goes down," sang the happy waterboy.

Denis leant luxuriously against the parapet and gazed at the strange stars. "The *Oceanic* sails the day after to-morrow," he murmured to himself.

Ah, this was peace. The first real peace he had known since coming to New York. The day after to-morrow. He had done what he could—but now he was going home. This blessed quiet.

Trinity Church struck one o'clock.

"Oh, father, father!" Denis whispered.

Lazily he turned to look eastward along the parapet. Two men were huddled together on an iron seat. One of them was snoring gently.

"God knows they could sleep in a worse place," said Denis.

Farther along, about fifty yards away, there was a gas lamp. Someone was leaning against it, Denis noticed. A woman, a girl.

A slender, noble figure with uncovered head.

Denis caught a sobbing breath as he leant to stare at her. She moved. Dreamily she turned her face so that the lamplight fell on it.

With a great cry Denis ran to where she stood.

"Christina! Christina!"

THE TWELFTH CHAPTER

CHRISTINA had recognised Denis a fraction of a second before she heard his voice calling her name. For a breath she stood still and fed herself on the sight of him running towards her, then turned and fled out of the arc of lamplight. But Denis was already too near for her to escape his sight thus easily, and his eyes, well used to the summer midnight, never lost her outline as she ran.

"Christina!" he shouted in rapturous excitement.

"If she thinks that with that small start she can outsprint a runner like me!"

He laughed and shot forward at a still faster pace.

Just as she swept round the corner of a dark street on the other side of the park, he caught her arm and brought her to a standstill.

Panting, laughing, trembling, he held her with both hands.

They clung together, for Christina without being aware of what she did had taken the lapels of Denis's coat in her two hands; they clung together, taking hard gulps of breath, and staring into each other's faces.

"Christina! What did you run like that for? Why did you do it, my darling?"

"The minute you let go I'll do it again!"

"That'll be never!"

"It's you, is it?" she fingered his coat timidly. "It's really you, Denis?"

"Ah, love, the dance you've led me!"

"You're looking tired."

The voice in which Christina spoke was very tired, and so were the eyes that scrutinised Denis's face.

"Not quarter as tired as you are. Come, love. Where can we sit down and talk?"

"Nowhere, child."

He put an arm round her shoulders and began to lead her gently along the empty, dark street.

"You can talk as nonsensically as you like," he told her, "it doesn't matter a scrap. I've got hold of you, Christina, and I'm going to hang on. I've found you, darling, darling, darling!"

He leant his cheek against her hair and they moved along the street with a dream motion as once they trod a dewy field under the moon. They came into Broadway and wandered north along it, still quiet, still leaning together. The great street was strangely peaceful—not emptied of life, for that it could never be, but for an hour suffering life to move on it somnambulistically, a drunken man here, a slow market wagon there, at the corner of Wall Street a pessimistic hackman.

They halted by Trinity Church.

"Why did you come out here, Denis?"

"To find you. I've been looking for you nearly eight weeks."

"Oh, I didn't want this to happen! Denis, how did you know where to come?"

"That's neither here nor there. Where are you living, Christina? Can we go there now and talk?"

"Indeed and we can't."

"Well, then, we must go to my hotel—you must sit down, Christina, you must have food—oh, heavens, how thin and tired you've grown!"

"I couldn't eat if you paid me," she said with a shudder. "I was serving food until half-past twelve."

"Where, where? I've haunted eating-shops?"

"Pahren's—a little underground sailors' place, off South Street."

"Ah—I was on the wrong tack. Mrs. McNulty said you were near the Washington Market."

"I was at first. This is better. And it's nearer the wharf. Sometimes before I go home I can walk along the waterfront when it's quiet."

"As you did to-night—oh, lucky chance! Come, darling—my hotel's near here. They'll give me a sitting-room where we can talk—or if you're too tired to-night, they'll give you a bedroom, and we can talk our heads off to-morrow when you're rested. Come, sweet."

She caught the lapels of his coat again and looked into his face with anguish.

"Will you do as I ask you, Denis—this once—in mercy's name? Will you go away now, this minute, and never look for me again?"

"You're asking too much," he said. "You're asking what I don't understand."

"I can't help that; will you do this one thing for me?"

"Anything else, Christina. Anything in life but that."

"Denis, that's all I want from you!"

"My darling, this is crazy! You're tired, you're too tired for anything now!"

"I'm no more tired than I'll be to-morrow. I'm strong—a day's work never finished me yet."

"You call it a day's work that ends after midnight?"

"It doesn't begin till nearly midday. Oh, Denis, my darling, let go of my hands!"

"I won't, I say! I've followed you across half the world, and now I've found you, all you can say is 'Let me go'! Christina, what are you dreaming of? Have you forgotten everything?"

She looked at him without an answer. Her eyes were blank.

Denis whistled to the pessimistic hackman across the street.

"I can't keep you standing like this after your hard day," he said, "but neither can I let you out of my sight until you talk sense."

He opened the door of the growler.

"Get in, Christina—please."

She got in.

"Drive anywhere you like," said Denis.

The hackman had looked suspiciously on the shabby working girl, but the young man's clothes and bearing made him cheerful about his fare. Besides he sensed that kind of situation in which people do not notice what they pay for cabs. He nodded understandingly.

During the hours that followed these children from the Vale of Honey made as complete a tour of the streets and avenues of New York as may ever have been accomplished in a growler.

Christina was to remember vividly for many years, though she was hardly conscious of them now, the physical impressions that touched her during that drive in the cab. The dusty smell of the cloth-covered seat, the cool air from each window slashing through the stuffiness, the vigorous jolts, the reeling swing of the vehicle on corners, the rattle of lowered glass, the murmured chat of the hackman to his horse—all these that her senses accepted and her brain ignored just now, reviving in her after life, when she rode in other cabs maybe, or caught the smell of unclean cloth upholstery, brought with them a sense of oppression and discomfort which puzzled her.

§ 2

TEN weeks lay between this meeting on the Battery and the day that Christina drove out from the Blackwell farm to take the train for Cork.

On that bright morning of departure, when she had locked her trunk and entrusted to her cousin John the only letter of farewell she had to write, when she climbed into the cart and was jogged up the lane, and along the high road between the golden fields of hay, under a sky which, vast though its blueness was, seemed yet only wide and high enough to hold the day's clamour of larks, when she looked westward to the silver Taigue and to the little wood beside it in which her lover would wait for her on Sunday evening, it seemed to Christina at one moment that the pain in her heart was so great that it must stifle her now and instantly and most happily destroy her—and in the next that this fortunate thing had come to pass, and that she was somehow dead, numbed of thought and feeling, looking indifferently on a scene from a forgotten world. These dear things around her were not actual, but a memory; she was not driving away from them now, but long since had lost them, and since that was so, and they, and with them Denis her lover, were gone from her, dead and gone for ever, then the worst of life's pain was over and the sea and the strange cities ahead and the waiting years held nothing that she need fear. Peace and love had belonged to her, and they were gone. The best and the worst were behind.

This cold idea held her in patience until she was far out at sea.

But then, one night and day from the last sight of land, storms rose in her that seemed to her soul that had a habit of quietude louder and more shameless than the din of drunkenness, obscenity, and lamentation which beat all round her in the steerage hold of the ship. This hell of noise, which at first in her state of numbness she had shrunk from in great fear, she welcomed now as sympathetic. The savage licence which these exiles took as dramatic compensation for their plight, their abandonment of every reserve of decency and self-control, their raptures of self-pity and furies of contention, their prayers, their easy tears and easier curses, all would once have been to her a very foreign manifestation of woe, but now had a natural and a consoling ring. Indeed they seemed a tame indication of what the heart can hold. Christina heard them even with a mild contempt for their inadequacy and from far off, beyond the wilder uproar of her heart. Sometimes it seemed to her as if this, so loud and terrible, must utterly drown every outer sound and force these other light lamenters to be silent and hear frenzy speak; sometimes it seemed to her that she was shouting her own pain at the full pitch of her voice for the ears of her fellow-exiles, and even if she was, she did not care. Let them listen, let them hear. But the exiles, busy with their own noise, heeded Christina only to remark to one another that she was as high and mighty as a queen—"and not a sound out of her, either. Is it the way that the creature is deaf and dumb, God help her?" The loud fury in her made no physical sound.

This storm that followed on numbness was mainly of self-hatred. Awake to her loss, with the grey sea curling round her, the sea that she had never looked upon before and that stretched now till it united with the sky on every side to defeat the searching of her eyes, awake to realisation of a probable fifty years yet to be lived and that she had chosen to live them in a strange land, in a strange city, forsaking and hurting a

love that had never hurt her in order to pursue this barren-
ness—awake to stare at this fate that she had made, Christina
turned upon herself and ranted. What sort of coward was she,
then, to run away from the rich thing she had for fear she
would not have it always? Love had to die. Ah, and so had
Denis to die—but would she leave him because of that dark
certainty? What did she want? A world built specially for her,
with no loss or change or danger in it? Too proud to argue
about love with a priest and an old woman, but too weak to
stay and fight for it? Ah, but there was more than that in it,
she pleaded in confusion, for she was so tired and tossed with
her own arguments that memories and intentions went astray
in her head—there was some better reason. . . . "I wasn't
frightened for myself, I wasn't! I knew he couldn't love me
for ever—why is this I was so sure I had to go? Ah, 'twas
for him—I remember—because he wanted to marry me and
I was afraid that I'd give way—I daren't marry him—I
daren't! What is he but a child, with all his hopes and pranks
before him?—Oh, Denis, Denis, what'll you do when you hear
of it? What'll you think of me, my darling, for doing this
terrible, sudden thing? Why did I do it? Why am I here, lost
and crazy like this in the heart of the sea when all I want is to
be in the wood with you—the wood I'll never see again! Oh,
am I mad, I wonder? Am I crazed in my head for ever, to be
driving through the sea like this—away on my own wish from
where all my love is? Denis, take me back! Let me come back
to you, child—and we'll be as we were or any way you like—
I'll marry you, I'll do anything you ask! But not this—where
am I going in this ship, like a coward and a fool? Why is this
I thought I had to go? . . . Oh, stop crying, let you, Nora
darling—stop crying, my little pet! . . . This isn't real—this
isn't true. I'll be home again soon . . . no, Denis, no—I'll
never marry you—I want you to be happy—but how do I
know what's best for you? No, child, no—I love you . . .
what's this I was trying to remember?"

She was stupid with the unresting noise and struggles in her
of grief and fear and doubt and wild regret. She was seasick
too, and suffered acutely from lack of privacy on the ship and
from its indecent conditions of filth. Afterwards she remem-

bered this journey only as a dark blur—confusion ringed about with confusion.

By the time she entered New York Harbor she was quiet again and in command of herself, knowing where she was and why she was there. Her fanatical faith had returned to her, that in taking first love and refusing to let it be more than it could be she had done well.

With a composure that annoyed the immigration officers she passed through the ordeal of Castle Garden. Then, leaving her trunk at the wharf, she made her way on foot to Spielman's Court off Christie Street, the Bowery.

She did not know whether she was glad or sorry that her aunt was no longer there.

She found New York both more and less bearable than she had imagined it would be. The noonday heat of its midsummer was a stinging shock, but in the hours when its worst torridity was eased, in the clean, early brightness of morning or when she escaped to walk on the waterfront at night and catch the inland-coming winds before the town staled them, she was aware of a strange, new vigour in this foreign air, something hard that had hope and energy in it and that did not pamper dreams. Christina found, almost resentfully, that the tonic strength of the air made her heart move lightly in the early morning and at midnight.

She found too that the much-preached-about moral dangers of a great city need be as little of a menace to those whom they did not attract as they had been to her when she sat under the pulpit at Glenwilliam church and listened to Father Considine's denunciations of them. It seemed to her as she walked the crowded, wild streets of the town at all hours of the day or night, that in order to suffer molestation, assault, abduction, robbery, in order to be insulted or drugged or raped, one would need to be either extraordinarily innocent or extraordinarily willing. Men flung half-expectant greetings to her sometimes as they passed and she, used to the "Good-day to you, miss" of strangers on the Irish roads, sometimes returned these other greetings out of sheer habit, and had passed on before remembering that such salutes might be called insults by the wise. She heard words flung about that her instincts told her were obscene, she saw the minor decencies outraged in ways that certainly did wound her Irish puritanism, and in her day's work in Washington Market, and afterwards in South Street, wagoners and sailors made propositions to her that, always lewd, were sometimes playful, sometimes menacingly urgent. She discovered, with inward amusement, that the way to handle these suggestions was matter-of-factly and with politeness. She began to think that a great deal of nonsense was talked about the dangers of city life.

But she was not altogether right in smiling at the moralists. When she did so she forgot that in her beauty there was a quality of formidableness, in her bearing and the poise of her head an expression that would make any man not quite demented pause and wonder; and that recent sorrow had increased this composure of her face and eyes. Also she forgot that she was no longer a virgin, and did not know that virginity of its very nature makes danger from within for its possessor.

After four nights in the noise and squalor of a lodging-house in the Bowery, Christina found a dark small room in Davy's Row, off Gansevoort Street. She stayed in this room because it was cheap, and, giving on a high blank wall, was blessedly quiet; also, once she had begun to work, as kitchen hand, waitress, what you will, in an eating-house of the Market Wagon, she had no time in which to seek a better shelter.

Within ten days of landing at Castle Garden she had left one job and found a second.

In the Market Wagon she was miserable, shocked by the squalor in which she had to work, flurried by its strangeness, made stupid by the impatience and abuse of the Italian for whom she worked, and who resented her quiet manner as much as she despised his leering and mercenary effusiveness. When for six working days of sixteen hours each she received two dollars and an injunction to work harder in future, she made no answer but departed without ceremony from the service of this master.

Three days later she was engaged as waitress in his East River dining-room by Emil Pahren.

She liked this small, firm man at sight, as she liked his poor, simple restaurant, with its open windows, scrubbed deal tables, and clean food.

Emil Pahren was a German Swiss who had come to the States in 1874, and was already making a modest profit in his business. His cook told Christina that the patron's wife and child were buried in Zurich, and that it must be living alone that made such a fussy old bachelor of him. He did indeed believe Calvinistically in the decencies, in order, probity, cleanliness, punctuality—and early perceiving in his new waitress a similar faith in these things, he took pains to make her work agreeable to her. He was a just and cheerful man of middle age, with an ugly, spirited face. He paid his servants reasonably, fed them well, and did not systematically overwork them. Christina, settling to her duties among his lively sailor customers, under his guidance became interested in the new routine and more efficient than she realised. And the eyes of Emil Pahren, who, besides being just and cheerful, was also an ambitious and emotional man, often rested on her thoughtfully as she moved about the restaurant.

In many ways, then, New York was proving less terrible than she had dreamt it. Wild and hot and vast it was, but also it was negotiable. It whirled with passion towards some greedy ruthless dream that no one seemed to have time to explain or to examine—there was a pressure of madness in its hurry—but underneath all that, a part of it, indeed, individuals walked about who would tell you the way to a street, hastily but civilly, if you asked them, who would let you have a bed to sleep in provided you could pay for it, who grew hungry and tired at intervals as people did at home, and whose children, running perilously about the streets, were not at all unlike the children who tumbled out of Glenwilliam school-house at the three o'clock bell. Christina found that it was possible to walk safely among the wolves, keeping one's own thoughts, and that though the paving-stones were hot and hard and the vistas nightmarishly unbroken by the colour of a hill or a ploughed field, two living rivers flowed about the terrible streets She discovered too that the harbour where the sea came up bearing ships was at midnight full of peace—not the same peace that she knew in the Vale of Honey, but another moving, mysterious peace that was new to her, and yet old and friendly.

There were churches too, she found, dark, holy, quiet, set
down in their aura of silence amid the very frenzies of the
slums. Strangely they seemed old here, where they must have
been new; the unchanging burden of men's petitions and confessions lay upon them like centuries of sadness. Christina was
startled by their homeliness—the musty smell of poverty, the
trail of incense, dim-gleaming stations of the cross, the candles
lighted imploringly to Our Lady of Sorrows, the bowed forms
of old women, the confessional boxes murmurous with contri-
tion; the red lamp of the sanctuary.

Oddly, it was in these churches, these quiet places where
everything was hers and what she knew, that New York
seemed least bearable to Christina. For here she could really
think and really remember. Here, where the immediate silence
was so deep as almost to make the remote voice of the town a
part of it, it was possible, it was unavoidable, to create illusion,
to play with the idea that the leafy high road to Mellick lay
outside, that the priest's white house with its glass porch and
yew trees was opposite the chapel gate, and that when she
genuflected and went out in a minute or two she would see,
away at the top of the hill, the thatch of the Keener's Cross
where Denis had left his horse, and downwards the long untidy street of Glenwilliam with its pink and white and yellow
houses, its children whipping tops or leaning to stare at the
bottles of sweets in Mrs. Lacey's window. West of it all Blackwell farm would be lying before her, sorry and poor in its own
small valley, and west again from that she would see the wood,
her wood where he was waiting now, by the silver river. Ah,
that was vivid and unbearable. To that clear picture every beat
of life that was in her leapt. That, that was what she wanted.
What she found over here was not too terrible—it was endurable after all; one could live in it and yet remain oneself—
for so much she was grateful, but oh, she cried to the Presence
beyond the sanctuary lamp, "take it away all the same and
give me back the other! Is life only to be bearable for the rest
of my days? Is there no hope of being happy too? Take it
away, all this other—let it be a dream! Let me find when I go
out that I'm at home again! O Lord, have mercy on me and
do this thing! Take this past month away, that's all! Lord, you
can do all things . . ."

But as she made her fantastic prayer she swung deeper down into her heart that in the busy hours she was learning to leave ignored. At her work and in the hurtling streets she refused to examine love, she neglected it—but here where she was quiet, with head buried in her hands, there could be no evasion.

If God, Who could do all things, did take this bitter month away and give her back the Vale of Honey, what would she do in her turn? Would she not go straight from this place of prayer and purity across the fields to where love waited shamelessly to take her?

Christina felt her cheeks burn against her hands, for all her blood was answering "Yes." Ah, if it could only be! If only once more she could give herself to Denis!

"Lord!" she prayed again and lifted her honest eyes to search the dimness beyond the sanctuary lamp—"Lord, you know that I'm not sorry for having loved him, and that I can't pretend I am! You made me and You know me—and if loving him as I did was a sin against You, if it is sin and wickedness for me to love him still—oh, Lord, I tell you I can't help it! I've given him up. I'll never see him again. Isn't that enough? Must I say I'm sorry too for what I did? Must I confess it, Lord, and ask forgiveness? I can't, I can't! It was no sin to me or him, but the best thing in the world! I can't call it a sin, Lord! If I were to try for ever, I couldn't feel ashamed of it!"

So she prayed in great perplexity—for this obstinate glorying in her love meant, she knew, that all the consolations of her faith must be cut off from her. If she could not see and humbly admit the sin of love, she would be barred from sweet and holy customs that were more than half her life, from Confession and Communion, from prayers to the saints, from the protection of Our Lady, from the friendship of the mystic tabernacle that in the past had made such kneeling moments as reassuring as long sleep.

"Ah, my darling!" she would say, flinging God and His exactions from her with impatience, "ah, my darling, what does all this matter? Denis, where are you? Let me find you a minute, dear love . . ." and the dark church would become the dark wood and the far-away voice of New York would be the light voice of the Taigue. Bent before the sanctuary lamp in an attitude of adoration, Christina would give herself up to reveries that the gaudy saints around forbade.

It was these fantasies, these hours of escape from New York, that she found, of all that New York held, most terrible and wounding, and yet she sought them repeatedly. Their pain was harder to bear than the negative rest of the day; their vigorous illusion roused, exhausted, and did not console her, but left her weary and frustrated, panic-stricken with awareness of the impotence of a faithful heart before its own desolation. But they were so precious as to be worth all that.

§ 3

"I won't scold you to-night," said Denis, "and I won't waste time asking a lot of questions." The cab jolted them together —Denis put his arm closely, eagerly about Christina. "No, no, don't wriggle. Oh, darling, is it true that I'm holding you in my arms again? And you and I really driving round New York in a smelly cab?" He gave a soft laugh and laid his forehead gently against her shoulder. "There's nothing that need be said now about all the things that have happened to us, is there, Christina? Nothing, except that what you did was crazy and what other people did was—well—beyond description. If I were to say what I think of that busy fellow, my Uncle Tom, the cabby might hear and refuse to drive me! Oh, love, love, love! The main thing, the only thing, has happened! Love!"

Christina, as she listened again, after weeks of alien chatter, to this soft, hurrying, tender voice, as she felt this well-remembered fall of heavy hair against her neck, was thinking too that the main thing, the only thing, had happened.

"How did you know where I had gone, Denis?"

"Made them tell me, silly! What sort of congenital deaf-mute did you take me for, to think that I wouldn't find out where you were? And then when I got here your blessed aunt had disappeared, and I had only Mrs. McNulty to rely on. A nice woman, Mrs. McNulty, but a bit vague. So I walked the streets these eight weeks, Christina, and asked questions, and stared and poked about and swore, and ate steak and fried potatoes in every single downtown restaurant except—except——"

"Pahren's."

"Pahren's. And here you are. Oh, love, do you love me still?"

She swept him down into her embrace. She bent above him, her fingers violently tender in his hair.

"Love you? Love you?"

"Then you'll marry me to-morrow, won't you? To-morrow, or the first possible minute? And we'll go home together?"

Marry him and go home! Tides of delight were rising round Christina. She felt them come and knew what their strength would be. And why not let them come? How in God's name was she to hold them back?

He loved her with greater than a boy's brief passion. He had proved that by this wild-goose chase, by his slow disheartening search for her. He proved it by the joy in his face as he ran to her along the wharf, by the hurrying, happy notes of his voice, by the warmth and comfort that his presence flung about her. He loved her. Let there be an end of obstinacy, then —she must take this sweet, undreamt-of chance—give him what he wanted now, which was all she wanted, and have done with wild, crazy guessing at his unborn desires. Could she not make it her whole work in life to make him happy on his terms, whether he acknowledged them or not? Could she not be clever enough to be his just as little or as much as she would know he needed her? It was likely that she would be defter at that than at serving steaks in Pahren's. And since he did still truly love her . . .

She bent above him, every question stilled. In perfect happiness she bent above him. Her eyes were stars. Denis loved her. Then let the hidden years come—she was enriched to meet them.

They kissed for the first time since they had said good-night ten weeks ago in a dewy field under the moon.

The kiss carried Christina over a wide range of debate. When she bent to take it from the boy who leant upon her breast she was too happy to feel the pain of happiness—simply happy. When it was over and they breathed apart again and stared into each other's altered faces, she was just as simply unhappy, unhappier than she had ever been.

Between the two moments she had discerned that which Denis had half hidden from himself and of which in this glad and tender hour he was determinedly incredulous, that he loved now but no longer imperiously desired her. She could never have told how this was made plain to her or how one embrace that seemed like other embraces could have said so much that was new about a complicated emotion.

Denis's mouth was hungry; his arms were strong about her, and all his muscles quivered with an excitement that Christina remembered; his eyes, wide open and staring close into her own, reflected in full the happy, honest relief which this finding of her meant to him. It could not be true to say that he did not desire her, and Christina, who never thought in clumsy sentences, but in a series of wordless intuitions, saw that in this moment desire, piercing its way through many other emotions, was indeed burning him. But perversely too, still staring into his staring eyes, she saw that now this hunger of his senses for her was an accident. Hitherto, woven with friendliness and respect and tenderness and curiosity and the need for companionship, it had been the very fabric of love—now, looking into the too-near eyes of which she could read every flicker and shadow, she saw this desire as a loose thread, unravelled from all other feelings. These eyes loved her still—loved her with gratitude and constancy and pity and great brotherliness, with the promise of fidelity and consolation, loved her in all these ways because she was Christina and no other, because he knew and honoured her, and had exacted overmuch from her, that she should be humiliated and driven to a far country for him—because in fact she had been made his charge, his duty, his dear responsibility that he was eager to bear—all that, though Denis was unconscious of it, was in his staring eyes. But passion was there, Christina thought, as an accident—not because this was Christina whom he kissed at last, but because she was beautiful and he had been long alone and unconsoled.

Hair-splitting. Folly. Fanaticism.

Christina closed her eyes.

This that had looked like the unasked-for opening of gates was only after all their final clanging-to. What had once seemed wise, and then for a moment paltry, was now inevitable. To have married Denis while his desire was still insatiable except by her would have seemed grasping, would have been to ask too much. To marry him now would be like murder, said her fanatic heart.

There was no reason in her. But her searchings into knowledge of Denis had always been irrational, harvested from touch and pause and intonation, from words unsaid, from light and shadow of his eyes. These gave her such clues as convinced her obstinately of her own right understanding of him. In nothing else would this girl have claimed infallibility—but here almost hysterically she assumed it. She knew him in all things—therefore in this embrace she knew him too. Desire was a part of it, but a man's desire already, adventurous and capable of slaking itself in other arms than hers. Let it do so then. Against this one ephemeral, dangerous hypothesis she would not weigh the many other gifts that she could give him, for these, she told herself half bitterly, he had already from his father, and would always have. She could give him what Anthony Considine would not—freedom. She had had him and could have him now and still wanting him would let him go. In this she would be greater than his father. Well, that would be something, she told herself, an old, unadmitted jealousy still moving uneasily in her.

Thus the kiss that had begun in welcome to returning love and the reopening Vale of Honey, the kiss that had been full of high resignation to happiness, changed to another resignation in farewell, became a last salute to things of whose existence there was after all no proof save in the beauty of this face she kissed and in a few faint images that might be dream or memory.

"Good-bye, Denis, good-bye."

That is what her kiss said as its debate concluded, and her mouth, denying itself to his at last, repeated the small phrase for his ears.

"Good-bye, Denis, good-bye."

"What are you saying, Christina?" She was drawn down again and held more strongly. "Oh, don't say topsy-turvy things to-night—like you used to in the wood. Don't tease me to-night of all nights, Christina!"

But she couldn't tease herself to-night of all nights. There must be now no sweet, half-careless arguments such as used to be in the wood. The only endurable thing was to be quick as lightning in killing the last chance of such a thing, and then get away for ever to the small, dark room that looked on the blank wall.

Christina searched her open mind for **some trick** of disingenuousness. If the only one she found was novelettish, she was too simple to know that. It seemed a brilliant lie to her, and she seized it with greedy despair.

"Sit up, Denis—no, straight up, like a good boy. Over there in the corner. That's right."

"Oh, Christina, must I really? For how long?"

Denis, in his delight at finding her, and in recognising that in spite of a look of weariness she was unchanged Christina, lovely, quiet, noble, had assumed a gay and babyish mood that he knew she loved particularly.

But his light-hearted manner hid a passion of excitement and he was aware that this excitement was as much of conflict as of joy. He dared admit to himself, and then fled from his admission, that the whirl aroused in him by this long-desired finding was not a confusion of pure happiness. But happiness was in it, he protested. And, growing angry, growing unaccountably afraid, he questioned if he knew what happiness was. Why should it not be this, this very flood of dark and light in which these moments swam? Relief after strain was happy, and so was success after failure. To be overcharged with tender thoughts of one who sat at hand in quietude, to be filled with will and power to cherish and reassure, to know that bad days of cruelty, blundering, and helplessness were over, these were happy things. To have found that which was lost was a happy thing.

But many things had been lost, and had he found them all?

He must woo her now. He would be gay and obstinate and play the baby. Dear Christina! Loved and deflowered, pursued in pity's rage across the sea—and here fantastically now in a New York cab, on an August night. A good and harsh adventure, worth fruitful ending. He would not believe himself so cruelly perverse as to shrink back from it. It was clearly impossible for a sane man to dread his pursued desire when at last it fell into his hands. A wife then! A wife for ever! No whimsical love, no secret of the woods, but love paraded, subjugated, with signature on paper! If that wife is Christina? Ah, Christina . . .

"Darling, I tell you I won't sit up in a stuffy old cab like this! Well, one minute then. Exactly one minute by the clock, you silly! What's the point?"

"I've something serious to say. I hope you'll be able to forgive me for it."

"Well, if I've forgiven you for skedaddling off the way you did, and I suppose I have—— Oh, don't you think that minute's up, dear love, dear darling——"

"Where are we now, Denis?"

"Turning into Twelfth Avenue, I think. Yes, here's the river. Look, Christina!"

The Hudson lay beyond the window of the cab, a black and empty mirror for the stars. The hackman had turned northward away from the lights of Hoboken and New Jersey. The far shore was as passive as the water, and ahead the street was empty. The sleepy noises of the cab seemed both vast and tiny against the widespread silence.

"Ah, it's grand!" said Christina softly.

This dumb subjugation of roaring, petty life to night, this abasement of a city under trampling stars touched her searchingly with self-contempt, and even gently with contempt for Denis. What was this fuss she was making about whether she spent life here or there, with this companion or with that? The best things were incommunicable, and thereby only tantalised companionship. They were imperishable too and could make a million Springtimes in the mind. All that they needed was such a quietude as this that lay about her, in order to prove that scenes of childhood remembered and love remembered had a reality that went deeper to the spirit than the reality of tactual life. This moment, this passive stretch of night and water caught in the cab window seemed to suggest that once the mind has known and wrestled with happiness, it has secured as good a shield as may be found against the loneliness of time—it has a dole on which to live, and must account itself lucky. That which once was is safe, and cannot suffer bank-ruptcy. That which was and is no more is hidden treasure.

Christina took Denis's hand in hers and with one half of her consciousness pondered the sensation of its contact. The other half was busy with the lie she was about to tell.

"I'm not going to marry you, Denis, because I've promised to marry someone else."

"You—you've what, Christina?"

"You heard it quite well. Someone that I've met out here, Denis. I'm going to marry him and stay here. That's what I'm going to do. It's the best thing."

"I—I simply don't believe it, Christina! Do you hear? I don't believe it?"

Christina, earnest to play her part well, wished she had the audacity to twit him for his vanity—but she knew that it wasn't vanity that made his face so blankly incredulous, but his conviction of the high faithfulness of her. She was at a loss when she stared into his eyes.

"It's true," she said wearily.

"It isn't. You know as well as I do that it isn't. For some mad, mad reason you're making up this lie! How dare you, Christina? Oh, but how dare you be so crazy?"

"Denis, listen to me. You know as well as I do that our love is over. Yes, over. You know as well as I do that, whatever we did and however we tried, it could never be the same again."

"I don't know what you think you know all of a sudden, but I know that for me it is the same, and will be the same, Christina."

"The same?"

There was ruthless penetration in her voice.

"No, not the same," he answered as if compelled—"but it's more than it was, Christina, it's greater now. You mean much more to me after all this——"

"Ah, in a way, perhaps. But it'll never be again like it was in the wood. You're not my lover any more."

"Who is then, may I ask?"

Christina noted, almost methodically, that this was the first time that his voice was cruel to her.

"No one, Denis. Don't be silly."

It occurred to her that in spite of herself she was making

it appear that he was to blame for the change in their relationship. She paused, aghast at this injustice, and fumbled for a more careful way of speech.

"Silly!" he echoed excitedly. "I must say I like that, Christina! It's you who're silly, if you think you can make me believe that you're an entirely different person from what I know you to be."

"Listen. I didn't know you were coming out after me. I didn't think anyone would let you know where I was, and I didn't want them to. I'd given you enough, Denis." She stumbled over the mean words, and Denis stared at her as if her outward aspect were changing in that minute before his eyes. "I'd given you enough, and I thought it was time for us both to get over that—that first love affair."

"Oh, my Christina, what are you saying to me?"

"No, no—don't touch me—please!"

"I must. You're mad! Listen—you don't look as if you knew what you're saying! You're saying these things against your will! Your face is exactly like it used to be—and you're shaking all over! You simply don't mean what you're saying! Since when have you taken to measuring love, and saying you've given enough, or given too much, and will give no more? You, who are generous beyond imagining! My love—you said this minute you loved me! You said it, Christina!"

"Ah that! That was just the first minute of seeing you again —it, it revived things."

"Revived?"

"I want to stay over here, Denis. I want to marry this man and stay over here."

"Why?" he shouted.

"Go easy, darling."

"What are you calling me 'darling' for?"

"I don't know."

"Why do you want to stay over here?"

"I can make good money here, to send home."

"Good money! Ah, if you're thinking of things like that, don't you know that I'm rich, Christina?"

"I like New York, I tell you."

"Liar!"

"I'm not a liar."

"To-night you are. The world's champion. Tell me again—look in my face and tell me that you like New York better than Glenwilliam, better than the Vale of Honey, better than little Coonagh wood!"

"Ah, it's a different kind of liking!"

"I should think it is. Not your kind, Christina."

"What's there so odd about me that I shouldn't like New York?"

"Everything's odd about you, my dear, my darling! Oh, Christina, there has never been anyone like you since the world began—never anyone so beautiful and honest and gentle and faithful! And now this trying to be like other people—it's, it's ridiculous! It's even odder than anything else about you! But give it up, Christina. Give it up, I say! You'll never convince me that you, of all people in the world, are on with a new love before you're properly off with the old! It's—it's simply not *you!*"

"I'm going to marry this man, I tell you—and there's an end of it."

"Why?"

"Well, because I want to. He's very—very nice and he's been very good to me."

"No doubt. Who is he—this very nice, very good gentleman?"

"Mr. Pahren," she said, bravely fulfilling her lie.

"Mr. Pahren? And who might Mr. Pahren be?"

"But I told you. I work for him, in South Street."

"Ah! A restaurant keeper—the owner of a low-down eating-house for sailors?"

"What's that got to do with it?" Amazingly Christina found herself as angry now as Denis was. "Who am I that a restaurant keeper isn't good enough for me? And I never wanted to marry a great Considine anyhow."

Denis shrank from her as if she had struck him.

"Christina," he whispered, "what has happened to you?"

Christina realised then that she had played this scene only too well. It had carried her away. Under the weary strain of too many emotions, an anger that she could not account for, rising to defend Emil Pahren from Denis's scorn, had made her say an inexplicable thing—something that offended against all her dear relationship with Denis, and made him look at her as if she were a changeling. In a sentence that was no part of her plan and no part of her normal nature, she had convinced her idealising lover that she was indeed something less than he had believed. In terror she turned inward on herself to try to find the source of this cheap taunt. What in God's name was Emil Pahren to her, or ever likely to be, that Denis's contempt for him should have so ensnared her into coarseness? What did she care for this commonplace, elderly Swiss, that she should rise so stupidly and so madly to defend him against one of whom she had made a god, and who had therefore a god's privilege to mock no matter whom at his pleasure?

As she pondered her own unaccountableness and stared at Denis, huddled in his corner, Denis for whom she believed she could deliver fifty Emil Pahrens up to torture, Christina became aware of something that her consciousness had hitherto ignored—that in fact Emil Pahren loved her, and that her unscrupulous use of him in this sad debate had arisen out of a hidden awareness that, should she in fact by marrying him seek to make her flight from love irretraceable, she had only to give him the sign. This discovery neither surprised nor interested her. Nor could she see in that sneer at Denis that had revealed it to her a prophetic cry of loyalty to her own future. All that mattered now was that she had succeeded in her present purpose. Ten words flung out heedlessly, because she was suffering overmuch and must end this scene quickly at any cost, had convinced Denis, as no measured protestations could, of a change in her nature and so of a change in her love.

She took his hand timidly again.

"You must forgive me," she said. "It'd be impossible for anyone to be the kind of person you always pretended I was."

"When are you going to marry him?"

"Oh, any day now."

What did it matter how many lies she told?

They rode awhile in silence. They had left Riverside Drive and seemed to be going southward. Christina caught a glimpse of water down a side street to the left.

"That must be Harlem River," she said.

"You seem to know your way round all right."

"How did you find out where they'd sent me?"

"I made them tell me. And when they realised all that had happened they were afraid you might be going to have a child, my child! Ah, if only you were, Christina!"

"Well, I'm not."

He looked at her with sharpness.

"You're sure, Christina? Oh, darling—you're not marrying that man for any reason like that?"

Christina, dazed and half-listening, almost said "What man?"; then caught herself up and shook her head.

"Tell him to go to Gansevoort Street, will you, Denis?"

"Why?"

"That's where I live—just off there."

"Oh, but——"

"Please, Denis. I simply must go home."

Denis gave the cabman her address.

They leant back in their corners then, amazed at the confusion that divided them.

"May I see you to-morrow, Christina?"

"No, no, child. Never again."

Denis jerked his head up sulkily—and folded himself in silence.

Christina smiled a little as she watched him.

But though one sulked and the other smiled, these signs were nothing—fidgety, outward gestures that served them now as well or ill as any others. Both were in despair and numb at heart, Denis because first love was indeed dead for him, and because in finding Christina he had not found again that which he had persuaded himself he would find, a golden, sweet-filled June, a happiness that, seeming magic-bountiful, had proved a haggler after all. Against all his brave and anxious protestations, first love had fled.

Christina, on the contrary, was numb and in despair because in her it still lived mercilessly.

"I'll love him for ever," she told herself, panic-stricken. "Oh, what'll I do if I love him for ever?"

The cab rattled down Fifth Avenue.

"Say something, Christina! Oh, speak to me, can't you?"

They turned and stared at each other piteously.

"I can't."

She opened her arms.

"Once more. Let me kiss you once more," she said.

Straining her to him, he sought with hunger again for the precious thing that he had lost. But it was not in her arms for him, and their mouths, even as they brushed together, fell apart.

"It's no good," Denis whispered. "I don't know on earth what's happened to us, Christina!" And his tears splashed on Christina's face.

She ran her fingers over his hair, over his wet eyes.

"Forget all this," she said. "It's like a bad dream we're having. Forget it all, Denis, and only remember the things that used to be between us—will you promise?"

"Will you remember, Christina? The first time ever you came out of the wood, after the swan had passed."

"She'll nest up there in Farrell's reeds next Spring."

"I won't go out to look for her!"

"I'll remember it all till I die!"

"Come back to it!"

"Never."

"Christina, you were more beautiful and noble than any dream or poem or woman that's ever been!"

"Remember me that way, then, and that you gave me such happiness as no one should dare to try and keep!"

"No, it won't stay," he said dreamily, "no matter what you do, you can't keep hold of it."

Christina kissed his hair, and held him quietly against her heart.

At last the cab stopped.

"Gansevoort Street," the cabman shouted.

They got out into the cold light of the small hours, and walked down the shabby street and into Davy's Row.

"To-morrow, Christina?"

"No, never again."

She looked at him as if gathering knowledge of his face to feed an eternity of dreams.

"Good-bye, my darling."

She vanished into a tall and slatternly house.

§ 4

THE next day Denis walked by the East River waterfront and looked for South Street. He was not sure that he wanted to find it; he was not sure that he wanted to see Christina again, and if he did, he had no idea of what he was going to say to her. What was this man like that—that she said she wanted to marry? Or had he dreamt all that happened last night?

At last, half against his own will, he stood in the little passage that led to Emil Pahren's dining-room. It was a quiet afternoon hour, and the restaurant seemed almost empty. Beyond the red curtain that hid it from where he stood he could only hear the murmur of one voice.

He fingered the red curtain and drew it an inch or two aside.

He saw a clean, big room, whose long deal tables, clothless but laid for a meal, had no customers seated at them. At the far side of the room near the window Christina stood, with her back to him, in a dark cotton dress and white apron. A grey-haired man, who also wore a white apron, was standing with her, his face towards Denis, but his bright, fine eyes bent questioningly on Christina. He was talking to her softly. Denis could catch no word of what he said, only its tone of tenderness. As the man spoke he took her hand.

Denis stared. There was no mistaking the great emotion in Emil Pahren's face.

The curtain fell into place again. Denis turned away and passed into the street.

"Good-bye, Christina," he said in a whisper. "Oh, my dear, dear Christina."

§ 5

HE WALKED along the waterfront and came again to Battery Park. He leant upon the parapet.

"Hereabouts she must have stood," he said, trying to reconstruct in noisy daylight the scene of fourteen hours ago that seemed already a fragment of another life.

He leant on the parapet and watched the busy, glittering water.

"That's a fine clipper out there! I wonder where she's off to? Spanish flag. A beauty like that could never sail up to Mellick. It's lovely in Aunt Teresa's house, the way you can see the ships from every window. What a fuss it's all been! Oh, Christina, my dear, what a fuss! Uncle Tom will never speak to me again, I imagine—and that's no loss. I must send a cable to father. Ah! Christina! What's it all been for? I'd like to see his face when he reads that cable. He might even have it this evening, after dinner."

Denis leant upon the parapet and strove to see his father's face. "What'll I say in the cable? 'Sailing to-morrow—love—Denis'? Sailing to-morrow, love. Denis."

THE THIRTEENTH CHAPTER

T HE Spring of 1877 was pleasantly sprinkled with happenings for the Considines.

There was the Pope's jubilee, for instance. Many of the elders made up parties for this event in May and travelled to Rome in order to look on the living face of His Holiness and kiss his authentic toe. The Joe Considines made this pilgrimage very pleasantly with their friends, the newly knighted Sir Jeremiah Daly-Downes and his lady. The Mulqueens took Aunt Agnes with them, and Teresa also persuaded Anthony to give her son Reggie leave of absence from Considine's in order to accompany her.

Every morning of her stay in Rome, while the rest of the party made dutiful circuits of the eternal city, Teresa knelt on the cold floor of Saint Peter's—a church whose vastness moved her passionately—and, praying in an abandonment that ignored all her own weariness and failing health, and even the especial pain that nagged unceasingly nowadays in her left breast, implored her compassionate God to allow her a miracle, to ordain that her afflicted son Reggie, whose disease earthly doctors could control but could not cure, should be made well now in this blessed month of jubilee when the shadow of Christ's vicar would fall across him. For Teresa still had one overweening mortal desire—to dandle the son of her favourite son before she died. She had grandchildren now. Her eldest daughter, Alice, married these four years to young Dr. Condon of Galway, was about to have her third child this summer.

Moreover, Daniel, Teresa's third son, who was on the Stock
Exchange, was engaged to a nice, healthy girl, and would no
doubt be quick to reproduce himself when he was wedded. And
Marie-Rose had become engaged at Easter. But all these things
were nothing. Teresa prayed in Saint Peter's and at the feet
of His Holiness for only one thing—that her son Reggie be
vouchsafed a miracle, so that he might marry and she might
see his sons before she died. But, as it happened, God did not
vouchsafe the miracle.

Caroline Lanigan did not go to Rome, although she asked
Eddy to take her there. He wrote rather ungraciously that
jubilees were the last things to jubilate over and Caroline was
so cross that even the beautiful old emerald-studded clasp that
he sent with his disagreeable remarks did not soothe her.
"Wear it to pin Denis's roses to your dress this summer,
Caro," Eddy wrote—but she threw the letter angrily on her
dressing-table.

Anthony had suggested rather anxiously to Denis that perhaps he would like to go to Rome by himself that Spring, but
Denis replied rudely that it was the Pope's jubilee that was on,
not his, and that it was unlikely that the Holy Father would
miss him in the crowd. Anthony laughed at that, betraying
neither annoyance nor perplexity at the irritability, and so he
had had his reward, for Denis, hurrying along the garden
after him, had put his hand under his arm and said, "Why
don't you kick me, father? But look here—don't mind the
Pope. You and I'll go to Italy on the quiet later on."

Thus Denis had been all the Spring towards his father—
see-sawing between exasperation and great tenderness.

There was this engagement of Marie-Rose Mulqueen also.

Marie-Rose and her younger sister Aggie had happened in
March to go to a race-meeting in Dublin with their sporting
Uncle Joe, where they fell in with the De Courcy O'Regans
of Coolcroagh, Malahide, County Dublin. The De Courcy
O'Regan family, fathered by Donatus de Courcy O'Regan,
J.P., M.P., possessed every kind of temporal virtue and ad-
vantage, and it was therefore a source of great satisfaction all
through the Considine family when young Vincent de Courcy
O'Regan, the heir to all the advantages, was seen to be authen-
tically in love with the chic and golden-haired little Marie-

Rose. During the rejoicings that followed the satisfactory fiançailles in Easter Week, it occurred to no one that in presenting one young man to two young ladies it is at least possible to establish unhappiness side by side with happiness— that is to say, no one noticed that Aggie, aged twenty-two now, two years younger than Marie-Rose, had fallen in love with her sister's fiancé. But if anyone had, he might have wondered how a young man as intelligent as Vincent de Courcy O'Regan, confronted by Aggie's tall, casual elegance, confronted by her vivid and benevolent young face that was dark and faintly sardonic, confronted by her honest, humorous, self-forgetting eyes, could have overlooked all these splendours to court a tiny moss-rose. However, so he did. And Aggie, who loved her soft, vain sister with cherishing tenderness, was very kind to her happiness. She was always kind to Marie-Rose.

There were small events among the River Hill children too. Jack had got his wish and was apprenticed to the great training stable of Bill Cusack at the Curragh. More than that, he had invested a part of his inheritance from his grandfather in a promising two-year-old chaser—a leggy colt called Happy Jap, by Hilarius out of Geisha Girl. This colt and the two victories of its first season, as well as the registered Considine racing colours (St. Patrick's blue, emerald sleeves and cap), were a source of enormous delight to all the family, even secretly thrilling Father Tom. They constituted for Dr. Joe a complete excuse for leading more and more the sporting life.

Mary, Anthony's eldest daughter, had "come out" in the winter of '76, and was proving a reasonable social success. She was a handsome girl with a bold carriage and a good opinion of herself. Anthony thought her too fat to be attractive, but she already had admirers. She was not likely to throw her advantages away on a bad match or do anything derogatory to her surname.

Paddy, the third River Hill son, was distinguishing himself at Clongowes both in Greek and in football, and looked like being the captain of the school in the following year. Tess, on the contrary, was, in the Easter of the triumphant betrothal of her cousin Marie-Rose, expelled from her convent school, or more accurately, Anthony received a letter from the mother superior expressing her desire that his daughter Teresa should not be restored to the convent's charge. The mother superior had a duty to her other pupils, and Teresa Considine's incorrigible disregard for discipline, her idleness, and the manner in which she encouraged her younger sister Florence in idleness made her a dangerous influence among the other young ladies. The mother superior regretted very much, etc. etc., conceding that the "dangerous influence" was in fact good-humoured, charming, and talented, but—the "buts" must indeed have been enormous to drive the authorities to this gesture of despair. "Miss Teresa Considine," the letter concluded, "is interested in only two topics, her brother's racehorse and the sound of her own singing voice."

Anthony raged at Tess about this letter, and all the aunts and uncles thundered. But Denis observed that his fifteen-year-old sister was not merely unmoved by all their clatter but did not listen to it. Having attained her object of not going back to school, she was in charming mood, and did not in the least mind being abused. Unceasingly she sang about the house and garden—in her thin, true, piercing voice—ballads, lieder, dirges, and funny little dancing songs, whose accompaniments she picked out cleverly and softly sometimes on the drawing-room piano.

Rage as he might, Anthony found her decorative and entertaining.

"How are you proposing to get through life without education, my fine young lady?"

"You haven't done badly, father."

"Don't be impertinent, miss."

"Education! Well, I ask you, father! William and Mary, and the mineral products of China—and 'parlez-vous français, mademoiselle'!"

"But if you can't parlez-vous français—what about it then? Won't you feel a nice fool in Paris?"

"I'll learn to parlez-vous my own way in Paris. Without all this grammar fuss. But first you have to send me to Germany, father!"

Anthony snorted.

"I'll send you nowhere, you baggage! Nowhere, do you hear? I won't spend another penny on you, so I won't!"

But Tess was already out of the window, and chanting as she crossed the lawn:

> *"I go to the Elysian shade*
> *Where sorrow ne'er shall wound me . . ."*

Denis laughed at Anthony.

"She has you on toast," he said. "It's great fun."

There was not much that was unusual happening to the Lanigan children at this time. Peter, a barrister, was doing well on the southern circuit. John, articled to his father, was rumoured to be behaving badly, drinking in low-class public-houses, it was said, and following the fortunes of more horses than Happy Jap. But at family gatherings he always appeared to be just a handsome, shy young man. Jimmy was still at Downside, but Lucy and Norrie, at home with a French governess, preparatory to be being sent to Paris "to finish," were a source of irritation to Caroline, who loved the pretty creatures very much and was constantly being wounded by the cold, unsympathetic silence that fell on them when she—headache-racked, as she told them—dropped into sharp or impatient words. She thought she observed a tendency in Lucy and Norrie to fuss about their father more than they did about her.

The only points worth noting in regard to the Joe Considines at this date are that Sophia's palpitations were making port wine more and more indispensable to her, that Isabel, the second daughter, was hanging fire as Millicent had once done, and that Victor, now practising in Dublin, was paying serious court to Anna, the eldest daughter of Dominic and Louise Hennessy.

So all the Considine households were placed in the May of Pio Nono's jubilee, and in the June of Marie-Rose's wedding to Vincent de Courcy O'Regan, when Teresa's laburnums were dripping gold about the lawns of Roseholm and over the bride's white veil.

That wedding passed off well on the whole.

"Love and a cough cannot be hid," said Danny contentedly when, the last wedding guest gone, he stood on the steps of his white house above the river and contemplated the day's happy doings. "Love and a cough cannot be hid."

There was no one at hand to heed him but his third daughter Aggie, and though she was by then despairingly in love with her sister's happy bridegroom, she knew better than to dispute a maxim of her father's.

Danny was well content. The only blemishes which he could observe on the wedding festivities were that young John Lanigan had got exceedingly drunk before they were over and that Denis had not appeared at them at all. This was badly done of Denis, Danny thought, and knew that all the other aunts and uncles would call it downright insolence. They had all intended to extend to him at last to-day that patronage of geniality which had been coldly withdrawn since his return from America. And what way was this to thwart their mood of friendliness? Denis was a queer cove, and no mistake.

§ 2

DENIS spent his cousin's wedding day riding alone across the lush, sweet Vale of Honey. Letting his horse take his ease under the pleasant sun, he guided him to long-familiar lanes and bridle-paths where peace was certain to be found. He was in no hurry and had no destination but quietude. He halted often to stare at haymakers or drink with tramps. He did not return to River Hill until the stars were in full ascendency. By that time he was in serene humour and was able to be gay with Anthony about the wedding which he had missed.

He wished his cousin Marie-Rose no ill. He knew little about her but, having seen her bridegroom, was inclined to think that she was probably getting far more than she had to give. And it was at least half out of good will towards her that he had stayed away from her wedding party. He had no wish to make a scene at it or behave unpleasantly, but he had felt in advance that his elders would make the convivial day an occasion for restoring him to their favour. Waking on the bright wedding morning he had realised that he was in no mood to take their unctuous patronage politely—and so had ridden away from River Hill after breakfast, telling Anthony to kiss the bridesmaids for him.

The nine months since his return from America had been difficult for Denis.

Restored to Anthony, he was at first almost feverishly happy in the generous, excited, uninquiring welcome that his father gave him and was both touched and amused by the arrogance with which that welcome enlarged itself to overcome the stiff disapproval of himself which the family hierarchy was not long in making manifest. At all the Considine gatherings of the Autumn and Winter Anthony made a great point of addressing Denis frequently and with especial love, teasing him and telling anecdotes in which he figured. He even questioned him in public about America and commanded him to tell his Aunt Teresa or his Uncle Tom this, that, or the other about his journeyings.

All this was embarrassing but it was also pretty good fun, particularly the invitations to tell traveller's tales to Uncle Tom, with whom Denis was now not even on the most formal speaking terms. But the impudent game exasperated Anthony's brothers and sisters, many of whom had no desire to be unkind to Denis, but believed that he deserved a really sharp lesson from them and must not lightly be forgiven.

"Father," said Denis one night, as they drove home in the phaëton from the Lanigans' house, where Aunt Caroline, growing sharper-tongued every day, it seemed, had jibed at Denis with scarcely veiled contempt, thus evoking a passion of partisanship in Anthony—"father, you'll end by making the entire family hate you!"

Anthony turned to his son with a smile, every brilliant detail of which was revealed in the hard moonlight.

"If I do, it seems I'll be in good company," he said.

Denis was deeply stirred.

"God! If you knew how I missed you in America," he murmured.

Instantly tears glinted in Anthony's eyes.

"River Hill was a tomb without you, my son," he said.

They drove on in silence, each thinking in his own terms that life seemed complete for the moment, a strong, unmutilated thing, ready for its own complications.

It did indeed seem that their old companionship had only been deeply refreshed by the upheaval of the Summer. Their walks to and from the office, and the lazy hour when they sipped port together, rid of Aunt Agnes's cantankerous table-talk, were full of new zest at first. Anthony never inquired about Christina or seemed to wish to do so, and Denis, bless-ing him for this, raked his mind for such news of America as he guessed would really entertain him. He told him of a new writing machine being used there now—Mark Twain was said to have written his last book on one of them instead of with a pen; he told of rumours that were about of an instrument which would make it possible to talk over a wire from street to street, and even from town to town; he described a marvel-lous bridge that was being built from New York to Brooklyn across East River; of Coney Island and its rowdy Saturday fun he talked, and of the amusing corruptions of the Presi-dential election, and of the topsy-turvy architecture of New York, and the tasteless, new amenities of Central Park; he described the wizardry of money-making in the petroleum fields, and what he knew of the Arabian Night splendours of the Vanderbilt crowd; he described the races at Jerome Park; he described the Bowery and the waterfront, and the Negro life in New York, and the bohemianism of Greenwich Village.

"I think you must take me over sometime and show me round," said Anthony.

"Oh, that'd be great!"

Thus, reassured by the dancing happiness of his father's eyes, and watching Autumn smoulder softly about the Golden Vale, touching his garden with red and gold, with midnight frosts and with morning mists of pearl, Denis felt that the nostalgia which had wrung him in New York was justified, and had now been lulled and fed.

But Winter came. The last petal fell in the garden, then the last leaf. Rain swelled the river so that its steely curve was mud-coloured; rain blurred the hills and made the cypresses look brown and sodden. The days of forage-selling succeeded one another unchangingly; the family persisted in contempt; there was no one at the office to take the place of Don José, no one among the cousins to be what Tony had been, no one in the rest of Mellick to offer such a companionship as

"Flasher" Devoy had once provided. And nowhere was there work or ambition or emotion to take the strength that lay wasting in him. Life was, after all, only a bearable monotony, with no particular quality in it for Denis and no particular stimulation except his father's love.

That love, which could carry much, and braced itself generously to take the external hardships of this time from Denis, was unable however to grapple with itself. Anthony, thinking by love to adjust all things, became, against all his watchfulness, too loving. He became with practice a shade too quick in defence, a shade too eager to acclaim; he grew over-sensitive to hurt or weariness or boredom in his son, and so, in his anxiety, conceded too much, indulged too much, surrendered too much. Aware that he had never really understood Denis's temperament, Anthony thought that now, in a difficult time, it was wisdom to give in to it before it had a chance to shout. He was wrong. When everything else was flat and featureless, Denis would have found relief in his father's more resistent, less observant moods. He needed to be stimulated, to feel the hard surface of life, to laugh and contradict and be enlivened. The watchfulness of Anthony's love began to unnerve him little by little; he found himself waiting for its gentle manifestations, found himself setting traps for it—but it touched him so much and he was so lonely in this grey reaction from first love, that he could not bring himself to protest against or repudiate it. Only in rare moments of something like fury, when seized with an unreasonable idea that he was being treated as if he were a lunatic or a dangerous prisoner, he shouted savagely at Anthony:

"Leave me alone, father! Oh, God, go away and leave me alone!"

But as Anthony obeyed and left him Denis had almost always to run after him and catch his arm. For he could not endure to hurt this man, whom no one but he could really hurt.

So through the Winter and Spring he grew more moody and listless and changeable of temper—see-sawing for ever between resentment and adoration of his father. Meanwhile the coldness of the family was maintained against him. Anthony seemed his only real friend.

§ 3

DENIS came of age on the 28th of June, two weeks after the wedding of Marie-Rose Mulqueen.

The anticipation that had fired Anthony's eyes for weeks before this day, and the movement of preparation for it that hummed through River Hill caused the young man to wake to his twenty-first birthday with a troublesome consciousness of ordeal ahead for which he was not braced and almost believing that some spiritual finality and climax attached to this conventionally emphasised date.

He turned on his pillow and blinked towards the glittering garden. He searched himself anxiously for appreciation of all that lay hidden in the next twenty-four hours—the gifts, the blessings, the jocose admonitions, the change of status in the firm which he was only too sure would be thrust on him, the increased salary and accession to something like wealth, the splendid family dinner, the dreaded toasts: "Our third chairman, May his days in Mellick be long and prosperous!"—the dance that would follow, the exciting music, the consoling wine, the breath of the garden troubling him at every window, the river insisting still, through all his perplexed acceptance of his birthright, that life is wide and wasteful and thousand-faced, cruel and transitory and of infinite beauty and infinitely to be explored—the river saying this, and the young girls, as they danced, telling him that on the contrary life is its full self in the quiet harbour of their arms and that here at home among sequestered ways all beauty can unfold itself. The young girls would be seductive to-night—he knew that by the state of fear in which he woke—seductive but hereafter only to be kissed at peril of the marriage bed. For their mothers' eyes would be upon him, announcing ruthlessly that now he was responsible, eligible, a citizen, someone marked down for their manœuvring flattery. And his father to-day, ah, he would move about all the birthday and most of all in its festivities, with an irresistible light upon him, the light of triumph, of safety in possession. By the tilt of his head, by the flash of his

WITHOUT MY CLOAK

432

eye, he would say to every comer, "This is my beloved son in whom I am well pleased."

Oh, damn him, damn him! Denis kicked away the bedclothes and turned and buried his hot face in the pillow. Suddenly it seemed to him that he hated his father, who had compelled from him so womanish and unnatural a love. He hated this undenying, terrible love that was more than half himself; he hated the dear, dear picture of Anthony as he would look to-night when he raised his glass gravely to "Denis John Mary."

"I hate him."

His body shook as he whispered the words. He clenched his fists and bit the pillow.

"A happy birthday, my son," said Anthony's voice then, more penetrating than the morning light, illumining Denis's dark pillow.

Denis turned to the source of the bright voice, aware of blind conflict in himself but defeatedly aware, as a drowning man might be that beats against the contemptuous sea.

He smiled at his enemy.

"You look as if it were your happy birthday," he said.

"And so it is! Get up, you lazy good-for-nothing! Get up and see what it's like to be a full-blown man!"

Denis slid out of bed.

"It's going to be a terrible day," he said. "I feel that in my ageing bones!"

"Well, and if it is, many terrible returns of it to the two of us!" said Anthony, and laid a hand on his son's shoulder.

Denis dropped his glance from a face that was radiant with safe prophecy.

"Thank you, father," he said and stared at his own naked toes.

"I wish I had my trousers on," he added.

Anthony chuckled.

"Here's a present for you," he said and thrust a small plant at Denis. The roots of the plant were wrapped in wool; a label hung from it. "This isn't the only present I have for you, but you're such a queer cove that you'll probably like it better than the others."

Denis read the label.

"Magnolia. The Chinese Yulan! But, father, how in the world——"

"I heard you muttering a week or two ago that you wanted some such crazy thing—so I thought I'd be a hell of a clever fellow! I stole the catalogue and copied out the gibberish where you'd marked it!"

Anthony's eyes danced excitedly.

"Is it right, my son? Or have I made a fool of myself?"

"Right?" said Denis, not knowing how to look into the eager face. "It's absolutely dead right. You're—you're a marvel."

He held the little tree gently, dreaming that it blossomed in his hands. He saw its heavy leaves spread out to an impassioned sun, saw the rose-white flowers of all its unborn summers asleep in a cloud of their own rich breath. But beyond the flowering tree, the mist of petals, and the sweet smell, he looked still into his father's radiant face.

"A lily tree! Man alive, you've ears on your fingers and toes!"

"Of course I have! Happy birthday to you, my son. And now I'll let you get into your trousers."

After Anthony had left the room, Denis stared a long while at the little plant in his hands. A small sign of tenderness, but it oppressed him like a bad omen.

And as he dressed fear of his birthday grew on him so that he could not keep his hands from shaking.

When he went downstairs he received the rest of Anthony's presents—promotion in the firm with doubled salary, promotion to a roll-top desk in O'Halloran's room, to be O'Halloran's lieutenant in general direction of all departments. With this went a seat among the directors of Considine's and a substantial parcel of Considine shares. There was also a cheque on Anthony's account for one thousand pounds. There was also an order on Anthony's London tailor for six new suits of clothes. There was a gold hunter watch, there was a beautiful dark brown mare, a thoroughbred two-year-old. There were a dozen cases of Hermitage 1876, which would replace those of his birth year, 1856, the first of which would be broached to-night. Beside such splendours Aunt Agnes's offering of a morocco-bound missal seemed prim, not to say meagre, but

Anthony had the face to keep his disgust at it to himself. Denis thanked Aunt Agnes glowingly, but even to-day the poor woman could not smile more than winterishly on the nephew who had committed unnamable sins.

But to-day all the other aunts and uncles forgot Christina Roche, and to Anthony's great pleasure, showed a forgiving generosity towards Denis. Letters, telegrams, and presents showered from them on the mistrusted one. The Joe Considines sent a cheque and a case of 1811 brandy; the Mulqueens an elaborately fitted dressing-case; the Lanigans a pearl-headed scarf-pin and the works of Alexander Pope in calf. Uncle Eddy arrived unexpectedly from Paris, bringing his nephew an exquisite piece of eighteenth-century needlework—Watteau-esque ladies in meditation by a lake against a grove of cypresses. Aunt Mary sent from the convent silver rosary beads in a morocco case. Uncle Tom sent an old French writing-table of rosewood inlaid with brass. The note that went with it said: "To my dear nephew Denis, wishing him long and happy years. Uncle Tom." Denis stared at these words in perplexity.

During the morning Lucy and Norrie Lanigan called with their French governess to greet Denis for Aunt Caroline, who had one of her headaches. Aunts Sophia and Teresa also called, as much to criticise Agnes's arrangements for the evening as to salute their nephew.

Aunt Teresa laid a knotty hand on his shoulder as he stood and greeted her on the noon-bright lawn.

"You're a man now, Denis, and we're right in expecting great things of you. You'll be an honour to us all, I'm sure!"

These sentiments were an icy wind on Denis's raw nerves. But Aunt Teresa looked old in the sunlight and as if in pain. Some transitory emotion stirring her, too, made her look, for all her plainness, most damnably like his father. He could not smile at her—his lips were rigid, but he kept quite still until she passed from him into the house. He moved then, unwittingly, flung up his hands to open and shut them frantically against the sky.

"An honour to us all, I'm sure!" he muttered. "Oh, God, we own one another here! Body and soul—do we possess one another for ever, us Considines? What in hell's the matter with us, that we insist on owning things we know nothing whatever about?"

Uncle Eddy, newly arrived off the mail train, was leaning wearily out of his bedroom window, and saw the gesture of Denis's hands.

"So it's as bad as that by now, is it?" he mused. "Or could the fate of a rich and spoilt young man ever be as bad as that?"

Unable to answer himself, Uncle Eddy turned from the window to his dressing-table, and, as he brushed his thinning hair, he stared indifferently at his own handsome, wasted face.

Denis meanwhile turned and ran over the grass.

"I'll ride," he heartened himself. Maybe his new mare could take him to a place that would cool this heat of fretfulness, this rising, burning panic.

But he ran into Uncle Tom, descended from a beautiful grey mount and coming towards him, hand outstretched, mouth smiling. He looked rather fine in his controlled embarrassment. Denis's mind groped backward over the dull year, seeking what he had once felt against this stealer of treasure. "Christina, Christina!" he prompted his lagging heart—but there was dust already on the story.

He put out his hand to Father Tom, aware that his action was neither useful nor quite useless. Not quite useless, he thought, if it pleased his father—but for this priest and himself, who performed it and to whom it was costing much, it had no significance. If they two were to shake hands twice a day for the rest of their lives, Denis reflected with astonishment, it would mean nothing to them, since they were born to be strangers, though clipped within one family formula, which could deliver to neither of them the other's clue. Why scruple to shake hands then, since, though the world might say they had each something to forgive, there could really be no question of that, neither even remotely guessing what the other had done to him.

Taking the priest's hand then and listening to a rounded sentence of good will, Denis looked into the face so near his own and saw a disturbance of gratitude and returning peace in it.

"Great God!" he thought. "The man's been bothering about

all this, and I haven't given a curse for it. Oh, we're an emotional set, all right. Can it really matter to him whether he and I are on speaking terms or not?"

He heard his own voice sounding graciously.

"It was ridiculous of you to send me such a beautiful present, Uncle Tom. I've never seen a lovelier table."

"I'm glad you like it, Denis. I took some trouble to please you."

Denis shrank under this happy unction, but Father Tom wanted more of it. He put his arm across the young man's shoulder and called to Anthony, who was descending the housesteps, to join them. He forced Denis forward triumphantly. This moment to be fulfilled must be paraded.

Denis went with him, keeping his eyes on the ground.

So the day moved, encounter heaping on encounter, chain dropped softly on chain.

Climax waited in it somewhere, Denis knew.

The year that was gone, the dead, decayed, and flowerless months of it were piling up their symbols and rewards for him to-day, under the ironic sun. And he wanted none of them, these gifts from a strange country in which he had lived too long, in which no one knew his loneliness or the fretting habit of his heart. That year must not repeat itself, he told himself madly—not by so much as one little day. A day! How precious it was! If he were to tell the Considines that a day was more valuable than a hundred thousand pounds, would they believe him? Would they measure its little strip of brightness against long death, or would they answer with murmurings of heaven and hereafter? Well, let them. The value of brief time could not be depreciated by such a consolation. Death that seemed impossible still seemed a fact, and the means by which one man consoled himself against it and fought for its temporary contradiction might well seem nonsense to his neighbour. But need that matter, since it was impossible for men in their crazy diversity to know one another, and since rules were for ever breaking down? Life could only be the antithesis of death—and a brief antithesis at that—when the questing mind was free at least of its own narrow acre.

He was feverish on his twenty-first birthday. The proprietorial fuss that was being made about him inflamed the hidden,

smouldering ill-humour of months that had been savourless
and lonely. The Winter and Spring just dead had laid a deadly
chill on him, and their routine, that used no quality of his
essential self, but chained him to those which he had only in
moderation and in common with a million other young men,
took on for him at last, though there was no element of
hardship in it, the taste of slavery. Not that his notions of
himself were lofty now. He had sought honestly enough, and
still sought, in spasms of despair, for that stimulus which lay
in buying and selling, the stimulus that kept his father's mind
leaping, his father's eyes bright. But he had never found it.
He did not wonder what others found in it, observing that
some found happiness, which was all he wanted. A common
need, which other Considines were finding in other places, in
the accumulation of wealth or the securing of social status, in
simple prayer, as Aunt Mary did, or in the Bishop's favour
and his own pulpit eloquence, as Father Tom did; in beautiful horseflesh which was his brother Jack's solution, or in port
wine, which was Aunt Sophia's; cousin Reggie fumbled for
it in bawdy jokes, and Chopin-strumming; Tony seemed to
have found it in complete denial of himself. Happiness, or the
hint of it, lay somewhere for most men, and Denis saw where
it lay for him. In no fantastic place. In no superior dream
of greater knowledge than his fellows, in no idealistic frenzy
to put the world right at any point, but simply in making gardens; in being allowed to assimilate the habits of mind and
emotion of his time—and to express these, and fantasies on
these, in gardens. All his reading and thinking led him back to
this. Visions of gardens crowded on him at night, waking
and inflaming him beyond all chance of rest. Notebooks and
portfolios into which no one ever looked were filled with plans
and sketches, but more schemes and beginnings of schemes
than he could ever set down floated in and out of his exasperated mind perpetually, like fragments of real life tantalis-
ing the delirious. With all this preoccupation he nowadays
scarcely touched his own garden at River Hill, which had become locally renowned, and of which Anthony was loudly
vain. He scarcely touched it, because it increased his sense of
frustration, because there was no room in it for one hundredth
part of his conceptions, because in any case it was made, an

idea of the past and done with—and finally, because, for all
its beauty of river and cypress trees and slowly moving terraces, the house above it was an irreparable scar across its
face. There were moments when Denis found consolation in
this first garden of his making—moments of Spring morning, Summer evening, Winter night, when its beauty spoke to
him reproachfully, asking if any mortal man should not rest
easy all his days in such a setting. But he did not want to rest
easy—he wanted to be up and about his business—that was
the long and the short of his trouble.

"Ah, Christina, Christina!" he would catch himself crying
sometimes in the night. "You were right, you see—I didn't
even love you properly, my darling—I didn't love you half
as well as I love these crazy ideas—I didn't want you half
as much as I want this simple thing—to be myself, Christina,
not a bit of a family tree—to be myself. Oh, tell them, Christina, tell them!"

And then he would laugh into his pillow.

"Tell them yourself, you theatrical fool! You've a tongue
in your head, haven't you?" And planning then to tell "them,"
to tell them first thing in the morning that he must go away
and live away, and wander the world as he chose, and do the
work he chose, he would see the light going out of his father's
eyes, and the set look of desolation creeping across his
father's face. Coldly then he would fold his mind in blank-
ness, refusing to admit that this look was the least bearable
thing in the world. But he could go no further with his passionate argument. He was the prisoner of his father.

To-day the prison was in festival.

§ 4

AT LUNCH his young brothers and sisters were very gay, teasing him, counting his presents, giving advice.

"Don't forget the deserving poor, Denis!"

"What on earth does he want with another horse, father?"

"Now you have that two-year-old, you'll be selling Abelard.
I'll make you an offer," said Jack.

"Selling Abelard? Just when he's got his Héloïse? Not I."

"Den," Paddy shouted, "can I have the old silver brushes, since Aunt Teresa's given you gold ones?"

"All I want out of your millions, Denis," said Tess, "is a thousand pounds and a first-class ticket to Munich!"

"Don't propose to anyone to-night," counselled Jim, who was thirteen. "Take your time about a thing like that."

"Propose indeed! At twenty-one?" Mary laughed haughtily. "Who ever heard of such a thing?"

"Not you anyway," said Jack. "Don't we all know that your latest is a senile old gaffer of twenty-two?"

"With buck teeth," chuckled Tess.

"What's this? What's this?" said Aunt Agnes in a fuss.

Mary tossed her handsome, bold head.

"I know who'll be doing the proposing to-night," said Reggie Mulqueen, who had come out on some errand from the office and had stayed to lunch. "Our irresistible cousin, Dr. Victor Considine."

"Oh, that's nothing new," said Denis amusedly. "Time enough to notice Victor's love affairs when someone shows a sign of accepting him."

"I'm not so sure—this time it looks like business!"

Denis laughed.

"Has the idiot been found who'll say 'yes' to our cousin Victor?"

"Jealousy badly becomes you," said Anthony, twinkling. "They actually tell me that he's on the point of being accepted by the most stand-offish young lady in Mellick. And I don't know what we'll do with your Aunt Sophia if her family lands another Hennessy!"

"A Hennessy, is it?" said Jack. "Which of them?"

"John Aloysius's favourite grandchild, no less. Dominic's eldest girl, Anna."

"A damn fine-looking girl," said Reggie, "but a terrible touch-me-not. All the chaps are terrified of her. They say she's a blue-stocking! Poor old Victor! He's biting off more than he'll ever be able to chew!"

Denis was amused. He disliked Victor Considine.

"Anna Hennessy! So she's a beauty, is she? I remember her as a cranky little cat at parties long ago. She must be about my age!"

"Older than you, Denis," said Mary. "High time she married someone, I think. She's been out three seasons now and has nothing much to show for it, for all her notions of herself!"

"Puss! Puss!" Denis teased his sister.

"The men are terrified to propose to her, I tell you," said Reggie. "Besides there are very few who dare to think themselves good enough for a Hennessy."

"Takes Victor to rush in," Denis laughed unkindly, "broken nose and all! Does he really think she'll accept his broken nose?"

"Well, there's no shame in breaking your nose with the Killing Kildares," said Jack. "You can say what you like, Den, but he's a good man to hounds."

Aunt Agnes chipped in acrimoniously.

"I hear that this young lady, Anna Hennessy, gets on badly with her mother, Mrs. Dominic. I'd be very sorry to believe such a thing of any mother and daughter, of course!"

"Oh, you can believe it all right," said Reggie.

"That's why she's stayed abroad so much," Mary chipped in, "in Austria and Italy and places, although she finished school there three or four years ago. She met Victor in Vienna last Winter, you know. She and her mother fight like cats!"

"Peter Lanigan says that's why she's encouraging Victor," said Reggie. "You see, Dominic and grandpa are making her stay at home now, and she loathes it. And Victor's a damn fine fellow, God bless him! Oh, yes, Denis, a grand, powerful husband for any young lady! And grandpa approves of him, and he's proud enough of himself to suit her pride, and he'd be an easy, creditable way of shaking off mamma! So there you are!"

"She's a lovely creature," said Tess suddenly. "She's like a lovely ghost!"

Anthony burst out laughing.

"Poor Victor! It'd be great fun to hear him proposing to a ghost!"

"Greater fun to see him married to one!" said Reggie.

Anthony stood up from the table.

"Remember, father," Mary threatened him, "you promised me mother's big ruby for to-night!"

"You're too fat for rubies, girl," he answered her, and then

smiled at Denis. "Come on, my son. You've eaten enough.
They're waiting for their new director at the office!"

§ 5

So THEY were. Waiting with an illuminated address, waiting
with engraved gifts of silver and mahogany and ormolu, for
this stripling director, to wish him long authority over them,
and such a prosperity as was his without their wishes, and of
which for themselves they had no earthly hope, waiting to
salute his youth as some of them had waited to salute his
grandfather's age on that dramatic day that was his last on
earth. The emotion of the long dead event stirred again in
this living one; O'Halloran, Flannery, Peter Farrell allowed
themselves the sweet spice of reminiscence; wagging their
heads luxuriously over days which at this distance seemed incomparably finer than the present, and which had over them
indeed the advantage of younger hope and a longer vista; they
recalled the old man, Honest John, and boasted his legend to
their juniors, truly believing as they talked that they had not
feared but loved him with playful confidence.

Their talk stirred a feeling of geniality which spread
through the whole staff, and took increase from a variety of
causes. The sunshine, the universal wearing of best clothes, the
knowledge that the chairman would not be in till after the
dinner hour, the knowledge that good bonuses would mark
the day, the satisfaction which there generally is in giving
presents, the good-natured liking which prevailed for Denis
in Charles Street, even among those who mocked his idiosyncrasies, all these things swelled the sentimentality of the older
men into an emotion which the entire staff of Considine &
Company could enjoy.

"God spare him many years to us, the bouchal," thought
blinking Flannery, as he held his place in the front row of the
press of clerks that crowded the chairman's room and peered
at the chairman's son. "God spare him long to us, but he'll
never be the man his grandfather was, heaven rest him!" And
as he prayed he drove his elbow with fury into the stomach of
a pusher behind him.

"Keep back out of that, young Quirk, before I make you!" he hissed. "Wouldn't anyone think that at least for the day that's in it, you'd try to ape the manners of decent people?"

"Tch, tch," said O'Halloran, in soft annoyance, "order there, if you please, Mr. Quirk!"

Denis stood at the chairman's desk, flanked by his father and Uncle Eddy, and stared at these familiar men who had just desisted from cheering him and were composing themselves now to listen with him to an illuminated address that would describe his limitless virtues. Peter Farrell was in a fuss, adjusting his eyeglasses for an ordeal through which it was impossible to hope his feeble sight would carry him. O'Halloran, tremendously fat these days, streamed with sweat as he besought, "Order, gentlemen, order!" from the rowdy clerks. Uncle Danny, peeping round Anthony's chest, looked as uneasily happy as if the ceremony were centred on himself. Reggie Mulqueen and Hubert Considine, who stood behind Denis, were poking him in the back in an effort to make him giggle. Uncle Eddy stood in gracious composure; so did Anthony, but with an added brightness in his eyes that contradicted his easy calm.

Denis looked at the clerks and was neither disposed to giggle like his cousins nor to be emotional like his father. He felt dry and dull.

These people, these familiars who were strangers, were about to be added, like horse and dressing-case and directorship and magnolia tree, to his possessions. Not content with thrusting on him their testimonies, which rose up already on Peter Farrell's quavering voice from Peter Farrell's gilt-framed document, not content with those offerings of silver and mahogany and ormolu which he could see bobbing about among them in the hands of their agitated presenters, these men, whether they knew it or not, were giving themselves to him. Symbolically maybe, and at long remove, the remove of his father's future years—but his nevertheless by to-day's ceremony they helplessly declared themselves.

He viewed them with weariness. What could he find to do with such a burden? They would know, more or less accurately, whatever it was necessary for them to know about hay and straw and oats and bran and mangolds, about prices and harvests, import and export, supply and demand. They would invoice and lade and check, ship and unship, train and detrain; they would thank for favours of ult. and inst. to hand, they would keep petty cash and strike balances; they would run to the bank with Considine money, would calculate Considine dividends, write Considine salary cheques, say "Yes, sir" and "No, sir," and hold the director's horse while he mounted; and draw their pay and go home to their Saturday tea. And they would be always his. In their most intimate selves they would be his, in their loves and wives; in their children, in their dreams for those children which should replace whatever dreams of their own had been frustrated. They would be his, held to him by the slender thread of the dull service they could do him, they or another, and swung by the same thread above despair and hunger.

It was absurd. He didn't want them. He stared into their upturned, smiling faces. What on earth was Peter Farrell stuttering at? ". . . the talented and beloved representative of the third generation. May he and all of us long enjoy the wise and paternal guardianship of our honoured chairman, his devoted father . . ."

Denis stared at the upturned faces, at the walls of varnished pine, at the fly-stained gasolier, the grotesque portrait of his grandfather, the photograph of his father in mayoral robes, the illuminated addresses of other Considine occasions, at the open window beyond which the river swept relentlessly, and back again to the upturned dependent faces. The presents were being hoisted more purposefully now, for Peter Farrell's voice was flowing homeward down the last slope of peroration. Denis's father cleared his throat softly and softly shuffled his feet. A moment of significance was at hand.

There was silence, a happy expectant silence, in the room. Peter Farrell, exhausted and triumphant, was laying his gilt-framed burden on the desk before Denis. The bearers of silver and mahogany and ormolu were pressing up behind him, smiling sheepishly above their gifts. The crowd of clerks was quiet and shy, waiting for the gracious condescension of the young man, their master, who would speak to them now and reward their loyalty out of his lordliness.

Anthony bent to study the illuminations on the address and

to hide the emotion in his face. Eddy leant forward to hitch
a small packing-case more easily on the arms of the young
clerk who held it. Uncle Danny got out his handkerchief but
forbore to blow his nose. Reggie Mulqueen and Hubert Considine, knowing that Denis must now be collecting his wits for
a speech, desisted charitably from poking him in the back.

Denis stared at the scene in front of him and was surprised
to notice a new, swaying motion of its outlines, a strange light
on it, as if water flowed all about it, as if he looked at it
through water. While he puzzled over this, he became aware
that his hands were icy cold, and that his heart was heeling
over slowly under his ribs. There was a sudden, terrifying
nausea in his throat. The outlines of men and objects swayed
softly, as if under the sea.

This was the climax that he had feared since waking. The
panic that had not ceased all day to press on his nerves leapt
up and mastered him. He became hysterical. He flung up his
hand against the swaying scene. He gave a great cry. He
turned and sped between his two astonished cousins towards
the office door.

"Never, never!" he shouted insanely as he ran. "Oh, never,
never, never, never, never!"

He was gone before his shouting ceased to echo in the room.

§ 6

HE RAN along Charles Street, southward out of the town. Hat-
less, breathless, he tore down the quiet, suburban road. Beyond the last houses, where the hawthorn hedges began, he
sprang into a fast-trotting baker's cart, and flung himself flat
among the baskets of hot bread.

He had no object in view. He was quite insane. He muttered and sobbed and laughed as he lay in the cart. The baker's
boy looked back at him uneasily several times, but did not dare
protest. All of the immediate situation that Denis was aware
of was that the cart was taking a road that he had greatly
loved a year ago and that had often seemed too long then at
sunset-time. For some reason now it made him happy to be
on that road.

"I hate him, oh, I hate him!" he sobbed and laughed.

Without premeditation he sprang from the cart near the Keener's Cross, and dropped into a field without becoming aware of the indignant baker's boy, or remembering to reward him for the long lift.

He ran as if pursued by devils until he reached the triangular meadow and the oak tree. He threw himself full length along the turf in the familiar pool of shade, and pressed his body passionately against the root-knotted earth.

"You've done it at last," he soothed himself, "and it's all over. You've flung it all back in his face for ever, and you're free! You're free, do you hear, you're free! No one will try to stop you after this! You've shown them you're a lunatic— and that they'll be well quit of you! You're free, free, free! He'll never want to look at you again! You can be off tonight, and have done with it all. You're free and free and free!"

He sobbed and laughed. He clutched the oak roots in his shaking hands.

THE FOURTEENTH CHAPTER

THE great family dinner-party at River Hill that night was a sad fiasco. No one ate anything worth mentioning; hardly anyone touched the excellent wines; everyone spoke in frightened undertones. Denis's chair was empty and so was Anthony's, for the host of River Hill, having waved his guests to their places, had left the dining-room without a word. For once the chairman of Considine & Company was unequal to a situation.

Small wonder indeed, as Teresa and Tom compassionately murmured to each other.

In the first place, it was now half-past seven o'clock and since four o'clock, when Denis had vanished from the office in Charles Street, there had not been sight or sign of him. In the second place the whole town was rampant with the tale of his behaviour in that office, a tale which had lost nothing in the thirty-odd versions of it which Considine's clerks had been nimble-tongued to spread. In the third place—but what need to catalogue? The position now was, as all the family knew, that Denis had vanished, in an outburst of shameful hysterics, that no one had an idea where he was, and that Mellick had decided (a) that he was drunk when the thing happened, (b) that he had gone out of his mind, (c) that he had thrown himself into the river, (d) that he was already locked up in a padded cell in the County Asylum, (e) that they had always known him to be wrong in the head, (f) that his father had had a paralytic stroke—and so on, with a calamitous legend to fit each letter of the alphabet.

The family admitted itself beaten this time.

The late hours of the afternoon had been filled with their vast alarums and excursions. Fruitless attempts were made to weave a story with which to stem the town's excited gossip, and panicky suggestions were flung out about consulting the police and arranging search parties. But Eddy, keeping his head and smiling at all his relatives, had begged them to have sense. He pointed out that a piece of juvenile melodrama was not a family tragedy, but Denis's own rather tiresome business, and that no great harm could come to an able-bodied youth of twenty-one, if he did choose to run wild awhile about the countryside; and that he was certain to turn up before the night was over and explain himself one way or another to his father.

Eddy's common-sense prevailed. He found it easy to persuade Teresa to take the situation passively, for ill-health and pain were nowadays spreading a blur on outward things for her. Tom also was chary of interfering so soon again in Denis's affairs. Indeed, all through the family, intrinsic dignity responded to Eddy. This preposterous business must take its course and they must bear what Mellick had to say of it. Poor Anthony! The nemesis they had so often prophesied for him, and sometimes half wished on him, was here and, dramatic though it was, no one seemed to find gratification in it.

Anthony kept out of everyone's way during the afternoon. He paced about the library alone, hardly pausing at all in his long impatient strides. When it was time to dress for dinner, he went upstairs and dressed. But he ate no dinner, returning to pace the library when his relatives were seated at the dining table.

§ 2

AT ELEVEN o'clock Denis had not returned to River Hill, but his coming-of-age ball was going forward merrily enough without him. His brothers and sisters and cousins, though varyingly annoyed and perturbed by his bad behaviour, could not for all that deny the mood which champagne, the Summer night, and the string quartette from Dublin exacted of them.

As for their young friends and guests, all the curled darlings of Mellick—they were frankly amused by the legend of Denis Considine's latest caper, and saw no reason at all why it should spoil a night's fun.

But the occasion was to be more than a night's fun for Victor Considine, who looked to its events with great seriousness. Sophia's eldest darling was in his thirtieth year now and the most important of Dublin's young physicians. He had a fine appearance, an excellent knowledge of his work, and a dignified if rather unbending bedside manner. He had distinguished himself, socially and intellectually, in Paris and Vienna, and was a finished man of the world. Last winter his fine aquiline nose had received an added aquilinity in the hunting field. Victor was tall and broad and held himself as if he guessed his own worth. His brown hair and moustaches were luxuriant and curly; he had a chivalrous manner and danced well. He lived in Baggot Street, Dublin, at present, and it was his wish to marry before the end of the year and move into Merrion Square. His practice justified such a scheme and would benefit by it.

Staying with some Austrian friends near Vienna for a New Year's house-party last winter, he had found Anna Hennessy, a Mellick girl, among his fellow-guests there. The younger daughters of his host had been her schoolmates in Bavaria. Victor had been overwhelmed by her difficult and aloof young beauty, and not unmindful either of her remarkable eligibility as a life-partner for himself. He regarded this meeting in a far country as fatally romantic. Since then he had come frequently to Mellick and paid anxious suitor's visits to St. Anne's, Dominic Hennessy's vast house on the Serpentine Road. All the Considines and all the Hennessys saw his intentions, and some of them were laying heavy bets on and against his chances. The feeling among the more observant Considines was that the Hennessys approved of him qua Considine, but were unenthusiastic about him as an individual, and Anthony's impression was that John Aloysius Hennessy would be politely disappointed if his favourite grandchild accepted the superb Dr. Victor. But as this grandchild was known to be difficult and to have scorned many eligible young men perhaps the wise grandfather would feel that a suitable if rather surpris-

ing marriage was better than none. Meantime there was no
guessing what answer Anna Hennessy would give to Victor
Considine.

He would put his hopes to the test to-night. He was by now
consumedly in love, and therefore by no means so self-
confident or conceited as his contemptuous young cousin Denis
always maintained he was. He was in an agony of humble
uneasiness, though no one would have guessed it, as he drew
on his white kid gloves in the hall of River Hill, and prepared
to enter the drawing-room, to-night the ballroom, in search of
Anna. Still, he took comfort from mirror-glimpses of his own
fine figure. He was, though Denis might not believe it, accustomed to triumph with the fair, and was by no means in the
habit of proposing marriage to young ladies and being refused.
Indeed, he had had to exercise care to escape their designs on
him so long.

He drew himself up on the threshold of the drawing-room,
took a deep breath, and advanced to bow before his white-
clad love. And Sophia, his mother, seated nearby, peered at
him through her lorgnette as he opened his courtship, and
prayed for him tenderly and proudly under her breath.

§ 3

ANTHONY took no notice of the revellings.

Eddy, as it happened, was playing host for him, greeting
arrivals, flattering the old and the important, charming the
shy, encouraging the musicians, seeing to the smooth running
of all the excellent arrangements. But Anthony neither noticed
that Eddy was doing this nor cared if his guests were in his
house or in Timbuctoo. He strode about the library and stared
out of the library windows, he strode through the hall and
onto the hall-door steps, he stared about the shadowy, starlit
garden, and turned and strode through the hall again and
back into the empty library. He did not seem to hear the music
or the familiar voices round him, or to see the silky, murmurous, gay crowds through which he cut his way, and which
fell back uneasily to let him pass. His face was shamelessly
grief-stricken. He did not care how much the world saw of
the wound his son had given him.

§ 4

THE second waltz of the night was in full tide. Young men and women glided contentedly over the drawing-room floor; there were no wallflowers anywhere; all the elderly and the non-dancers were disposed in comfort about the brightly illumined house, gossiping, chaperoning, sipping sherry, arranging whist-tables. Violins, 'cello, and piano were passionately, superbly in time and tune; the moon was rising over the garden.

Eddy turned from his duties awhile and took Cousin Rosie into the dining-room to steal an early sandwich.

"You and I are old fogeys to-night, Rosie," he told her.

"Much I care what we are," said Rosie, who looked fat and shabby and perplexed. "I don't like being here at all, so I don't, and poor old Denis missing and in disgrace the way he is. I think it's heartless of the lot of us to come out here at all."

"Nonsense, woman. Can't he be allowed to make a fool of himself now and again if he wants to, without upsetting all our arrangements? Don't be fussy. Everyone's making far too much of a fit of tantrums."

"Ah, trust you to be diplomatic at all costs. But don't you know well the way poor Anthony is fretting. It was a shame for the boy, so it was, to go and make such a fool of him to-day of all days."

"That's neither here nor there."

"Look at him striding out to the garden again! He's like a hen on a hot griddle."

"Won't do him a ha'porth of harm. Won't do either of them a ha'porth of harm to upset each other thoroughly for once."

"But supposing the young ruffian's run off for good? Supposing he never comes back?"

"Well, supposing?"

"Ah, don't be trying to madden me, man!"

Caroline's voice could be heard talking softly and angrily in the doorway. "Oh, please stop apologising, Jim. I distinctly said my *green* shawl, but I'm used to your blundering. It doesn't matter."

A shadow fell over Eddy's face. He turned towards the door to see Caroline enter the room alone. She looked lovely and distinguished in spite of greying hairs and irritable mouth. Her gown was of the blue of summer dusk, her eyes were as starry as the great emerald on her hand. She moved towards the window and half-smiled at Eddy.

"Do you think I could have some tea, Ted?"

Eddy signalled to a maidservant.

"Headache, Caro?"

"Raging."

"Oh, you poor thing," said Rosie, "it's terrible the way your head is always at you these times."

"Makes me so cross," said Caroline, with an apologetic appeal in her eyes for Eddy.

"Enough to make a saint cross, darling Caro."

She leant against the window, her arm stretched on its frame, her face towards Eddy. The thin, decrescent moon was behind her head and looked like a diadem set rakishly in her hair.

"What a dreadful, dismal party," she said.

"Doesn't sound like that," said Eddy.

"Are we never to be done with the tomfooleries of this stupid Denis? Ah, Rosie, why did we have sons? There's Peter making a complete fool of himself to-night with that terribly fast creature, Mrs. Haddington—and John has already had more champagne than is good for him."

"Sure, they'll only be young once," said Rosie good-naturedly.

"I sometimes wish they'd all been monks, like poor old Tony," Caroline murmured, closing her eyes.

Eddy stared at her dreamily and at the moon that was still entangled with her hair.

Reggie Mulqueen came into the room.

"Well, Mrs. Barry," he said to Rosie, "what odds are you giving on the favourite now? Even money?"

"What's this, Reggie?"

"I thought you were making a book on the Anna Hennessy Stakes."

"I am, faith. And he hasn't a chance of her, has Master Victor."

"Well, if I were you, I'd study his form to-night. He's finding the going pretty easy, believe you me!"

"Here's your tea, Caro," said Eddy. "Come and sit down and rest that aching head."

§ 5

JOHN ALOYSIUS HENNESSY did not often accept invitations to evening parties, but he had consented to come to River Hill for Denis's coming-of-age ball, out of a special compliment to Anthony Considine, whom he liked particularly. He also came in order to observe the courtship of his granddaughter by the unexceptionable Victor Considine.

John Aloysius was nowadays Mellick's Grand Old Man —the same age as the century, as he liked to say, and outwardly a fair example of the qualities and achievements that the majority of its important people stood for. But he inherited a thin, proud blood, that had known power and pride in other centuries, and was tinged with their traditions, a blood in which the attributes of soldier and priest and fanatic and worldling and wit ran with the attributes of a successful merchant. He stood for the autocracy of wealth and the supremacy of the bourgeoisie, but he was in spirit, faintly and deprecatorily as he might suggest it, an aristocrat. He cared little for distinctions of rank, which seemed to him to settle themselves arbitrarily in the womb, but he cared much for the tradition of fine behaviour and fine breeding in the Hennessys. He exacted a harsh standard of conduct from his dependents, not out of little but out of much understanding of life, being as fully aware of the rebellious hearts of men as he was convinced that it was necessary for them to conform to arbitrarily set conventions. He had a deeper knowledge of character than he ever betrayed, and high spirits attracted him, if only because of the necessity he saw to tame them. He was not especially interested in Victor Considine, whom he believed to have been born ready-made for the exemplary life he was to lead. It would not thrill him to give a grandchild who was so endearingly like himself into such safe keeping.

To-night he held a small court in the morning-room of River Hill. Tall and austere in his black clothes, one small white hand resting on his ebony stick, the other, signet-ringed, stroking his small white beard, his dark eyes and his thin lips smiling faintly, his second wife, the Englishwoman out of Debrett who was thirty years younger than he, standing at his side, beautiful and beautifully dressed and exasperatedly afraid of him—he received the homage of everyone who was anyone in Catholic Mellick, among them of his own distinguished-looking sons and daughters and of the simultaneously pleased and agitated Considines.

The Considines were pleased, of course, that the great man had honoured them by his presence, a condescension rarely bestowed on any but a Hennessy household—but they were agitated by the blot that Denis's folly had put upon so auspicious an occasion.

No remark was made, either by John Aloysius himself or by the groups that formed around him, of Denis's deplorable absence or of Anthony's distracted state. Clearly the Grand Old Man knew the whole story. The Considines, as they greeted him, did not dare surmise what he was thinking of such an inexcusable gesture as Denis had made, such a betrayal of caste before the lower orders, such a mad discourtesy, such a hysterical surrender of one's name to gossip and mockery.

As John Aloysius talked and smiled, his faintly smiling eyes often looked beyond the heads of his companions towards the hall and across it to the library door through which Anthony kept passing and re-passing in his restlessness.

"If you will excuse me a moment——" he suddenly said to Father Tom and Clement Haddington. "I shall return to you very shortly, my dear," he added, bowing to his wife. Then he walked out of the morning-room and across the hall to the library.

Anthony turned from the window and looked surprised when he saw John Aloysius carefully closing the door.

"May I smoke a cigar with you, Considine?"

"Why, of course," said Anthony, moving towards the cabinet.

"But will you sit down and be polite to me meantime?"

Anthony smiled.

"I'll try to," he said.

They lighted cigars and sat down near an open window.

"That was a bad bit of manners your son Denis treated the town to to-day."

Anthony drew himself up. His lips tightened. If this old josser thought he had the right to preach a sermon on Denis's manners, well, he was in the wrong box, that was all.

"Where is he now?"

"I don't know," said Anthony.

"It's badly done of him not to have come home by this and apologised to you. I suppose he's feeling too much embarrassed to face the crowd you have here. Well, no one asked him to bring the embarrassment on himself."

"I'm sorry," said Anthony, "but I can't discuss Denis with you."

"I'm not asking you to. I'm making my own comments, that's all. I like your picturesque son."

Anthony stared at John Aloysius Hennessy, believing for a moment that the last remark had angered him. Who was asking the old tyrant what he thought of Denis? And surely the word "picturesque" was a contemptuous one? But as he considered it Anthony felt that, whatever its secondary implications, it was accurate. Denis was picturesque. The sight of him filled the eyes as nothing else could, Anthony thought. And calling up his image now, he groaned to it in his heart, "Come back to me, my son; only come back and tell me what's the matter! Come back to me, Denis." He twisted in his chair. He ached to get up and stride about.

John Aloysius Hennessy smiled faintly to himself.

"Since it looks as if your nephew, Victor Considine, may soon be related to me, I don't mind telling you that I wish he were more like your mad son, Denis."

Anthony chuckled.

"I wish poor old Victor heard you," he said, and then unable to resist the question, "Why do you like Denis?" he asked.

"Oh, an air he has—of being different from the next man. You could never mistake him for anyone else. And he looks like a thoroughbred. As you know, I account such things important. I am regarded as a snob in this town. My snobbery is at least original. We Hennessys as a matter of fact prefer to call it a philosophy, but that's neither here nor there. All that I mean by this long-windedness is merely this, that I am much more sympathetic to your troublesome, hysterical Denis than I fear I shall ever be to my excellent prospective grandson-in-law. I would have preferred to have flattered you about him to his face to-night, in the conventional, coming-of-age manner—but it is only by breaking a few conventions that an intelligent young man can learn their irreplaceable value. And Denis is certainly intelligent."

Anthony drew luxuriously on his cigar. This old windbag's talk had much pompous folly in it, but in the main, what balm it was! What blessedness to hear this unsought praise, from such a source, of the disgraced one!

"If you want my advice," John Aloysius went on, "you'll lecture him heavily about this episode when he comes home—and you'll see to it that no other busybody says 'Boo' on the subject. It's between you and him and it's for him alone to patch up the ridiculous insult he's given your employees. Let him make the best he can of that, and give him no particular assistance. He'll manage them gracefully enough, I've no doubt. The excitable young idiot!"

The Grand Old Man laughed softly and stood up.

"I must go back to my wife now," he said. "Why don't you join us?"

But Anthony shook his head. This was Denis's night, and without him could be nothing. When his visitor had left the room, he returned to the window and leant his head upon the frame.

"My son, my son," he kept muttering, "what happened you at all? What's troubling you, my dear, my son?"

§ 6

It was close on midnight when, Victor Considine being temporarily engrossed by some dutiful attention to his mother, Anna Hennessy escaped from her mother's light, indifferent chaperonage and vanished through the French window of the drawing-room into the long sedate rose garden that stretched beside it.

She wanted to collect her thoughts. At any moment now she would have to accept or reject the love of Victor Considine. Never hitherto had she needed to commune with herself before saying "No" to the marriage proposals of young men; there had been no other answer in her for them, and she had assumed that in this question of love there could be only "Yes" or "No" and that either answer would be complete and instinctive. She was puzzled therefore to discover in herself neither an honest "No" nor a leaping "Yes" for Victor Considine, and she wondered very much what there was about him that distinguished him from other young men at least sufficiently to make her unwilling to dismiss him with finality. She could not discover why he attracted her more than she was wont to be attracted. She found his conversation dull, his face heavy, his attentions to herself embarrassingly self-conscious. He did not amuse her and, to her finicking taste, his concern with social niceties and social triumphs was naïvely vulgar. But when she danced with him, when she felt his arm round her, felt the ripple of his muscles and the slight lift of his ribs as he breathed, as she studied the firm set of his ear above his brown neck, and inhaled his clean odour of tobacco and good soap and she knew not what of live virility, as he bent so that his breath stirred her hair and she could catch his deep, soft, secret humming of the waltz tune, she knew that he had a power over her that no man had had before, and that if he were to take her and kiss her without breaking through that power with speech, she would be unable to resist his kiss.

But Anna, if not a blue-stocking as Mellick described her, was a young person whose mind worked sensitively and critically, and she knew that the sway that Victor had over her senses was not enough for marriage, not nearly enough for the kind of marriage she desired.

She was what is called a difficult girl, over-educated according to the notions of her day, and lonely and proud. Her grandfather's devotion to the Hennessy legend flowered dangerously in her. She despised her pretty, fading, refusing-to-fade mother, looking at her and through her with the hard,

contemptuous eyes of youth. Hardness, integrity, fastidiousness, and pride controlled in Anna Hennessy a deep-flowing
emotional capacity. She had read too much and seen too much
to be content in the genteel, virginal idleness that filled the
days of her contemporaries and that was all that was expected
of her now. She disliked her mother's elderly friends, who
were mostly military gentlemen; her sisters were at school,
her brothers at universities, her father busy and abstracted.
Her chief solace since leaving school had been in the companionship of her adoring grandfather, and in long visits to
school friends in her beloved Austria and Italy. Now in the
dark troubling of her senses that Victor brought to her, she
felt a new, fluctuating release from the exasperations and
futilities that so often wearied her, an escape from her strange
fears of the future and of hurrying death. But she knew that
his passion was not enough. She knew that in it she would
never find the fine adventures of emotion, the dangers of tenderness and understanding and delicate fierce love that life and
her own heart were for ever hinting at and that she believed
in and desired to know. Still, there was much in the warmth
his touch could give her and that no man had disturbed in her
before. There was much. Perhaps there was enough. Perhaps
there was nothing more in this business of love than the
straightforward passion she could take from and give to Victor Considine.

She paced by the low stone parapet of Denis's rose garden,
and coming to the end of it leant on a leaden urn and gazed
over the wide, long vista of shelving lawns and beyond the
cypress trees to the curving, tumbling river, steel-bright under
the moon. She smelt the red rose that flowered in the urn and
her eyes appraised and gradually approved Denis's austere
and tranquil garden.

"It's—it's unconfused," she thought, fumbling for an
accurate word. "I wonder if he's like that himself," she went
on enviously, and smiled at the story of his unbalanced behaviour of that day. "It doesn't seem as if he is. I wonder
what he's like."

Anna's brother Paul always said that Denis Considine was
stark mad, and that he had a swollen head into the bargain.
Anna herself did not know him. They had not met since they

both gave up attending children's parties. All she knew was
that he was six months younger than herself, and said to be
unreliable and eccentric. She knew the local fame of his garden and had heard disputes as to whether or not he was good-
looking. Paul and her mother did not think so—too effemi-
nate, they said. On the other hand she had heard her father
say that his face was positively beautiful. "Exactly what I
mean," Paul answered to that, "he is positively beautiful.
Which is ridiculous."

Anna was sorry that Denis was not present to-night. She
was vaguely curious to see him again, but she despised him
for having made a public fool of himself in the afternoon.
She felt that if any relative of hers had behaved in such a
manner she would be unable to forgive him, for she believed
even more fantastically than her grandfather in the duty of
the individual to submit himself to the rule of his tradition.
However, such an outburst of bad taste coming from a Considine was not the volcanic thing that it would have been from
a Hennessy.

She veered back to her own concerns. Was she going to
marry this other Considine who wanted her? At any rate, she
need fear no unconventionality from him, no public outbursts
or shirking of formal obligation, no womanish hysterics. He
would be only too ready to adopt her exacting code. Poor Victor! What was it that she wanted that he had not to give?

A tune from "Die Fledermaus," reminding her of her dear
Vienna, came sweetly now over the long avenues of roses.
This number was Hubert Considine's on her programme; he
would not worry if she was missing for it. She leant on the
leaden urn, and drinking up the breath of the red rose composed herself to think about her suitor.

It was then that Denis spoke to her, breaking the silence
in which he had watched her since her coming to that place.

§ 7

DEW was falling before Denis rose and left the oak tree, feeling colder and saner than when he had flung himself under it.
Hungry and thirsty too.

He walked to the Keener's Cross, took possession of The Snug, and called for bread-and-butter and whisky.

He was embarrassed now by his doings of the afternoon, but he did not permit himself to regret them. If that was the only way in which he could bring himself to declare his weariness of the life he was tied to, well, it was at least a clear and conclusive one. Sadly as its witnesses might deplore his lack of self-control, at least they must see his argument ablaze in it. There would be no necessity now to plead his unfitness for responsibility in Charles Street. They would realise themselves well rid of such a fool. (All through his reflections under the oak tree, Denis had used the euphemisms "they" and "them" with which to hold off the image of his father.)

There was nothing to bother about in the past now, he had told himself as he lay under the tree, nothing to gain by chewing the cud. He had tried to fit into their schemes for him, he could say that he had tried honestly—and he had failed. In fine and scandalous fashion his failure was now demonstrated. And he laughed, no longer hysterically, picturing his own absurd, theatrical figure as he fled shouting from the crowded office. What a comic variety of consternation he must have left behind on all those faces! He saw them all and laughed at them all now, except one, which he refused to admit into his picture.

Well, it was over. Something had been accomplished, however clumsily. He could go his own way now to his own life, and no one much the worse for it after all. What a fuss about nothing!

He stretched along the harsh and friendly oak roots and thought of the swan of last summer, wondering if she had come again to nest in Farrell's reeds; he stared at the caddis-flies above the stream; he turned to stare at the edge of the little wood.

"I suppose I'll never lie here again, Christina, any more than you will. I wonder what you'd have thought of the shindy I made to-day. You're so calm, Christina. You're always able to think before you act. Will I ever do that, I wonder? Or will I always do things in violent, silly jerks, or not at all? Oh, Christina, I'm a damned fool, a bloody fool! But at least

I have settled something now—my way. The worst way in the world, I admit, but the only way I seem to know. . . ."

He talked for a long time to himself and to Christina, growing soothed and lazy.

". . . Funny how I still talk to her. I—I—wish I loved her. I wish I could go rushing to her now the way I used to. I wish I could go rushing to someone. My God! I believe I'm mad. The minute I'm free of everyone, all I can think of is rushing to someone else. Am I mad—or is there no such thing as being alone, being settled in that state, I mean? Ah, but there is, for sane people, people like Christina. It's just that I'm not sane yet, I suppose, but I'm free anyway and that's a start. I'm free of them all."

But in The Snug, while he waited for his whisky his soliloquy failed to sustain its burden of "they" and "them." Anthony, his father, swept these aside. His image stared unrelentingly at Denis.

Denis faced it.

"I see," he said to it, "oh, yes, I see what I've done to you. I know, I tell you. But what about me? Why did you make two people of me like this? You shouldn't have done it. It's all your fault, I tell you, your fault from beginning to end, this bloody mess we're in. Father, I tell you it's your fault!"

The whisky came and he gulped at it. But Anthony's image remained with him in The Snug. He called for more whisky and went on arguing with his father. He went on drinking whisky and arguing for a long time. At last he stood up.

"All right," he said. "I'll go home first and apologise to you. I'll explain it all. I'm—I'm bloody sorry. I'll admit that much. But you see now, don't you? You do see, father, that it's all your fault? Oh, I'll go home and explain that to you, I'll explain that to you clearly, and then, then I'll get off on the first old train, the very first train. Because it's your fault, mind you, I tell you it's your fault, father!"

He was staggeringly drunk.

It was dark and cool on the road. He lurched along it towards Mellick, growing drunker in the fresh air. Several times he sat down in the grassy hedgerows, still arguing softly or singing to shake off argument. Once he sat for a long while on a gate, and stared into the sky.

"Poor old Tony! I wonder does he ever have a look at the stars or is that forbidden too? God knows it might well be. It's a damned sight more pleasant than looking at the average woman. If I were the abbot I'd forbid it. I'd make sure to forbid it. How unperturbed it is, that tremendous, terrible sky. Oh, God, what is this solemnness at the heart of everything? What is the rule that keeps all these monstrous, lovely affairs in place like this? 'Child of light'," he murmured, drunkenly— " 'Child of light, thy limbs are burning—Child of light——' Now where did I hear that, or did I make it up myself?"

By the time he reached Mellick his body was sober, that is to say his legs and hands were steady again and his eyes were clear, but his brain, unused to spirits, was fierily intoxicated, and he was absorbing new intoxication from the mounting beauty of the night. He strode through the quiet town cock-surely, his head in the air, a sense of power and freedom driving him, a mad expectancy of rapture rising like a flame in his breast.

He came to the open gates of River Hill and swung under the lime trees. Then he left the drive and dropped into the neighbouring meadow. It was his intention to approach the house by the herb and strawberry gardens through a side door, thus avoiding all the guests whose waltz tunes he already heard with derision. He would contrive to get hold of his father then without seeing other people. He would explain himself to Anthony, apologise, collect some books and clothes and money, and be gone. Nothing easier. But he must be quick. Rapture was waiting somewhere in the exquisite night —was waiting very near—he must not miss it.

His path took him by the far end of the rose garden, and as he glanced through a clearing in the masses of American Beauties, he saw a girl walking towards him by the low stone parapet. She was all in white, and the dying moon poured light on her.

Denis stood. The beauty of the girl he looked at beggared him of movement, of the will to move. He saw her move with a dream motion, unselfconsciously, as once the swan had moved, he remembered, towards Farrell's reeds. He saw her come to rest very near him by the leaden urn. Her profile was given to him then, as she turned to contemplate the garden.

Anna Hennessy possessed all those first essentials of physical beauty which the dullest observer can take in at a glance. She was tall and slender and had the ease of youth in her limbs; her skin gleamed under the moon in an unbroken whiteness with her dress; her elegance was subdued and accurate. Her small dark head rode patricianly on her curving neck. So much was easy to observe. Longer looking showed in her disciplined features and in the sweet, light angularity of her profile a mingling of sensuousness, spirituality, and penetrative fire that seemed somehow tragic in so young a face.

Denis, staring in astonishment, fumbled for words with which to tell himself of all these things and more that shone from this unknown girl. But he could find no phrases of his own; the lines that he had flung irrelevantly at the sky a while ago were tumbling round his brain again:

> *"Child of light, thy limbs are burning*
> *Through the vest that seems to hide them——"*

"Ah, something like that," he told himself. "It's as if she were burning, through the vests of her flesh and her silk—burning like a lost soul, like a poet or a saint or a sinner, like an unhappy soul in purgatory! Or a light she is, a light set out in the jungle to hypnotise wild beasts."

His heart was shaking him. His intoxicated brain leapt painfully. "Child of light," it went on chanting to him. "Thy limbs are burning," and "Lamp of earth, where'er thou movest—— Oh, what in God's name has she to do with me? Why can't I take my eyes from her and go about my business? Child of light, child of light—ah, but she's lovelier than that rose she's smelling, she's lovelier than all this sky! Who is she? God, who is she?"

He vaulted gently through the gap in the American Beauties, and came soft-footed to stand below the parapet.

§ 8

"Who are you?"
   "My name is Anna Hennessy."
   "Ah, the girl my cousin Victor wants!"

"You're Denis Considine, aren't you?"

"The little cranky girl that used to come to parties! Tess said you were like a ghost, a lovely ghost, she said, but she's wrong. There's nothing ghostly about you, you're alive. You're simply on fire with being alive! I'd have said a lamp or a star if I were Tess. It's no wonder that men are afraid of you! How could anyone possibly blame them? Listen to me, Anna Hennessy. Don't touch my cousin Victor. Don't touch him ever, do you hear? He's only a poor man of flesh, he'd shrivel in your fingers!"

"My brother says that you're mad."

"I'm not mad. To-night I'm drunk. Does that offend you? Should I tell a lie, or would it be any good? Surely you know long ago all the things I'd like to hide from you?"

"Why are you drunk?"

"They say that you're a blue-stocking. That's idiotic. I don't believe you know a thing that blue-stockings know."

"Who says I'm a blue-stocking?"

"They say that Victor has met his match in you! My God, his match! They say you'll manage him well, that you'll be a managing woman! Well, manage away is what I say to you! Manage the whole world, Anna Hennessy. It's you that should! If you're not to have the saddle, who's to have it? But Victor thinking he's met his match! I always despised the poor prig, but now I almost pity him! Poor creature of flesh, poor heavy Victor, married to you!"

"You're extraordinarily rude," said Anna softly. "But then I've never spoken to a drunken man before."

She smiled as she ended this speech, surprising herself by a sudden desire to smile very sweetly on this intoxicated boy, surprised and startled to catch herself thinking that in this ridiculous conversation she might find the answer to her debate on Victor Considine. A great deal of her hidden troubled self passed into the smile she gave Denis.

He watched it, holding his breath.

It came to him first out of her luminous eyes, then curled itself slowly, sweetly across her hesitating mouth. Fully unfolded, it lingered as if to let him appraise all its revelation of sharp, shy sympathy. It searched him wonderingly; it seemed to wound her too.

Words from *Prometheus* entangled themselves again about the air—"And the souls of whom thou lovest walk upon the winds with lightness . . ."

The smile flickered out.

Denis drew a long, hard breath as if rising from under the sea. He stretched up his hand to the urn and the rose she was fingering.

"Will you give me that rose?" he said. He touched her hand lightly. "Your hand is as cool as this flower." He laughed. "Give me the whole of it." He pressed her fingers against the stem of the rose until it broke. "Did it prick you? Never mind that. I want this rose, because I'm going on a long journey, like the romantic mediæval fellows!"

"Don't go."

"I'm off to-night. I was on my way to—to see about it, when you got in the way and delayed me. I don't mind that, but I daren't let you keep me longer. Ah, if I ever come back, and we meet again, Anna Hennessy, will there be anything in your face, I wonder, to remind me of this queer meeting?"

"What do you mean by 'going on a long journey'?"

"What I say. Away from Mellick. Round the world."

"Why?"

"That's a long story. But I happened to make a bit of a fool of myself to-day, and so now is the time to be off, while they're all acutely aware that there's no great gain in keeping me! Now is my chance, my last chance!"

"Yes, I heard that you made more than a bit of a fool of yourself to-day."

He winced.

"And now you're running away!"

"Put it like that if you like. I'm no stoic."

Her face was stern.

"It's an untidy way to behave."

"What does that matter?"

"It matters enormously, I think."

"What matters is to be oneself."

"Must one make scenes for that, and get drunk and run off in the night?"

"If you happen to be me, you must."

"I'd hate to make scenes and get drunk and call attention to myself."

"You have no need to do such things."

"How do you know?"

"Good-bye now. Give me the rose and let me go."

Her fingers tightened on his hand. "What do you expect to find at the end of your long journey?"

He leant against the urn, his face uplifted full to her. He raised his other hand to hers and spoke on a soft, imploring tone.

"I hardly know, Anna. Only to explore myself, I suppose, and find out, once for all, if there's anything good or valuable in me, or any meaning in my life."

"You foolish boy," she said. "You needn't go far to discover that."

"But that's not all of it anyway, because what does it matter, here or there, about me? What I really want is to get hold of the world somehow, take a good shake at it and knock some sort of answer out of it!"

She laughed.

"You could do that at home."

"No, no!"

"No matter where you went you couldn't get a real answer out of the world. The answer is—another world. And you know that already, after all."

"Ah!"

"I know it."

"You're lucky."

"I'd like you to be lucky too."

"I'd have no objection to it myself—but no two people's luck seems to be the same!"

"Stay at home, Denis."

His heart thudded in panic. Their hands twisted together.

"But it isn't fair," he cried. "You're drowning me! It isn't fair!"

"It is fair. Wherever you go and whatever you do you'll only get a very small bit of what you want. That's true. You know it's true. Wherever you go, the most of life will have to happen in your mind."

"I tell you I've tried to be happy with that old cant! I've told myself that until I'm sick of the sound of it."

"It seems to me," she said, "that everyone has to try and be happy with that old cant."

"Why are you saying that, you of all people?"

"You're settling a question for me to-night," she said. "I want to settle one for you. I want to be even with you."

She smiled again, the slow hesitating smile that seemed to hurt her with its own sweetness.

"What in God's name is that smile you've got?" he asked her. "Where did you get it? Do you smile that way often? If I were to see it often, Anna, I think something would burst in me. And if I were never to see it again——"

She bent over the urn, taking both his hands tightly. There was something like cruelty in her face.

"You see," she said—"you see you'll have to stay at home."

His heart thudded again—in panic, but hurried also by a deeper and more hidden emotion. For even as Denis stared now into Anna's face and into the situation which had leapt up about him and her, a part of him looked further off—to the image of his father, over which until now his resolution of escape had imperatively flung darkness. He looked at this newly uncovered image and was aware of relief, even of rest, in seeing it again. "Would this do?" he heard himself asking Anthony, half in despair, half in hope. "Could we settle it this way, father?"

Meantime his voice cried out to Anna:

"You're mad! This is mad! A minute ago we didn't know each other."

"We know each other now."

He shook off her hands and clasped his own together prayerfully across the little rose tree. "You're drowning me," he cried. "Oh, Anna, what are you doing to me?"

"I don't know," she said. "What are you doing to me?"

"Let it be a bargain then! Let it be a quid pro quo between us. If I stay—oh, but why?—oh, Anna, if I stay, will your answer be 'No' and 'No' and 'No' and 'No' to Victor Considine?"

"That's been my answer to him since you spoke to me."

He laughed out wildly, seeing as he did so, as clearly as he saw the girl's, his father's eyes, filled with bright happiness.

"And then . . . ?" said Anna.

"Leave all the 'then' for to-night!" he cried. "Leave all the 'then' till I come courting in the daylight. Isn't it enough, ah, God! isn't it too much that for this night you belong to no one, and that you have chained me here to look into your face. Leave all the 'then,' you terrible strange girl, until my muddy hands are clean and my hair is combed like Victor Considine's!"

She touched his hair lightly.

He leant against the urn without moving. She continued to stroke his hair. They were silent and still a long minute.

The band tuned up again in the drawing-room.

"I must go in," said Anna. "The chaperones will be flurried."

Denis raised his head.

"Whom are you to dance it with?"

"With Victor."

"Ha! That's with no one at all!"

"Will you dance it with me?"

"I, Anna? In these clothes, these shoes?"

"Will you?"

He sprang to the stone parapet beside her.

"I'll dance with you till you cry out for mercy; I'll dance with you till you faint on the floor at my feet."

He snatched her hand and hurried her down the long avenue of roses. It seemed imperative to get back at once under the roof of River Hill.

§ 9

FOR the second supper extra the string quartette was playing what the programme called a "Weber Potpourri."

The elders, who had gone into supper first, were grouped about the dance-room walls gossiping lazily, while some of their memories climbed back maybe along the jumble of old tunes, to supper extras of their youth. There were only about six couples of young people on the floor. The rest were at supper or even, possibly, sitting out.

John Aloysius Hennessy leant on his ebony stick by the door and wondered where his favourite grandchild was. Victor Considine, erect beside his mother's chair, wondered too, had been wondering for some time where Anna was, but knowing her irritability against fuss and her fierce independence, was restraining himself from going in search of her. He bit his lip in anxiety. This was the hour of the night in which he had intended to ask her to be his wife. Where was she, the lovely one? Oh, where on earth? Victor wished his father wouldn't sing the waltz tunes quite so loudly. He wished too, with an anxious eye at the formidable John Aloysius, that his mother was not so visibly under the influence of port wine.

"Do I see Anna anywhere about, Victor darling?" Sophia kept saying, lifting her lorgnette and letting it fall with a little laugh, and lifting it again.

At the other side of the room Eddy bent over Caroline's chair.

"I suppose it would be silly of us to dance it, Caro?"

"Very silly, Ted; an old grey-haired brother and sister."

There was a movement by the big French window.

Victor started. Here was Anna.

The whole room started. Here was Denis.

Without a word, without looking to left or right, or seeming to feel one glance of all the excitedly focused glances of the room, Denis and Anna slipped into the waltz, just as the quartette broke into "Invitation."

Denis's grey suit was dusty and crumpled. His shoes were white with dust, his hair fell wildly across his forehead. Anna was exquisite in shimmering evening white, with pearls on her neck, and silver slippers on her feet. But neither of them seemed to think it strange that she should give up her snow-white dress and snow-white hand to his ungloved and mud-stained hands. A dark red rose lay crushed **between** their joined fingers.

Weber's waltz climbed steadily, its rhythm undisturbed by the rigid consternation in the room. The only sound that crossed it was a soft cry of surprise from someone in the hall. "It's Denis," a girl's voice said. A moment later Anthony came and stood in the doorway. John Aloysius stepped aside from it to let him have a full view of the room.

Denis and Anna danced the discreet waltz of their day, danced it with a beautiful, grave precision, with perfect circumspection, with composed and masklike faces. But to the alert nerves of the lookers-on, it was as if what they did was shameless. It was as if they danced to a vaster music than Weber's, to a music of fate and death, and triumph and resignation. The fire that was between them escaped to blaze about the room, so that the most obtuse might know that here were lovers.

Victor Considine was not the most obtuse.

Neither was John Aloysius Hennessy obtuse. As he watched the dance, his thin lips and his dark eyes smiled their faint, thin smile.

Anthony stared at his son; his brilliant eyes blazed love on him.

THE END

The first Virago Modern Classic was published in London in 1978, launching a list dedicated to the celebration of women writers and to the rediscovery and reprinting of their works. While the series is called "Modern Classics" it is not true that these works of fiction are universally and equally considered "great," although that is often the case. Published with new critical and biographical introductions, books appear in the series for different reasons: sometimes for their importance in literary history; sometimes because they illuminate particular aspects of women's lives, both personal and public. They may be classics of comedy or storytelling; their interest can be historical, feminist, political, or literary. In any case, in their variety and richness they promise to confuse forever the question of what women's fiction is about, while at the same time affirming a true female tradition in literature.

Initially, the Virago Modern Classics concentrated on English novels and short stories published in the early decades of the century. As the series has grown, it has broadened to include works of fiction from different centuries and from different countries, cultures, and literary traditions; there are books written by black women, by Catholic and Jewish women, by women of almost every English-speaking country, and there are several relevant novels by men.

Nearly 200 Virago Modern Classics will have been published in England by the end of 1985. During that same year, Penguin Books began to publish Virago Modern Classics in the United States, with the expectation of having some 40 titles from the series available by the end of 1986. Some of the earlier books in the series were published in the United States by The Dial Press.